Murray saw the shock in Marcus's eyes.

This was supposed to be an easy win for the Grievar, a fight to pad his record. His Tasker probably told him to finish the blind boy in a brutal fashion. Instead, Marcus was the one fighting for survival, looking like he was treading water in a tank of razor sharks. Marcus grunted as he pushed himself off the ground. He stood and tried to shuck the boy off his back, bucking wildly, but the climber wrapped around him even tighter.

The blind boy began to snake his hands across Marcus's neck, shooting his forearm beneath the chin to apply a choke. Either as a last resort or out of pure helplessness, Marcus dropped backward like a felled tree, slamming the boy on his back into the dirt with a thud. A cloud of dust billowed into the air on impact. The crowd hushed as the little boy was crushed beneath his larger opponent's bulk.

Murray held his breath as the dust settled.

By Alexander Darwin

THE COMBAT CODES

The Combat Codes
Grievar's Blood
Blacklight Born

THE COMBAT CODES

THE COMBAT CODES: BOOK ONE

ALEXANDER DARWIN

orbit

orbitbooks.net

Cover design by Lauren Panepinto
Cover art by Peter Bollinger

Author photograph by Jeanette Fuller

Orbit
Hachette Book Group
1290 Avenue of the Americas
New York, NY 10104
orbitbooks.net

First Orbit Edition: June 2023
Originally published by Insight Forge Press in October 2015

Orbit is an imprint of Hachette Book Group.
The Orbit name and logo are trademarks of Little, Brown Book Group Limited.

Library of Congress Cataloging-in-Publication Data:
Names: Darwin, Alexander, author.
Title: The combat codes / Alexander Darwin.
Description: First Orbit edition. | New York : Orbit, 2023. | Series: The combat codes ; Book one. | Originally published by Insight Forge Press in October 2015.
Identifiers: LCCN 2022037450 | ISBN 9780316493000 (trade paperback) | ISBN 9780316493130 (ebook)
Subjects: LCGFT: Science fiction.
Classification: LCC PS3604.A794 C66 2023 | DDC 813/.6—dc23
LC record available at https://lccn.loc.gov/2022037450

ISBNs: 9780316493000 (trade paperback), 9780316493130 (ebook)

Printed in the United States of America

LSC-C

Printing 1, 2023

To Katie, who always holds my hand when
I've lost my glasses.

To the gentle art of jiu jitsu, which isn't often gentle,
but soothes the soul.

CHAPTER 1

Into the Deep

We fight neither to inflict pain nor to prolong suffering. We fight neither to mollify anger nor to satisfy vendetta. We fight neither to accumulate wealth nor to promote social standing. We fight so the rest shall not have to.

First Precept of the Combat Codes

Murray wasn't fond of the crowd at Thaloo's. Mostly scum with no respect for combat who liked to think themselves experts in the craft.

His boots clung to the sticky floor as he shouldered his way to the bar. Patrons lined the counter, drinking, smoking, and shouting at the overhead lightboards broadcasting SystemView feeds.

Murray grabbed a head-sized draught of ale before making his way toward the center of the den, where the crowd grew thicker. Beams of light cut through clouds of pipe smoke and penetrated the gaps between clustered, sweaty bodies.

His heart fluttered and the hairs on the back of his neck bristled as he approached. He wiped a trickle of sweat from his brow. Even after all these years, even in a pitiful place like this, the light still got to him.

He pushed past the inner throng of spectators and emerged at the edge of the action.

Thaloo's Circle was eight meters in diameter, made of auralite-compound steel fused into the dirt. Standard Underground dimensions. On the Surface, Circles tended to be wider, usually ten meters in diameter, which Murray preferred. More room to maneuver.

Glowing blue streaks veined the steel Circle, and a central cluster of lights pulsed above the ring like a heartbeat, shining down on two boys grappling in the dirt.

"Aha! The big Scout's back. You runnin' out of kids already?" A man at the edge of the Circle clapped Murray on the shoulder. "Name's Calsans."

Murray ignored the greeting and focused on the two boys fighting. One of them looked to be barely ten years old and had the gaunt build of a lacklight street urchin. His rib cage heaved in and out from beneath the bulk of a boy who outweighed him by at least sixty pounds.

Many of the onlookers flicked their eyes between the action and a large lightboard that hung from the ceiling. Biometric readings for each boy in the Circle flashed across the screen: heart rate, brain wave speed, oxygen saturation, blood pressure, hydration levels. The bottom of the board displayed an image of each boy's skeletal and muscular frame, down to their chipped teeth.

As the large boy lifted his elbow and drove it into the smaller boy's chin, a red fracture lit up on the board. The little boy's heart rate shot up.

The large boy threw knees into his opponent's rib cage as he continued to hold him down in the dirt. The little boy writhed, turning his back to his opponent and curling into a ball.

"Shouldn't give your back like that," Murray muttered, as if trying to communicate with the battered boy.

The large boy dropped another vicious elbow on his downed

prey. Murray winced as he heard the sharp crack of bone on skull. Two more elbows found their target before the little one stiffened, his eyes rolling into his head as he fell limp.

The ball of light floating above the Circle flickered before it dissipated into a swarm of smoldering wisps that fanned out into the crowd.

"They call the big one there N'jal; he's been cleaning up like that all week. One of Thaloo's newest in-housers," Calsans said as the boy raised his arms in victory.

Beyond a few clapping drunks, there was little fanfare. N'jal walked to the side of his Tasker at the sidelines, a bearded man who patted the boy on the head like a dog. The loser's crew entered the Circle and dragged the fallen fighter out by his feet.

"Thaloo's been buyin' up some hard Grievar this cycle," Calsans continued, trying to strike up conversation with Murray again. "Bet he's tryin' to work a bulk sale to the Citadel, y'know? Even though they won't all pan out with that level of competition, there's bound to be a gem in the lot of 'em."

Murray barely acknowledged the man, but Calsans kept speaking.

"It's not like it used to be, y'know? Everything kept under strict Citadel regulations. All the organized breeding, the training camps," Calsans said. "I mean, course you know all about that. But now that the Kirothians are breathin' down our necks, Deep Circles are hoppin' again, and folk like Thaloo and you are making the best of it."

"I'm nothing like Thaloo," Murray growled, his shoulders tensing.

Calsans shrank back, as if suddenly aware of how large Murray was beside him. "No, no, of course not, friend. You two are completely different. Thaloo's like every other Circle slaver trying to make a bit, and you're a . . . or used to be . . . a Grievar Knight . . ." His voice trailed off.

The glowing spectral wisps returned to the Circle like flies gathering on a fresh kill. They landed on the cold auralite steel ring and balled up again in a floating cluster above. As more of the wisps arrived, the light shining on the Circle grew brighter. Fresh biometrics flashed onto the feed.

It was time for the next fight, and Murray needed another ale.

* * *

Murray drew the cowl of his cloak over his head as he exited Thaloo's den, stepping directly into the clamor of Markspar Row.

Stores, bars, and inns lined the street, with smaller carts selling acrid-scented foods on the cobbles out front. Gaudily dressed hawkers peddled their wares, yapping like bayhounds in a variety of tongues. Buyers jostled past him as ragged, soot-faced children darted underfoot.

Much had changed since Murray had first returned to the Underground.

Two decades ago, he'd proudly walked Markspar Row with an entourage of trainers in tow. He'd been met with cheers, claps on the back, the awed eyes of Deep brood looking up at him. He'd been proud to represent the Grievar from below.

Now Murray made a habit of staying off the main thoroughfares. He came to the Deep alone and quietly. He doubted anyone would recognize him after all these years, with his overgrown beard and sagging stomach.

A man in a nearby stall shrieked at Murray, "Top-shelf protein! Tested for the Cimmerian Shade! Vat-grown in Ezo's central plant! Certified for real taste by the Growers Guild!" The small bald hawker held up a case with a mess of labels stamped across it.

Compared to the wiry hawker, Murray was large. Though his gut had expanded over the past decade and his ruffled beard was now grey-streaked, he posed a formidable presence. From beneath the cut-off sleeves of his cloak, his knotted forearms and callused hands hung like twin cudgels. Flux tattoos crisscrossed the length of Murray's arms from elbows to fingertips, shifting their pigmented curves as he clenched his fists. His sharp nose twisted at the center, many times broken, and his ears swelled like fat toads. His face was overcast, with two alarmingly bright yellow eyes penetrating from beneath his brow.

Murray turned in to a narrow stone passageway sheltered from the central clamor of the row. He passed another hawker, a white-haired lady hidden behind her stand of fruit.

"The best heartbeat grapes. Clerics say eat just a few per day and you'll outlive an archivist." She smiled at him and gestured to her selection of fruit, each swollen and pulsing with ripeness. Halfway down the alley, as the sounds of the market continued to fade, Murray stopped in front of a beat-up oaken door. A picture of a bat with its teeth bared was barely visible on the faded awning overhead.

The Bat always smelled of spilled ale and sweat. An assortment of Grievar and Grunt patrons crowded the floor. Mercs keeping an ear to the ground for contract jobs, harvesters taking a break from planting on the steppe, diggers dressed in dirt from a nearby excavation project.

SystemView was live and blaring from several old boards hanging from the far wall.

And now... broadcasting from Ezo's Capital, in magnificent Albright Stadium...

The one thing that brought together the different breeds was a good SystemView fight. Though most of the folk living in the Underground were Ezonian citizens, their allegiances often were more aligned with the wagers they placed in the Circles.

Most of the Bat's patrons were tuned in to the screens, some swaying and nearly falling out of their chairs, with empty bottles surrounding them. Two dirt-encrusted Grunts slurred their words as Murray pushed past them toward the bar.

"Fegar's got the darkin' reach! No way 'e'll be able to take my boy down!"

"You tappin' those neuros too hard, man? He took Samson down an' he's ten times the wrestler!"

Grunts weren't known for their smarts. They were bred for hard labor like mining, hauling, harvesting, or clearing, though Murray often wondered if drinking might be their real talent. He didn't mind the Grunts, though—they did their jobs and didn't bother anyone. They didn't meddle with Grievar lives. They didn't govern from the shadows. They weren't Daimyo.

The man behind the bar was tall and corded, with near-obsidian skin. The left side of his face drooped, and his bald head gleamed with sweat as he wiped down the counter.

Murray approached the bar and caught the man's good eye. "Your finest Deep ale."

The man poured a stein of the only ale on tap, then broke into a wide half grin. "Old Grievar, what brings you to my fine establishment on such a sunny day in the Deep?"

Murray took a swig of the ale, wiping the foam off his lips. "Same thing every year, Anderson. I'm here to lay back and sweat out my worries at the hot springs. Then I figure I'll stop by the Courtesan Houses for a week or so 'fore returning to my Adar Hills mansion back Upworld."

Anderson chuckled, giving Murray a firm wrist-to-wrist grasp from across the bar. "Good to see you, old friend. Though you're uglier than I remember."

"Same to you." Murray feigned a grimace. "That face of yours reminds me of how you always forgot to cover up the right high kick."

Anderson grinned as he wiped down the bar. Both men were quiet as they watched the SystemView broadcast on the lightboard above.

The feed panned across Albright Stadium, showing thousands of cheering spectators in the stands before swooping toward the gleaming Circle at the heart of the arena. Two Grievar squared off in the Circle—one standing for Ezo and the other for the empire of Kiroth.

Murray downed his ale and set the cup on the bar for Anderson to refill.

A list of grievances popped up in one corner of the screen to remind viewers of what was at stake in the bout: rubellium reserves in one of the long-disputed border regions between Ezo and Kiroth, worth millions of bits, thousands of jobs, and the servitude of the pastoral harvesters who lived out there.

The fate of nations held in the sway of our fists.

The fight began, and Murray watched quietly, respectfully, as a Grievar should. Not like crowds modernday—booing and clapping, hissing and spitting. No respect for combat.

Anderson sighed as Ezo's Grievar Knight attacked the Kirothian with a flurry of punches. "Do you remember it? Even taking those hits, those were good days."

"Prefer not to remember it." Murray took another gulp of his ale.

"I know you don't, friend. But I hold on to my memories. Blood, sweat, and broken bones. Locking on a choke or putting a guy down with a solid cross. That feeling after, lying awake and knowing you'd done something—made a difference."

"What's the darkin' difference? I don't see any. Same lofty bat shit going on up above." Murray sniffed the air. "Still got that same dank smell down here."

"You know what I mean," Anderson said. "Fighting for the good of the nation. Making sure Ezo stays on top."

"I know what you mean, and that's just what those Daimyo politiks up there say all the time. *For the good of the nation.* That's why I'm down here. Every year, the same thing for a decade now. Sent Deep to find fresh Grievar meat."

"You don't think the Scout program is working?" Anderson asked.

Murray took another long swig. "We'll discover the next Artemis Halberd. That's what that smug bastard Callen always says. The man doesn't know how to piss straight in a Circle, yet he's got command of an entire wing of Citadel."

"You never saw eye to eye with Commander Albright—"

"The man's a coward! How can he lead? The Daimyo might as well have installed one of their own to Command. Either way, doesn't make a difference. Scouts—the whole division is deepshit. Grievar-kin are born to fight. Thousands of years of breeding says so. We're not made to creep around corners, dealing out bits like hawkers."

"Times are different, old friend," Anderson said. "Things are more complicated. Citadel has got to keep up; otherwise, Ezo falls behind. Kiroth's had a Scout program for two decades now. They say even the Desovians are on their way to developing one."

"They know it's just the scraps down here, Anderson," Murray said. "Kids that don't fare a chance. And even if one of them did make it? What have we got to show for it? Me and you. For all those years we put in together in service. The sacrifices—"

Their conversation was interrupted as the door to the bar swung open with a thud. Three men walked in. Grievar.

Anderson sighed and put his hand on Murray's shoulder. "Take it easy."

The first to enter had piercings running along his jawline, glinting beside a series of dark flux tattoos stamped on his cheekbones. The other two were as thick as Murray and looked to be twins, with matching grizzled faces and cauliflowered ears.

The fluxed man immediately caught Murray's stare from the bar. "Ah! If it isn't the mighty one himself!"

Murray left his seat with alarming speed and moved toward the man.

Anderson shouted a warning from behind the bar. The man threw a wide haymaker at Murray, who casually tucked his shoulder, deflecting the blow, before dropping levels and exploding from a crouch into the man's midline. Murray wrapped his arms around the man's knees, hoisted him into the air, then drove him straight through a nearby table, which splintered in every direction.

Murray blinked. He was still in his seat by the bar, the pierced Grievar hovering over him with a derisive smirk on his face.

"Nothing to say anymore, huh, old man? I can't imagine what it's like. Getting sent down here to do the dirty work. Digging through the trash every year."

Murray ignored the man and took another swig of his ale. "Think any of your trash will even make it through the Trials this year?" the man taunted. "Didn't one of your kids make it once? What ever happened to him? Oh, I remember now…"

Anderson pushed three ales across the bar. "Cydek, these are on the house. Why don't you and your boys find a place over in that corner there so we don't have any trouble?"

Cydek smirked as he took the drinks. He turned to Murray as he was walking away. "I'm scouting Lampai tomorrow. Why don't you tail me and I can show you how it's done? You can see some real Grievar in action. Nice change of pace from watching kids fighting in the dirt."

Murray kept his eyes fixed on the lightboard above the bar. SystemView was now replaying the fight's finish in slow motion. The broadcaster's voice cut through the quieted Ezonian crowd at Albright Stadium.

What an upset! And with the simple justice of a swift knee, Kiroth takes the Adarian Reserves!

Anderson leaned against the bar in front of Murray and poured himself an ale as he watched the knockout on replay. "The way things are going, I hope the Scout program starts working…or anything, for that matter. Otherwise, we'll be drinking that Kirothian swill they call mead next time I see you."

Murray let a smile crease his face, though he felt the tension racking his muscles. He downed his ale.

* * *

Murray realized he'd had a few too many, even for a man of his size, as he stumbled down Markspar Row. The duskshift was at its end and the arrays that lined the cavern ceiling bathed the Underground in a dying red glow. Murray had stayed at the Bat chatting about old times with Anderson for the entire evening.

Though he often denied it, he did miss the light. He wished he were back in fighting form, as he had been during his service.

That's the thing with us Grievar. We rot.

He cracked his knuckles as he walked in no particular direction.

Murray felt his body decaying like the old foundations of this crumbling Underground city. His back always hurt. Nerve pain shot up his sides whether sitting, standing, sleeping—it didn't matter. His neck was always stiff as a board. His wrists, elbows, and ankles had been broken multiple times and seemed like they could give way at any moment. Even his face was numb, a leathery exterior that didn't feel like his own anymore. He remembered a time when his body was fluid. His arms and legs had moved as if there were a slick layer of oil between every joint, seamlessly connecting takedowns into punches into submissions.

He'd seen his fair share of trips to medwards to sew up gashes and mend broken bones, but he'd always felt smooth, hydraulic. Now Murray's joints and bones scraped together with dry friction as he walked.

It was his own fault, though. Murray had his chance to stay young and he'd missed it. The first generation of neurostimulants had debuted when he was at the top of his fight game. Most of his team had started popping the stims under the *recommendation* of then–Deputy Commander Memnon. "We need the edge over the enemy," Memnon had urged the team of Grievar Knights.

Coach hadn't agreed with Memnon—the two had been at each

other's throats for those last few years. Coach believed taking stims was sacrilege, against the Combat Codes. The simplest precept of them all: *No tools, no tech.*

The man would often mutter to Murray, "Live and die like we're born—screaming, with two clenched, bloody fists."

It wasn't long after the stims started circulating that Coach left his post. The breach in Command had grown too wide. Memnon would do anything to give Ezo the edge, even if that meant harnessing Daimyo tech. Coach would rather die than forsake the Codes.

Even after Coach left, Murray kept to his master's teachings. He'd refused to take stims. A few of his teammates had stayed clean too—Anderson, Leyna, Hanrin, old Two-Tooth. At first, they'd kept up with the rest of the team. Murray had even held on to the captain's belt. It wasn't until a few years later that he'd felt it.

It had been barely perceptible: a takedown getting stuffed, a jab snapping in front of his face before he realized it was coming. Those moments started adding up, though. Murray aged. He got slower and weaker while the rest of Ezo's Grievar Knights maintained their strength under the neurostimulants.

And then came the end. That fight in Kiroth. His whole team, his whole nation, depending on Murray. Everything riding on his back. And he'd failed.

Wherever Coach was right now, he'd be spitting in the dirt if he could see what Murray had become. Skulking in the shadows, stuck with a lowly Grievar Scout job, to be forgotten. Another cog in the Daimyo machine.

Before Murray realized it, the light had nearly faded. The streets were quiet as most Deep folk returned to their homes for the blackshift.

Murray was walking on autopilot toward Lampai Stadium, now only a stone's throw away, looming above him like a hibernating beast. Shadows clung to him here, deep pockets of darkness filling the folds of his cloak as he made his way to the base of the stadium.

Murray stopped abruptly, standing in front of Lampai's entrance. He stared at the old concrete wall and the black wrought-iron gates. He craned his head at the stadium's rafters towering above him.

Murray placed his hand against a gold plaque on the gate.

It was cold to the touch. It read:

LAMPAI STADIUM, CONSTRUCTION DATE: 121 P.A.

LET THIS BE THE FIRST OF MANY ARENAS, TO SERVE AS A SYMBOL OF OUR SWORN ARMISTICE AND A CONSTANT REMINDER OF THE DESTRUCTION WE ARE CAPABLE OF. HERE SHALL GRIEVAR GIVE THEIR BLOOD, IN HONOR AND PRIVILEGE. THEY FIGHT SO THE REST SHALL NOT HAVE TO.

"We fight so the rest shall not have to," Murray whispered. He had once believed those words. The first precept of the Codes. He would repeat the mantra over and over before his fights, shouting it as he made entrances into stadiums around the world.

The Mighty Murray Pearson. He'd been a force of nature, a terror in the Circle. Now he was just another shadow under these rafters.

Murray inhaled deeply, his chest filling with air. He pushed it all out again.

* * *

Murray returned to Thaloo's every day that week and saw more of the same. Just like it had been every year before. The well-nourished, stronger Grievar brood beating down the weaker lacklights. There was little skill involved; the brutal process pitted the weak against the strong. The strong always won.

Eventually, the weaker brood wore down. Patrons didn't want to buy the broken ones, which meant that Thaloo's team of Taskers was wasting their time training them. Thaloo was wasting bits on their upkeep. So, like rotten fruit, the slave Circle owner would throw the kids back to the streets where he found them. Their chance of survival was slim.

Murray's head throbbed as he stepped back to the edge of the Circle. Spectral wisps gathered above as the light intensified on the dirt fighting floor.

The first Grievar emerged from the side entrance, stopping by his Tasker's corner. He looked to be about fifteen, tall for his age, with all the hallmarks of purelight Grievar blood—cauliflowered ears, a thick brow, bulging forearms, bright eyes.

The boy's head was shaved like all the brood at Thaloo's to show off the brand fluxed on his scalp. Like any other product in the Deep, patrons needed to see his bit-price. This kid looked to be of some value—several of the vultures were eyeing him like a slab of meat.

The Tasker slapped the boy in the face several times, gripping his shoulders and shaking him before prodding him into the Circle. The boy responded to the aggression with his own, gnashing his teeth and slamming his fist against his chest as he stalked the perimeter. The crowd clapped and hooted with anticipation.

The second boy did not look like he belonged in the Circle. He was younger than his opponent and gaunt, his thin arms dangling at his sides. A mop of black hair hung over the boy's brow. Murray shook his head. They'd just taken the kid off the streets, and hadn't even put in the effort to brand him yet.

The boy walked into the Circle without expression, avoiding eye contact with his opponent and the crowd around him. He found his designated start position and stood completely still as the glowing spectrals rose from the Circle's frame and began to cluster above.

"The taller, dark one—name's Marcus. Saw 'im yesterday." Calsans pulled up to Murray's side, just as he'd done every day this week. Murray expected the parasite to ask him for a favor any moment now. Or perhaps he was one of Callen's spies, sent to ensure Murray didn't go rogue.

"Nearly kicked right through some lacklight." Calsans smirked. "This little sod is gonna get thrashed."

The skinny boy stood motionless, his arms straight by his sides. At first, Murray thought the boy's eyes were cast at the dirt floor, but at second glance, Murray saw his eyes were closed. Clamped shut.

"Thaloo's putting blind kids in the Circle now..." Murray growled.

"Sometimes, he likes to give the patrons a show," Calsans said. "Bet he's workin' on building Marcus's bit-price. Fattening him up for sale."

The fight began as Marcus assumed a combat stance and bobbed forward, feinting jabs and bouncing on the balls of his feet.

"It's like one of them Ezonian eels about to eat a guppy," Calsans remarked.

Murray looked curiously at the blind boy as his opponent stalked toward him. The boy still wasn't moving. Though his posture wasn't aggressive, he didn't look afraid. He almost looked... relaxed.

"Wouldn't be so sure," Murray replied.

Marcus approached striking distance and feigned a punch at the blind boy before whipping a high round kick toward his head. A split second before the shin connected, the boy dropped below the kick and shot forward like a coiled spring, wrapping around one of the kicker's legs. The boy clung to the leg as his opponent tried to shake him off vigorously, but he stayed attached. He drove his shoulder into Marcus's knee, throwing him off-balance into the dirt.

The boy began to climb his opponent's body, immobilizing his legs and crawling onto his torso.

"Now this is getting good," Murray said as he watched the blind boy go to work.

Marcus heaved forward with his full strength, pushing the boy off him while reversing to top position. Hungry for a finish again, Marcus straddled the younger boy's torso, reared up, and hurled a punch downward. The boy slipped the punch, angling his chin at just the right moment, his opponent's fist glancing off his jaw.

Marcus howled in pain as his hand crunched against the hard dirt. Biometrics flashed red on the lightboard above.

Capitalizing on bottom position, the blind boy grasped Marcus's elbow and dragged the limp arm across his body, using the leverage to pull himself up and around onto his opponent's back.

Murray raised an eyebrow. "Well, look at that. Darkin' smooth back take."

The crowd suddenly was paying close attention to the turn of events. Several spectators hooted in approval of the upset while others jeered at a potential bit-loss on their bets.

Murray saw the shock in Marcus's eyes. This was supposed to be an easy win for the Grievar, a fight to pad his record. His Tasker probably told him to finish the blind boy in a brutal fashion. Instead, Marcus was the one fighting for survival, looking like he was treading water in a tank of razor sharks. Marcus grunted as he pushed himself off the ground. He stood and tried to shuck the boy off his back, bucking wildly, but the climber wrapped around him even tighter.

The blind boy began to snake his hands across Marcus's neck, shooting his forearm beneath the chin to apply a choke. Either as a last resort or out of pure helplessness, Marcus dropped backward like a felled tree, slamming the boy on his back into the dirt with a thud. A cloud of dust billowed into the air on impact. The crowd hushed as the little boy was crushed beneath his larger opponent's bulk.

Murray held his breath as the dust settled.

The blind boy was still clinging to his opponent, his two bony arms latched around his neck, constricting, ratcheting tighter. The boy squeezed until Marcus's eyes rolled back into his head and his arms went limp.

The light flared and died out, the spectrals breaking from their cluster and dissipating into the den.

The boy rolled out from beneath his unconscious opponent, his face covered in dirt and blood, his eyes clamped shut.

CHAPTER 2

Dreams from the Underground

A Grievar needs neither tools nor technologies to enhance their physical prowess. One that resorts to shortcuts on the path to mastery will find themselves weakened. When such an individual faces true adversity, their trappings of strength will falter.

Passage One, Twelfth Precept of the Combat Codes

Just a few minutes more.

The sun peeked over the window frame and cast a shard of light at the boy.

He squeezed his eyes shut.

He half expected to hear the old master's gruff voice from outside the loft, yelling at them to get up and begin another day of training. Though the boy was curled up on his pallet, he could already feel his muscles aching in anticipation of the arduous day ahead: sprinting across the black sand beach, carrying boulders beneath the waves, climbing to the top of the seaside cliffs.

Arry licked his face with her wet tongue, trying to wake him.

The salty breeze wafted through the window, bringing with it the pungent smell of fish drying on the stone slab outside. The sigil sparrows began their morning chatter, and as usual, Arry tried to join the birds' chorus, yelping in his ear.

He rolled over, grabbing Arry to silence her, burying his face in her warm fur. She smelled like a tuft of washed-up seagrass.

Just a few minutes more.

The sun crested the window, the light pulsing against the boy's clenched eyelids. He wanted to hold on to the peaceful darkness. He wanted to let the tide lull him back to sleep. He wanted to lie still while the world around him moved on.

He opened his eyes.

* * *

The boy sat in the dim cell, watching the little wisp dance. He stared at the floating ball of light until it filled his field of vision with a white shroud. He concentrated on his breath, focusing on deep inhales and slow exhales.

He could only stare at the wisp for so long. Eventually, the boy flinched in pain and pulled his eyes from the light.

When he looked away, the deep shadows of his cell returned, curtains of darkness that hung around him. He stretched out his arms and touched the cold stone walls, tracing his hands along every familiar fissure.

The boy didn't mind the darkness of his cell. He felt at home in the shadows. It was the light that had taken time to get used to.

When he had first stumbled into the Underground, the light had burned his eyes. The white beams had rained down on him from the arrays above. He'd clamped his eyes shut, clawed at his face, screamed in agony.

Despite being dressed only in dried blood, he hadn't garnered more than a passing glance on the Underground's streets. No one had stopped to offer him help when he'd curled up in the shadows of some looming building, desperately trying to escape the light. They'd assumed he was just another Grievar kid, used up in the slave Circles and tossed out on the streets. Eventually, he'd get swept up by the mechs like any other piece of garbage. Someone must have been convinced that the boy still had some life in him, though, some worth that could be wrung out of his frail body. Maybe they'd been convinced by his screams as they attempted to pull him from the shadows.

He'd woken up in this cell. The little wisp of light had appeared on his first day here, hovering in the corner amid the cobwebs.

Today, he'd kept his eyes on the wisp for one hundred breaths before flinching away.

Every day in the cell, he'd trained himself to stare at the light. Slowly and agonizingly, the burning effects had faded. The explosions of white had become smaller and the blasts of brightness softer.

It was a momentous feat for the boy, considering he'd kept his eyes wired shut for weeks to avoid the light. Even when his captors dragged him out to fight, he kept his eyes shut, much to their dismay.

Not that being blind had mattered during the boy's fights so far. The opponents they put him up against were slow. He could hear them lumbering toward him, their labored breath betraying their movements. Though the boy was hardly an effective striker without his vision, his grappling was unhindered. Once he got ahold of his opponent, he didn't need to see.

He heard footsteps coming from outside his cell door, and on cue, the wisp disappeared, leaving him in the familiar darkness.

"Get yerself eatin', you lacklight twig!"

The boy had been called many names down here so far, derogatory terms in a variety of languages he didn't understand and every manner of insult he could imagine. *Lacklight, scumslagger, scrapdog, blindbrood.* But the boy remembered his real name. He hadn't lost that, like so much else. *Cego.*

A slot opened at the base of the door and a metal plate covered in green slop slid through. His captors called the food *fighting greens.*

The slot stayed open for a moment longer and Cego could feel the familiar eyes of the guard peering in at him, waiting for him to spoon the slop into his mouth.

Cego kept his eyes shut, pretending to grope at the stone floor for his food. He let his captors think he was blind.

A perceived weakness is strength, and a flaunted strength is weakness. The old master's baritone voice echoed in Cego's head.

"Darkin' *blindbrood.* Eat, don't eat, see if I care."

The slot rattled shut and Cego heard the guard spit on the floor outside his cell.

"Think yer doin' good so far, eh, boy?"

Cego didn't respond. They'd heard his screams when they took him off the streets, but he hadn't given them anything since.

"Seen yer type before. Boss probably thinks you'll bring in the bits," the guard said from outside the door. "Like when we had that one-legged kid; patrons liked that too. Freak would hop around the Circle pretty fast, actually won a fight throwin' jabs. Then boss matched him up with a good kicker with sharpened shins. Snapped his good leg clean right at the knee. No-leg is what we called him after that." The guard chuckled as he walked away.

Cego waited until he was sure the man was gone before he opened his eyes and stared at the rusted metal plate in front of him. He reached forward and pawed some of the watery green mush into his mouth, chewing and swallowing it lifelessly. Cego hadn't eaten his first few days down here and he'd paid for it, nearly blacking out during his first bout. Now he forced himself to eat, as disgusting as the greens looked.

Making sure he was eating regularly was just one of many things that Cego was getting used to.

He pulled a tattered blanket tight to his shoulders as he tossed the metal plate aside. Though Cego was more than familiar with pain, the cold here was different from pain. The cold lingered; it crept into his bones and made his nose run. Cego longed to stand beneath the warm sun, feeling the sand between his toes.

Here in the Underground, Cego had realized he could wither away. He'd been helpless on the streets for days, unable even to push himself off the ground. If not for his captors hauling him off the pavement, he'd have likely starved to death.

Cego threw the blanket off his shoulders and dropped to the floor. He started with push-ups, sit-ups, and planks. He reached up and grasped the edge of the doorframe for a set of pull-ups, ignoring the splinters that dug into his fingers. He bloodied his knees on the cold stone floor as he shot for takedowns—crouching low, stepping deep, and driving forward with his hips. He thrashed back and forth in the tiny cell like a tanked shark.

Cego shadowboxed imaginary opponents until his arms shivered with weariness. He threw round kicks, the tight stone walls tearing the skin from his feet as he spun around. Sweat and blood pooled in the cobbled crevices of his cell.

He would not wither away.

Though many things were alien to Cego in this Underground world—the light, the cold, the food, the folk, their languages—combat was not one of them.

Combat's familiar scent was fragrant here, wafting down the dark stone hallways and blooming in the raucous dens. Combat blared on the boards hanging from the walls and echoed in the conversations of every guard, patron, drunk reveler, and bit-rich hawker. Combat glimmered in the eyes of the Grievar, men and women like Cego, some barrel-chested and visibly scarred from battle, some hidden beneath their cloaks, lurking in the shadows.

Combat was alive here in the Underground, and Cego was born to fight.

* * *

Though it hurt to stare at the wisp for too long, Cego was fond of the little thing. It appeared on routine in the corner of his cell, hovering and pulsing as if trying to communicate with him.

"There are many more of you, aren't there?"

Cego had gotten in the habit of talking to the wisp. Though it never replied, it felt good to use his voice after keeping silent for so long. He made sure the guard was out of earshot before he started up his one-sided conversations.

"I saw more of your kind out there. Floating around the giant machines, heading up top where the lights are. It hurt to look at," Cego admitted. The memory of the blinding light shining down on the Underground streets was seared into Cego's mind.

"Why aren't you flying around with the rest?" Cego asked.

Only now could he start to remember what he'd seen when he stumbled into the Underground. Vast ceilings so far up that they looked like craggy grey skies. Buildings towering above him and strange mechs whirring past him. Thousands of folk strolling by and ignoring Cego's bloody, crumpled body on the pavement.

Perhaps this little wisp was his only friend down here. Though the guard took a particular interest in swearing at Cego from outside the cell door, he didn't think that was a likely sign of friendship.

"If I were you, I'd go back to my family," Cego said, sweeping his hand at the wisp as if trying to shoo it away.

The wisp didn't budge—it pulsed in the corner stubbornly.

Cego halted his conversation as he heard footsteps echoing down the corridor outside his cell. The wisp blinked away.

There were several footfalls this time: two men. He listened to the dull thud of their boots on the stone. One of them was large, probably near two hundred fifty pounds.

Cego squeezed his eyes shut and sat up on the wooden plank as he heard the door rattle.

"Lacklight scumslagger, yer time's come!"

The door opened and rough hands grabbed his shoulders. Cego's muscles tensed.

They pulled him up and dragged him out of the cell. "Kid smells like a Deep rat nest."

"All asses can't be as clean as yours, Aldo," the other replied as they pulled Cego down a long hallway.

"I'm tellin' you, shower spouts is the good stuff. None of that cold bucket of water o'er the head Deep-native shit for me anymore."

"Who says I put *any* water on my head?" the other man said. "Soap-eaters got you talkin' like them, smellin' like them, even. *Clean.* All the girls smell like soap and flowers now. Rather my woman smelled like dirt and blood. Natural, like a real Grievar."

The one called Aldo snorted. "Whatever. Boss wants us to clean this blindbrood up, whether you like it or not. Gotta get 'em processed."

They continued until Cego felt the guards' grips tighten on his shoulders. They shoved him through a doorframe, and the stone floor under his feet was replaced with a cold metallic surface.

"Let's get you clean," Aldo said menacingly.

They pushed Cego onto a metal table. He didn't struggle. Cego heard a buzzing noise getting closer to his head.

Something cold cut into him and he felt a chunk of his hair drop to the ground. They were shaving him.

"This is gonna hurt a bit." One of the men chuckled after Cego's head was shaved clean. They held him down tightly. He clenched his teeth as something seared into his scalp. He could smell his burning flesh, but he didn't cry out.

They made Cego strip his dirty clothes off and step into a large vat of cold water. They laughed as they forced his head beneath the water, his raw scalp stinging as he went under. After Cego came out of the vat, dripping wet, the guards weighed him and measured his height. They scrubbed a layer of skin off his body with a wire brush. They provided him with a pair of pants with a drawstring to keep them up before pulling him out of the room.

The guards were quiet as they pulled Cego into an adjacent room. The two were suddenly bereft of their routine cackles.

Cego felt a bulbous hand grab his face, lifting his chin to the air.

"He's not blind, you idiots," a toadlike voice croaked. Cego felt someone's rotten breath close to his face.

"What? Boss—he can't even piss straight in his cell pot, we're sure he's—"

"He's not blind." The one called boss interrupted the guard.

"But—but how about his fights? Why'd he...?"

"That's what I'm wondering too," the boss said. "See the movement under his lids? He's shut his eyes but they're still trying to see. The eyes of a real blindbrood would have given up long ago."

"The little shitstain, foolin' us like that," one of the guards murmured.

"Open your eyes," the boss commanded Cego flatly.

Cego didn't respond. His feigned blindness was the only advantage he had over his captors right now. The only technique he had hidden in his back pocket.

"Open your eyes or I'll have Aldo here stick a knife in them to see if you care that they're really gone."

The tone of the boss's voice made Cego believe the threat. The old master's voice echoed in Cego's head. *Know when to hold on to your position tightly and when to let go. Grasp for too long and you'll end up in an inferior position.*

Cego opened his eyes.

The man in front of him was enormous. His girth seemed to strain against the chair's sides. He looked at Cego like a piece of meat on display, smacking his lips.

"Hmmm. Golden eyes. Haven't seen that one before. He's Grievar brood for sure, but I can't tell what sort," the boss said. He examined Cego and spoke to him condescendingly. "Who's your mammy, little gold-eyes? What sort of line are you from? Got some Grunt in you, maybe?"

Cego stared at him blankly.

"Just another street boy, then." The man turned to Aldo. "You said you found him down by Lampai? Are you sure he isn't one of ours, or maybe escaped from Saulo's Circle across town?"

Aldo shook his head. "Neither, boss. We scanned him, checked the archives—nothing in there. Real strange. Usually got some light trail on these kids."

"Where did you come from, boy?" The man continued to eye Cego.

Cego met his gaze silently.

"Always such anger from some of these boys." Spittle flew from the man's lips as he spoke. "You don't realize that Pappy Thaloo here is helping you, little gold-eyes. I could throw you back on the streets. Let you end up sweeping the floors or serving food on a platter for some bit-rich Daimyo. You'd go through life with a hole in your heart, always feeling the pull of the light, not knowing why you felt so empty."

The man called Thaloo paused, licking his lips. "You can fulfill your lightpath here, your destiny. Fighting is what you were born to do, little gold-eyes. I'm helping you; can't you see it? If you do well, you'll be treated well. Maybe even end up getting bought by a patron, serving a family or business with honor. Doing some good in this world! Don't you understand?"

Cego's gut told him to stay silent.

"They never see." Thaloo sighed, a horrid croak of a noise. "You'll thank me someday, little gold-eyes." Thaloo swiveled his chair and started to thumb through images on a handheld screen. "Put him on a crew. Let's see how he does with Tasker Ozark, shall we?"

Thaloo turned back to Cego as the guards began to pull him out of the room. "Keep your eyes open this time, boy. You'll need them."

* * *

The yard had tall stone walls with high grated windows that opened to the Underground's street level. Trails of faintly glowing moss ran along some of the walls, and the yard's ground was made of compacted red dirt.

Eight boys with shaved heads were running in a circle around the perimeter of the yard. They were tied together with a knotted rope looped around their waists.

When one boy at the end of the line tripped, he was dragged along the dirt floor by the other boys who kept moving, unknowing or uncaring of the fallen. The boy running in front looked like an ox, his leg muscles bulging and a vein in his forehead pulsing as he yanked the rest of the line forward.

A man stood in the center of the circle. He yelled in a gravelly voice at the boys to move faster, to pull harder, and to get up off the floor. He did not seem like a pleasant man.

The guard brought Cego over to him. "Tasker Ozark. Got a new recruit here for your crew."

"My crew is already full; must be a mistake," Ozark replied without taking his eyes off the runners. Cego could see Ozark had a strange audio device implanted in his throat from which his grating voice vibrated.

The guard pushed further. "Boss's orders, Ozark; he says this boy here is to be placed in your crew for acclimation and training."

"If the boss says so, fine. That means these boys will be splitting their food for nine instead of eight." Ozark turned his faded yellow eyes on Cego. The man's face appeared to be locked in a permanent frown. "Other boys won't be happy about it, though."

The guard nodded and left Cego standing in the yard with Ozark.

"Whoever you think you are, or think you were, forget it now, boy. What you now are is the property of Thaloo, and as his property, you are now my property. I'm your Tasker, meaning my word is your task. When I say crawl, you crawl. If I say swing, you swing."

Ozark stopped to yell at the boy at the end of the line. "Get out of the dirt and start moving again, you little maggot! Move or you'll end up doing sloth carries until blackshift!" The little boy looked like he was about to pass out. He had tears running down his dirt-streaked face as he was dragged behind the line. He barely managed to pull himself up with the rope before beginning to move again.

Ozark continued, "I have one task, and that is to make you strong enough to win in the Circle. You winning means I did my job. You winning means you are worth more for Thaloo-loo-loo-loo-loo-loo—" Ozark's voice box was stuck in some sort of loop. He slapped the back of his neck and it stopped repeating. Cego couldn't help but crack a smile at the strange occurrence.

Ozark's frown cut even deeper, which Cego hadn't thought possible until he saw it. "Halt!" the Tasker called out robotically, and the eight boys came to a sudden stop, panting with relief. Some keeled over and others fell to the ground in exhaustion.

"Circle Crew Nine! You have a new member. I'd like to introduce him to you. His name is..." Ozark waited.

Cego hesitated to meet the eyes of the eight fatigued boys. "Cego."

"Cego. Your new friend here, Cego, thinks what you're doing is funny. He was over here laughing at you, telling me that you looked like a bunch of half-wits running around in circles. Says he could do twice the job of any one of you."

The boys glared back at Cego. The big, heavily muscled one in front of the line flexed his shoulders and stomped the dirt like a bull ready to charge.

"How do you think we should welcome Cego to Circle Crew Nine? After all, he'll be spending every minute with you now, training alongside you, eating your food, pissing in your pot. He deserves a fair welcome, no?"

Ozark tugged at the scruff on his chin, made up of several long, wiry hairs. "Ah, I know. In honor of Cego's welcome, we'll continue your training for an extra two hours. You'll probably miss your duskshift meal and go to bed hungry, but I think we should put Cego's interest in catching up first."

A visible slumping of shoulders shuddered through the crew. They already looked worn as it was.

"Let's get our friend Cego right onto task. Back to rope runs," Ozark barked.

Cego was tied in toward the middle of the pack. The rope had small metal hooks that latched directly into the loops on Cego's pants. Ozark tightened the rope to decrease the slack between each boy.

The boy in front of Cego, who had a scar running across his jaw, turned around and whispered, "You be slaggin' us bad. Crew's gonna make you pay."

The big ox at the front of the line eyed Cego before surging forward with a jerk, causing a chain reaction of boys bouncing into each other. One boy at the front of the line stumbled forward, and Cego saw a boy behind him fall to the ground and immediately get dragged in the dirt without any chance to get back to his feet, which created more work for the entire group.

Ozark sat back with a dirty grin, watching the entire ordeal, yelling at the crew to pick up their pace.

After Ozark was sufficiently pleased with the crew's fatigue from rope runs—most were barely able to stand—he screamed, "Sloth carries!"

Each of the crew was to lift and carry another boy around the room until he fell to his knees.

Cego was paired with the scar-faced boy, who glared at him and refused to cooperate. When it was time to pick him up and run, the boy made it extremely difficult for Cego to get under him, shifting his weight and falling like a sack of turnips.

Cego breathed out, frustrated, while the boy stood back up with a smug grin on his face. Just as the scar-faced boy turned away, Cego shot toward his legs quickly and threw him onto his shoulders—a classic entry into the kata guruma shoulder throw.

The boy let out a grunt of surprise. He settled in to let Cego jog around the room with the rest of the crew. As he ran, Cego had a vivid memory of the old master making him drill kata guruma over and over for hours.

These boys were using a variety of inefficient methods to carry their partners. The ox was sweating profusely as he carried one of the smaller boys under his arm.

Ozark's final task was called *last boy hanging.* There were a series of ropes draped from the ceiling around the perimeter of the room. The boys were to climb to the top of a rope and hang there for as long as possible.

"The boy who falls first has piss pot duty for the next week," Ozark threatened.

Cego didn't exactly know what piss pot duty was, but he knew he didn't want it.

He scaled his rope within seconds, using his hands and feet in unison to crawl up it like an island ferrcat. From the top of the rope he could see the street's light filtering through the window grates. It cast crimson shadows on Circle Crew Nine, each boy hanging from his rope, muscles shuddering from hours of hard work.

Why shouldn't he beat them? Cego knew he could hang there for longer than the rest of the crew, perhaps well into the night. He could show them he was strong. Perhaps then they wouldn't turn on him.

Cego looked to his right at the small boy hanging next to him, the same one who had been dragged at the back of the rope line. The little boy's body shivered with strain and Cego saw tears streaming from the corners of his eyes.

Another of the boys, one with haughty yellow jackal eyes, taunted the crying boy. "Weep! Weep! You might as well drop now; you know you'll be the first anyway. You lacklights were made to clean piss pots."

Cego saw the little boy's arms trembling. He wouldn't last more than a few moments longer.

The old master's voice echoed in Cego's head again, this time louder than he'd ever heard it before, as if he were standing in the yard. *We fight so the rest shall not have to.*

Cego dropped to the ground, landing nimbly on his feet. He had been the first boy to fall.

He met Ozark's stare.

* * *

Cego's plan didn't work out as he had envisioned. By showing weakness, he thought to make the crew forget the extra hours of training and shared food rationing. Instead, like a pack of wolves that smelled blood, they went after him.

After the grueling training session, Tasker Ozark held Cego back to drag all the equipment from the yard into storage for the night. Cego's stomach rumbled as he finished the work. He hadn't eaten since yesterday.

Cego finally returned to the Crew Nine bunks and found himself without any place to rest.

Although there was an extra cot for him, a strange assortment of metal cans lay strung together on top of the bed. The scar-faced boy popped his head out from the bunk above. Using his finger, he spooned a glop of green sludge out of a can and let out a loud burp. "That there be Modek's bed."

"Modek?" Cego asked.

"Right there, that be Modek," the scar-faced boy replied, nodding at the pile of tin cans on the bed. The boy had an accent that Cego couldn't place. "Crew decided he gets your greens tonight."

The ox from the front of the rope line chimed in from the bunk across from them. His voice sounded like Cego thought it would, like a hollowed-out log. "Modek probably could've held on to that rope longer than you, weakling. That's why he's got your bed and you've gotta sleep on the floor," he said matter-of-factly.

Another one of the boys slowly walked over to Cego with his arms crossed and his lips pursed. Cego recognized him as the jackal-eyed boy who had taunted the crying little one in the yard.

"Ah, now, Dozer, Knees, let's see that our new crew member has a better welcome than this, as Tasker Ozark instructed," the boy hissed. "No need for childish games. After all, we all will be tasking with... Cego, here, for who knows how long."

The ox named Dozer interjected, hooting, "Till I get a patron!"

The jackal boy stared Dozer down. "Shut up, Dozer. Don't interrupt me. And you won't be getting a patron anytime soon."

Dozer looked down at the floor. "But Shiar..."

"As I was saying, we need to welcome Cego to our crew, especially because he's been so kind as to volunteer his piss pot skills for us," Shiar said. "Why don't we further our welcome to Cego and let him take on his new task tonight? After all, I am especially stuffed after polishing off all those cans of greens." Shiar licked his lips. "Dozer, why don't you start off with that famed stench of yours and get over to the pot?"

Dozer clapped his hands together and headed for the adjacent bathroom, glaring at Cego as he lumbered past. Shiar moved closer to Cego and whispered in his ear, "Don't think I couldn't see you let go of that rope on purpose. You won't find any pity here, lacklight."

A few other boys made their moves to the chamber pot after Dozer. The scar-faced boy, Knees, smirked as he brushed past Cego. "You be deepshittin' it now."

Shiar was the last to go and returned with a small wire brush, which he offered to Cego. "The pot is almost overflowing out there. I think more than half of it is Dozer's. You'll need to make sure it gets emptied out in the drain and then made sparkling clean with that brush. The dawnshift guard is quite the stickler, so make sure you get every spot in there."

Several of the crew laughed in glee. Dozer thudded his hands against the metal bunk post.

Cego didn't take the brush. He kept his hands down by his sides.

Cego knew fighting techniques, ways of movement, breathing, and energy conservation, but never had he been taught how to deal with other boys like this.

As if on cue, the old master's voice spoke to Cego. *You may need to give up position to gain position. Don't be afraid to retreat, give in, let your opponent dictate your pace for a moment. Then, when they think they are in control, use momentum to your advantage.*

Cego looked Shiar in the eye for a moment and then, with lightning speed, snatched the little brush from his hand. Shiar flinched but laughed it off. Cego took on the task, emptying and cleaning the pot with the tiny brush. He was surprised at how difficult it was to hold his breath while trying to scrub out every stain on the chamber pot. By the time he was done, his arms felt weak and he saw white spots from the lack of air.

Cego returned to the bunk. The rest of the boys appeared to be sleeping soundly.

He found a spot in the corner of the room and curled up on the cold stone floor, adjacent to the littlest boy's cot. He quickly found out why the rest of the crew called the boy Weep—he was shuddering with sobs, trying to be silent, with a tattered sheet pulled over his face.

Cego forced his eyes shut, attempting to fall asleep as he listened to the boy cry.

CHAPTER 3

Momentum

A Grievar shall not accumulate land, wealth, servants, or worldly possessions beyond what is necessary for survival. In the act of relinquishing all but dedication to martial prowess, a Grievar will become unburdened, free to attack and defend without hesitation.

Seventh Precept of the Combat Codes

Green luminescence shimmered on Cego's skin as he swam through the water. He cut through the waves effortlessly, feeling them swell and pass beneath him, setting their course to whip up on some distant shore.

A swarm of leathery-skinned bats skimmed the water beside him, careening like dive-bombers from above to snatch at the plankton that foamed all around him. The glowing swath of plankton continued far out into the distance, providing Cego a shimmering path to swim along.

About ten yards ahead, another figure was traveling the same path, a dark silhouette thrashing through the waves. Cego tried to push his pace to catch up to the figure, but every time he swam faster, the silhouette also sped up to maintain the gap between them.

Cego attempted to find his rhythm—a steady pace of exertion that the old master stressed no matter what the physical exercise was. Whether fighting, running, climbing, or swimming, it needed to be efficient.

Cego's feet, hands, and body twisted through the current in unison, each stroke feeding off the previous one's energy, his breath timed to every movement.

Cego didn't think about the murky depths around him. Beyond the glowing path of plankton, darkness was everywhere. Above him, the sky was as black and as unfathomable as the depths below. Cego followed his rhythm and swam.

Suddenly, he heard a scream. The figure ahead of him had disappeared from the surface of the water.

Cego dove beneath the waves and tried to swim toward the sinking body. He felt the water resisting him, though; it became viscous, pushing back against his efforts. Every stroke Cego took, the liquid became thicker, congealing around his limbs.

Cego gurgled as he was pulled down. He desperately tried to swim toward the sinking figure, but he wasn't moving. The liquid wrapped around Cego's body, slithering into his mouth and ears, choking him and blotting out his vision.

He sank into the darkness.

* * *

Cego awoke again in the cold, sterile bunk in the Underground.

He thought about the little wisp that used to visit him in his cell. He hadn't seen the thing since he'd arrived at the Crew Nine bunks. He missed the one-sided conversations with the wisp—his new bunkmates were not nearly as good listeners.

The other boys roused as an old guard entered the room, rattling their bed frames as he went by. "Time to get at it, you snivelers." He shook Weep's post particularly violently.

The man tossed each boy a can stuffed with fighting greens. Cego popped the lid, turning his head to avoid the noxious smell.

The guard caught Cego's reaction from the corner of his eye. "Don't think you aren't darkin' lucky, with yer own cots and food in yer belly every morning. Go out to the dregs, see them cleaver addicts, their lightless spawn. You'll see how lucky you are."

The boys were hungry after another cold night and they dug into the greens with a determined but passionless vigor. Dozer finished first, throwing the can against the wall across from his bunk. The large boy pulled his drawstring pants up and let out a beefy burp. "Can't wait to get outside today and show 'em what I've got." He feigned a few punches at an imaginary opponent.

"You won't be havin' a patron pick you up with punches like those," taunted Knees, the boy with the scar. He picked up Dozer's empty can and tossed it back at him.

Dozer knocked the can to the ground. "Yeah, right, and you're gonna get one by losing all your fights, huh, Venturian?"

"Just one fight and that kid be outweighin' me by thirty. He be like you, all vat-beefed up, no skill. Just sittin' on me," Knees said.

"Who cares; you lost. Patrons gonna see that. While you're still playing in that yard every day, I'll be on my way to the Lyceum. I'm gonna be a Knight someday. And I'm gonna get a real darkin' flux tattoo," Dozer said.

Knees guffawed, nearly choking on his greens.

Dozer's face reddened. "What? What makes you think I won't make it into the Lyceum?"

"When I be thinkin' *Grievar Knight,* you definitely don't pop. Maybe some patron be pickin' you up at a discount." Knees smirked.

Dozer stiffened and was beginning to move toward Knees when the old guard came back into the room. "Save your fights for the Circle. Now get to the yard. I hear Tasker Ozark's going to have you doing something special today." The guard chuckled ominously.

Cego pulled his pants on and waited for his turn to shave his head with the razor the boys were passing around. Thaloo required all the boys to be fully shaved every morning to display the flux brand on each of their scalps.

Cego had discovered that each brand displayed a boy's bit-price. Patrons watching the fights could easily determine if the kids were worth buying. If a boy won his fights handily, his price would increase and the flux brand would reflect that. Cego's brand displayed zero currently; all his previous fights had only ensured he was hearty enough to be assigned to a Tasker.

The crew fell into formation behind the guard and began to walk toward the yard. Shiar gave Cego an impish stare as he pushed to the front of the formation. Currently, Shiar was on top of the crew's rankings. Dozer wasn't far behind him.

As he listened to Crew Nine talk during their breaks, Cego had attempted to understand the purpose of it all. Thaloo had acquired the boys through unscrupulous means. Dozer had been bought at a bargain price from some hawkers trying to unload their wares before going Upworld. Knees had come along with a shipment of Venturian Grunts sent Deep for mining work. Weep had been grabbed fresh from an orphanage right after both his parents had died of the Cimmerian Shade. Some of the boys, like Cego, were simply picked up off the streets.

Shiar, as he incessantly reminded everyone, had been the son of an Underground purelight family that had fallen on hard times. Cego gathered they'd been forced to sell their property along with some of their children, Shiar included.

After purchase, Thaloo put the boys through fight acclimation—a period of cost-efficient training to increase his product's value. Men like Tasker Ozark were hired to facilitate the training and were promised a small cut of successful sales. Thaloo then showcased the young Grievar in his Circle, letting them fight while potential patrons watched and bid on them. Patrons liked to buy Grievar at a young age to instill loyalty.

Though Cego was starting to understand this strange Underground world, he knew he had much to learn.

The crew arrived at the yard, where Tasker Ozark waited for them, his face drawn into the same perpetual frown. "Well, let's get you scumlings at it. Time to ramp it up. Few of you have got fights coming up and I want you winning. You winning means I win. Means Thaloo wins."

Ozark directed his gaze at Cego. "You lose, though…and you're not gonna last. Thaloo will have you chewed up and spat out, no time. Back on the streets where the Cimmerian Shade can take you."

Here at Thaloo's, the training was mostly drills made to harden the boys for their fights. They weren't taught techniques or skills for any long-term development. Thaloo had short-term sales in mind for most of his assets.

Ozark shouted at the crew to do fifty push-ups, his metallic voice scraping against the yard's stone walls. He had them do dog crawls, running on all fours around the perimeter of the room until their legs couldn't hold out. Next, it was sloth carries again.

Every once in a while, Ozark would have them shadowbox or show him a round kick to measure progress. The gaunt man enjoyed watching the boys fall over as they tried to spin around on a misguided kick. He didn't give them any advice; he laughed at them in a hyena-like wheeze.

Cego knew the old master had taught him real technique, the tiniest movements that made a world of difference. How power in either a punch or kick came from the hips. How to generate leverage. How to use his opponent's momentum to his benefit.

Cego had been staying quiet for the past few days, cleaning out piss pots and doing whatever else was required of him. The crew had continued to make things difficult for him along the way, stealing his food, reporting his disobedience to Ozark, throwing sneaky elbows at him during their training in the yard.

He knew it was almost time to use that momentum. Cego needed to show strength when he entered the Circle.

* * *

Cego's first fight on Circle Crew Nine came fast. Tasker Ozark wanted to test him as soon as possible to see how much he'd be worth.

He had rings under his eyes from the long hours training in the yard, and his body felt stiff from sleeping on the hard stone floor every night. The rest of Crew Nine stared Cego down as he walked out of the bunk.

Ozark led him toward the Circle den with the rest of the crew trailing behind. "Don't start off on the wrong foot today, scumling. Losers stay losers," the gaunt man warned him. They entered the large den at the center of Thaloo's compound. Though Cego had already fought there several times, the place was different with his eyes open.

The room around him was a blur of chaos. People were sitting along the bar, shouting, looking up at dozens of flashing lightboards. Men and women stood around the perimeter of the Circle, clanking their glasses against each other, pounding their hands on the railing, barking in a variety of languages Cego did not understand.

The floor smelled like rotten ale. Foul smoke wafted to the ceiling from lit pipes. At the back of the room, strange meats were smoking on a heat pad, lending another acrid smell to the stifling air.

Cego could hardly breathe and he hadn't even started moving yet. He attempted to calm himself as he walked to the edge of the Circle, expelling the air from his lungs as the old master had taught him. But he kept breathing in, his chest tightening.

Ozark shoved him forward into the steel Circle, which was pulsing an azure blue now.

He saw his opponent across from him. The boy was about Cego's size, maybe a few inches taller, with a scrunched-up nose and narrow eyes. Cego could see the brand on his head, his bit-price reflecting the several fights he'd already won in this Circle. The boy's Tasker was at his side, whispering in his ear.

A large lightboard flashed to life above the Circle. There was an image of Cego and his opponent up there along with a series of fluctuating numbers he couldn't focus on. Cego could feel his heart beating rapidly in his chest. Could his opponent see that? He tried to take another deep breath, unsuccessfully.

Cego didn't know why he was fighting here. Had the old master trained him so diligently to fight in a den for a bunch of drunken Deep folk? To get bought by some patron and spend the rest of his days in their servitude? It didn't make any sense; his head was spinning.

Suddenly, a swarm of glowing blue wisps rose in the air and clustered above the Circle. Cego had heard them called *spectrals.* They were similar to the little glowing wisp in his cell, but somehow, these spectrals were very different.

Cego felt their light immediately. It streamed into his eyes and grew warm on the surface of his skin. It was like nothing he'd experienced before. The chaos around him dissipated into silence, as if a soundproof bubble had enveloped the Circle.

He could breathe. The trapped air flowed from his lungs. Cego drank the air, brought it in through his nose, let it settle in every inch of his body—running up his spine, relaxing in his shoulders, tingling in his fingertips and toes.

As Cego's breath and heartbeat calmed, the world around him slowed. He saw his opponent clearly on the other side of the Circle. No one else was in the room, just two boys standing across from one another. Everything felt right. His past, his stiff body, the troubles with his crew, Tasker Ozark—they all seemed unimportant now.

The other boy was lumbering toward him. Why was he moving so slowly? Cego stood perfectly still.

Finally, the boy was in front of Cego, swinging at his head with a clublike right hand. Cego easily slipped the punch.

He saw the unsure expression on the boy's face, the sweat

droplets on his brow, the wildness in his citrine-tinged eyes as he moved forward.

The boy threw another looping punch. This time, Cego caught the arm at the elbow and moved in with a quick step, wrapping his arms around his opponent and hugging him tightly. He circled his leg behind the boy's knee and took him to the floor.

Cego was on top of the boy, rearing up to punch him. "Put 'is head through the dirt!" someone nearby shouted.

The crowd was screaming for blood, slamming their hands against the metal railing. They wanted to see him beat the life out of the boy. Cego knew that the bloodier and more vicious a finish, the louder their approval would be.

Cego felt Tasker Ozark's eyes on him, urging him to put on a show of dominance. Winning in a spectacular fashion would result in pushing his bit-price higher and selling to a patron faster.

He sensed Crew Nine watching from the sidelines. Cego could make an example of his opponent and show jackals like Shiar what would happen if they messed with him. He could make Dozer and Knees respect him.

Cego wanted to please the crowd. He wanted to teach the boy beneath him a lesson for being weak. He felt the crowd's energy within him, tendrils of anger urging him to pummel his opponent until he was a lifeless husk.

True fear is often masked by strength and true strength is often mistaken for fear. The old master's voice rang above the crowd's clamor.

Cego saw the fear in the eyes of the boy beneath him. They reminded him of Weep as he shivered on the rope in the dusklight. He felt the fear in the crowd around him. They yelled for blood because they were also scared, unsure of the path they followed.

Cego realized he was afraid too—that's why he wanted to please the crowd, his crew, his Tasker.

He snapped out of the trance.

Instead of raining punches down on his opponent, Cego clapped his hands against both sides of the boy's head.

The boy panicked, trying to turn away from the openhanded strikes. Cego loosened his hips slightly and let the boy beneath him turn. He pinned the boy facedown. He'd want a quick finish, without humiliation.

Cego thrust his hips down, pushing the boy into the dirt. He snaked one of his arms under the boy's chin, grasping around his neck. *Mata Leon*—the Lion Killer. This boy was hardly a lion, but Cego squeezed until he felt the boy stop struggling. He'd be awake in less than a minute, without a scratch on his face.

Cego stood, the boy's limp body prone on the floor. He could feel the light shining down on him, even brighter now. He wondered if the little spectral from his cell was up there in the mass of pulsing light.

Cego's eyes were wide and alive as he felt a strange tingling from the flux brand on his scalp. The light was communicating with his body, taking in every detail of the fight: how many heartbeats had passed, how many breaths he'd taken, the exact saturation of the oxygen running through his blood vessels.

At its apex, the light suddenly dimmed as the spectrals dispersed, some floating toward the crowd and others sinking onto the Circle's cool surface. Cego was again standing in the noisy room. The drunken spectators were still yelling, the air still tinged with smoke and stifling body odors. His opponent's crew entered the Circle, dragging the unconscious boy across the floor and out of the room. Cego felt a pit in his stomach.

Ozark still had that deep-cut frown on his face.

The Tasker grabbed his arm, dragging him out of the den. "Don't ever play with my chances of getting you sold off as fast as possible, boy, or I'll make your life more miserable than it already is."

* * *

Cego's bit-price rose with every fight, his flux brand constantly shifting.

He looked at his reflection in the dirty mirror of their bunk. The strange brand on his head was alive. The ink was in constant movement, the pixels never staying in one place, swirling and waiting for the next command from the light.

Cego had most recently beaten a boy from Circle Crew Two who had been previously undefeated. The boy had come at him with a series of thudding leg kicks. He rubbed his thigh where a huge welt in the shape of the boy's shin had swelled. Walking, let alone training, would be tough today.

As Cego won more fights, the rest of the crew began to tone down their tormenting. Although they ignored him for the most part, they removed the tin cans from his cot and no longer touched his food.

Weep and another boy from Crew Nine had lost their last fights, so Ozark was especially vindictive with the day's training. With the damage his leg had sustained, Cego could barely make it through the drills.

"Think you're going to lose on my watch? Think I'm going to just let that go?" Ozark screamed at the boys as they crawled on all fours in the red dirt.

Weep fell to his belly in exhaustion. Ozark marched over to the little boy and placed his boot on his back, holding him to the ground. "Want to take a rest, you little sniveler, do you? All right, how about I take a rest too and stand right here for a while?" Ozark had his weight pressed on Weep's back, crushing his boot down on him.

As he watched Weep struggle, Cego felt the hairs on the back of his neck prickle. His jaw clenched and his fingers curled into fists. He forgot about his sore body and the task at hand. He was crouched on all fours in the dirt, his golden eyes locked on Ozark.

Anger is like a boiling pot of water. Useful if you can keep the boil steady, but if turned too hot, it will overflow and become useless.

The old master was right, as usual. Attacking Ozark would be disastrous for the whole crew, Weep included. Cego breathed out deeply.

Ozark removed his boot and yanked Weep back to his feet. "Keep moving," he yelled as he prodded the little boy forward. A long rope run was to be the final drill for the day—the crew was barely standing at this point. The boys wearily attached the gnarled rope to their harnesses, pulling the line taut between them.

Ozark was taking them past the limit this time. The Tasker wanted to make them stronger so they could win, so *he* could win. But this was beyond training. This was torture.

The run began as it usually did: chaotically. Dozer surged forward, pulling the rest of the boys, some staggering and tripping over one another's feet, others stumbling to the ground. They would never make it through the entire drill like this.

Cego was the middle link. He needed to do something now. He placed his hands on Knees's shoulders in front of him. The scar-faced boy was startled at first, turning back to look at Cego suspiciously. Cego didn't say anything; he just looked at Knees and kept steady.

For every step Cego took, he put slight pressure with his hand on Knees's same-side shoulder, also using his outstretched arms for support.

After a circle around the perimeter, Knees turned back at him and nodded—he understood. Knees placed his hands on Shiar's shoulders and did the same thing.

Cego looked back at a boy named Yusef and got his attention to the front of the line, where Shiar now had his hands on Dozer's broad shoulders. Yusef was staggering with fatigue, but he grabbed hold of Cego's shoulders.

Soon, the entire rope line was running in sync. No boys crashed into one another. Their legs moved in rhythm. They were using the entire group's momentum to slither forward like a sea eel.

Cego saw Ozark watching the crew, his calculating eyes darting back and forth.

"Halt!"

The rope crew came to a stop, the boys panting. "Weakness! You scumlings aren't fit for my task, so you've decided you need to cheat, to hold each other's hands. Will you have each other to hold on to in the Circle? When a Grievar is on top of you, smashing your face into a pulp, where will your friends be then?" Ozark spat into the dirt. "I will not tolerate such weakness. Sloth carries. Now!" Ozark screamed.

The crew was on the brink. Dozer staggered forward, his legs shivering from the constant strain that came from leading the pack. Cego could even see desperation in Shiar's eyes as he turned back, panting. They were nearly broken.

With a malicious glint in his eye, Ozark paired Weep with Dozer for the sloth carry. The frail boy clearly could not support Dozer's weight, not even for one second. He tried futilely to get under Dozer, heaving with his shoulders until he fell to the ground.

Cego had Knees as a partner again—he lowered his center of gravity and was able to hoist Knees up, though moving with him on his shoulders was nearly unbearable.

Ozark walked to Weep's side, looking down at him. "Stop crying, boy. Your mammy isn't here to patch you up." The Tasker prodded the boy with his boot. Weep rolled over onto his back, the side of his face wet with tears.

The anger swelled in Cego again at seeing the man standing over Weep, a boot against his rib cage. He dropped Knees to the ground and moved across the yard toward Ozark. *Don't let the pot boil over.*

"Let me show him how to pick Dozer up."

Ozark looked down at Cego, at first surprised to see him out of position and then seething at the challenge to his command. "Oh, if it isn't the champion himself. Just because you've won a few fights, you think you're a Grievar Knight. You think you can do my job for me?" The Tasker's eyes narrowed. "Get back in line and do your task, you little larva. Run, fight, and shut your mouth."

"If Weep can't pick up Dozer after I show him how to properly do it, I'll take Dozer on my back every day from now on," Cego said steadily. He had to make the feint for his opponent's hands to come down.

Tasker Ozark eyed Cego suspiciously, clearly thinking he was trying to outsmart him. Ozark then looked down at Weep, still heaving, barely able to get himself off the ground, let alone lift a boy more than twice his size. Ozark shook his head in agreement. "Okay, little champion, you've got it."

Cego knelt at Weep's side. "You all right?"

Weep wiped the snot from his nose, looking up at Cego with watery eyes. "I'm okay."

"I'm going to show you how to do this," Cego whispered. "It's as easy as standing up." Cego heard the old master's voice again as he said the words.

Weep nodded obediently. Ozark watched from the corner of his eye as he yelled gratingly at the other boys to keep moving. "First, breathe out. You're trying to take in too much air but you're not letting enough out. Breathe out first; get rid of it all."

Weep sat up, closing his eyes, and blew out of his mouth, more snot coming out of his nose as he did so.

"Okay, keep breathing like that. Dozer, come stand here; don't do anything. This will be good for you too." Dozer surprisingly did as he was told.

"I want you to think about it like this," Cego said. "You aren't picking up Dozer. You aren't picking anyone up. You're getting under him and then standing up."

Weep was confused; he shook his head. "But I am trying to pick him up. There's no way I can carry Dozer; he's way bigger than I am. And I'm not strong. I couldn't even pick you up, Cego."

"Watch me," Cego said.

Cego moved toward Dozer. The bulky boy outweighed him by at least seventy pounds. He bent his knees, crouching directly under Dozer, with one arm circling through his legs, grasping his back. He kept his posture straight. Cego then lifted from his knees, causing the front half of Dozer's body to fall forward onto his shoulder. He wrapped Dozer's arm around his neck and stood up effortlessly. He took a few steps around the yard with the huge boy on his back before letting him down.

He looked at Weep. "See how easy it is? You can do this." Weep nodded, wiping his nose and standing. "Just remember, you aren't trying to lift Dozer. Don't use your back or your arms. You are standing up under him."

Cego showed Weep where to crouch and place his arms again.

"Now give it a try." Cego clasped Weep's shoulder. "It's just standing up, like you do every morning."

Everyone in the yard stopped to view the spectacle, even Tasker Ozark.

Weep mimicked Cego's movements. He crouched under Dozer, his knees bent. He tried to stand up.

Cego held his breath as Weep's knees buckled for a moment, but suddenly, the large boy was on top of the tiny boy's shoulders. It was an unnatural sight, as if a grass mouse were lifting a prize pig. Weep appeared the most surprised of everyone in the yard, his eyes bulging. He took a cautious step forward.

Weep walked steadily around the yard with Dozer awkwardly draped on top of his shoulders. Knees stamped his feet in the dirt and laughed, watching the strange sight. "The tiny one be all jacked up!"

The rest of the boys in the yard hooted as Weep slowly made it back to the starting point before collapsing to the ground.

Ozark narrowed his eyes and glared at Cego, as if he'd somehow cheated.

Cego knew he'd pay for his intervention, but it was worth it. A smile crept across his face as he returned Ozark's glare. The gaunt Tasker screamed, "All right, that's enough of this. Shut it and let's get on to the next!"

* * *

After that day in the yard, the other boys began to act differently around Cego.

Dozer was the first to break the standoff. It was the middle of the night when Cego awoke to the large boy standing over him. Cego stared at him for a moment with bleary eyes before Dozer extended his hand. Cego grasped it and was promptly yanked into the air, dangling like a newborn ferrcat. The large boy deposited him on the floor and put his finger to his lips. The other boys were still sleeping.

He followed Dozer across the room to the wall next to his bunk, where the bulky boy knelt on the floor and shifted a small piece of concrete. He reached his arm about halfway into the opening, grasping and pulling out about a dozen cans of greens. Some were half-eaten, and there were even a few unopened ones.

Dozer smiled at him, nodding and passing him one of the unopened cans. He whispered, "Sometimes, I get hungry."

Cego returned the smile and padded back to his bed with his early breakfast.

Knees didn't protest anymore when getting partnered with Cego in the yard. Cego actually caught the scar-faced Venturian carefully watching him explain another technique to Weep. Later, he saw Knees slowly attempting to replicate the technique with another crew member.

Eventually, the other boys began to come directly to Cego for advice on techniques for their upcoming fights.

In the corner of their bunkroom, beyond the view of the old guard, Cego showed Knees and Dozer a simple back take. Grab behind the elbow, drag the arm across the body, and use the momentum to expose the opponent's back.

To Cego, these things were second nature. He felt it in his muscles—he'd drilled that back take thousands of times. To these boys, though, even the simplest techniques were marvels. They were awed at the efficiency of good movement. The boys had Grievar blood in them, but they certainly weren't fighters yet.

Ozark eventually caught wind of Cego helping out the crew. Though he made Cego pay for the stand-down in the yard every chance he got, Ozark didn't intervene with the off-hours training.

Since Cego had arrived, the crew's overall winning percentage had increased and they'd been moving ahead in the crew rankings, which comprised the wins of all members. Cego could nearly see the bits flashing in Ozark's eyes as he watched his product appreciate in value.

Weep had even stopped crying at night. Before bed, Cego watched the little boy sitting against the wall, breathing steadily as he'd been taught in the yard. Though he hadn't won any fights, Weep had won some confidence.

Shiar was the only one who did not accept Cego. The jackal got even worse.

After one of Shiar's fights, he returned to the bunk and stared Cego down. Shiar had blood on his hands, having just mercilessly pounded his opponent into the ground with glee. He licked the blood from his knuckles while keeping his burning eyes on Cego.

Shiar's insults toward Weep became more stinging, and he even turned his vehemence toward Dozer. Shiar treated Dozer like an unwanted pet, shooing him away and calling him a mound of useless muscle and a blockheaded dolt, and yet Dozer still followed his lead.

And then Shiar called Dozer *lightless.*

Before that day, Dozer had brashly repeated he would graduate from the Lyceum and become a Knight. That was his goal, his destiny, his lightpath.

The scales of destiny weren't balanced for all, though. For some like Dozer, who wasn't born of pure Grievar blood, who didn't have the best trainers and equipment at his disposal, that destiny was nearly impossible to reach.

Shiar had made it perfectly clear to the rest of the crew on numerous occasions that he was the only purelight in the bunk, perhaps even at Thaloo's. Both his mother and father were from a long line of Grievar. They "hadn't strayed from the light," as Shiar arrogantly said. Though he'd had the misfortune of getting tossed in this slave Circle, Shiar said it wouldn't be long before he ended up at his rightful place at the Lyceum.

By contrast, most of the other boys at Thaloo's were lacklights; they were some impure mixture of breeds. They didn't have the supposed pure Grievar line that gave them an edge to place at the Lyceum.

After Shiar called him lightless, Dozer fell silent, no longer posturing before his fights and boasting in victory. In fact, the entire bunk was far quieter without the large boy's constant bravado and thumping around. Though Cego appreciated the newfound silence, he also saw the toll the insult had taken on Dozer.

The large boy sat on his cot with his shoulders slumped. He barely ate, and during training, Dozer went through the grueling tasks with a lifeless monotony.

Dozer's bit-price began to fall along with his confidence—he'd lost two of his last three fights, one against a top specimen called N'jal. Cego had watched that fight from the sidelines.

N'jal had taken Dozer down from the outset and unleashed a flurry of ground-and-pound for nearly ten minutes as Dozer tried helplessly to cover up. Cego cringed, thinking about how the crew had dragged Dozer out of the Circle, his big body looking like a slab of raw meat.

Afterward, Ozark had given Dozer the bare minimum in meds from stock. Dozer was lying inert in his cot, wrapped head to toe in bandages, when Cego went to his side.

"You did good covering up, but you could've gone out the back door." Cego spoke softly, taking a seat at the edge of Dozer's cot.

Dozer looked at the light overhead without expression. His face was a craterous landscape, with welts and hematomas covering the surface.

Cego continued, though Dozer stayed silent. "When N'jal postured up to throw down those heavy shots, your hips were under his. You needed to buck, put his head in the dirt, and escape out the back side. You'd risk taking a direct hit in the process, but it was the only way. N'jal was hoping you'd concentrate on defense—he's made to smash through your forearms, grind you down slowly. You needed to take the risk to escape. You needed to commit," Cego said.

Dozer's straw-colored eyes finally met Cego's. "What's the point in all this? Learning this stuff? Getting better? I'm not going anywhere. You heard Shiar. I'm a... I'm..." The big boy looked down at his chest as his body shuddered. "It's not fair. Lacklights like us... It's not fair that we weren't born purelights when we want the same thing as them."

Cego nodded silently, agreeing. He didn't think any of this was fair. Thaloo imprisoning them, throwing them in the Circle, and having them fight for his own profit.

But Cego did know one thing now. He understood what Thaloo had said to him when he'd first arrived.

You don't realize that Pappy Thaloo here is helping you.

In some twisted way, Thaloo *was* helping these kids. Though his motivations were self-serving, Cego knew that there was some truth to them.

He'd felt the spectral light in the Circle, the thrill of the fight. He knew that all Grievar had that connection, that same universal pulse of combat. They all wanted the same thing but would arrive on different paths.

"Taking the back," Cego suddenly said. Dozer looked at him quizzically.

"Remember the technique I showed you the other day? Taking your opponent's back."

Dozer nodded slowly, clearly puzzled at the line of questioning.

"Well. I've probably learned about thirty ways to take the back so far. Drag an arm across, spin around from north–south, lure them into a throw. I could keep going and I know there are far more techniques with the same goal of taking the back that I haven't learned yet," Cego explained. "Dozer. It's like us. Every technique is different. Some are better than others, depending on the situation. But each one has the same goal—taking the back. They all end up in the same place, with the same finish."

Dozer was still nodding slowly, though he didn't appear to understand where Cego was going.

Cego continued. "We're all different, Dozer. Lacklights, purelights, bit-rich or poor, Deep folk, Upworlders, Islanders. We're all coming from different places but are trying to get to the same spot, find the same path, take the back. You just need to find the right technique. You need to find your own path. It doesn't need to be same path as Shiar's or mine or anyone else's. You need to find Dozer's path."

"Dozer's path," the large boy repeated slowly.

Knees also stepped to Dozer's side. "All that Cego said be true, plus, we know Shiar be lying through his teeth when he talks of his blood. We pretty much all got Grunt flowing in our veins. You want to know the real difference between purelight and lacklight?"

"What?" Dozer asked.

"Purelights think they know it all, that it be their blood-given right to be on top," Knees said. "Lacklights like us? We know we got to work for our wins. We be training and learning and bleeding for it, and we won't stop till we're under the dry earth."

A slight smile and then a huge, toothy grin broke across Dozer's face. He bellowed and slapped Cego on the back, surprising him and nearly knocking him off the cot.

"Hey, Shiar!" Dozer burst out of his bed, bandages and all. "Hear that? I'll see you at the Lyceum!"

CHAPTER 4

A Light and a Path

When first attaining the mounted position, one would be foolish to try to attack too soon. Though any well-built roof can withstand the initial downpour of a rainstorm, it is the prolonged accumulation of water, the filling of gutters, the soaking of soils, and the pressure on the roof that finally bring it to collapse. The mount should force such a collapse. Listen to an opponent's rhythm of breathing and apply pressure to the diaphragm during each attempted inhalation. Block their mouth and nose so that what air they do find is a struggle. Cover their eyes so that they welcome the darkness when it comes to them.

Passage Two, Eighteenth Technique of the Combat Codes

Cego opened his eyes and thought he was truly blind. A white shroud veiled the entirety of his vision. But he felt a familiar warmth on his face, and as his eyes adjusted, he saw a fuzzy form take shape. It was a spectral, nearly sitting at the tip of his nose. Not just any of the commonplace wisps—it was Cego's spectral from the cell, the one that had kept him sane through hours of one-sided conversation. Somehow, he knew it just as he knew any other old friend.

"You're back," Cego whispered, keeping his voice low to not wake the rest of Crew Nine. He glanced over at Weep's bed to see the boy wrapped tightly in his covers. Dozer was snoring loudly, as usual.

The spectral flickered and began to drift away from Cego's cot. He stared at it through the darkness and it stopped. He could feel it pulling at him, beckoning.

Cego slid off the bunk, feeling the cold stone floor against his feet as he padded after the floating wisp. He thought about the guard usually posted outside their door, but unsurprisingly, he wasn't there. Cego had overheard the man talking with another guard earlier about visiting a place called Courtesan House during blackshift.

He followed the wisp past the exit and turned the corner to see it drifting down another hall. Cego recognized the route as one he'd been prodded down every day for the past month. The spectral was leading him toward the practice yard.

Cego paused to make sure no one was following him before stepping out onto the red dirt of the yard. He watched the little wisp ascend toward the street-level grates at the top of the room.

He heard a sudden grunt in the darkness. Cego could make out a single form at the center of the wide yard. Someone was shadowboxing, throwing out a series of jabs followed by a spinning kick. Cego recognized the movement, the lanky limbs, the fluid attacks melding together one after another.

A mech transport rumbled by at street level and cast its headlights onto the yard for a moment, illuminating a face with a wicked scar crossing it. Knees.

Cego stepped farther in to make his presence known. Knees abruptly stopped moving.

"It's you." The boy stared at him. "Thought the old guard be deciding to come back from the Courtesan Houses early."

"Still a risk," Cego said as he approached. "Ozark probably would punish us for coming out here at blackshift."

"Right, even though he already be punishing us by making us do exactly this." Knees smirked as he threw several more punches. "Having us spend extra time training here, running laps, shadowboxing."

"It's about control," Cego said. "Ozark doesn't care if you're improving, or helping the crew, or even helping him. He wants to be the one to make the decisions."

"You be right." Knees nodded. "So, if you don't mind, I'd like to be getting back to my illegal training session."

"Why are you here?" Cego asked. "Ozark already had us worn to the bone with a full day... Aren't you tired?"

"Yeah," Knees said. "I am. But if the rest of you be sleeping, then I'm getting ahead."

"You want to get a patron that much?" Cego asked.

"I don't care about no patron," Knees said.

"So, why?"

"I want to be stronger." The boy's eyes glimmered in the dark.

"To become a Knight?" Cego asked. "Like Dozer wants?"

"No... I be wantin' revenge," Knees said. "Against those stronger than me. Against those I couldn't do anything against when I was still small, still weak."

Knees started to throw his hands again, harder, clenching his teeth as if striking at some imaginary opponent. Cego knew that look in Knees's eyes.

"I understand wanting to get stronger. But it can change you," Cego said. "Like Shiar, he preys on the weak. He looks for blood, for injury, for any opening he can take advantage of. But it's because he's fearful. Because he's full of hatred."

Knees looked at the ground, but when he stared back at Cego, there was no shame in his eyes. "Shiar always be the strongest down here. I wanted to be like him. That's why I followed him."

"And now?"

"And now..." Knees trailed off. "Maybe he don't seem as strong anymore."

Another flash of light from a passing transport illuminated Knees's face.

"There's a cost to becoming better, you know that, right?" Cego said.

Knees glared back at him. "I already paid the price."

"I understand," Cego said. "We've all had to leave our homes… the places we remember. We're here now—"

"My price is not that I be here in this shithole," Knees interrupted. "My uncle put me up for sale soon as I be havin' some muscle to me. Man likely spent the bits on ale. My price already be paid. Myself and my little sis, havin' to live with that man, under that monster's roof."

"I'm sorry," Cego said. The old master had always been hard on Cego, forcing him to train until he couldn't stand anymore, but he'd never gone beyond that.

"Don't be," Knees growled as he started to throw punches again. "I'll return to where I'm from someday…to Venturi. And I'll be ready. My past be makin' me stronger."

Cego nodded as he looked for the little spectral that had brought him here, out to the yard and to Knees. It was gone.

"Guys?" A timid voice emerged from the shadows near the yard's entrance. A small form stepped forward. Weep hadn't been asleep after all.

"You be shittin' me." Knees shook his head, narrowing his eyes at Cego. "What, you be tellin' the entire crew to follow me out here?"

"Cego, I saw you leave the bunk and wanted to see what you were doing." Weep looked down at the dirt.

"Weep, I was just following…" Cego thought it best if he didn't mention the strange spectral that kept visiting him. "I just wanted to check where Knees went off to."

"I thought you might be showing off some more techniques I could use," Weep said as he stepped closer. The little boy had a black eye from training and he was walking with a limp.

"Weep..." Cego was about to tell the boy he should get some rest, but he stopped himself. "Weep, why are we even calling you that name anymore? Look how far you've come. What's your real name?"

Weep took a moment to think about the question, as if he were trying to remember his name before he'd been sold to the slave Circles. "It doesn't matter."

"It matters, we don't want to—" Cego started, but Weep spoke up with a sudden confidence.

"It doesn't matter, because my old name is a part of my past now. And whatever is in our past, whatever we once were, it can make us stronger." The boy looked at Knees and raised his chin proudly. He'd been listening.

Cego breathed out and nodded. Down here in the slave Circles, where they were all sold like pieces of meat to the highest bidder, it seemed none of their pasts mattered.

"Seems as good a time as any to be learnin' more of those secret techniques of yours." Knees nodded to Cego. "I could also be usin' them."

Cego looked at the two members of Crew Nine standing next to him. Perhaps he had made some new friends down here besides the little glowing spectral.

"Yes, there's a certain spiral arm lock I'd like to show you..." Cego began.

* * *

The fighting at Thaloo's blurred together for Murray. The Circle's spectral light collapsed and hundreds of punches and kicks melded into one seamless whirlwind of violence. The stench of sweat and smoke, the ceaseless clamor of the crowd, the faceless figures dressed in dirt and blood—Murray was done with it.

He'd already decided to return Surface-side empty-handed this year. Better than hauling one of these broken kids back with him again. Better than building a kid up, mending their wounds, training them, giving them hope, only to see them break again during the Trials.

The Scout commander wanted him to fail—he'd be happy when Murray returned without any talent in tow. He could already picture the sneer across Callen Albright's face as he reprimanded him.

Murray had just downed his seventh ale and was about to head for the exit when he saw the blind boy again. He'd been keeping an eye out for the boy for the past several weeks but hadn't seen him back in the Circle yet.

The boy's head was now shaved and he wore standard crew-issued white pants. He'd been processed, designated as fit enough to be assigned to a Tasker.

At first, Murray thought he'd had far too much to drink when he saw the boy's eyes—wide-open and glimmering like golden nuggets. There was no mistaking him. The boy maintained the same relaxed posture, looking like he was about to sit down for tea instead of fight for his survival. The boy was as blind as Murray was sober. He shook his head and smiled as he made his way to the Circle's edge.

This time, the boy was up against N'jal, one of Thaloo's in-house Grievar. Thaloo had shipped the thick fighter all the way from the ice flats of Myrkos. N'jal was notorious for his ground-and-pound style of combat. Murray had seen the type before: N'jal would wrap both his opponent's legs up in a double-leg takedown, pin them to the ground, and throw powerful body and head shots to finish them. It was an extremely effective style that Murray himself had employed on many occasions during his path.

The crowd grew for this fight, many folk shouting N'jal's name in recognition. All of Thaloo's in-house crew were fairly well-known, and many ended up fighting at Lampai. Most of the crowd probably had bits riding on N'jal and hoped to continue their streak.

The Circle flared to life and biometrics flashed on the lightboard above. The disparity could not have been more apparent. N'jal, although only fourteen, weighed nearly two hundred fifty pounds. He stalked into the Circle like a budding silverback, his shoulders thickly muscled and his shovel-like forearms already covered with flux ink.

The golden-eyed boy once again looked calm, not even glancing at his formidable opponent. Murray breathed as he steadied himself. He felt nervous for this fight, for this boy in particular. He could feel the spectral light from within the Circle perking him up as if he were the one about to fight.

Thaloo himself sat on one edge of the Circle in a gold-studded chair, one of his cronies fanning him with a large teva leaf. The boss appeared mildly disinterested as he tossed small dried fruits into his mouth.

Thaloo casually waved his hand as the light pulsed and the fight began.

N'jal set himself to a low crouch with his elbows tucked, moving toward the boy with deliberate aggression. The boy waited for him, unmoving, breathing as Murray had seen him do in his last fight. Unused to the lack of aggression, N'jal hesitated for a moment as he closed in on the boy. However, instinct took over and he shot in for the takedown.

The boy, lightning fast, threw his legs backward in a sprawl, distributing his upper body weight to the ground to prevent N'jal from getting underneath him. N'jal surged forward, grasping for a leg as the boy bore down on his shoulders. They moved across the Circle, the boy shuffling his feet and using his full body weight to keep N'jal from getting the takedown.

The boy was too small to keep the pressure on, though. N'jal burst forward and grabbed hold of the boy's knee, driving him onto his back down in the dirt.

N'jal smirked and launched a quick volley of punches at the boy's head. The boy managed to block several of them with his hands to his face but took one square in the side of the nose, opening up a steady stream of blood. Unfazed, the boy squirmed his hips out from under N'jal, pushing against his attacker's head as he got back to his feet. The boy's face was covered in red.

Seeing blood, N'jal moved forward more haphazardly this time, abandoning the crouch and swatting at the boy with a winging right hook before trying to wrap his body up. The boy ducked the punch and threw a quick cross to N'jal's midsection, which produced an *oomph* from the bigger Grievar. Again, N'jal shot in, only to be sidestepped by the boy and caught with a quick body punch, to the liver this time, followed by a heel stomp delivered to the top of the foot.

The boy was dancing on the balls of his feet now, feinting in and out as his golden eyes twinkled.

N'jal growled in pain, incensed, and charged, this time with his head down, swatting at the boy with his outstretched arms. The boy anticipated N'jal's overhead swings, ducking under and going for a takedown of his own.

The boy grasped behind N'jal's knees, driving forward with his full body weight. His opponent was too strong, though. N'jal kicked one of his legs out from the boy's grasp and brought it back sharply as a knee to the head. The knee caught the boy squarely in the temple, throwing him back to the dirt in a heap.

N'jal went in for the kill as the boy lay stunned on the ground. He threw his full weight behind an overhand right, drilling his fist through the air toward his downed opponent. The boy barely got an arm in the way, which was smashed to the side as the punch glanced across his bloody face. Now N'jal was on top of him, squeezing the breath from the boy as he reared up for his specialty: ground-and-pound.

Murray knew this would be the end. N'jal was too large, too high in his mount, the boy too inexperienced to know how to escape. The question was, how much damage would the golden-eyed boy sustain? Murray knew Thaloo and other Circle owners were notorious for setting dangerously high biometric thresholds for their slave brood, not caring if they were badly injured or killed.

N'jal began the onslaught with glee, sitting on top of the boy's midsection to throw shots at his face, aiming to drive the boy's head through the dirt with his fists. The boy did his best to defend, moving his head, grasping for N'jal's arms, bucking left and right.

Several glancing blows caught the boy on the side of his face, streaking the blood and dirt already there. A new gash opened up just above the boy's eyebrow. He didn't panic—he continued to parry and move with the little room he had.

N'jal looked at the boy beneath him, perhaps puzzled that his victim hadn't broken yet. He attempted to grab the boy's throat with one hand to hold his head down, but the boy wriggled free—a tiny victory.

Murray looked to Thaloo, who now had a smirk on his face as his Grievar continued to deliver blow after blow to the downed boy.

N'jal growled, breathing hard now from his onslaught as he arced a sweeping elbow down into the boy's defending arms. He followed up with a straight elbow, the sharp part of the bone drilling directly toward the boy's head, who barely managed to get two cupped hands in front of his face to soften the blow. N'jal pinned one of the boy's wrists to the ground and dropped another elbow.

Just as the elbow fell and N'jal's balance was centered forward, the boy bucked his hips, throwing N'jal's head toward the ground. He squeezed out from underneath N'jal's legs. The boy somersaulted forward and nimbly sprang to his feet. Blood was now pouring from the boy's nose and the nasty gash over his eyebrow.

Murray shook his head in amazement.

The sag in N'jal's shoulders was noticeable as he edged toward his opponent, heaving as he tried to catch a quick breath. The smaller boy was light on his feet despite the fact that he was drenched in his own blood. He bounced and feinted in and out of N'jal's range like a cat.

The boy connected with a series of quick low kicks to N'jal's shin, more annoying than damaging to the bigger Grievar. Just before he threw each kick, the boy looked down at the spot he was aiming for. N'jal grinned slightly as he caught the boy looking down. Catching one of those kicks would mean getting the boy back on the dirt, where he could finish the fight.

The boy looked down again, and this time, N'jal preempted the kick, dropping his hand to catch the incoming foot. To his surprise, the boy instead came in with a quick cross, finding N'jal's eye socket and sending him reeling. The boy followed his opponent, hitting him with two more jabs to the face that brought N'jal's hands high and then a winging left that thudded into N'jal's liver.

Murray had seen and felt many well-placed liver shots before, and this was one of them: a second or two of delay after the punch connected, followed by overwhelming pain and the body's refusal to answer the brain's commands. N'jal toppled face-first into the dirt and curled into a ball.

The boy stood above his downed opponent, wobbling on his feet. The dirt under him was steeped in red.

Murray looked over to Thaloo, who now had a frown on his walrus-like face. N'jal would need to sustain far more damage for the Circle to recognize a finish.

The boy seemed conflicted, standing over N'jal with a blank stare on his face. Most Grievar would have waded in without hesitation, paying no heed to the Codes. A kick to the head would do the job. *Listened to the light*, they would say afterward to excuse themselves from the dishonorable attack.

Instead, the boy fell toward N'jal, his legs giving way as he landed next to his opponent in the dirt. He grasped N'jal's bulky body with one arm, tugging himself against the big Grievar's shoulders and reaching for his neck.

N'jal was still conscious. He feebly attempted to defend the north–south choke, fighting off the circling hand, but the boy's bloodied forearm slipped beneath the big Grievar's head. The boy dropped his shoulder into N'jal's neck and squeezed, his eyes closed, using the last of his energy to go for the finish.

N'jal went out. The light above dimmed as the mass of spectrals broke apart.

Murray released his breath, which he realized he'd been holding for the last minute of the fight.

The golden-eyed boy had won. He'd beaten one of Thaloo's in-house Grievar, one ranked far above him. That kind of upset in a slave Circle was unheard of. The strong always beat the weak here.

Murray heard some of Tasker Ozark's crew cheering from the sidelines. They were yelling, "Cego." More often, the boys rooted against members of their own crew.

The boy, Cego, attempted to stand, but his knees wobbled and his eyes rolled back into his head. He fell to the dirt beside his unconscious opponent.

* * *

Murray downed his ale and headed toward the back of the large den.

Two mercs stood posted in front of an ornate doorframe. "I'm here to see Thaloo," Murray growled.

They clearly recognized him. The one on the right stared at Murray's flux tattoo sleeve cut with Grievar Knight ink in obvious admiration. The merc quickly recovered and asked suspiciously, "Do you have an appointment with the boss?"

"No, but he'll see me just fine."

"No one is allowed to see the boss without a—" the merc started, but Murray shouldered his way past the two, moving with a quickness that wouldn't be suspected of a big man.

Murray entered a lavish room filled with plush pillows and thick carpets. Marble statues stood in the nooks lining the back wall. Golden standing lamps shined dull light into the room, illuminating the pockmarked face of the fat man sitting at a polished desk.

"Thaloo," Murray said. The man did not seem surprised to see Murray barge into his office with two guards at his tail.

"Ah, the Mighty Murray Pearson; a pleasure as always." Thaloo's jowls undulated as he spoke. He looked up indifferently with his dulled yellow eyes.

"Boss...he pushed past us." One of the mercs moved toward Murray as if to grab him. Murray's eyes latched on to the man midmovement, stopping him in his tracks, promising him that making contact would be a very bad move.

"Leave us." Thaloo waved his hand and the mercs made a hasty exit.

Thaloo smacked his lips like a hungry toad as he stared up at Murray. "Come to make a bit in my Circle? I know certain influential folk that have been waiting a long time to put some bits on the back of the Mighty Murray Pearson."

"As much as I'd like to pad your purse with my blood, that's not why I'm here," Murray said.

Thaloo frowned. "Ah. That's a pity. You were a pleasure to watch, once upon a time." The man swiveled his chair to face the statues along the wall and stood. "Perhaps you were once even good enough to stand here along with Ezo's other great champions."

Murray narrowed his eyes, breathing out, reminding himself why he was visiting this man. "I'm not here to reminisce, Thaloo. I'm here for patron rights; I want to make a purchase."

"You know what made all these Knights great champions, Pearson?" Thaloo asked, not waiting for a response. "They stuck to their lightpath." Thaloo ran his hand along one of the statues lovingly. "It's all a script. A path written for us. Those highbred Daimyo say the script is written by their Bit-Minders. From the Codex, they program the spectrals and plot our destinies, like gods from above. Do you believe that, Pearson?"

Murray opened his mouth, but Thaloo continued to speak. "Now, the Grunts, those harvesters and builders and drudgers, the diggers and reapers and haulers...toiling ceaselessly. Most Grunts believe the spectral light came from the stars, floating down from the night sky like angels to guide them on their lightpath. Those brainless fools actually believe they were put on this world to grovel for the Daimyo." Thaloo chuckled. "And the Grievar. Well...you know what the Grievar believe, of course. The spectrals came from deep within the earth, their light illuminating the darkness of the Underground, casting away the shadows on the snowy peaks, cutting through the thick jungles of the Emerald Isles...shining down on the Circles and finding us...the chosen ones. The champions to lead the rest. That garbage from the Codes, about fighting so the rest shall not have to." Thaloo theatrically rolled his eyes.

Thaloo sat and swiveled his chair back toward Murray. "I know you're smarter than the average merc, Pearson. Unlike those dolts outside my door, you're a Citadel-trained Grievar. Exposed to those highbrow Surface-side minds. What do you believe?"

Murray snorted. "I believe that you don't care what I think, Thaloo. I believe that you're just running your mouth while you figure out how you can get something out of me."

Thaloo completely ignored Murray and continued to forge ahead with his monologue. "What do I believe, you ask?" Thaloo croaked. "I don't care where the light came from. All I know is everyone has a script. I'm a Grievar, yes, but I was never a real fighter; I knew that right off. Don't like to get hit. I like the business of fighting, though. That's my path, Pearson.

"Do you know how many out-of-work Grievar come my way looking for bit-heavy patrons? I connect them. Or how many of these little scumling lacklight kids I bring through my door, sniveling off the street without a bit to their name? I play my part and I put them on their path. Most of them won't make it or even survive, but I give them a chance to do nature's bidding, to find their place in this world of ours."

Murray didn't try to speak, knowing the toad would continue smacking his lips until he caught his fly.

"I know that we each must play our part. I'm not meant for the Circle, but without me, how would others survive? You just needed to play your part, too, Pearson. You are a Grievar Knight through and through, meant for the Circle, meant for the Citadel. And yet...you forgot how to follow your path. You forgot how to play your part."

"I didn't forget anything. That's exactly why I'm here. To play my part. I'm a Grievar Scout and the Citadel has tasked me with bringing prospects Upworld," Murray said.

Thaloo grabbed a small wad of gummy material from a vat on his desk, shoving it into his mouth and chewing voraciously. "Your part is to take the batch of kids we've set aside for you, like every year. And yet, like you did during your Knight days, you are trying to deviate from that path."

"Those kids you send up with me every year aren't Citadel material. You know that. They can barely walk, let alone fight. We both know the deal you have here. You send the Citadel your scraps and keep the meat to yourself, and for that luxury, you have the honor of lining their war chest with every sale you make."

"Very perceptive, Pearson." Thaloo slurped. "What would you have me do? Send my finest Grievar with you? Why not take my top ten? What you ask does not make sense. However, with the Citadel's purse behind you, you could take my very best."

"I only want one, though. A boy called Cego—he arrived recently."

Thaloo raised an eyebrow. "Ah. The blind boy who suddenly opened his eyes. He certainly surprised many of our patrons, defeating N'jal like that."

Murray knew he had to downplay the potential he saw in Cego. "He's fast and quick-witted. I think I can make something of him."

Thaloo was silent for several moments, his dull eyes shifting side to side. "Clearly, you see something more than is apparent in this Cego. Why else would you force your way into my office and cause such a stir? Why deviate from your path again, Pearson? Perhaps you have an eye for things like this. Perhaps you have foreseen this boy to be next Artemis Halberd himself."

"I'll give you the standard purse for just Cego," Murray said. "Usually I bring up a dozen kids for that price."

"Clearly, you aren't authorized to expand the Citadel's purse beyond these meager sums; otherwise, you would have just bought him outright. So, why should I just give him to you? What will you give me for this favor, Pearson?"

Murray breathed out. He knew it would come to this. "I'll fight for him."

Thaloo stopped chewing. A wide, toothy grin spread across the man's face.

* * *

Cego listened to the lapping of the tide against the shore. He dug his hands into the black sand beneath him, feeling the tiny granules slip between his fingers and fall back to the beach.

He sat cross-legged in the surf, the breeze flattening his hair across his forehead. The sky was a crisp, unwavering blue and the sea lay before him like a treasure trove of sparkling emeralds. Cego tried to match his breath to the tide, exhaling as a wave crashed onto the shore, the water flicking at his toes and caressing his calves, and inhaling as the tide receded, rolling back out into deep.

Over and over, the tide rolled in and receded again, and Cego attempted to match the water's rhythm with his own breathing, just as the old master had taught them. Without beginning or end, rolling like a wave, *he'd say.*

Cego couldn't do it as well as Silas always had. His elder brother had been better at most of the master's teachings—ki-breath included. Silas could sit on the shore for hours without moving an inch, looking like an immovable statue swept with sand by the end of the exercise.

The three brothers used to practice ki-breath together every morning. They were instructed to never shut their eyes, to always keep their gaze to the sea even when the breeze kicked up stinging sand.

Little Sam would always be the first to break, his wild beach-grass eyes darting to some distraction, a scuttling crab or silvery fish in the surf he would chase. Cego would try to concentrate and keep pace with Silas, but he never lasted long. He would feel a restlessness build within him, urging him to leap up and sprint across the beach after Sam.

Silas had always been the strongest of the three brothers. He was always one step ahead in the Circle. He'd flash that wry, mocking grin at Cego, standing above him after knocking him down repeatedly.

Cego placed his hand to his lip, rubbing the jagged scar he'd received from his last bout with his brother.

And now Silas was gone.

Cego trained his golden eyes across the sea, toward the horizon. During daylight, he could only make out a faint glimmer, but when night fell on the island, the crest of every wave glowed with a vibrant green luminescence.

When he was younger, Silas had told him that the glowing trail was a great serpent slithering toward the horizon. Though he'd believed his elder brother then, Cego had discovered diving beneath the waves that the luminescence came from a much smaller creature—tiny wisps of plankton blooming along the ocean's surface.

The old master called the glowing trail the Path.

Cego and Sam had watched from the black sand beach as their elder brother swam the Path a thousand nights ago, following the trail of luminescence until he disappeared from view. Cego remembered Silas appearing small, just another shadow rolling atop the breakers. That was the only time he could remember Silas seeming small like that.

Since then, the old master had kept the remaining two brothers on their same rigorous training routine. Cego had expected something to change—a shifting of schedule or a mere mention of Silas's departure. Instead, the master acted as if nothing had changed at all. He ignored the fact that there were only two boys remaining on the island.

Today would be no different from any other day.

Morning ki-breath, followed by techniques with the master. Then endurance training on the black sand beach, including sprints and boulder carries beneath the waves. Shin conditioning by kicking the trees in the ironwood grove as the sun reached its height. Hard sparring throughout the afternoon. More technique refinement as the daylight faded.

Today wasn't the same, though. It hadn't been the same since Silas had left.

Cego stood up in the sand, his ki-breath exercise clearly finished because of his wandering mind.

Where had Sam run off to this time?

Cego dusted the sand off his tanned legs and briskly jogged down the beach toward the cliffs on the western edge of the island. Sam liked to explore the tide pools at the base of the cliffs, where the water was calmer and a plethora of strange creatures made their homes in the stony nooks.

The island only had one expanse of black sand beach on the northern edge. The old master's compound perched atop it. The smaller outlets on the southern side of the island were mostly made of jagged rock.

Though the black sand beach was certainly beautiful, it made Cego think of training. Racing full speed along the shore until his breath became ragged, swimming out into the strong current until he needed to float on his back to regain his strength, carrying heavy boulders beneath the waves until his lungs were on fire. The beach was not a place of relaxation for the brothers.

A sharp series of barks broke Cego from his reverie. Arry would always give away Sam's location.

Just as Cego suspected, his little brother was crouched in one of the tide pools beneath the cliffs, peering into the murky water. The grey pup, Arry, was at the edge of the pool, barking at Sam but too timid to join him in the cold water.

"Sam, it's time to head back," Cego said as his brother tried his hardest to ignore him. "Come on!"

"I've almost got one of the big blue crabs, though! He's pinned down inside his lair," the small flaxen-haired boy pleaded as he jabbed a piece of driftwood into the water.

"Farmer's gonna pin you down worse than that crab if you don't come quick," Cego said flatly.

Sam stood, his eyes darting to Cego. "Silas never would have made me come back so early..."

Sam had been using Silas as an excuse lately. He'd always let the littlest brother get away with small delinquencies. Probably because Silas had never cared about Sam. Not like Cego did.

Cego sharpened his voice. "Silas is gone. It's just us and Farmer now. And he wouldn't be happy to hear you're stalling on your training."

A familiar wrinkle curled on Sam's forehead as he held his ground stubbornly in the water. "Why are we even training? Why do we have to keep fighting?"

Cego hardened his gaze and replied with the same answer the old master had given him so many times. "We fight so the rest shall not have to."

It wasn't a real answer. Cego didn't really know what it meant. The mantra had become the master's all-encompassing response to their many questions. Why were they training? Why did Silas have to leave? Where did the Path end? The old master would always return the same answer, flicking out each syllable like a well-honed jab.

We fight so the rest shall not have to.

Who were the rest the old master spoke of, and why were they fighting for them? Beyond the two brothers and their old master, the island was only ever visited by nearby Hlai fishermen looking to trade their wares. Cego couldn't believe the Hlai fishers, on their rickety boats with their stinky sacks of sarpin, were the reason that he and his brother were constantly honing their combat skills.

Sam huffed and made his way through the tide pool to Cego's side. The answer had been sufficient, as usual.

The two brothers jogged back toward the compound, Arry in tow, the ocean wind blowing against them and whipping sand into their faces. Several times during the run, Cego caught his brother glancing uneasily toward the sea. The little boy was uncharacteristically quiet, not full of the incessant questions he'd usually pester Cego with.

The brothers ran up the tall sand dune and passed through the old master's rock garden set at the periphery of the compound. The garden was filled with tiny potted trees and makeshift trickling streams where the man would often sit and stare for hours at the sea while the boys were training.

The various sections of the home were connected via an outdoor gravel path. The rooms were framed with ironwood planks and separated by thin, translucent walls that glowed in the sunlight.

The two boys cut between the living quarters toward the large courtyard at the center of the compound.

As usual, they found the old master sitting within the ironwood Circle, waiting for them with his eyes closed.

Farmer.

The old master's grey hair fell to his shoulders from a topknot. He breathed quietly and forcefully all at once, his entire body heaving and cresting like the ocean's current. His eyes fluttered open, brilliant, glowing, and locked on to Cego.

* * *

Cego awoke in a cold sweat.

He tried to hold on to the dream, mark it in his memory like a new technique, but it faded rapidly as the fight rushed back to him.

N'jal on top of him for what seemed like hours, raining down punches and elbows. Blood on his face, barely able to see. Trying to win little victories, concentrating on every fist that came his way.

Cego wiggled his fingers and toes. Surprisingly, he didn't hurt badly, though he knew he should be in considerable pain. He brought a hand up to his face, gingerly touching his nose. It was there for sure and only ached a bit.

He slowly turned his neck to see a mountain of a man sitting by the bed, staring at him with tiger-yellow eyes.

The bearded man barely fit in the small chair by the cot. He looked uncomfortable. Flux tattoos flowed from the tops of his forearms to his hands. The man was grinding his knuckles together, staring forward like he expected Cego to say something.

Cego pushed himself up, looking around the small room. It was primarily red and white, with a metallic counter against the wall.

"Clerics had you all neuro'd up, if you're wondering why everything is a bit hazy." The bearded man spoke in a baritone.

Cego figured he was talking to him, since no one else was in the room. "Clerics?"

The man pointed to the door. "They finished workin' on you an hour ago."

Cego nodded. *Why is this man here? Where is* here*?*

The bearded man spoke again. "They said you had a few broken ribs, orbital bone fracture, broken nose, lot of lost blood—nothing they couldn't fix up, though. They're Daimyo, so don't get to trusting them... but the clerics do a fine job of fixing folk."

Cego sat up in his little cot. Besides his back being a bit stiff, he felt all right.

"That was a darkin' stupid move." The bearded man looked at him seriously.

Cego had no idea what this man was talking about.

"You risked getting pounded senseless with N'jal mounted on

you for so long. Trying to wear him down? Too risky. How could you know that he didn't have the gas tank to finish the job? Sure, it paid off and he got tired, but I'd say you're lucky you didn't get finished under him."

The man continued, as if he'd been waiting to lecture Cego. "You should've given him your back right off. He had a solid mount, but I doubt he'd be able to get his hooks in if you turned on him. Thick types like him, especially from the Northlands, they don't often get the hooks in. I should know. You could've walked out of that Circle instead of getting carried out."

Cego thought about it seriously, reviewing the fight in his mind. Would that have worked?

The man seemed to sense his questions. "I'll show it to you; you'll see."

They sat in the room for several minutes in silence, neither boy nor man thrilled to engage the other in conversation. Cego could hear whispering voices from outside the door.

Cego finally broke the silence. "Where are we?" After he'd choked N'jal, he couldn't remember leaving the Circle or anything beyond that.

"Cleric's medward, south of the steppe. I paid for your fixin'," the man stated.

"Why?"

"I figure I didn't want my new Grievar kid to be all busted up."

"You...you bought me?" Cego asked, his eyes wide.

"Far as Underground Circles are concerned, yeah." The man sighed. "But no, I'm not your patron. Dark all this patron talk. Thaloo and his whole operation—doing all this for the bits. It's a disgrace to the Grievar. No honor in it. I didn't buy you to make bits off you like that Deep scum."

Cego had seen some other kids get bought, but their prospective patrons had visited first and haggled with a Tasker over the course of several days before finally agreeing on a price.

"Why did you buy me, then?" Cego asked.

The man scratched his grey beard. "I've been watching you, kid. I've seen you fight. You move well. Your hips, your head—you know how to use them."

"There's a lot of kids that move well down here," Cego responded.

"True," the man said. "You could use fixin' in places. But that's fine; you've got the right framework. Like a new rig before some two-bit maker messes with it too much, you can be fixed."

Cego looked at the big man quizzically. His head felt even hazier than when he'd first woken.

"Speaking of rigs," the man said. "That was impressive what you did out there. Blocked the auralite's effect altogether. Where'd you learn to do that?"

"Auralite effect?" Cego asked.

"You know...the crowd push—" the man started, then paused. He shook his head and sighed. "I forget scum like Thaloo don't bother to teach their kids about the Circles they fight in, let alone any decent technique. I can't explain it well as some Circle engineer, but I'll give you an old Grievar's version."

Cego nodded.

"Thaloo's Circle is built mostly of auralite-compound steel. Not the purest sort, but does the job. It's one of the alloys that interacts with the spectrals—which is why you see them swarming around it during your fights," the man said.

Cego thought back to his fights—seeing the spectrals buzzing around the Circle. He'd never even considered *why* they were there.

"Different alloys attract different sorts of spectrals. Each gives off a different light. *Varying wavelengths* is what Tachi would say," the man muttered. "Each type of spectral light influences a Grievar fighting in the Circle differently."

It made sense to Cego as he thought back to his fights. He'd felt the light seeping into him, communicating with his body.

"Circles like Thaloo's—built of auralite alloy—attract bluelight spectrals. Makes a Grievar... convincible. The crowd around you gets louder. Makes you want to do what they say, to please 'em whether they're cheering or hissing at you. Auralite effect is a hard one to overcome, which is why I say I'm impressed you resisted the urge twice now to kick some kid when he was down even though the crowd was pushing for it," the man said.

"There are other types of Circles out there?" Cego asked. Though he was more than familiar with combat, it was starting to seem more complicated than simply beating his opponent.

"Yeah. Auralite, rubellium, emeralyis, cytrine... just to name a few. Each one does somethin' different to you. My team will train you for all that when we get back Surface-side, though," the man said.

"We're going... to the Surface?" Cego asked, his eyes wide.

"Well, that's the plan. If I can work *this* rusty rig into combat shape real soon." The man slapped at his protruding stomach. "I'm not buying you—I'm fighting for you. In three weeks' time, under the lights of Lampai."

Cego knew he shouldn't trust this man. Why would he fight for him? Ever since Cego had ended up in the Underground, folk had only used him. They had locked him away in the darkness. They had tossed him in the Circle and made him fight for their own greed.

How could he know this man was any different? He was surely using him in some way, no different from anyone else in the Underground.

"I'm bringing you Upworld, kid. Surface-side to the Citadel. To the Lyceum," the man said.

The Lyceum. Since he'd first arrived at Thaloo's, Cego had heard other kids often whispering of the Lyceum. It was Ezo's national combat school—a prestigious place of learning where the greatest Grievar passed techniques down only to the best students. Dozer had said that many of Ezo's famed Knights were now professors at the Lyceum. Dozer had also told Crew Nine that the Lyceum kept wild tuskers down in its catacombs, so Cego wasn't sure what to believe.

The Lyceum didn't matter, though. Cego didn't understand this man's motives. What could he possibly gain from his release from Thaloo's? Why would the man risk his own life and fight for Cego?

"We fight so the rest shall not have to," the man whispered.

The familiar mantra triggered a wave of memories that rushed back to Cego. He breathed the salty sea air and heard the lapping of the tide. He saw Sam running beside him on the shore of the black sand beach and Silas swimming out atop the green glow of the Path. He saw the old master's face, rough and wrinkled like tree bark.

In the back of his mind, Cego had known it since he'd arrived, bloody and beaten on the Underground's streets. He'd known it sitting alone in his little dungeon cell beneath Thaloo's. He'd known it training in the yard and fighting in the slave Circle. He was far from home.

Though he had no idea how to get back, this man was the first person that had reminded him that home even existed. The burly Grievar had said the words with conviction, as if he truly believed them.

We fight so the rest shall not have to.

Cego nodded at the bearded Grievar. He would go with him to the Surface. He would find his brothers, Sam and Silas. He would get back to the old master.

The man reached forward with a gnarled hand, grasping Cego's. His grip was like a vise, but it was warm.

"Murray Pearson."

CHAPTER 5

Work as Usual

The Grievar who is born strong faces more difficulty on the path to mastery than his smaller and weaker brethren. Such a Grievar may resort to brute strength to defeat opponents and thus is less likely to learn the principles of leverage and efficiency. The strong Grievar follows the harried path; they must control their strength to learn true technique.

Passage Five, One Hundred Fifty-Second
Precept of the Combat Codes

Cego was still unsteady on his feet when Dozer slapped him on the back, nearly sending him crashing into the wall.

"Someone finally made it!" Dozer was red-faced and smiling again. The news had spread fast that Cego had gotten picked up by a patron. Though Cego wasn't technically under Murray's charge unless the man won at Lampai, the rest of Crew Nine treated the deal as if it were already done when they greeted him on his return from the medward.

"You're going to the Surface! I hear on the Surface they ride giant birds around called rocs!" Dozer exclaimed.

Knees patted Cego on the shoulder and turned to Dozer. "You blockheadin' it again. Rocs be rare, almost extinct now. I'm from the Surface, and I've never even seen one."

Dozer shook his head. "You're from the desert out in Venturi, birds don't like heat like that. I'm going to get myself a roc. Grow it up from a hatchling until it's big enough to carry me around."

"You better hope it becomes a big darkin' roc if it be carrying you." Knees smacked Dozer's bandaged belly.

Cego laughed deeply at his friends, though his rib cage hurt.

Weep was there, shy but standing taller now as he grasped Cego's wrist firmly. "I'm glad it was you, Cego. If anyone was to get out of here, I'm glad it was you."

Cego felt a weight bearing down on his shoulders. Somehow, this Murray Pearson had decided he was the kid worth fighting for. Why should he have a chance to get out of the Underground when Weep, who had gone through so much already, would still be sitting in this tiny bunk every night? Weep, who had almost no chance of getting picked up by a patron, would inevitably end up on the streets alone.

Cego looked Weep in the eye. "You're getting out of here too. I promise you."

Knees interjected as Weep turned away to hide the tears welling in his eyes. "That be some fight you had, Cego. I was thinkin' you finished when N'jal be throwin' those hammers from top. Then I'm blinkin' and you're back standin'—feeding him the real heat!" Knees feinted in and out like Cego had, throwing shadow punches at Dozer's barrel-like chest as he emulated the fight.

Dozer took a playful swipe at Knees, who ducked under and tried to wrap his arms around the big boy, though he only could get about halfway around his girth.

"You're weak. And lucky." Shiar emerged from the corner of the bunk. The jackal stood in front of Cego, his eyes blazing with hatred.

Cego stayed silent, though he returned Shiar's stare without flinching.

"Yeah, if he's so weak, how come he beat N'jal? How come Cego's bit-price is above yours now and he's gotten himself a patron?" Dozer moved up next to Shiar, looking down at him.

"That's where the luck comes in. Caught N'jal on a bad day. He had some lucky shots. Anyone could see that, even an imbecile like you," Shiar hissed at Dozer.

Cego didn't want this to escalate. A fight here could hurt the rest of the crew's chances of getting out, especially if someone got hurt. Tasker Ozark wouldn't stand for fighting when it wasn't for his own benefit.

Cego conceded. "You're right, Shiar. I was lucky against N'jal. I think he might've got the rotworm or something; he didn't look himself."

Shiar shook his head. "If that's the case, you are just as I said—a weakling. I saw the end of the fight. You could've finished it standing up like a real Grievar. You were barely able to put him away though he was finished."

Cego remembered that part of the fight clearly. Though he'd been on the verge of passing out, he'd looked at N'jal's curled-up body on the dirt. The once-fearsome Grievar had seemed like a helpless child.

Cego knew he could've finished it faster. A swift kick to the head or another few punches from mount to knock N'jal's brain around in his skull. He'd felt the crowd urging him to finish it that way—the amplified effect of the auralite Circle around him.

He'd resisted the urge, though, pushed the anger and fear down as he'd done before. Why badly damage N'jal when he could finish the fight with a choke, ending it all the same?

Cego heard Farmer's voice in his head as he turned toward Shiar. "We fight neither to inflict pain nor to prolong suffering. We fight neither to mollify anger nor to satisfy vendetta. We fight neither to accumulate wealth nor to promote social standing. We fight so the rest shall not have to."

Crew Nine stood around Cego, listening to his words, to Farmer's words. Somehow, Cego knew words like these were not often heard in slave Circles, where the sole purpose of fighting was for entertainment and patron sales. The words Cego spoke were old, older than their training yard. Older than Thaloo's fighting den. Even older than this crumbling Underground city.

Knees nodded in agreement and Dozer puffed his chest out proudly, his head held high.

"Pffft. You speak the Codes now?" Shiar spat. "I've heard it before. Drivel written by those Grievar long passed, dust and bone now. It's only about being strong and winning. That stuff doesn't mean anything, especially coming from a lacklight like you." Shiar turned and walked back to the other corner of the bunkroom.

Dozer nearly took a swing at Shiar as he walked by, but Cego stepped forward and put his hand on the big Grievar's shoulder. "He's not worth your time."

* * *

Murray's opponent was announced promptly after his contract with Thaloo was signed. The Dragoon—one of Thaloo's most feared in-house Grievar, known for his unconventional and deadly leaping attacks.

In the past, Thaloo had outsourced the Dragoon for a number of the Underground's most publicized disputes. The Dragoon had most recently settled a grievance between two prominent Daimyo. The fight bestowed the winning Daimyo the rights to a new mining operation along the western cavern, a contract worth millions of bits.

The Dragoon had knocked out his opponent in fewer than forty seconds with a spectacular flying knee.

Although Murray didn't trust the man, Thaloo certainly knew how to leverage his connections. And that made him a great fight promoter. The word about Mighty Murray Pearson's return to the Circle spread quickly.

The Deep Hawkers Guild was the first to promote the fight across the Underground. Within a day of the fight announcement, an ad was aired on SystemView showing footage of Murray's old fights spliced with the Dragoon's most recent wins. Murray was made to look like a young Grievar who had a decent chance against the notorious merc.

The hawkers also packaged fight tickets with some of their wares. "Need a Surfacing Day gift for the brood? Treat yourself to something as well, all for one great price! Buy the latest from Ark-Tech Labs and get two free tickets to Lampai's biggest fight of the season!"

Builders were quick to erect massive lightboards along the Underground's bustling thoroughfares. In a matter of days, Murray saw his face plastered across Markspar Row, flashing at him from the huge displays. Again, they used clips from his early years at the Citadel. Murray barely recognized the chiseled Grievar smiling down at him.

Drawing even more attention than Murray's comeback was the fact that he was fighting for some slave Circle kid, an unknown Grievar brood. A lacklight. The gossip was tremendous, aided by the sensational rumors the hawkers spread to sell the fight: The boy was his bastard son. The boy was a Kirothian asset. Or any other shocking story the hawkers could come up with to draw attention to the fight. At the Bat, Murray even heard some folk speculating on the Citadel's secret involvement, how they planned to use the fight as a catalyst to usurp the Underground's Circles. That was one story Murray thought not too far-fetched, especially as the Underground used to be fully under Ezonian control until the powerful Daimyo merchants and slave Circle owners expanded the black markets.

Deep folk started to recognize Murray again, pointing at him, shaking his hand, asking for his attention on the street. He was one of the Grievar from below, representing the underdogs, the downtrodden, the lacklights. Murray didn't get it. Why was everyone making such a big deal? This was his fight, not theirs.

The more he thought about it, though, the more he realized it was a big deal. He hadn't been in the Circle for over a decade. He'd left it with a loss—the worst of his career.

Now was his chance to dispel those bad memories, to feel the light again. He could redeem himself. Show people that there was more to being a Grievar than pulling in the highest bit-purse. It was about honor. Adhering to the Combat Codes. But he was going up against the Dragoon. Even the Citadelians spoke about the Dragoon with respect. The former Grievar Knight had won several land disputes between smaller villages just outside of Ezo early on in his career but ended up taking the merc path like so many others, deciding he'd rather pad his purse than honor his nation.

Despite his lack of honor, the Dragoon was dangerous. Deadly.

Murray needed to train.

* * *

Murray exhaled deeply as he followed the cobbled road to Anderson's home in the Farmoss District, passing beneath the large swaths of lumin lichen on the cavern ceiling that cast everything in a sleepy green hue. He passed by traditional Grievar homes carved out of the cavern walls, intermixed with modern steel-framed buildings set farther out along the streets.

Farmoss was the one place in the Deep that Murray still considered Grievar land. Unlike most of the Underground districts that faced the constant glare of the spectral arrays, Farmoss was shielded from the light by the slope of the steppe perched above it. The Daimyo had tried to desecrate it just like the other districts, but somehow, Farmoss had rejected their incursions.

Every other major district was directly under the arrays, gargantuan fixtures set along the cavern ceiling that lit the darkness of the Deep. The arrays slowly rotated throughout the day to deploy one of five distinct elemental alloys, each of which attracted swarms of spectrals.

The arrays streamed yellowlight at dawn to take the edge off the Grunts' hangovers, bluelight at midshift to keep the droves in line, followed by verdant greenlight for inspiration, then redlight to give the masses a final hard adrenaline kick at dusk. Night was covered by the invisible blanket of blacklight. Everything moved like clockwork according to Daimyo programming.

But when they'd made numerous attempts to install their arrays in Farmoss, the spongy roof had slowly expelled the metals, diluting the mortar and stripping the screws and eventually spitting out the chewed-up refuse like a finicky eater. Sometimes, Murray truly believed he could settle in Farmoss, tucked away from the light and far from the Citadel's reach. Anderson had done so. His old friend had said he'd rather not live out his later years in the constant pull of spectral light. Many Grievar could never remove themselves from the light. They constantly felt its gravity, pulling them back to those beautiful moments of action and glory they'd felt in the Circle. It eventually ate away at them.

Murray didn't know if he could do the same as Anderson. Though he appreciated the quiet calm of Farmoss, he knew there was a reason he still kept close to the light.

He located Anderson's address by memory. The home was a traditional Grievar build, the clay exterior pale grey except for the dark wooden door at the center.

Leyna, Anderson's wife, opened the door and gave Murray a vigorous hug.

"My Murray! How long has it been?" Leyna led him into their sitting room. Though the exterior of the home was built of clay, the interior walls were reinforced with the redwood strips cut from the forest of roots that hung in the western cavern.

"Too long, Leyna—it's good to see you. And you look the same as I remember. Better than can be said of me," Murray said as he ran a hand through his scraggly beard. Leyna truly did look like she hadn't aged a year. Same soft honey-yellow eyes set on sharp cheekbones.

Murray, Anderson, and Leyna had come up together at the Lyceum. They'd started as fresh-faced Level Ones and graduated together as hardened Knights. In the Citadel, they'd been there for each other's greatest victories and most devastating losses.

Murray sat at a grooved wooden table that matched the walls. Leyna emerged from the kitchen with three ales. "I assume you're still liking these, given Anderson told me you've already paid him a visit or two at the Bat this trip down?"

Murray shook his head. "This fight. I need to hold off on those for a bit, Leyna."

"Ah, yes. Just like the old days! Eating right, abstaining from the drink. Why, I remember Anderson and I even shucked off our playtime for a month prior to fights."

Murray chuckled. "Well, luckily, that part of it won't be a problem for me right now..." He looked down at the table, rubbing his knuckles together.

"Oh, so you mean to say there isn't any lucky lady paying homage to the famed Mighty Murray right now? I find it hard to believe that. Once upon a time Upworld...I can remember not a single lass able to keep her skirt down in your presence."

"Well, as you can see for yourself, I'm not the man I once was." Murray patted his gut, giving Leyna a playful grin.

"Ah, so we are all getting wrinkles. Doesn't mean you won't wipe the mats with this dragon boy, or whatever they call him. Looks to be all flash to me—these flying techniques, all the Grievar are trying them out modernday. No basic technique in the lot of 'em."

"As flashy as they seem, my dear, the Dragoon has knocked out some top-notch opponents this past year with those very techniques." Anderson emerged from the basement. He had his spectacles on and a dirty apron draped over his chest. Murray couldn't believe this was the Grievar who had once brought crowds to their feet in the Citadel, clamoring and chanting for *the Bat*.

"How many times have I told you to leave that dirty rag downstairs—you're going to get soot all over the kitchen," Leyna scolded Anderson, taking his apron off as he held his arms outstretched.

Anderson clasped hands with Murray, examining him from over the rim of his spectacles.

"Seems like you've really gotten yourself into it this time, brother."

"As usual." Murray grimaced. "I didn't know who else to come to. I mean, we had Coach back in the day. I've been out of the game for so long, though...I don't even know where to start with the darkin' thing."

"This boy must be real important to you. For Mighty Murray to come back to the Circle after all these years..."

Murray lowered his voice to a near whisper. "He could be the one, Anderson. I've watched him fight. The kid moves like...like him. I don't how to place it; it's just the way he fights."

Anderson was quiet for a moment. "He's gone, you realize. He said he wasn't coming back and I don't think he ever will. You could just be seeing him in places."

"It's different this time, Anderson. This kid, he fights by the Codes. You need to see the way he takes the light. I have a feeling about this one."

Anderson nodded. "Well, what do we have, then, three weeks?"

"My body, my mind—I don't feel like I used to," Murray said grimly.

"We've done worse," Anderson said. "I remember a time when Mighty Murray won us the Tamal Plains. When me and Hanrin Tuvlov broke down your tavern door the morning of the fight, you were out like the great void, a girl tangled in the sheets with you. All it took was a bucket of cold water and a hearty meal—you were ready to go. Took that Desovian down within a minute and went to work as usual. It'll be the same this time around, old friend. Work as usual."

Murray nodded affirmatively. "Work as usual."

Anderson gestured toward the basement. "I've got the old mats and pads down below; shall we get started?"

"Never a time like right now," Murray muttered wearily.

The two old Grievar creaked down the stairs into the basement.

* * *

Cego was dreading his final day in the yard.

Tasker Ozark had lost any potential cut of the profit from Murray's deal with Thaloo because of its unique unpaid nature. Ozark took out his frustration on Circle Crew Nine.

The training in the yard was even more grueling than usual. Ozark had the entire crew doubling up on all the standard drills. A few of the boys were worked so hard that they didn't make it back to the bunks on their own two feet.

Weep took the worst of it. He was in and out of Thaloo's makeshift medward for exhaustion, muscle fatigue, and dehydration. They usually shot him up with some generic neurogen that convinced the boy's brain he was fit to train, despite the fact that his body was giving way. Weep would disappear for part of the day and return to the yard with deep circles under his glazed-over eyes.

Ozark wasn't even taking enjoyment in the crew's suffering, which worried Cego. Usually, Ozark would laugh when one of the boys went down in the dirt from exhaustion. Now, as the crew toiled, Ozark was expressionless.

Part of the deal Murray had negotiated stated that Cego would be released from Thaloo's captivity several days prior to the Lampai fight. Murray would ensure Cego didn't escape during that time, and if he lost the fight, Cego would be returned to Thaloo. Either way, Cego hoped his departure would provide the rest of the crew some relief from Ozark's spite.

Which was why Cego was particularly dreading his final day in the yard.

Ozark was planning something bad. Cego really wasn't sure what the Tasker was capable of—how far he'd be willing to take it. Although lining his bit-purse had always been Ozark's primary incentive, he now seemed capable of a level of cruelty that went beyond bits.

That day, Ozark had them doing all the standard tasks: sloth carries, rope runs, dog crawls, last boy hanging. So far, nothing beyond the standard level of exhaustion.

Cego hung on to his rope as the last rays of dusklight cut through the yard's street-level grates. He dropped nimbly into a crouch as Weep began to shiver beside him.

Ozark was facing away from the crew, staring at the rays of crimson light streaming into the yard. He slowly turned, looking directly at Cego.

Perhaps it wasn't that Cego had usurped Ozark's control over the crew or made him appear incompetent. Maybe it wasn't even that Cego's patronage left Ozark out of the deal.

Cego could see that this cut deeper for Ozark. Like any Grievar, Ozark strove to find his lightpath. Ozark probably wasn't skilled enough to fight for the Citadel or become a well-paid merc. So he'd turned to one of the least honorable careers a Grievar could find—Tasker.

A Tasker didn't even make an honest living with his own two fists. Instead, he profited off the skill of other fighters.

Ozark licked up Thaloo's scraps every day, hungering for wins and sales. It was a pitiful existence, one that filled the man with uncertainty, fear, and anger.

Ozark's robotic voice echoed off the yard's stone walls. "We're going to make some changes on this fine duskshift, little scumlings. You all look weak in the Circle. Even when you win, it looks weak." He stared directly at Cego, his crooked teeth bared. "No killer instinct in the lot of you. I need you to start going for the kill. Patrons pay for killers, not for weak-willed scumlings."

The Tasker continued, "We need more live combat, more than just these tasks. Think of it like fighting in the Circle, except without the light and the crowd. Just two Grievar fighting for the finish like it was meant to be."

Cego didn't like where this was going.

"We start this now," Ozark said. "Form a ring, two of you in the middle."

Ozark stared down the line of boys and his eyes fell again on Cego. "You, get in there."

Cego knew he had to keep his calm. He stepped into the middle as the rest of the boys circled around him.

Ozark's voice grated, "Weep, get in there with him."

The little boy walked into the middle of the circle robotically. Weep looked like he could barely stand. His blank stare was focused into the distance, as if the neuros had him occupying a completely different world.

Ozark barked, "In this yard, I am the light. Only I tell you when it's done. If I don't say stop, you keep fighting. Disobey me and things get worse."

Cego's mind raced. That had been Ozark's attack—having him fight Weep. Farmer always said there was a parry to every punch, an escape to every submission. What was the escape here?

There was no way Cego would hurt Weep. But if he refused to fight, Cego knew it would end up far worse for the entire crew. If anything, he wanted to let Weep win, whatever it took. But Weep wasn't in any condition to win convincingly, even though he'd improved considerably during their blackshift training sessions. Now Weep could barely stand, let alone fight. He should have been in the medward.

"Go!" Ozark stood with his arms crossed as he waited for the two boys to fight for him.

Cego looked into Weep's eyes. He needed to communicate with the boy somehow, wake him up. Cego needed Weep to attack him and beat him.

Cego put his hands up and got into a fighting posture, slowly circling Weep. He threw a few feints—maybe he could get him to snap out of the stupor. The little boy didn't respond, though; he stood lifelessly, not even flinching as Cego's fist passed right in front of his face.

Cego thought back to the moment in the yard when Weep had first lifted Dozer onto his shoulders. It was months ago, but it felt like a lifetime since he'd first come to Thaloo's, to the Underground.

Cego's time in the Deep had taught him of the greed, corruption, and fear that made this place work. Folk like Tasker Ozark ruled this Underground world. Those who stood on the sidelines, away from the action and the real hardship, yet constantly frothed at the mouth and shouted for the kill. Folk like Thaloo thrived here—those who profited and got fatter off the sweat and blood of young Grievar.

But there had been light in the darkness. When Weep had carried Dozer on his shoulders in the yard that day, Cego had seen it. When Weep had bravely followed Cego at blackshift and insisted he needed to train more, Cego had seen it. At those moments, Weep's eyes had been luminous, as if he could suddenly sense the path laid out in front of him.

Seeing Weep like that had given Cego strength. The whole crew finally working together, running as one cohesive unit and using leverage to their advantage—the thought of that moment filled Cego with light. Watching Dozer and Knees opening their minds to learn new techniques and finally standing up to Shiar. There *had* been light in the darkness. Cego could almost feel it now, filling his belly with each breath.

Suddenly, Cego realized he *was* feeling the light. A lone, pulsing spectral hovered above Weep and Cego. It was *Cego's* spectral, returned to the yard again, casting its light on the crew. He knew the white flicker of its ethereal tendrils, the gentle warmth that flushed his face as it neared.

The crew and Ozark stared at the spectral with their mouths agape. There was no elemental alloy in the yard to attract spectrals like in Thaloo's Circle. Here in the yard, where street urchins and orphans toiled and followed broken lightpaths, spectrals never appeared.

Cego knew he was not the one who needed the light, though. Weep needed it like water, like nourishment, like life. Weep needed the strength to attack him, to beat him, and to finish him so that this day could be over.

As if the spectral could hear Cego's thoughts, it slowly floated toward Weep, shining brightly down on him. The little boy's eyes suddenly became lifelike again—first a glimmer and then a bright yellow flare within his irises, like he'd woken from a dream. Weep looked around the yard and breathed deeply.

Cego caught Weep's eye successfully this time. He knew the two would have to act quickly if this fight was to be convincing. He began to move in on Weep again, throwing feints in his direction. Weep now responded accordingly, moving his head side to side and shuffling his feet to match Cego's stance as if the two were dance partners. The spectral buzzed around Weep, following his every movement.

Cego threw a quick jab at Weep, aimed just below the chin, which the boy blocked, though barely. Cego couldn't slow down his strikes too much or Ozark would discover the game they were playing.

Cego threw a combination this time, a quick jab and a cross, as Weep continued to defend with his hands up. The boy blocked one of the strikes but the other grazed his ear, knocking his head to the side jarringly.

Cego shot in for a quick double-leg takedown. He slowed just enough to telegraph the shot so that Weep could parry by sprawling his legs backward.

Weep was doing well, better than Cego had expected. The boy even followed up his sprawl with a series of sharp elbows to the side of Cego's exposed head as he drove in. The elbows reopened the scar tissue on a gash just above Cego's eye, creating an immediate streak of blood on his face.

Cego knew exactly what he needed to do to get Weep to capitalize on the position and go for the finish. The final steps of this dance were laid out in front of him.

Cego gave up on the takedown attempt, falling as if his legs had given out with Weep bearing down on him. He ended up on his knees and elbows with his head on the floor—turtle position. Weep would know what do here; Cego had practiced this maneuver with him nearly every blackshift in the yard during their illicit training sessions.

Just as expected, Weep capitalized on Cego's turtle defense. He swiveled around Cego while keeping his weight on him, then threw one foot over Cego's hip, hooking just above the knee. Weep grasped his hands around Cego's shoulder with an over-under grip, and slid under him as he threw another hook in.

Weep had taken his back beautifully.

The crew around them cheered as Weep started to fight for a choke. Cego played the proper defense, making it difficult for Weep to slide his forearm across his neck, constantly pulling the boy's hands off as he tried to dig them in. Cego felt the spectral hovering over them, basking the two boys in its warm glow.

Finally, Weep convincingly caught one of Cego's defending arms under his leg, making it a two-on-one race to the finish. Now was the time. Weep needed to capitalize on the advantage and go for the finish. There wouldn't be a better moment.

In one fluid movement, Weep stripped away Cego's remaining

arm with one hand and slid his other hand under Cego's chin. He'd locked on the choke. Weep started to squeeze, constricting the arteries on both sides of Cego's neck to stop the flow of blood to the brain. Excellent form. Cego could feel himself start to get light-headed. He needed to hold back his smile at the thought of Weep choking him unconscious.

Just as the blackness closed around him, Cego heard Ozark shout from the sidelines.

"Don't let go of that choke."

* * *

Sam shot in and Cego threw his legs back into a quick sprawl, pressing his weight down on his little brother's shoulders until he curled onto his knees. Cego swiveled around to Sam's side.

Farmer watched from just outside the ironwood Circle, the old master's glowing eyes appraising the techniques of his students as they sparred. He wore his usual robe with sleeves that cut off just under the elbow, and his grey hair fell to his shoulders. Arry sat obediently at the old master's side, standing on her hind legs and yipping when one of the brothers made a sudden movement.

This Circle was their home. The brothers spent most of every day in it, training from when the sun peeked over the emerald sea to when they lay exhausted on the wooden floor in the fading dusk light.

Cego pressed down on Sam, throwing a warning punch at his brother's ear, reminding him to cover up. Sam wasn't reacting the way he normally did. He'd normally give Cego a spirited fight, leaving them both panting on their backs.

His brothers had always been his opponents in the Circle. They fought viciously until one of them was unable to continue—unconscious on the floor or with a limb wrenched at the wrong angle. Cego was never angry at his brothers for hurting him, though.

Farmer had always said your opponent is your teacher, and, as usual, the old master was right. Though Farmer had taught Cego all his techniques, his skills had been honed by constantly battling his two brothers. Testing new attacks and combinations on Sam. Getting smashed by Silas—defending or just trying to survive.

"You are thinking. Hesitating. Do not think," Farmer advised stoically, snapping Cego back to his present sparring session with Sam.

Sam was still hunkered down in his defensive position.

Why was he stalling?

Cego took action and swiveled to Sam's back, flattening his brother to the ground. Cego had practiced the attack thousands of times. Executing it was as simple as placing one foot in front of the other.

He snaked his hand across Sam's neck and locked on the choke, squeezing until his brother slapped the wooden floor in submission. Cego rolled away and faced his brother as he sat up.

"You need to try to escape before I'm so far in," Cego said in frustration.

"I know," Sam said, looking down. "I tried to." Though Sam was the smallest of the three brothers, he usually fought like a cornered island ferrcat, clawing for survival against impossible odds. Lately, though, Sam had been giving up.

"You didn't try. You haven't been trying for some time now." Cego raised his voice as he stood over his brother. "How many times have we fought? I know when you're trying."

"I did," Sam responded listlessly again, looking at the ground. "You're just better than I am."

Cego felt the hair stand up at the back of his neck as he faced off with Sam. Farmer had taught the boys to leave emotion out of the Circle, but Cego couldn't help it; heat rose in his chest.

Maybe Cego was angry because Sam was hurting his advancement—he wouldn't learn anything against an unresisting opponent. They trained to get better. And now he'd hit a standstill.

"What's wrong with you?" Cego yelled at his brother. "Don't you want to get stronger?"

Sam shook his head. "I don't know."

Sam was usually full of questions, throwing them out like pestering jabs at Cego through the entire day. Why did some crabs have soft shells when it made them more vulnerable? Why did Farmer never smile? Where did the Path lead? But now, when it was Cego's turn to ask such a simple question, the boy couldn't answer. He just had that pitiful look on his face.

Or maybe Cego was angry because Silas had left. Silas had always tested Cego's abilities to the fullest, making him work for every inch of ground. Sam couldn't do the same. He seemed almost useless in the Circle. Cego felt the anger bubbling up within him and boiling over.

"Silas is gone; he left us," Cego spat at Sam. He wanted to make his little brother as angry as he was. "You were holding Silas back. That's why he's gone!"

Sam charged at Cego, his nostrils flaring, throwing a flurry of punches as he came in. Cego managed to block one strike, but another came through and snapped his head back violently. Cego put his hand to his mouth, tasting the blood on his tongue. He missed that. He hadn't taken a hit like that since Silas had left.

"That's what I'm talking about," Cego said, smiling at Sam through his bloody teeth. Cego raised his hands and stalked toward Sam.

Sam wasn't smiling.

Cego feinted in with a quick jab and followed up with an elbow that sliced across Sam's brow. Cego yanked his brother forward with two hands behind his head and threw a quick knee to the midsection. Sam responded with a head butt, slamming his forehead into Cego's sternum, knocking him backward.

"There you go!" Cego yelled. He spat blood onto the floor. Farmer had taught them to respect the interior of the Circle, having the brothers methodically clean it after every session.

Cego fired a lunging cross at his brother, expecting him to dodge it, and then came under with a quick body shot that thudded into Sam's ribs. Sam grimaced and looped his arm around Cego's back, shoving his hip into him and tossing Cego to the wood with a well-timed o-goshi throw.

"There! See?" Cego yelled from the ground. "This is how we sharpen each other! This is how we get better!"

Arry let out a high-pitched howl.

"What are you even talking about?" Sam stood over Cego now. "Get better for what? What's the point of all this?"

Cego abruptly remembered that Farmer was watching the heated bout silently from the sideline. He felt his face flush with shame—he'd gone out of bounds, screaming and spitting in their sacred ironwood Circle. Cego sat up and looked at the old master, steadying his breath.

Farmer nodded at Cego, repeating Sam's question in his baritone voice. "What is the point of all this?"

Cego breathed out slowly, letting his adrenaline fade. What was he doing? He didn't have any reason to be so angry at Sam. Sam hadn't done anything wrong. He wasn't the reason Silas had left. They were brothers—and he only had one left on the island.

"We fight so the rest shall not have to," Cego replied slowly.

"Yes, I know. I've heard it a thousand times," Sam said, still heated. The little boy directed his defiant eyes at Farmer now. "We fight so the rest shall not have to. We're training to take the Path."

"Yes, Sam," Cego said.

Sam wasn't convinced. "But why are we fighting, really? We've been training our whole lives to take the Path, but how do we even know if something is actually out there? I've never seen it. Have you? What if Silas swam out there and there wasn't anything but more water?"

Cego looked at his little brother. This was why Sam had been acting so peculiar lately. He didn't believe. He didn't think the Path led anywhere. Sam didn't think Silas was alive.

Cego waited for Farmer to respond, but this time the old master stayed silent. He was testing Cego—he wanted him to answer Sam.

"How do we know the sky or the bottom of the sea exists? I've never climbed high enough to feel the clouds or swum down to touch the bottom of the deepest trenches, but that doesn't mean they aren't there. The end to the Path is the same. We have to believe it's there, just like Silas did," Cego said.

Sam looked down at the floor, a tear welling up in the corner of his eye. He breathed out slowly.

Cego stood and put his hand on his brother's shoulder. "I'm sorry I pressed you like that," he said. "I'm not sure what got into me."

Sam nodded. He looked at Farmer and then back to Cego, his hay-flower eyes sparkling with wetness.

"I'm sorry too. I just miss Silas," Sam conceded. "I'll try harder next time, I promise."

"Good," Cego said as he looked to Farmer for instruction. The old master nodded again, and Cego knew what to do. He squeezed Sam's shoulder.

"Let's get back to training," Cego said, though his voice wavered as the words came out of his mouth.

* * *

Cego awoke. He'd been choked unconscious before, numerous times in Farmer's capable hands. Though he knew he'd only been out for a minute or two, it always felt like a lifetime.

The darkness faded from the edges of Cego's vision as the world slowly came back into view. He was lying on the floor in the yard.

Cego could see the boys were still standing in a circle with two fighting at the center. Weep was in there again, this time fighting Shiar. Tasker Ozark stood on the sidelines, yelling for Shiar to go for the finish.

Don't let go of that choke.

The Tasker had ordered Weep to finish Cego.

Cego was alive, though. If Weep hadn't let go of the choke, Cego would be dead. Weep must have disobeyed Ozark's orders, which was why he was still fighting. This time, he was up against Shiar, who Ozark knew would show no mercy.

Cego saw Weep fall to the dirt, Shiar easily tossing the smaller boy to the ground. The spectral was gone and Weep looked like he'd lost the glimmer in his eyes along with it.

Cego tried to stand. He would help Weep, no matter what happened. He wouldn't let Shiar hurt him anymore.

Cego couldn't move, though; he lay paralyzed on the floor. He felt the hazy fog that came with the neuro they'd injected him with, the same sedating drug they'd given him when they first dragged him off the streets. He could do nothing but watch his friend get beaten.

Shiar was on Weep, throwing punches and kicks at the boy, who desperately tried to cover up from the ground. With a jackal-like grin on his face, Shiar drove his knee into Weep's belly, bearing his full weight down into the boy's solar plexus. From there, Shiar threw blow after blow like a jackhammer, driving Weep's head into the dirt. Weep turned over onto his stomach and curled up into a ball, trying to escape the vicious onslaught.

Cego looked out to the rest of Crew Nine, saw all of them standing frozen, not lifting a hand to help Weep. Knees had his eyes squeezed shut as if he had escaped to some other place in his mind.

Cego saw Dozer's bulky form step forward from the circle of boys, staring pleadingly at Ozark. "Stop this! He's going to kill him."

"Stay where you are or you'll end up where that little scumling is now," Ozark growled back.

Dozer shook his head and stepped forward again toward Shiar, who was still mercilessly slamming his fists into Weep's ribs. Ozark moved to block the big boy, and suddenly a glowing metallic stick was in the Tasker's hand. The rod blazed with menace as a red current ran up and down it.

Dozer stopped in his tracks, staring wide-eyed at the strange sight: a weapon, wielded by a Grievar. A direct violation of the Codes. But no surprise to Cego, knowing who Tasker Ozark was, knowing what this man was enabling right in front of their eyes.

Shiar laughed and stood over Weep. Cego saw the jackal turn toward him and catch his eyes just before he threw the first kick from above, which thudded into Weep's rib cage. The next kick caught Weep on the side of the head, bouncing it back and forth like a tethered ball.

Cego tried to scream but nothing came out. With every bit of energy in his body, Cego wanted to stand and save Weep. He'd fight Shiar; he'd fight Ozark, even—whatever it took. But he couldn't do anything. Cego lay on the floor, immobilized, helpless again.

Weep's eyes met his, their heads level on the yard's red dirt. For a moment, Cego thought he saw a glimmer of light behind Weep's eyes. The same defiance he'd seen in Sam's eyes. Asking those same questions: *Why am I here? Why am I fighting?*

Another kick crashed into the boy's body, and the light was gone.

* * *

Though they were torturous, those days training in Anderson's basement felt good to Murray. He felt like he was doing something worthwhile after so many years spent dredging up Grievar brood on a hopeless mission.

Though he remembered Anderson as a good training partner back in the day, Murray never realized his friend could be such a hard-nosed coach. The lanky Grievar's laid-back demeanor evaporated when Murray told him how important this all was—taking the fight to the Dragoon and winning Cego's freedom.

From that point forward, Murray was on the mats, huffing, sweating, grunting, keeling over, vomiting in the can in the corner of the room, and generally feeling like he was dying.

The basement had the bare basics of combat training equipment, but it was more than enough for two old Grievar Knights. A tattered jump rope, Anderson staring hard-eyed at Murray, analyzing his footwork and mobility as he warmed up, alternating his stances, cadence, and speed. A frayed heavy bag, Anderson standing behind it, shouting at Murray for one more minute of repeated hooks, constant knees, cutting elbows. Well-worn striking pads, Anderson expertly wielding them on both hands, calling out for Murray to throw, one-, two-, three-, four-, five-, and six-punch combinations. A thin tatami, frayed through to the floor in spots, Anderson screaming for Murray to sprawl onto it and shoot forward for single- and double-leg takedowns. A heavy, patched-up grappling dummy, Anderson standing over Murray, yelling at him that it was the last minute of his fight with the Dragoon and he needed to finish his floored opponent with ground-and-pound. Two to the body, one to the head, two to the body, one to the head, over and over again.

And when Murray was at his worst, panting like a dog, trying to savor every breath, it was suddenly time for sparring rounds. Though Anderson was older now, the lanky man still threw jabs with frightening speed, catching Murray on the nose, jolting his head back as he repeatedly tried to get inside.

They would grapple on the mats with Anderson wrapping Murray up in his legs, threatening submission after submission, seamlessly flowing from triangle neck attacks to omoplata shoulder locks to straight arm bars.

At the end of one session, the two old Grievar lay side by side on the mats, sweat and blood dripping from their skin.

Murray turned to look at his old friend. "Why do you think he left?"

Anderson looked up at the ceiling, his chest expanding and contracting, his arms sprawled at his sides.

Murray continued, "It was right after I lost. I know Coach said it wasn't because of that, but I've never been able to shake the feeling that it was somehow my fault."

Anderson sighed. "Every path has got to end sometime. Maybe Coach knew it was time for him. Things changed fast—the Citadel no longer following the Codes to the letter. You, me, Leyna, Coach, any Grievar—we're all working on fading light, anyways. You know that."

"Yeah, fading... *Fade from the light gracefully.* That's what some Citadel clerk said to me that day when they transferred me from service. Should've been straight and said they're tossing me into a vat of bat shit instead."

"A Scout job is respectable," Anderson said.

Murray snorted. "Bah, respectable. Scouting for the Citadel is something, but going after these kids in the dark—they knew, Memnon knew what he was doing to me. He's still holding that loss against me."

"I hope the high commander of the Citadel has more to do than hold grudges after all these years," Anderson said.

"Fade from the light gracefully," Murray repeated. "Follow the path, do it for the good of the nation. All that stuff—I got it. I just keep coming back to how everything fell apart all of a sudden. One moment, we were all standing beneath the stadium lights—so bright, fans cheering, the stability of the entire region riding on our shoulders, and the next thing you know, here we are, lying on your basement floor in the Deep, over ten years later," Murray said.

Anderson turned toward Murray. "Maybe so; I sometimes get the same feeling, like I'm spinning after taking a hit. But you need to adapt, as Coach would say. You fall into an opponent's trap, make it work for you. Sure, maybe Memnon knew what he was doing to you. Throwing one of the best Grievar Knights in the past few decades into the Deep, turning him into a lowly Scout. Make him pay for it, Murray. You say you're onto something here with this boy Cego. That's a start."

Murray nodded, exhaling. "Yeah, it's a darkin' start."

* * *

The boy walked alongside the burly man, the top of his shaved head only coming up to Murray's midsection.

Lampai Stadium glowed in the distance at the end of Markspar Row. The greenlight coated the surface of the Underground's streets in an emerald sheen. The cawing and cooing of hawkers from the nearby market echoed on the stone walls around the two companions.

"Let's get away from the hawkers... Never know what you'll end up buying from the crafty ones after midshift," Murray said. He'd been trying to get the kid talking, have him open up about his past, but it had been difficult to get him to even open his mouth.

As they approached the stadium, the bustle on the street grew thicker, with swarms jostling their way toward the daily fights at Lampai. Murray watched Cego swivel his head at the sights, sounds, and smells that infiltrated every street corner.

An assortment of old mechs crawled down the streets—rusted transports hauling alloys from the mines or foul-smelling sweepers heading for the trash heap. Murray even saw the grounded form of a scrapped Flyer with a pack of glowing spectrals trailing the exhaust.

"Straight from Arklight!" A hawker stood atop the mech, screeching. "This beauty only flew five runs for Governance before she was decommissioned. Rubellium blast cannon still intact, only needs a minor Maker to fix her up!"

The Deep didn't get near the quality of gear Upworld, but there was still a thriving black market for anything and everything getting pawned off as Arklight tech.

Amid the crowded mass of mechs and laborers and hawkers walked the Grievar. Thickly muscled, scarred, and gnarled, the Grievar strode boldly under the light, their chests puffed out and their muscles bulging, intricate flux tattoos adorning their bodies like works of art.

Murray caught Cego staring at some of the bare-chested Grievar.

A lion flux on an exposed chest reared up on its hind legs and swiped its paws menacingly. An octopus on another Grievar's back expanded and unfurled, reaching with its tentacles down the man's arms and legs.

Murray felt his own flux tattoos shifting under the light, even from underneath his thick cloak. He sensed each tattoo as if it had a personality, a unique characteristic he'd acquired during his path.

"Flux tattoos," Murray said to Cego. "They used to mean something. Now Grievar get whatever fits their darkin' fancy."

Closer to the stadium, the two passed a Daimyo caravan pulled by a pack of Grunts, thick-shouldered haulers whose sole purpose was to drag their lord around. Even though the Daimyo had mechs for transport, many preferred to *show off* with an entire mobile caravan, complete with Grunts pulling the vehicles from the helm, courtesans draped across the inner chambers, and armed mercenaries surrounding the entire procession.

The Daimyo noble at the center of the caravan was shielded from the street with a translucent pod surrounding him, likely charged to the touch.

Murray could see the blue-veined man staring out from behind the glass, watching the rabble on the street with his black, fathomless eyes. Even with the shield between them, Murray wondered if he could put his fist through the glass and crush the frail creature's skull if he timed it right. His heart quickened at the thought.

Though Ezo had won the Deep long ago, Murray knew that these rogue Daimyo lords were the actual rulers down here. Those Daimyo with no allegiance but their own pockets; running the dens, the Courtesan Houses, the stim trade, and the illicit mining operations. Those hiding in the shadows while their mercenary Grievar fought for their interests.

One such merc guarding the caravan eyed Murray suspiciously as they passed each other. The man looked to be a Grievar, yet he carried Daimyo tech—a thick steel rod that pulsed with a menacing blue current. Murray had felt the effects of an auralite-forged weapon before. The second the rod made contact, it took your knees out from under you, made you want to curl into a ball and give up.

"No tools, no tech," Murray growled as he passed by the merc.

"Back off, old-timer." The merc held the glowing weapon up. "Lord Mamaru would have no problem with me settin' you to a sizzle."

Murray kept his eyes on the man until the procession turned a corner.

Before they reached the bustling square in front of Lampai, Murray guided Cego away from the main thoroughfare toward a smaller side street that looped around the back of the stadium.

Cego never asked questions about where they were going, but Murray could tell the kid was thirsty for knowledge. Murray had been the same way when Coach had brought his team out on their first expeditions around Ezo or to foreign lands beyond the borders. Everything was new, each sight unique.

Murray had planned on taking the kid straight to Anderson's, maybe let Leyna make him some of those famed Deep cakes of hers. Certainly would be an improvement over that green slop they called food at Thaloo's. First, though, Murray decided he'd bring the kid to a place he himself hadn't visited in ages.

The pair walked in silence beyond the clamor of the stadium and followed the small path toward Daeomons Hill, a steep, rocky incline that led up to the back side of the steppe.

When he'd just set out on his path, Murray remembered sprinting up Daeomons Hill for endurance training, purposely setting his lungs on fire so that the burn wouldn't seem so bad in the Circle. With his fight with the Dragoon looming, Murray wanted to test himself again.

"Ready for a bit of a workout?" Murray looked at the boy, who nodded silently.

Murray tried to think about the Dragoon as he and the boy started up the hill. Though he'd made progress with Anderson over the past two weeks, he still was nowhere near the shape he'd need to be in to keep up with a much younger Grievar.

Murray's heart started to thump in his chest as he visualized the upcoming fight. The spectral light filtering from Lampai's giant arrays, the crowd boisterous and zoned in on the two Grievar in the Circle. The thrill and anticipation right before the bout began, a steady tingling in his belly that would give way to a euphoria that filled his chest, surging through his arms and legs, guiding him toward his opponent.

Murray pushed his pace as the hill rose sharply, cutting away the view of the steppe above. He looked at Cego at his side, who seemed to be thinking the same thing as he—*get to the top*. The boy's eyes gleamed with determination, his short legs taking two strides for every one of Murray's.

Soon, Murray and the boy were running full steam, scrambling up the rocky ravine toward the top of the cliff face. Murray could feel the strain of his old body, his joints creaking as his legs pumped faster.

Though he was worn down, something felt different. He was going somewhere. He wanted this fight. He looked to the boy, striding up the hill without fear, only looking forward to his next step.

Murray's heart beat rapidly in his chest as he launched himself ahead. The two left an avalanche of gravel behind them as they scrambled up the hill. The last ascent was the steepest—the pair needed to throw their hands to the rocky surface to keep their balance as they clawed for the top.

Murray's body wanted to give way like an old roof strained past its years, ready to collapse beneath the weight of seasons of weathering. The Dragoon wouldn't stop, though. The Dragoon wouldn't be forgiving like this hill. Cego's freedom wouldn't be forgiven either—the boy depended on Murray. He needed him to fight through the burn, get past the suffering.

Murray let out a deep howl.

Finally, at the top of the hill, he fell to his knees. His chest heaved up and down like bellows trying to keep a dying fire lit. Cego stood next to him, breathing hard but calm.

Murray huffed. "Used to be easier."

The pair surveyed their surroundings. From the top of Daeomons Hill, the view of the Underground was unique.

The cavern glowed with green iridescence cast by the arrays laid into the scrimshaw ceiling thousands of meters up. Spectrals danced around the lights like swarms of glowing moths. Grey structures sprouted from the bedrock, and paved streets zigzagged between the buildings, broadening into wide thoroughfares and narrowing into thin alleys.

To the north, the Lift looked like a giant tree, its roots burrowing into the cavern floor, creeping under the gridded streets, its trunk rising into the cave ceiling. To the east, the greenlight bathed the market district in an undulating current, ebbing and flowing along with the bustle of the streets. And to the west, Murray could just make out the forms of giant mechs ripping into the cavern wall, digging along with hordes of Grunts to unearth deposits of valuable elemental alloys.

But Murray liked to imagine the sprawling cavern before any of this. Before the politiking and posturing, before he was born, before his father had built their little cavernside home, before the arrays and the Lift had been constructed, when the only way to come Deep had been on blind, long treks through winding tunnels.

It was down here, in this voluminous cavern, that empires had first chosen their champions, the Grievar, to fight for their interests. Many arenas had since been built across the Surface world. There were grander venues like Albright, or ingenious designs like Aquarius, or those in more unforgiving climates like Starkguard.

But none compared to Lampai, where the way of the Grievar had been born.

Murray's eyes shifted to the center of the city, where Lampai Stadium burst from the bedrock like a gem glittering in the Deep. Hordes would stream into Lampai every day at the height of the shift to watch the Underground's top Grievar in action. In one week, Murray would be standing within a Circle at Lampai's apex, facing the Dragoon.

Murray breathed out slowly as they turned from the view of the city toward the steppe, now directly in front of them. Layers of fertile growth were built alongside a central stairway with rows of glowing crops clinging to the bedrock on each level. The crops were fed by Dagmar Falls, which spewed from an opening above and was then channeled along to the rows of each level for irrigation.

The two began to climb the ancient staircase, moving past luminous rows of growth on each level. Cego stared as the crops pulsed in a dizzying array of green hues, ranging from the gaudy bright fluorescence of lichens to the dark, forest bloom of the mosses. Growers were heaving out large bags of fertilizer from storage sheds, and hundreds of harvesters were out working in the crops.

When they reached the base of the falls, Murray turned to Cego, his breath misty in the damp air.

"Hey. Do you know how to swim, kid?"

Cego nodded silently and Murray breathed a sigh of relief.

"Follow me." Murray motioned to Cego. White spray soaked the two as they moved single file around the edge of the falls and then behind the rushing water.

The pair emerged into a wide cavern. In front of them, a glassy lake shimmered a coral hue, illuminated by the now-nascent dusk-light streaming through a hole in the cavern ceiling. With a sweeping gesture, Murray signaled their arrival. "Lake Dagmar." Though the majority of the lake to the east was often crowded with visitors, this particular section was kept secret by a select few.

Murray broke the silence again. "Thought you'd enjoy a swim."

Cego surprised Murray then, speaking methodically as he looked out at the lake. "It reminds me of home."

"Where you from, kid?" Murray took the opportunity. He knew Thaloo and the other den owners had shipments coming from all over the world, but he hadn't had a chance to figure out where Cego was from yet.

Cego was silent again, his lips pursed.

"You from the Isles, maybe?" Murray said, prodding. "I did a tour of the Emerald a while ago. Good folk, good fighters out there. Though, can't say I'm a fan of Aquarius Arena. That place still gives me nightmares."

Cego slowly nodded.

After the trauma many slave brood went through, getting ripped away from their families or worse, it wouldn't surprise him if Cego had blocked out the past. Murray decided to drop the line of questioning.

"Well, you'd best go for it before blackshift."

Murray watched Cego sprint along the shore and dive beneath the glassy sheen of the lake. The kid swam like an otter, staying beneath the water for minutes at a time before surfacing for air. *Must be an Islander,* Murray thought, *to swim like that.* Cego looked like he belonged in the water, just as he'd appeared to belong in the Circle.

The way that Cego had stood motionless waiting for his opponent, using only the minimal amount of energy to finish them, replayed in Murray's head. The boy had moved with such fluidity, the sort that Murray rarely saw even in Grievar who had fought for an entire career.

Murray caught Cego's eyes for a moment, the kid looking back at him with that strange blank stare, as if he were occupying a completely different world. Cego closed his eyes and dove back beneath the water.

* * *

Cego was thrashing through the waves again.

The night sky blanketed the world as the two brothers swam the Path. Cego and Sam followed the green trail of plankton toward the distant horizon, the same Path that Silas had taken over one thousand days ago.

They'd left the island behind. They'd left the old master behind.

Something was wrong, though.

Silas had completed his training before he'd taken the Path. He'd fought Farmer.

Watching Silas fight Farmer had been like watching a boulder falling from the top of a cliff. Though Silas had been the strongest of the three brothers, it had been viscerally apparent that the old master would reach his destination as certainly as the falling boulder rode gravity to the ground. That wry smile had been missing from Silas's face that day.

That fight with Farmer had been Silas's last training exercise—a ritual that signified he was ready to leave the island and follow the Path.

Sam was far from ready, though. The youngest brother had left without Farmer's approval. Sam had always been too curious; he didn't have the patience to wait his turn. He'd recklessly leapt into the waves and Cego had followed him.

Cego told himself he followed Sam because he wanted to save him. Sam was weaker than he; Sam needed protection. In truth, though, Cego knew he was just as curious. He didn't want to stay on the island with the old master any longer. He wanted to follow the Path and see what awaited him on the distant horizon. He wanted to see where Silas had gone.

Cego tried to pick up his pace to catch up with Sam, but his brother maintained the distance between them. Against the green luminescence of the Path, Sam's figure was a dark silhouette.

The two swam endlessly until the island disappeared from view behind them. For a moment, the world was in balance, the darkness of the sky above an equal to the murky depths below, the horizon suddenly as close as the shore they'd left, the green, glimmering Path connecting their past and future.

Maybe they'd make it. Maybe they were ready.

Sam disappeared from the surface of the water. Cego could only see the crest and fall of the waves where his little brother had last been swimming.

Cego threw himself forward with all his strength. His swim out had been a calculated effort, trading speed for efficiency. Now Cego forgot about efficiency. He used every fiber of his coiled body to propel himself through the water.

Cego approximated where he'd last seen Sam on the surface and exhaled deeply before letting air fill his lungs to capacity. He dove under and launched himself toward Sam's sinking body, but the water hardened. The viscous liquid held Cego in place.

He couldn't move as he watched Sam's little body sink in front of him. He tried in vain to reach toward Sam, but the water was too thick for him to extend his hand. The liquid wrapped around his body like a serpent, immobilizing his muscles, slowly choking him.

As the world faded, Cego looked toward the surface for a glimmer of light. There was nothing but darkness above.

* * *

Cego stayed quiet on the walk back down the steppe with Murray. The dusklight was subsiding and hordes of harvesters were packing up their day's work among the crops.

As he trudged downward, Cego tried to forget about what had happened the previous day in the yard, but he couldn't. Weep's lifeless eyes kept coming back to him.

The day's trip into the markets, the run up Daeomons Hill, the tour of the steppe, and the swim in Lake Dagmar had all served to distract Cego from remembering the trauma. Now, though, as the two started down Daeomons Hill in silence, the fresh memories began to haunt him.

Cego had been helpless, frozen on the floor as he watched his friend get viciously beaten. Weep, who had come so far, was dead because Cego had been unable to do anything.

The moment played over and over in Cego's head. The sulfurous smell of the red dirt in the yard. Ozark's spiteful eyes surveying his handiwork. Shiar's cackle as he threw kick after kick into the little boy's body. The pleading look in Weep's eyes as the light faded from them.

Cego had stayed on the ground even after the paralyzing effect of the neurogen had worn off. Knees had tried to rouse him, telling Cego he needed to get up and carry on. But Cego hadn't moved.

He had watched from the floor as Dozer carried Weep from the yard, the big boy racked with sobs as he delicately draped the body over his shoulder. Cego had slept on the yard's dirt that night, not moving until the next crew physically removed him in the morning.

A tear streaked Cego's cheek. He turned to his side and wiped it discreetly with his sleeve. He couldn't let Murray see any weakness.

Cego could tell the man was trying to help him out. He still didn't know why the burly Grievar was doing it, but he could see something different in him. Murray wasn't in it for the bits—after all, he was fighting for Cego's freedom, putting his own head on the line.

We fight so the rest shall not have to.

The familiar mantra was a reminder that this man was the closest thing to home or family that Cego had down here. He'd grown close to some on Crew Nine, but they weren't here now, and they wouldn't be with him if he made it to the Surface.

The two reached level ground and turned onto a cobbled path that wrapped around the other side of Daeomons Hill. Homes were elegantly built into the slope here, carved and constructed as if they grew naturally from the landscape.

Cego sighed as they passed under the soft glow of the lichens.

Tendrils sprouting plentifully along the cave ceiling cast undulating light on the cobbled road. A curious sort of tree lined the path, with luminous buds sprouting from the ends of each wiry branch.

Murray pulled to a stop in front of a grey home with an oaken door, rapping on it with his fist. A silver-haired woman with a strong jaw and honey-colored eyes opened it.

The woman and Murray greeted each other with a wrist-to-wrist grasp. Murray looked down to Cego, who was standing silently in the doorframe.

"Leyna, I'd like you to meet Cego."

* * *

Cego's week with Leyna and Anderson was confusing. He wasn't used to the comforts in the cozy home, not after his grueling experience at Thaloo's.

Like a doting mother, Leyna made sure Cego had every amenity available—delicious foods at all hours of the day, a warm bath at night, and fluffed pillows in his bed.

Leyna constantly fed Cego, telling him he was far too skinny for a growing Grievar boy. After a steady diet of green slop for months at Thaloo's, it took his stomach a day or two to get used to the rich foods that Leyna laid out in front of him. He didn't let that slow him down, though.

Cego wolfed down every crumb of her delicious cooking, dishes like minced mushroom pies encrusted with beelbub nuts, spiral-root sautés over beds of moss, and fluffy Deep cakes frosted in lichen butter.

Cego didn't see much of Anderson or Murray that week. The men spent most of the days training in the basement, and when mealtime came, they talked fight strategy. Murray ate only special training-approved dishes that Leyna cooked for him, which looked far less appetizing than Cego's feasts.

Anderson gave Cego warm smiles and even a pat on top of the head, but the tall, dark Grievar was quiet around him. Once, Cego caught Anderson staring at him, examining him, but he quickly looked away when Cego met his gaze.

Cego spent several days working with Leyna in her garden behind the house. There, the Grievar lady cultivated a variety of Deep roots, mosses, and lichens that she used in her cooking. She even had a beelbub tree in the center of the garden.

Cego watched as Leyna harvested the luminous nuts. She hummed a wistful tune as she worked. As soon as she plucked each nut from the branch of the tree, its glow slowly faded.

"Why does the light fade like that?" Cego felt comfortable asking the Grievar lady questions, almost as if he were talking to the lone spectral in his cell again, except with Leyna, he got real responses.

"Good question." Leyna placed another nut into the basket Cego was holding for her. "Our beelbub tree gets nutrients from the ground—water and minerals that it pulls up in its roots. The nutrients travel to each of the tree's branches and eventually out to the very ends of each branch to feed the nuts."

Leyna brushed her silver hair over one ear, which was cauliflowered and studded with several earrings. She continued, "The tree uses some of those nutrients to generate luminescence in the nuts. Out in the Deep caverns, this sort of tree uses light to attract bats that feed on the nuts. The bats then deposit the beelbub seeds in another cavern where new trees can grow."

"But when the nut gets pulled off the tree, the light goes out. Doesn't that mean it dies?" Cego asked, a tinge of sadness in his voice.

Leyna looked at him with earnest eyes, her expression softening. "Well, yes and no. In a sense, it is dead because it is cut off from the tree's roots, from the ground. But when the nut is plucked from the tree and deposited somewhere else, it grows into a whole new tree."

Cego thought about how the old master had responded when

Sam had asked him one of his many questions about death. Farmer's words filled Cego's head, and he found himself speaking out loud. "A Grievar is not born to build legacy or history, to make name or impact. Only to fight and die in the Circle. Death should be considered—"

Leyna cut in. "Just as the wilting of a flower before the frost, noted and soon forgotten."

"How…how did you know?" Cego stared at the Grievar lady, wide-eyed.

"I think I should be asking you the same," Leyna replied. "Of course, I'm speaking the Codes. But it's more curious to me that a boy fighting in Thaloo's den can recite the Codes like that."

She met Cego's eyes, and for a moment, he became afraid that Leyna would ask him where he'd learned those words.

"Where did you learn to speak the Codes?" Cego fired the question like a counter jab to get ahead of anything coming his way.

"I picked up bits here and there growing up," Leyna said. "But most of my learning came from my years studying at the Lyceum, from the Codes professor who still holds that position at the school today—Aon Farstead."

"Where did the Codes come from?" Cego suddenly felt like Sam, with so many questions bubbling up.

Leyna stopped plucking at the tree and took the basket from Cego. "The Ancients wrote them, supposedly."

"The Ancients?"

"Yes. The Grievar who came before. Before all of this Underground you see today. Before the roads and buildings and stadiums and slave dens and arrays."

"What was there before all of this?" Cego asked.

"They say there was a time long past when you could still hear the Deep wind, the soft swish of cave bats flying overhead—not just the whirring of mechs eating away at the earth. A time before the great arrays above, when only the gentle glow of lichen illuminated the cavern floors. A time when our Circles were simple formations of rock, wood, or moss spread on the ground, not the overcrowded dens, amphitheaters, and arenas they've since become."

"What happened to all that?"

"The Daimyo happened," Murray said gruffly from the entrance to the garden. "Their archivists still brag about everything they gave us when they came Deep. Tech, slaves, language, culture, light. They *fixed* us. That's what they say."

Murray walked over to the beelbub tree, running his hand along one of its smooth branches.

"Truth is, they gave us nothing," Murray said. "They only took from us. They took our quiet caverns, our peaceful darkness, our language, our culture, our Codes. Same thing happened everywhere else they went—the Kirothian highlands, the Desovian peaks, the Emerald Isles, and of course the whole of Ezo—the Daimyo took everything from the Grievar. We are not free to fight, free to live, as they would have us believe."

"There's those in the North still," Leyna said. "Our kin on the Ice still have their sovereign lands."

Murray shook his head. "The time for Myrkonian freedom is near gone. As we speak, the Kirothian Empire is pushing into the North, bringing their Enforcers and Flyers with them. A darkin' airship even, I hear."

"But they need to make a challenge." Leyna frowned and crossed her arms. "Tharsis Bertoth won't let his lands go so easy."

"Bah." Murray waved a hand. "Smoke and mirrors. They'll find some Grievar pawn to stand in the Circle across from Bertoth, and meanwhile, Kirothian mechs will be ready to blast the Ice Tribes to dust if anything goes wrong."

Leyna shook her head. "All right now, we're boring Cego with this talk. And it makes me glad that Anderson and I decided to retire Deep, away from all such politiks. The fight never seems to end."

"I'd be happy to do the same, Leyna." Murray sighed. "But right now, doesn't seem I can stop fighting. And even though you and Anderson are out of the light, such matters are happening down here, too, just under your nose."

"We can only fight in the Circles we stand in," Leyna replied.

"That's the darkin' truth," Murray said as he grasped one of the beelbub nuts in his fist and plucked it from the tree.

Cego watched carefully as its light faded.

CHAPTER 6

Return to Lampai

Certain attacks may seem potent to the untrained eye. Groin strikes, eye gouges, clawing the skin, ripping the hair: though painful, these acts will only serve to bolster the spirit of the more experienced Grievar. The wild cat scratching at the hide of the great bear will soon find its home in the dirt. When faced with such cowardly attacks, a Grievar should return suit with the force of real technique.

Thirty-Second Precept of the Combat Codes

While in Leyna's care, amid the newfound comforts, Cego nearly forgot that his time in Farmoss was only temporary. The day of Murray's fight came as a harsh reminder to Cego that he was still on the precipice of ending up back at Thaloo's, living his days out in the tiny bunk and fighting for his survival.

Cego swallowed a dose of guilt as he thought about Dozer and Knees sweating in the yard while he'd had his head buried in a plush pillow, thinking about what he'd have for breakfast every day. He'd even asked Murray if there was anything he could do to get his friends out of Thaloo's, perhaps add them to the deal if he won at Lampai, but the burly Grievar had looked doubtful.

Leyna and Cego arrived at Lampai Stadium as crowds streamed through the open iron gates and filtered up the ramps like ants set on breadcrumbs. The dusklight crested toward the height of its strength and Cego craned his head at the rubellium arrays above, where swarms of crimson spectrals congregated. Many of the wisps descended from the cavern ceiling toward the heart of the stadium. Cego closed his eyes to the brightness and could still see the red pulsing beneath his lids.

Cego opened his eyes to Lampai's towering stone stands. Statues of Grievar champions stood on top of the walls, muscles and scars chiseled with precision, the redlight filling empty eye sockets. Cego thought about the old master again. Had he ever fought down here at Lampai? Looking across the row of ancient statues, he almost expected to see Farmer's venerated face staring down at him.

Leyna led Cego through the gates and into the outer ramp of the stadium. He could already hear the crowd from within, low murmurs giving way to roars of applause.

"Preliminary fights kicked off already," Leyna said.

Murray's fight with the Dragoon would be the main event today, scheduled to start just as the Underground's redlight reached its height. As they made their way around the ramp, Leyna explained the many sights of Lampai.

The stadium was sectioned off according to bit-price, which meant the best seats went to the Daimyo, set along the edge of the arena at the highest viewpoints. Some Daimyo lords owned elaborately crafted raised boxes. Of course, the Underground's most prominent Circle owner, slaver, and overall jack-of-all-trades, Thaloo, had his place up on the grandstand as well. Thaloo was the only Grievar with a box at Lampai, his designed to look like a tented palace, filled with plush couches, rugs, and servants carrying platters of heartbeat grapes. Cego wondered whether Thaloo was sitting up in his box now, looking down at the Circle with his crafty yellow eyes.

"Don't worry; nothing worth seeing in there. It's a waste of space." Leyna dismissed it as they moved by the strongly perfumed entrance to the Daimyo section, which was marked by a series of ornate golden doorframes.

They passed the entryway to the cheapest seats, where Grunt laborers filled the stands. Cego noticed that many of the Grunts were packed into the bar outside the entryway. They watched the preliminary fights on boards above the bar, clanking their bottles together and yelling at the screens.

Some of the lightboards plastered across the walls displayed the odds of each fight. Cego's heart sank as he saw that Murray was listed as a huge underdog, the Dragoon a six-to-one favorite over the older Grievar.

Leyna led Cego to the Grievar section, which was spartan. Beyond the bare basics of vat-jerky and Deep-ale stands, the Grievar had designed their interior as a simple hallway to funnel folk toward Lampai's true purpose—the fights. The two walked through the tunnel, listening to the echo of footsteps, before they emerged into the chaos of the open-air arena.

Cego looked down at the mass of folk slowly gathering for the main event. The crowd looked like a whirlpool, swirling around the circumference of the stadium and getting thicker toward the center of gravity, the Circle. Though it seemed small from this height, the Circle was a shining silver beacon with fiery streaks painted across it. The spectrals from the arrays above descended in a beam of crimson light and joined those rising off the Circle. Some spectrals sporadically broke from the stream, swirling around it and then jumping back in like spawning salmon.

"Rubellium," Cego whispered. Since Murray had informed him about the different elemental alloys, he'd attempted to recognize the various sorts on sight. This burning red Circle was not difficult to classify.

"Yes," Leyna replied as they climbed cracked stone stairs. "This

Circle is imported from the mines in Venturi, smelted from some of the purest rubellium reserves in the world, so it's stronger than most."

Even from here, Cego could feel the prickle of redlight on his skin. The hairs on his neck stood and he found himself clenching his jaw as if he were bracing it to take a punch.

Cego and Leyna made their way up another aisle before they found their seats. Though Murray had done his best bargaining to get them good tickets, they were fairly far out in the outposts of the Grievar section.

He looked around at the Grievar crowd in attendance. They were quieter than Cego expected, their eyes honed in on the preliminary fight down below, occasionally glancing up at the massive lightboard in the center of the stadium that displayed the biometrics of each combatant.

The Grievar around Cego joined together in a sudden chorus—*"O Toh, Yeo Toh, Le Toh!"* Their deep voices cut through the clamor of the stadium.

Cego was surprised to hear Leyna beside him echoing the call.

"What are they saying?" Cego asked.

"Fight for peace, fight for blood, fight to die," Leyna replied. "Spoken in Tikretian, language of the Ancients."

She smiled at him and motioned for him to join along. The Grievar repeated the chant whenever one of the fighters below showed strength or skill, no matter how subtle or small the action was. They were joining in the fight as if they were a part of the rhythm of combat.

In comparison, the other sections of the stadium were far less controlled. Spectators hooted and hollered as their favorites gained control or booed and spat on the ground when a fighter they had bits riding on lost. Folk constantly ran to and from their seats to make last-minute changes on their bets or to refill their tankards of ale.

Cego felt the tension building in the crowd as the final preliminary fight ended. The main event was nearly underway.

He wondered what Murray and Anderson were doing right now. Maybe waiting in some tiny locker room in the bowels of the stadium. Was Murray warming up, hitting pads as Anderson called out combinations, like they did in the basement? Or maybe Murray was sitting calmly with his eyes closed, breathing deeply as Cego had watched him do earlier that week.

Farmer had always told Cego to steady his heartbeat prior to fighting. The old master would say, *Your opponent will know if your heart is racing, your palms sweaty, your muscles tightened, your eyes fearful. You must quiet your heart and all else will follow.*

During Cego's fights at Thaloo's, that advice had been instrumental not only for staying calm but also for keeping his biometric data in check so his opponent couldn't capitalize on any perceived weakness.

Cego overheard two nearby Grievar talking about the upcoming matchup.

"Murray's last fight, he already looked worn out then. Like he gave up. Can't imagine how he'll look over ten years later!"

A second Grievar agreed. "Yeah. My uncle was Upworld at the Citadel when he fell. He was such a Mighty Murray fan, still talks about it like he was the one who lost the darkin' thing. Says the same thing, though...Murray walked into Albright Stadium like he'd lost already, shoulders sagging, eyes down on the canvas."

The other Grievar took a swig of something so strong that Cego could smell it from his seat. "Must be crazy, though, fighting for some boy after all these years. Don't think old man Murray knows what he's gotten himself into here. I mean, didn't he even watch the Dragoon's last fight? He darkin' put a Knight out in the first two minutes. I'm not talking about some washed-up Knight, either—Hardy was freshly graduated from the Lyceum."

"Yeah, I remember that fi—" Suddenly, the lights went out.

The crowd quieted, a hush rolling over even the most boisterous fans.

For a moment in the eerie black, Cego forgot he was in Lampai Stadium with so many other folk. He forgot he was in the Underground, even, a man-made city with a constant pulse. Though he could still hear the distant echo of the mechs digging at the western wall, Cego realized he was sitting in a massive cavern. He thought he could hear the Deep wind swishing and chattering overhead, swarms of bats fluttering through the darkness.

Crimson wisps of light emerged on either end of the stadium—spectrals, dozens of them on each side, floating toward the Circle. Even in the darkness, Cego knew that Murray was walking within one of those swarms.

The lights blasted back on, roaring to life all at once across the arena, beaming down again on the Circle. Murray was there, standing on one side of the silvery ring with spectrals buzzing around him. Across from him stood the Dragoon.

Both Grievars' images flashed on the huge lightboard in the center of the stadium, along with their biometric readings.

The Dragoon was massive. Compared to Murray, he looked to be at least two heads taller, with long, corded arms and legs. The Dragoon's signature flux tattoo was in full movement under the light. A red dragon curled around one of his shoulders, breathing a fireball across his back.

The huge Grievar flipped his long hair over his shoulder and smirked, raising his arm to the crowd's thunderous approval.

Murray looked undaunted. Though by far the smaller and older Grievar, he stood firmly in place, his chest deeply rising and falling as he steadied his breath. With Murray's shirt off, Cego could see the intricately patterned flux tattoos that started on top of his shoulders and ran down his back and arms. Each tattoo was a separate entity moving of its own accord, yet all the tattoos flowed together as if with some unified purpose.

As he looked at the lightboard image of Murray, Cego tried to discern the tattoos on Murray's bare skin. Usually, the burly Grievar wore a sleeved cloak that concealed all but the last few tattoos on his wrists and hands. Now Cego saw every design clearly, rendered fully under the light. A howling wolf. A floating, blinking eyeball. A bear rearing up and swiping its paws. A serpentine silver dragon unfurling across his back.

Cego turned to Leyna. "What do Murray's tattoos mean?"

She kept her eyes on the Circle as the two Grievar took their final preparations below. The Dragoon showboated to the crowd by dropping into a split while Murray stood, quietly staring at his opponent.

"Murray's fluxes are badges gained in the Citadel. He earned some for achievements when we were studying together at the Lyceum, and the others he won fighting for Ezo as a Knight. It's not the same modernday, though. The newer Grievar, like dragon boy down there, they just flux on whatever fits their fancy. Always trying to win the crowd over so they can command a higher bitpurse. Not like it used to be." Leyna shook her head slowly.

She smiled wryly at Cego as she pulled the shoulder of her tunic down, revealing the same howling black wolf on her skin. "That one was for passing sixth-year finals at the Lyceum—becoming a Knight. Hurt like the dark."

Cego was astounded to see that Leyna, so caring and warm, had been a Knight as well. He couldn't quite picture her in any vicious battles or traveling to foreign lands to fight for Ezo.

She caught Cego's wide eyes and laughed. "Hard to imagine me a Knight once upon a time, eh? Well, let me tell you, young Grievar...I stood with the best of them." Leyna looked like she was ready to launch into a story, but a loud tone echoed across the stadium, signaling that the redlight was at its height.

The fight began.

* * *

Murray was confused as he stood under the pillar of crimson spectral light. The light felt incredible, beyond what he'd dreamed of every night for the past ten years as he restlessly turned in bed and relived his days as a Grievar Knight. Murray could acutely sense every inch of his body, the connections between sinew, muscle, ligament, and bone running from the tips of his toes to the top of his skull. The light beam blasted away any doubts he had about fighting the Dragoon, the huge Grievar standing across from him, ready to take his head off with a kick.

And yet, the light brought back memories. His last year fighting for the Citadel, so often under the Circle's influence that he felt more comfortable there than in his own bed. Pushing those he loved away in the name of Ezo and his path. Coach leaving, the team breaking up.

Murray had lived through it. He knew the light took more than his biometric feedback. Murray knew the light had taken his life, almost everything he had once held dear. And yet he knew he couldn't live without it.

He embraced the redlight at Lampai fully and wholeheartedly, letting it seep into his skin, his blood, his breath, and his heartbeat. He opened his eyes and looked at the Dragoon. He was moving toward the huge Grievar then, every muscle of his body in balance as he cut across the Circle.

Anderson had laid out a gem of a game plan for Murray, one that capitalized on each potential factor of the fight. Murray was to stay away from the Dragoon's long reach, in particular avoiding the jabs and leg kicks that the man could throw to keep his opponents at range. To do this, Anderson wanted Murray to circle the Dragoon, staying just outside of his reach. Eventually, the Dragoon would be baited to move in with one of his famed flying knees—a leaping attack that he launched to rapidly close the distance and potentially catch his opponent off guard. Murray had watched SystemView replays of the Dragoon's last several fights, three of which had ended with a devastating knockout due to a flying knee. It was at this critical point in the fight that Murray needed to anticipate the move and go in for the takedown. Get the Dragoon on the ground and get to work. That was the plan.

Murray fully trusted Anderson's logic. The game plan made perfect sense. It played to Murray's strengths and the Dragoon's weaknesses. Murray was at huge disadvantage in the standing game, so he needed to get the Dragoon to the ground. Simple.

And yet, as the redlight streamed down on Murray and he moved toward the Dragoon, the plan disappeared like a candle-flame snuffed out. He'd spent years on end in rubellium Circles, acclimating himself to their effects. He knew what it felt like to be pulled by the redlight. He could sense the rage rising in his stomach, the adrenaline coursing through him as his heart thumped in his chest and pulsed in his temples. He knew he was getting pulled by the light. But he didn't care.

Murray didn't want to play to his opponent's weaknesses. He wanted to fight him like a Grievar. Murray was a Knight; this was what he did. This was his path.

Murray charged in at the Dragoon, the tall man looking down at him in surprise, not expecting such immediate aggression from the former champ. Just as expected, the Dragoon fired off two quick jabs at Murray, one catching him under the eye and the second brushing across his shoulder. Murray didn't even feel them. He was already inside the Dragoon's range, throwing a powerful overhand right, catching the Dragoon right on the chin.

The Dragoon stumbled back, stunned as Murray stayed on him, pushing him to the ground and leaping at him with a frenzy of punches. The Dragoon was barely able to close his guard, wrapping his long legs around Murray's waist, but the old champ kept attacking.

Murray heard the chorus of chants coming from the Grievar's section, an acknowledgment of his frenetic pace.

The Dragoon attempted to wrap up Murray's hands and pull him tight into his guard, but Murray broke free each time, posturing up and battering his opponent with quick elbows and punches from the top. He slammed two body shots into the Dragoon's rib cage and then followed with another quick strike to the head. It felt good to get back to work.

The Dragoon stiff-armed Murray with one of his long limbs, pushing him at the throat to jack his head backward. When Murray kept the pressure on, the Dragoon changed his tactic, jabbing two fingers directly into Murray's eye socket.

Pain shot down Murray's spine like an electric current, making him rear his head back and scream aloud. The crowd hushed.

Though any technique was legal in the Circle, eye attacks were frowned upon and seen as a dishonorable way for a Grievar to win a fight. By the precepts of the Combat Codes, at least. The Dragoon wasn't playing by those rules.

With the space he created, the Dragoon pushed his hips out from under Murray and leapt back to his feet, immediately starting to circle and throw jabs again.

Though he'd proven he could surprise and even hurt the Dragoon, Murray knew he was at a huge disadvantage now. He was completely blind in one eye.

Murray checked a quick leg kick, though it stung badly as it slammed into his shin. Another kick went unchecked, slamming into Murray's thigh. He'd seen this before—the Dragoon was softening him up, trying to take his legs out from under him so he wouldn't have the steam to shoot in for a takedown. And it was working. Murray could already feel some of the strength in his legs fading as each kick connected.

The Dragoon continued to pepper Murray with stinging jabs and leg kicks, interchanging them to keep Murray guessing. His blind spot prevented him from seeing many of the strikes coming his way. Murray attempted to grab hold of a kick, but the

Dragoon expertly pulled his leg back and followed up with a cross that crumpled Murray's nose.

He could feel the tide turning, but Murray was undaunted.

He needed to get out of kicking range; his legs wouldn't be able to take much more of the punishment. Murray waded in again, this time bobbing and weaving his head as the Dragoon launched jab after jab. The punches breezed by his face, some narrowly skimming his cheek. Now within range, Murray followed up with his own stiff jabs, snapping the Dragoon's head back and then following up with a series of thudding body shots.

Murray clinched with the Dragoon as he was on his heels, wrapping an underhook behind the Grievar's back and attempting a quick hip toss to throw him off-balance. The Dragoon agilely countered the toss, swiveling to center up with Murray, then reached with both hands to grasp behind the crown of Murray's head in a classic plum clinch.

Murray knew he was in grave danger here. The lanky Grievar jerked Murray's head forward with both hands to unbalance him and threw a series of knees at his face, using his height to generate incredible leverage. Murray barely got his hands in front of his face to cover up, the knees smashing into his forearms, one busting through into his rib cage. Murray felt something snap in his left arm, a sharp pain that was echoed by another deep cry from the Grievar's section as they watched the lightboard flash red above.

Murray didn't have time to look up at the board and see how bad it was. He dropped his good arm, purposely letting a thudding knee slam into his chest and immediately wrapping up the Dragoon's leg, driving forward with all his strength for the takedown. The Dragoon hopped around the Circle as Murray pushed forward, using his feline balance to stay upright on one foot as he simultaneously threw looping uppercuts into Murray's head.

Murray dropped levels and scooped up the Dragoon's other foot, finally slamming him onto his back. This time, he was ready for the Dragoon's guard. He kept hold of one of the Grievar's feet and dragged it across his body, swiveling his hips and passing to the Dragoon's side.

The crowd wildly applauded at the back-and-forth fight, clearly astonished that the old Grievar still had it in him to take it this far.

Murray, bleeding and battered, ground his shoulder into the Dragoon's face as he threw his own thudding knees into the Grievar's ribs. His left arm was useless now, so he used it to stabilize his position at the Dragoon's side.

Murray needed to be patient and wait for the opening. He couldn't rush the opportunity and risk losing position. If the Dragoon stood again, Murray knew he wouldn't be able to hold him off. He continued to throw sharp knees into his opponent's body.

There it was. The Dragoon turned toward him and extended his hand to protect his exposed body from the knees. Taking advantage of the position, Murray smoothly slid his knee across the Dragoon's belly, and then to the other side.

He had full mount, his legs straddling either side of the Dragoon's chest. This was his position. This was where Mighty Murray Pearson had been born in the Circle, smashing his opponents from above.

The Dragoon recognized the immediate danger and bucked his hips wildly, trying to throw Murray off-balance so that he could reverse the position. Murray was ready for it, though; he thrust his hips to the floor and hooked his legs behind the Dragoon's knees, clinging to the grounded Grievar like a constrictor.

Murray went back to work, methodically throwing punches and elbows down at the Dragoon, who desperately tried to cover up. Murray couldn't feel his left arm, but that didn't stop him from using it to drop elbows in combination with his pounding right hands.

The Dragoon was bleeding badly now, his breathing labored. Murray knew he'd have to take this one to the limit—the Dragoon's biometric threshold was likely set to the point of no return.

The Dragoon reached up in desperation, grasping at Murray's face, his fingers seeking the eye socket again. Murray grabbed two of the Dragoon's fingers and snapped them back viciously. He pinned the Dragoon's arms to the floor.

Murray growled, "That's not how Grievar fight," before he reared up and slammed his forehead down into the Dragoon's face. The Dragoon smiled at him through his broken teeth, so Murray slammed his head down repeatedly until his opponent wasn't smiling anymore, until the face beneath him looked like the pulp of a ripened fruit.

The light beam pulsed one final time like a heartbeat and then went dim as swarms of crimson spectrals dispersed throughout the stadium. The crowd was quiet, seemingly in shock, as they watched the old champion breathing heavily over the Dragoon's lifeless body.

Murray slowly stood, blood streaming from his mangled eye socket and his left arm hanging limply at his side.

He clenched his hands into fists, crossing his forearms to his chest and then lifting them to the air, as painful as it was. He began to walk the perimeter of the Circle with his arms raised. The Grievar Knight salute.

The crowd cheered as the Grievar in attendance rhythmically chanted. Murray walked the Circle.

CHAPTER 7

To the Surface

Osoto gari is surely a superior sweep when applied against an opponent whose near-side foot is planted firmly on the ground. However, a skilled opponent may sense the outer reap and retreat their leg to thwart osoto gari. This defense provides another opportunity for a perceptive Grievar. Sasae tsurikomi ashi may now be applied to block the opposite foot while pivoting an opponent toward the ground. Against an opponent that reacts to osoto gari by pushing forward, the harai goshi throw may prove an even better option.

Passage Two, Thirty-Third Technique of the Combat Codes

Cego waited for Murray at the base of the Lift as the dawnshift swelled.

He watched as hundreds of Deep folk piled onto circular platforms that rotated around the base of the massive structure. As each platform was pulled into the center of the Lift, it immediately spiraled upward, glowing faintly at the edges. Within the dark confines of the Lift tube, the many platforms moving toward the top and back down blurred together like a glowing corkscrew.

A continuous stream of transport mechs arrived at the other side of the structure, dumping giant piles of rocks into shipping containers. Clouds of dust billowed around the Lift and stung Cego's eyes. The containers were sealed by scrambling Grunt workers and pushed into the center of the Lift, where they were hooked in and pulled up on a long chain.

"Ore will be tumbled up at the Surface depot."

Murray was standing beside Cego with a large duffel set at his side. He didn't look as bad as he did after the fight, but he was rough around the edges. A white gem was set in the place of his left eye.

Murray looked down at Cego, who couldn't help but stare at the banged-up Grievar. "Anderson convinced me to stick somethin' in there," he said guiltily. "I didn't want the clerics putting no vat-grown ball in my head, that's for sure. I settled for one of these gems." Murray cleared his throat.

Cego could tell Murray was uncomfortable talking about his missing eye, so he changed the subject, looking back at the giant chain running up the center of the Lift "All this is for rocks?"

"They say it took them five decades to put this thing up." Murray shook his head at the Lift. "Back when the Underground was multinational. Kiroth and Desovi also had a stake down here, before Ezo won the Deep, so it was a joint effort. But yeah, there's alloy buried in those piles of rocks. Mostly rubellium and auralite, coming from the Deep mines. Once the alloys are sorted, cleaned, and smelted, they'll get used for everything you can imagine. Engines for mechs, lightboards, sizzlers, blast cannons, handheld rods, all sorts of useless Daimyo things. Except for the Circles. Much of the purest stuff gets smelted into Circles."

They stood quietly for a moment, staring at the platforms as they spiraled toward the cavern ceiling.

"But the Lift also brings people up to the Surface?" Cego asked.

"Yeah," Murray said. "Faster than going through the Deep

tunnels, that's for sure. Few broken-down transport lines still take the long way, and even fewer folk walk the darkness."

"Have you ever walked the tunnels?" Cego's stomach fluttered at the thought.

Murray nodded and sighed. "Used to, haven't for a long time. Seen some nasty things in those tunnels."

Cego was about to ask what nasty things the old Grievar was referring to, but he held his tongue as Murray set his duffel bag across his shoulder.

"Ready?" Murray asked.

Cego realized then that his friends from Circle Crew Nine weren't there with him. He'd secretly hoped that Murray would emerge with Dozer and Knees in tow, miraculously freed from Thaloo's captivity. Things were never that easy, though.

Cego hadn't even had the chance to say goodbye to the crew. As soon as Murray had won the fight, Leyna had rushed Cego back to the house in Farmoss, looking over her shoulder the whole way. The Grievar lady had muttered something about Thaloo not having a track record of honoring his deals. She and Anderson had kept Cego there, working back in the garden, filling his belly with more hot meals as if nothing had happened. As if Murray hadn't just fought and won Cego's freedom. As if he hadn't been a slave in Thaloo's den just over a week ago, fighting for his survival alongside Dozer and Knees. As if he hadn't watched Weep beaten to death on the red dirt of the yard.

Cego set his jaw and swallowed the guilt that welled up in his chest. He would come back for them. He'd come back to honor Weep. "Yes," Cego said. He wasn't sure if he was telling Murray he was ready to head to the Surface or affirming the promise to return to the Deep for his friends.

The two began to climb the stairs at the base of the Lift heading toward the boarding area. Murray had a limp in his left leg, probably from all the Dragoon's kicks. Cego still didn't understand why Murray had done this for him. It was only after the fight that Leyna had revealed the stakes beyond Cego's own freedom: Murray's life. The biometric threshold of the fight with the Dragoon had been set to expire only when one of the combatants surrendered or was killed. And Cego had a strong feeling Murray would not have surrendered under any circumstance.

The Lift boarding area was a circular walkway with a variety of colorful flags set on the rail atop it. A constant stream of folk pushed past Cego and Murray. Hawkers chattering about big sales headed to a blue-flagged boarding zone. Grunts shipping up for Surface-side labor squeezed into a red-flagged section like netted fish. And Grievar travelers strode proudly into a yellow-flagged boarding zone, many seeming to size each other up as if they were about to step into a Circle.

In a chained-off area marked with a black flag, Cego watched a diminutive man hobble toward the Lift entry with two burly mercenaries by his side, their heads swiveling. The man seemed frail and ill-suited for even the short walk he'd just made from his parked transport. He turned and met Cego's gaze from across the wide boarding area. Blue veins creased his face, and his eyes were black orbs.

Murray frowned. "Even Daimyo need to take the Lift, though they get the best of it, like with everything else in this darkin' world."

Cego pulled his eyes from the Daimyo as he and Murray boarded the Grievar platform. They pushed to one side of it, right up against the curved glass window. Other Grievar streamed around Cego to fill every available gap, jostling for position.

The platform slowly started to move around the perimeter of the Lift, in a queue until it reached the entryway. As it shifted into the interior of the tube, the platform was blanketed with darkness. Cego felt his stomach drop as they began to rise, spiraling upward.

It was eerily quiet within the Lift. The platforms made no sound as they rose, and the passengers within seemed pacified, as if silenced by some force in the darkness. Cego looked up, watching the hundreds of other platforms floating toward the cave ceiling, concentric circles of light becoming fainter in the distance.

Cego could make out Murray's bulky form hovering over him. He could hear the big Grievar breathing deliberately, hissing air from his mouth in quick bursts. Ki-breath—it was same method Farmer had taught Cego to relax his muscles. He wondered whether the breathing technique was something taught at the Lyceum. Perhaps Farmer and Murray had learned from the same source—the source he was heading to now.

Cego's body was tense with anticipation. He fell into Murray's rhythm of breathing, matching his inhales and exhales. It was said there was a world of difference between the Grievar fighting in the slave Circles and those qualified to enter the Lyceum.

Nearly all those accepted to the prestigious combat school were purelights, their mothers and fathers passing down combat genetics from generation to generation. Most were already versed in the Lyceum's curriculum, their parents preparing them with countless techniques. Leyna had even said that some of the kids were using neurostimulants to give them the edge.

Cego was confident in his fighting prowess; he'd handled himself well in the Deep. But he wasn't so certain how he'd fare in this new world he was fast approaching.

He watched Murray, staring at the white pearl set in place of the man's eye. Cego's mind again landed on the fact that this burly Grievar had fought for him, had put his life on the line.

"Why?" Cego blurted the word out.

"What's that?" Murray looked down at him.

"Why…" Cego whispered. "Why did you fight for me? I know about the threshold. How you would have died if you didn't win."

"Dying is what we do, ain't it?" Murray replied. "Like it says in the Codes: We should fondly watch death, fully expect to embrace darkness at every moment, never vainly seek the next breath."

"But I barely know you," Cego said. "I don't understand—"

"Listen," Murray said. "We Grievar fight for all sorts of things. For pride and honor. To prove our skill. For our homes, our nations. For wealth and greed. But few days ago, that duskshift in Lampai, I chose to fight for you, Cego. In my mind, you're as good a cause to fight for, to die for, as any. A better cause, even."

"I don't know how to repay you..." Cego felt the guilt sitting heavy in his chest again.

"You don't owe me anything," Murray said. "But if you do put some of those stuck-up Surface-side kids in their place while we're up there, I'll be smiling from the sidelines."

Cego nodded and took another deep breath. He could now make out a faint halo of light above, getting closer as the platform continued to rise toward the Surface. He steadied his excitement. How long had it been since he'd taken in fresh air? How many days since he'd felt the rays of warm sunlight on his skin? He pictured himself sitting on the black sand beach with the crisp blue sky above.

The platform neared the halo of light, and Cego pressed his face against the glass window. He closed his eyes, ready to return.

Something slammed into the side of the Lift, not far from Cego's face, jarring his eyes open. A torrent of freezing rain pelted the glass, disrupting the silence with the sound of a thousand drums.

"Darkin' greatstorm. Should've known our entry would be ruined by weather," Murray muttered. The rest of the passengers on the platform didn't seem particularly disturbed. "Hopefully it settles before our trek to the Capital."

Through the maelstrom of rain, Cego could see the Surface world as they continued to rise into the air. Something was wrong.

The sky, if it could even be called a sky, was grey, as if it were shrouded in ash. Cego had only ever seen varying shades of blue skies on the island. A dull light filtered through the grey sky, painting the pale landscape beneath it. Cego couldn't feel the light on his skin warming him like the sun he remembered.

Cego looked up at Murray, whose face was calm. Nothing was wrong. This was the Surface Murray expected.

Cego stared back outside as the greatstorm raged around the Lift, gusts of wind uprooting skeletal trees below and tossing them like playthings. In the distance, Cego saw the blurry outline of a sprawling city, its lights twinkling under the bleak sky.

Cego shook his head in disbelief. This place—this Surface world—was as alien as the Underground. Several angular black shapes streaked across the sky, joining the storm with a loud crack of thunder as they passed overhead.

"Governance has been running more Flyer drills on the borders than usual," Murray muttered to himself. The big man looked down at Cego. "You okay? Looks like you've seen a darkin' spirit."

"Yeah," Cego managed to whisper. He wanted to ask Murray the question coursing through his mind, but he held his tongue.

Where is my home?

CHAPTER 8

Finding Warmth

The novice is more likely to wag their tongue than the master. A Grievar who truly understands the path will speak simply by living.

Twenty-Fourth Precept of the Combat Codes

Murray fidgeted in his chair. His Scout uniform was too tight. Grievar weren't meant to sit like this, in this sort of room.

He stared at the ornate high ceilings adorned with auralite chandeliers, hanging like translucent jellies and splaying spectral light throughout the room. Above him, a balcony ran around the perimeter of the great hall where he sat, its platinum railings shining from a servicer's daily polish. Tall shield windows were spaced across the walls on each level, providing sprawling vistas to the eastern and western fronts of the Citadel. Between each window, elaborate portraits dotted the walls.

Murray stared out an east-facing window toward the Capital, about a mile in the distance beyond the Citadel's grounds. Under the grey sky, he could distinguish the hardlight districts of the city by their stark spectral contrasts. The gridded squares of the hawker's market set to bluelight, the bowl-shaped heart of Central Square ringed with redlight, and the towering skyscrapers of the Tendrum District with greenlight coursing up and down the structures.

In the middle of it all were the dregs, grey-streaked and dilapidated, without any noticeable light source. Dark clouds congregated over the dregs, and the domed roof of the Courthouse was barely visible, emerging from the shadows as if it were gasping for air.

Murray turned from the bleak view and appraised his surroundings. An audience of Grievar Scouts sat around him, uniformed and stiff-backed in their chairs, waiting for Commander Callen Albright to emerge on the podium for their cycle briefing. Some Scouts whispered and eyed each other with suspicious stares.

Murray remembered when this room was still the Knights' mess hall. There had been a grand fireplace embedded in the brick wall, and tattered heavy bags hung in every corner. He would sit with Anderson, Leyna, and Hanrin at the beat-up long tables that used to line the room, enthusiastically recounting their fights over a hearty stew and a round of ales.

They'd been the young fists of Ezo's Knights then, freshly graduated from the Lyceum. Brash kids full of hope and honor and adventures to come. Murray remembered how hard they used to laugh, loud enough to attract the ire of the veteran Knights from nearby tables who were carefully discussing Circle strategy. Murray hadn't needed strategy then. His life had been simpler, run by instinct and bravado. And he'd had a purpose.

In that old mess hall, Murray had felt as if he were a part of something bigger. They'd been a team, one unit fighting in the Circle for a defined purpose. Defending Ezo. Upholding the Combat Codes. They'd been unified beneath the wisdom of a real leader, Coach, who would watch his Knights quietly from a perch at the back of the room.

Since then, the old mess hall had been completely gutted and remodeled to accommodate the state-of-the-art Scout conference center. The long tables had been replaced with rows of sterile steel seats. The fiery hearth at the center of the room was gone and in its stead a large lightboard was plastered on the wall.

The Scouts quieted as Commander Callen Albright took the podium on the balcony above. Callen was smaller than most Grievar, wiry in build, with flat, dark hair and bright yellow eyes. He wore a firmly pressed black uniform and stared down at the room of Scouts with an air of superiority.

Murray shook his head, looking at his so-called commander. Callen was young. Too young for his post.

The Albright family was one of the long-standing purelight Grievar lines in Ezo, one of the Twelve Houses, their ancestors tied to the Citadel for centuries. When the position for Scout commander became vacant, Callen was a shoo-in. Though he barely knew the inside of a Circle, the Albright heir had jumped to a lofty position within the newly formed Scouts branch, which his father had conveniently created several years prior.

And now Callen was one of the Citadel's four commanders.

Callen cleared his throat, making sure he had the full attention of the Scouts. Murray continued fidgeting in his chair. Though it had been over a month since his fight with the Dragoon, his back still felt like a mech had run it over.

"Scouts! I applaud your efforts this cycle. As you all know, we've cultivated some promising talent." Callen spoke with an airy voice, enunciating every syllable of the words. "Let's begin our review with acknowledgment of some notable achievements.

"Scout Aeric managed to recruit a gem in the rough, a boy from the borderlands that was wasted on service work, lost amid a sea of harvesters." Callen nodded, and Scout Aeric stood to acknowledge his praise.

Callen held his hand over the lightdeck in front of him, and the boards across the room flickered on. The feed showed a large blond boy working in Ezo's borderlands among the harvesters. The boy swung a threshing hoe like it was a garden rake—he was massive. "He's only ten, and though he certainly has Grunt blood, he's larger than most of us in this room already," Callen said in praise. "This giant will be taking on the Trials in short order to enter the Lyceum. I have no doubt he will pass and enter our funnel for the Knight team."

The Scouts around Murray began to clap, another custom the Grievar had recently picked up from the Daimyo. Murray refrained from joining. If he actually believed in what the Scouts were doing here, a hearty *O Toh* would suffice, as it always had.

Callen continued his speech. "Though it is her first year with us, Scout Piara got her hands on an established Grievar Knight we've sought for a long time. She stole this gem from right under the noses of the Desovian council." Callen flicked his hand at the deck again, displaying another feed.

The broadcast cut between scenes of a dark-skinned man fighting in a series of Circles around the world. He dismantled each opponent he faced with a combination of devastating precision strikes. Callen paused for dramatic effect, letting the Scouts absorb the highlight reel before announcing the Grievar's name. "The Falcon himself, Sit Fanyong!"

Scout Piara, a square-jawed recruit fresh out of the Lyceum, stood and accepted her praise, nodding and smiling.

Callen continued to list the team's achievements. "Although Scout Cydek was denied a great opportunity with his attempt at the Dragoon's recruitment..." Callen paused and caught Murray's eye from the podium, looking down at him with obvious disdain. "He was able to recoup his losses and come up with what some may consider an even better prospect."

The feed displayed a boy with a shaved head viciously kicking a downed opponent, his eyes gleaming with delight as each blow landed. Murray recognized the boy. He'd seen him at Thaloo's, fighting out of Crew Nine. Cego's crew.

"Young Shiar may have been the only true purelight brood in the Underground, his inherent talents getting wasted in the slave Circles. Now Shiar can enter the Trials and be properly nurtured at the Lyceum, perhaps even becoming our next champion someday. Scout Cydek was able to realize this great opportunity. Let us commend him for that," Callen said as the Scouts continued to clap.

Cydek stood up across the room, his piercings glinting under the chandelier's light. He met Murray's eye and smirked at him.

Murray chuckled. He didn't mean to laugh, yet he couldn't help it. All this pomp and circumstance. Grievar, dressed from head to toe in foolish formal wear, clapping as if they were Daimyo. Accepting praise for talent they had nothing to do with. These Scouts didn't put their life on the line in the Circle. Yet they stood proudly, as if it were they who were fighting.

The rest of the room fell silent. All heads turned toward Murray, who was now laughing deeply, slapping the armrest on his chair.

Commander Callen's eyes bulged before he visibly composed himself. "Scout Pearson," Callen said dryly. "Apparently, you find the hard work of your fellow Scouts to be laughable."

Murray wiped a tear from his eye as his laughter subsided.

"You know, that *is* quite funny." Callen feigned a chuckle of his own. "It's funny that you, who have served as a Grievar Scout for longer than any of this team—nearly a decade now—you, the eldest Scout, have not contributed a single ounce of talent to the Citadel since your arrival. You've brought us a series of broken lacklights every year, street scum who don't even deserve to walk the Lyceum's hallowed halls. And you've continued this tradition of yours to this day with the latest lacklight you've dragged off the streets," Callen spat hatefully. "In fact, Scout Pearson, I'm still not convinced that you've ever contributed talent to the Citadel, even during your glory days as a Knight, which I'm sure you are reliving every moment of in those bleary eyes... eye of yours, stealing away our valuable resources due to your inability to move on," Callen said.

Murray stood up. He didn't stand like the other Scouts had, puffing their chests out and waving their arms as they accepted praise. He stood like a Grievar Knight whose honor had been insulted. Murray glared from beneath his furrowed brow, catching Callen's eyes with a piercing stare as he calculated the distance to the podium and the time it would take to cross it and crush the commander's windpipe.

Callen stuttered, though he stood several meters from Murray, high above on the podium. "Ahem, Scout Pearson, you can sit down now. We aren't in a Circle where you can smash your way through your problems. Which actually brings me to one of the points of our meeting today. Thank you for that," Callen said.

Murray slowly took his seat, keeping his eye locked on Callen like a predatory animal.

"We are Grievar Scouts. This team was formed two decades ago by my father for a purpose. Ezo was losing. Our Knights were failing us in the Circle. Desovi and Kiroth were simply better for years, which cost us dearly. Our in-house development programs were good, but the numbers didn't add up. There were too many Grievar in Ezo to not tap the full potential of the population. The purelights that got away, gems lost amid piles of rubble. The lacklight freaks, those few who somehow gained an edge from their impure breeding. We needed to find those Grievar, and so my father formed the Scouts, the fourth branch of the Citadel, and brought Ezo back from the brink," Callen said.

What a darkin' fool. Did he actually believe this trash?

Ezo survived because the Citadel had pulled up every competent Grievar from PublicJustice, drafting the very best to serve as Knights on the international front. Command had claimed they didn't need Ezo's top talent wasting their best years fighting for the justice of convicts and bit-less peasants. The Scout program had only been established because Callen's father, Stenly Albright, had donated ridiculous sums to the Citadel and wanted a brand-new Command position all to himself.

"We are Scouts," Callen repeated with emphasis. "Which means we operate in a very specific capacity. The Citadel has provided us with an allotted war chest to purchase talent. Each of you has your own purse, refilled every cycle for this exact purpose. We do *not* acquire talent by other means—fighting in the Circle like a common merc, for example." Callen shot his eyes toward Murray.

"This makes us look foolish. Weak, even. Imagine if the Kirothians saw our Scouts fighting in the Circle like uncultured brutes, as if we didn't have any organization. They would capitalize on that," Callen said.

Callen stared directly down at Murray again. "This sort of insubordination from Scouts is unacceptable. Cases will be handled on an individual basis, but hear me now—none will go unpunished."

Callen left the podium, walking down the spiral staircase at the corner of the balcony and greeting the rest of the Scouts at ground level. The Scouts stood, some congratulating one another while others were already on the hunt for leads, feeding themselves with rumors for their next talent run. Murray stayed seated.

"I hear Gylshtak Toliat is unhappy with his team, might be open to jumping ship from Desovi," one nearby Scout whispered to another. Murray snorted. It was a clear attempt at misdirection, trying to send his so-called team members out into the highlands of Desovi on an impossible recruiting mission while he clearly had his eye on another nearby target.

This was exactly what Murray hated. There was no honor among these Scouts. It was about getting ahead for yourself, lining your bit-purse with the commission from talent discoveries, all to get promoted to some decorative higher rank within the branch.

Grievar were not made for this work, for whispering from the shadows. Grievar were made to fight.

Murray was about to leave, eager to make the trip back to his barracks, when Commander Callen pulled up to his seat.

"Of course, because you aren't as dense as you look, Scout Pearson, you know that I was referring to you as one of our insubordinate Scouts," Callen said condescendingly.

Murray stood. He towered over the wiry commander. "Commander. Say what you need to and let me be on my way home. I've got work to do."

Callen cocked his head. "Oh, work, you say? You mean as a Scout? Please don't tell me you are attempting to train that lacklight find of yours before the Trials. If that is the case, Scout Pearson, perhaps I was wrong in doubting the density of your skull."

Callen casually brushed off the shoulders of his pressed uniform. "Perhaps if the boy was a giant like Scout Aeric's find, or an incredibly strong lacklight at the least, he would make it through the Trials. From what I've heard, though, your boy is just that—a boy who managed to win a few fights in a minor slave Circle. And for some reason, you took it upon yourself to secure him, risking the reputation of the entire Scout branch in doing so."

Murray remained silent, staring down at the commander. "The stupidity of your actions aside, what you did made the Citadel look very bad. Unprofessional. If it were my call, you'd be out. In fact, if it were my call, you would have been out long ago, after your first year of subpar Scout work. Unfortunately, you appear to have some comrades in Command who think you aren't completely useless. Old Aon won't always be by your side, Scout Pearson. Keep that in mind. Another act of insubordination and I shall make it my personal mission to see you doing servicer work for the entirety of your path."

"Is that all, Commander Callen?" Murray said with noted sarcasm as he turned toward the exit.

"Yes," Callen said.

As Murray walked away, Callen called after him, "Oh, one more thing, Scout. Your pay is docked for the cycle. You obviously don't have any commission, but you won't be getting your standard stipend, either."

Callen clearly wanted Murray to argue, to barter, to plead like a common market hawker.

Murray kept walking.

* * *

Cego leapt across the Circle into a front roll, springing from the dirt and shooting for a low single-leg, nearly flattening onto his belly as he dove for Masa's ankle. Masa easily yanked his foot away and pushed Cego's head into the dirt.

Cego popped back to his feet. He bobbed toward Masa, switching his stance to southpaw and then back to traditional, checking for his opponent's reaction.

Though Masa had the yellow eyes of a Grievar, his were strangely dark, an olive hue that Cego couldn't read, unlike a normal opponent. Cego knew Masa was at least thirty, but he looked like a young Grievar. His long mane of dark hair whipped around his shoulders as he moved.

Cego threw a series of feint jabs, clearly outside striking range. Normally, he'd follow up with an inside leg kick, something to get him within range and throw his opponent off-balance. With Masa, though, he knew he'd need something different. Something less traditional.

Cego spun, twirling his body in a full circle, using the momentum to whip his leg at Masa's head. Masa easily ducked the wheel kick, following up with a deft foot sweep that took Cego's remaining leg out from under him. Cego hit the floor hard.

Masa was already on top of him with his knee pressing into Cego's sternum. The olive-eyed Grievar looked down at him.

"Too much, Cego-Ko," Masa said quietly in his halting Jadean accent. "Normal combination. Two jab, low kick, cross. Stay regular. Not spinning like that."

Cego took Masa's hand and stood. He shook his head in frustration. "I didn't think I could get through with my standard combos. I wanted to catch you off guard with something."

Masa nodded, pointing at the Circle around them. "Circle. You follow its light. Need to follow *your* light." The Circle glowed with a faint indigo hue, illuminating the shadowy corners of the barracks they trained in.

Since his arrival at Murray's barracks in the Capital, Cego had been preparing for the Trials at the Lyceum, which were now only one week away. He had assumed the Trials would be similar to his experience in the Underground—pure tests of combat prowess in the Circle, the best Grievar emerging victorious. It didn't turn out to be that simple.

The Trials would mirror the schools of study at the Lyceum, concentrated on different phases of combat. Cego was very familiar with some of these phases already, such as striking or grappling.

One phase that he had struggled to learn over the past month was Circles. Grievar Knights around the world fought in different types of Circles, each forged with varying proportions of the base elemental alloys. The composition of a Circle determined the sorts of spectrals that would be attracted, and, in turn, the wavelength of spectral light would affect a Grievar's actions within the Circle. Murray's Circle, which Cego currently stood in with Masa, was a mixture of rubellium and auralite alloys, smelted alongside standard non-elemental metals. But the spectrals that this Circle attracted were unlike any Cego had seen, a result of the unique mixture of alloys. Several deep purple wisps lazily flickered back and forth overhead.

Despite the apparent disinterested nature of the spectrals, under their soft indigo glow, Cego felt confident—too confident. He felt like he could throw flashy techniques, move at lightning speed, play with his opponent if he wanted to.

Though confidence was one important part of fighting, too much confidence left Cego vulnerable. He'd strayed from his standard techniques to try to surprise Masa, unsuccessfully. The Circle had influenced him.

Murray had explained that a Grievar Knight needed to discern how their mind was being influenced by the Circle around them. With the proper training, a Knight could use a Circle's influence to their advantage, gaining confidence when it was needed.

Cego understood the theory, but when he'd actually stood in the Circle, it was hard for him to distinguish his own thoughts from those that were being influenced.

One problem was that he only had access to the hybrid Circle in Murray's barracks. The purelight kids Cego would be going up against had far superior resources. Some of their parents owned Circles of every element. If he couldn't even compensate in this Circle, one he'd been practicing in for the past month, how would he ever succeed under the influence of unknown Circles he'd never felt before? Cego breathed out steadily, trying to calm his nerves as Masa squared up with him again.

Despite Cego's frustrations, Masa had been a great aid to his training so far. Though Murray was his head coach, the old Grievar had constant Scout duties to fulfill within the Citadel. Most often, Murray would provide Masa with instructions to lead Cego's morning and afternoon sessions and would return in the evening to review progress.

Masa waited for Cego to attack again, slowly circling him with his hands raised. Cego breathed out, attempting to feel the pull of the Circle. He did still feel confident, though Masa had bested him several times in a row now. If anything, that was a good indicator that he was being influenced by the light.

Though he wanted to dive in with a leaping cross, Cego instead concentrated on Masa's footwork. He was circling to Cego's right in a traditional stance with his left leg leading. Cego matched his stance and moved in synchronization with Masa.

As Masa lifted his leg for a step, Cego shot out a quick inside leg kick, catching Masa beneath the knee and throwing him off-balance. Masa smiled and began to circle in the other direction, switching to a southpaw stance, with his right leg leading. He threw his own leg kick, which Cego checked with his shin.

Cego wanted to be done with this slow, strategic game of matching leg kicks and constantly analyzing his opponent's stance and the direction he was moving. Cego wanted to go for a finish; he felt like he could easily do so.

Clear your mind; free yourself of influence. Cego heard Farmer's voice, as he so often did since he'd blindly stumbled onto the Underground's streets.

Cego exhaled again. He needed to stick with his strategy. He shifted along with Masa, waiting for him to lift his right leg this time, timing it with a perfectly executed inside leg kick.

This time, as Masa was thrown off-balance, Cego added two quick jabs to the attack, one grazing his partner's forehead.

The dance continued, the two combatants circling each other warily.

Cego feigned the inside leg kick, this time swiveling his hips but not sending his leg out. Just as he expected, Masa reacted, ready for the kick, bringing his hips back and his head forward. Cego was already moving, though, launching a cross that he attempted to pull at the last moment to avoid serious contact with his partner. He still connected solidly, catching Masa just under the eye and knocking him to the ground.

"Sorry!" Cego reached down to help Masa up, who accepted his hand.

"No apologize," Masa said, rubbing the bruise that was already swelling. "You did good, Cego-Ko. No follow Circle light this time."

"Impressive," Murray said from the entrance to the barracks. "Masa is hard to catch."

Murray was standing beside a near-identical replica to Masa, minus the long hair. This Grievar's head was completely bald.

"Tachi, what do you think? Is Cego ready?" Murray asked the young man beside him.

"Cego-Ko…not ready," Tachi replied without thinking. Murray chuckled, looking at Cego's frustrated expression. Tachi was the polar opposite of his twin brother.

Instead of taking it slow to let Cego learn and testing his responses to various attacks, Tachi went at him full force every time. Though Cego could sometimes get the better of him, he often ended up battered and limping after his sparring sessions with Tachi.

"Well, I think you're ready. Just do what you just did in there. Stick to your plan," Murray said.

"What about the other types of Circles? What…what if I'm fighting in cytrine during the Trials? How will I know how to react?" Cego asked.

"Every Circle is different, but for each, you need to listen just the same." Murray walked over to the Circle. He knelt and placed his hands on its steel frame. "Just like with Violet here. Different Circles will speak to you in different voices. Some whisper, some shout, some sing to you. Circles are no different from folk; you just need to know which ones you can trust. Though I'd say I'd rather trust any Circle than most of the folk in this town…."

Cego was still getting used to Murray's strange affinity with his Circle, whom he'd formally introduced to Cego as *Violet* when he'd first arrived at the barracks.

"Speaking of…" Murray said as he produced a glinting coil of red metal from the cloth bag he was carrying and handed it to Tachi. "Let's make that replacement we've been talking about, Tachi."

Cego watched as Tachi knelt beside the Circle and began to unscrew one of the thick steel plates at its base. The purple spectrals suddenly seemed curious as to what Tachi was doing, hovering over him, one even landing atop his shoulder.

Murray had told Cego he'd first seen Violet when he was traveling across the Isles on assignment as a Knight. He'd taken a boat into the famed aquatic markets. As he rowed past ramshackle stilted huts, the hawkers cawing in a language he didn't understand, Murray had caught a glimpse of purple-hued steel from the corner of his eye. Deep in the recesses of a hut, under the fading island light, he'd seen Violet.

After his fight at Aquarius Arena on the Emerald Isles, Murray had made a point of rowing back out to that hut and striking a deal with the hawker. Though Violet was broken down and rusted, Murray had spent several fight paydays for her.

Despite being over three decades old now, Violet was in great condition. Murray polished her every morning, meticulously ensuring her frame was gleaming. He spent hours per week detailing the engraved sigils laid across Violet's face, fighting back the rust.

Aside from keeping Violet's exterior shining, Murray continually updated her inner mechanisms as well, bringing fresh clasps, coils, and gears back with him from the Deep. Cego hadn't even been aware that a Circle was more than a solid hunk of metal until he saw Tachi, Murray's resident engineer, open Violet up.

Cego watched in amazement as Tachi's dexterous fingers performed surgery on Violet, removing a corroded rubellium coil. Murray hovered over the whole operation in nervous anticipation—Cego couldn't remember ever seeing the burly Grievar so worried.

"What's it all do?" Cego asked, peering into Violet's mechanical innards.

"Most stuff in there for spectral light amplification," Tachi replied, speaking rapidly, his eyes never leaving Violet. "Inner tube needs to conduct light without interruption, from coil to coil in loop, then feed back out to talk with spectrals."

"Talk?" Cego suddenly thought about the little spectral that he used to speak with in his cell. He'd seen no sign of the wisp since he'd come up from the Deep.

"Tachi means communicate," Murray responded. "The Circle's alloy makeup and how it's set up inside help it communicate with the right sort of spectrals."

"What if...it's set up wrong?" Cego continued to pepper the usually quiet man with questions.

"Most Circles aren't done perfectly," Murray said nervously as Tachi slowly inserted the new coil. "But I've seen some real broken Circles cause havoc, mess with a Grievar's head, even drive 'em crazy."

Murray breathed a sigh of relief as Tachi nodded at him and began to close the hole in Violet's exterior.

"Aren't Circles like Violet...Daimyo tech?" Cego asked. He'd become accustomed to Murray's distrust of Daimyo tools, weapons, mechs, or meds. However, the old Grievar's obsession with Violet seemed to counter those beliefs.

Murray shot a steely glare at Cego.

"A Grievar takes pride in the Circle they train in, maintains it, treats it with respect—like it's a part of their own body." Murray knelt and ran his hand along Violet's polished surface again. "We may fight for the Daimyo, but the Circles are ours."

Cego thought back to his memories of the island and training in Farmer's Circle. He could remember the old master instilling in the three brothers a similar respect for the simple ironwood frame.

This Circle is your home; treat it so.

Cego watched the purple spectrals dance overhead, seemingly pleased that Violet's surgery had been successful.

"But the spectrals...Do they only affect us? Don't the Daimyo feel their light too?" Cego asked.

"Yeah, they feel it," Murray said as he swiped at one of the little wisps playfully. "The Daimyo use alloys and light everywhere in their cities. Bluelight to keep the Grunts from revolting. Yellowlight in the neurogens and cleavers to keep the addicts smiling. Even redlight in their SystemView feeds to keep folk fearful, on edge. But we Grievar feel the light more than any other breed. It's always been a part of us."

Murray dragged a cloth cover out from the corner and laid it over Violet. The spectrals drifted to the ground and seemed to settle down with the cloth. Perhaps they were tired from all the excitement, Cego speculated.

Murray waved for Cego to follow him into the living quarters. "All right, kid, let's get going inside. Mealtime, then we need to wrap up your Codes lessons."

* * *

Murray's barracks were spartan, as was fitting for a Grievar. Just the essentials for living. A bare-bones kitchen with two small rooms branching from it and a heavy oaken table at its center. Masa and Tachi, the twin brothers, occupied one room, and Murray, the other. Cego had opted to stay out in the training shed—the dusty interior reminded him of the lofted room on the island.

Cego, Masa, Tachi, and Murray sat at the oak table in the kitchen. They ate Grievar fare. Though far more nutritious than the fighting greens Cego had subsisted on in the Deep, the food wasn't much tastier. Tonight, they had chewy, vat-grown venison strips with rehydrated teva leaf. Murray wasn't the creative cook that Leyna was either; he'd dragged in the bulk storage container and thrown something onto the sizzler.

Almost all of Ezo subsisted on stored and processed foods, vat-meats and rehydrated plant fare that tasted like bark. Murray told Cego that fresh meats were a luxury only the Daimyo could afford regularly.

Living on the Surface was a sharp contrast to the fragments of life Cego remembered from the island. Though the memories were difficult to grasp—they slipped from his mind like fine grains of sand through the fingers—some vivid images stuck with him.

Silas's long, lean body thrashing through the waves, swimming back to the beach after hunting sarpin miles offshore. Silas had always been the fisher. He'd been by far the strongest swimmer of the three brothers. He'd return to the black sand beach with a line of sarpin strung across his back, his toothy smile flashing with the setting sun.

Cego had been the forager. Farmer would send him to scale every cliff along the edge of the island to collect various herbs and sprouts. Cego took to climbing naturally, finding grips with his hands and feet as if they were meant to be there. He'd enjoyed the heights, feeling the sea wind brushing the cliff face, gazing at the emerald waters that surrounded the island.

Sam would contribute to the meal with a bucket of blue crabs he caught from the nearby tide pools. Farmer and the three brothers would roast the fish and crabs over a bonfire as they watched dusk fall on the island.

After their meal, the brothers would put two crabs in the center of a makeshift driftwood ring and watch the creatures fight. Cego and Sam would take sides and bet on the victor, yelling in excitement when one of the crabs broke through its opponent's defenses with a quick-pincered jab or a deft scuttle maneuver. Silas would sit away from the firelight, shaking his head at their childish games.

Cego's island home was starting to seem more like a dream than a memory, though. Waking up in the loft with Arry's wet nose on his face. Sitting on the black sand beach and breathing with the tide. Diving beneath the waves as the old master watched from his perch atop the dunes.

Cego had spent his first week on the Surface in complete shock, staring at the bleak world around him. Though the sun occasionally peeked from the grey skies over the Capital, it was only a glimmer compared to the bright orb that rose every day over the island. Everything felt different here, as if Cego had emerged from the Deep to a completely changed world.

Cego still hadn't told Murray or anyone else about the island. He didn't speak out loud about the black sand beaches or the emerald waters. He kept silent about his brothers and the old master. Those scattered memories were all he had anymore; they were his only home.

"Thank you," Cego said as Tachi passed him the plate of vat-meat. Among these new companions—two Jadeans who most often spoke to each other in their own tongue, and Murray, who could be silent for hours at a time—dinner conversation was not the liveliest affair.

"You two work on throws earlier?" Murray uncharacteristically broke the silence, looking at Masa and Cego.

Masa nodded. "Yes, Murray-Ki," he said, using the Jadean honorific for *teacher*. Cego had slowly been picking up on the strange intricacies of the Jadean language. Masa and Tachi referred to Cego as "Ko," to denote his position as their student, and Murray as "Ki" as their master. However, when Cego asked what he should refer to Murray as, Masa told him "Murray-Ku," which also denoted master, but with a higher level of deference than Cego had with the twin brothers.

"Cego, your throws are solid, but I think your harai goshi could use some reps," Murray said as he ripped a piece of vat-meat in his hand.

Cego picked at the dry ferns in his wooden bowl. What he would give for fresh fish, sliced down the center and grilled over the spit.

"Yes, I still need to get used to the gi, though," Cego said. Though he'd practiced some of the throws before, he'd never donned a gi in the past—a thick, woven long-sleeved uniform that enabled strong grips by him or his opponent. Fighting slowed down in the gi; it was less of a scramble and more of a strategic match of constant reactions and counterreactions. He'd rather be unencumbered.

"Why do I need to practice in the gi, anyway?" Cego asked. "It seems silly to train in that uniform when I'll be fighting without it."

"The gi teaches your mind to slow down. You can concentrate on the details instead of just blasting through the techniques,"

Murray replied. "Plus, some of your Trials will likely be in the gi, so get used to it. In Myrkos, foreign Knights fight in the heavy gi—most would likely freeze on that barren tundra without any layers."

Cego nodded. After training with Farmer and then fighting in the Underground, he figured he would be better prepared for the Trials. Recently, though, Cego's confidence had wavered.

There were so many things about Grievar combat that he still didn't understand. Combat in various types of Circles, each affecting his mental state in a different way. The clothing he wore during his fights that could change his strategy, how he'd have to approach each opponent. There was potential for fights in various environments to mimic the conditions of the other nations, within Circles set in the bitter cold or in the sweltering heat.

Why hadn't Farmer prepared him for any of this? Though his training in the basics of combat had been thorough, it now seemed rudimentary given the vast number of variables he would need to take into account when going into the Trials and, if he got beyond that, training in the Lyceum.

Murray must have noticed Cego's furrowed forehead. "Don't worry, kid. I know it's a lot to pick up in this amount of time. Most purelights you'll be going up against have had a lifetime to learn this stuff."

Cego stopped chewing. Murray sometimes had a strange way of boosting his confidence.

Murray looked up at Cego from his empty plate. "What I mean is... you're picking this stuff up fast. Just keep your basics in mind; that's where you have the advantage over these other kids. You're strong there."

Cego nodded again. Murray's teachings were like his home—spartan. His house was made for efficiency. The things he owned, the sizzler, the small rooms, the training loft, Violet—each served a singular purpose. Even the food they ate, though it wasn't tasty, served the purpose of giving them the energy they needed. Murray didn't give much with his teachings, but what he did give was efficient; it had a purpose.

"All right, twins, you clean up here, Cego and I are getting a jump on Codes before lights-out," Murray said.

"Yes, Murray-Ki," Masa and Tachi replied in unison.

* * *

It was raining again.

Sitting on a small wooden stool in Murray's room, Cego listened to the drumming on the tin roof. A fire was lit in a diminutive hearth in the corner of the room. Cego rubbed his hands together; even indoors, he could see his breath as the Capital's night air became colder. The fire didn't seem to provide much warmth, not like the huge bonfires on the black sand beach of the island.

Murray sat at the edge of his cot, reading from a book with a worn leather cover. There were hundreds of similar books stacked in piles along the walls of his room.

Codes was another portion of his new training that Cego needed to pick up in time for the Trials. Murray took Codes very seriously, perhaps more so than the combat training itself.

The Combat Codes were written in old-fashioned language and the meaning of each passage often needed to be puzzled out. Murray said the Ancients had written the Codes as a doctrine for all Grievar to uphold—both in the heat of combat and during everyday life.

"A Grievar shall learn from the rainstorm. Upon finding oneself under a sudden downpour, there is the inclination to run below the eaves of nearby structures. But when pacing between buildings, hiding from the storm, one will still find themselves involuntarily soaked. Standing firm in the rain from the start, a Grievar has made a choice, at least," Murray read.

Cego nodded.

"What is the rainstorm?" Murray asked. He followed each passage of the Codes with a series of questions to test Cego.

Though Cego hadn't heard this particular passage before, he had a knack for interpreting the Codes. They were strikingly similar to the words he often heard echoing in his head—Farmer's words.

"The rainstorm is the opponent," Cego answered. Murray nodded and Cego thought for a moment before continuing. "The Grievar wants to run away from the rainstorm and hide under the shelter of the buildings. But if he does that, he'll get wet anyways. He might as well stand outside in the rain, because in that case, at least he made his own choice to get wet instead of the storm forcing him to take the action."

Murray nodded again, clearly impressed. "Spot on, kid. Now, what about combat applications?"

Cego was ready for this one. "Opening your guard. If your opponent is about to break open your guard, and you can feel that he is about to do so, there is no point in using your energy to fight it. You're better off making your own choice to open your guard, which gives you the edge and timing, maybe leading to a sweep or attack as your next move."

"O Toh," Murray responded in approval. "Great example, kid. Now, how about worldly applications?"

Cego wasn't so sure about this one. Beyond the example in the passage itself, how did it apply to the world around him? The Surface world was still alien to him, and Cego had never fully grasped how the Underground operated, so he latched on to something from home, something he was familiar with. "When climbing a rock face, you can't just take the straight path up. You need to make choices about which holds to grab on to, and sometimes the best path can seem the most difficult."

Murray shook his head. "You need to think about how the Codes apply to life. Being a Grievar isn't just about fighting or learning techniques. It's about the folk that we're fighting for, as darkin' foul as some of those folk may be modernday..."

"You made the choice to fight for me," Cego said abruptly.

Murray looked at him curiously, finally thrown off guard by one of Cego's answers.

"You made the choice to fight for me, which changed everything. Going into the fight at Lampai, you knew you were standing in the Circle because you wanted to be there. Not because someone was forcing you to fight."

Murray let out a deep breath. "Kid, I know sometimes it's best to leave what's done behind, not talk about a past we can't change. But I also know that wherever you're from, you got taught some sense, some good."

Cego felt a sudden urge to tell Murray about the island. But instead, he asked a question, a defensive habit he'd developed recently.

"Why are you doing this, Murray-Ku?" The Jadean formality slipped out of Cego's mouth without thinking. "Why did you become a Scout? If so many kids down there are broken before you even pick them up, why do you keep doing it?"

Murray paused, the flames from the hearth dancing in his yellow eye. "I'm no Scout. Was never made to be one. You know that, everyone at the Citadel knows that, yet I kept doing it," he said.

The burly Grievar looked up at Cego. "For so many years, I felt like I wasn't making any choices. Just had to stay close to the light, had to take the next step though I didn't know where I was heading. But now, things feel different. It's because of you, kid. You're right, I made the choice to fight at Lampai. I made the decision that you were worth fighting for because I see something in you. Something I don't see much of anymore.

"I saw it when you were fighting N'jal, when you didn't straight out put a foot through his skull when he was helpless on the floor. I saw it when you were watching the harvesters on the steppe; you were genuinely interested in what other folk did out there. I made a choice to bring you up here, and I'll see that through. We're going to get you into the Lyceum."

It was the most Cego had ever heard Murray speak of himself. Cego realized he'd never said it before, though he should have so many times along the way. "Thank you, Murray-Ku."

Murray nodded. "All right, on to the next," the old Grievar said as he flipped the book to the following passage of Codes.

Cego stared into the fireplace, rubbing his hands together. He was finally starting to feel some warmth.

CHAPTER 9

Movement

There are many middling Grievar who blame others for their failures. These Grievar are blind to their own weakness. They cannot see their failures as faults of their own, and so they are forever confined to mediocrity.

Passage One, Ninety-Ninth Precept of the Combat Codes

Murray whisked Cego out of his barracks just as dawn broke, hooding himself and Cego with thick cloaks to shield against the cutting sheets of rain.

They'd spent the entirety of the last month cooped up in his barracks, and Murray wanted Cego to see the city from the ground before the Trials, which were just one week away.

Murray's barracks were located on the east side of the Capital, on the edge of Karsh, a small Grievar-designated district whose inhabitants were mostly Desovian immigrants. Most of the Desovians in the Capital were secluded in the dregs of the city; living elsewhere, they would face the bigotry of proud Ezonians. The immigrants were hated because Desovi was one of Ezo's rival nations, another powerhouse of Grievar might that controlled much of the world's resources.

Over the past century, the two nations had gone head-to-head in numerous bouts. The disputes were fiercest over an area rich in elemental deposits along the Adar ridge, aptly called the Auralite Spine. The borders of the mountainous region had shifted between Desovi, Kiroth, and Ezo numerous times, each nation wresting control from another and then conceding land again as the strength of its current Grievar champions ebbed and waned.

Nearly two decades ago, Murray could remember winning a chunk of the Spine for Ezo in a grueling fight against Drogo Myrat, one of Desovi's best fighters at the time. Murray had returned home to the Capital to the blast of a thousand horns, the citizenry cheering him on as he was paraded down the central artery.

Since he'd left the service, Murray had taken residence in Karsh to escape the fanfare of the city. Though it was considered the dregs, Murray enjoyed living among the immigrant population. He'd come to realize the Desovians here were no different from him. They'd come to Ezo during a time of relative prosperity, seeking a better life for themselves and their children. They were following their path.

A curly-haired lady sitting under the awning of her house smiled at the two as they passed by. She used a pumice to rhythmically grind away at the contents of a large clay pot set in front of her.

A thin balding man lifted a gate to a shotgun building. The man flashed a wide smile at Murray as he passed. "Mighty Murray, bright morn!" the man yelled in a thick Desovian accent as he waved enthusiastically through the rain.

"Bright morn to you, Santil," Murray said, nodding back. The morning was anything but bright, yet Santil always managed to have a wide smile on his face.

The two continued through the neighborhood, passing shops and homes that were just waking up. The familiar smell of baked sponge bread wafted to his nose. The Desovians only cooked the delicacy once every month, rationing out small portions of the bread every day to their hungry families.

Murray looked down at Cego, who also sniffed at the yeasty aroma in the air.

The kid saw everything with fresh eyes. Even in Murray's drab barracks, Cego had observed each object with fascination, inquiring about the simplest items, like his sizzler or the shelf of tattered books in his room. The kid had even started to pick up Jadean, peppering Masa and Tachi about the meaning of various words in the foreign language. Murray wasn't surprised Cego was such a natural fighting talent, the way he constantly sought new knowledge.

Two Desovian kids, a few years younger than Cego, fell across their path, play-fighting in the rain outside their house. Cego stopped abruptly, his shoulders tensing in anticipation.

One of the kids tossed the other to the muddy ground. The other boy, likely his brother, quickly pushed away and sprang back to his feet, laughing.

Cego watched the boys with wide eyes. "Brothers... fighting."

"Yeah. That's how it's supposed to be," Murray responded. "We're born to fight. With our enemies, friends, even brothers and sisters. Now things are complicated, too much darkin' politiks."

"I know," Cego responded. "I have brothers."

Murray nearly stopped in his tracks. After restraining himself from asking Cego about his past for the last month, here he was, finally getting something straight from the kid's mouth without even a push.

"Yeah?" Murray tried to respond calmly. "Bet fighting your brothers helped you get better."

Cego appeared thoughtful for a moment, raindrops hanging from the brim of his hood. "It did."

"How many did you have?" Murray asked.

"One older, one younger," Cego said.

"Bet you're missin' them now," Murray said.

"Sometimes," Cego said quietly.

Murray left it at that as the two continued to trudge through the muddy streets. When it came to dredging up his own past, Murray could only handle so much before he needed the next drink. A little bit at a time would do with Cego.

They moved beyond Karsh into the Capital's central sector. The Courthouse's domed roof came into view over the tightly packed tops of dilapidated buildings.

Some of the buildings were completely torn apart—eroded by weather and time and never fixed. The servicers didn't come this way for repairs; there weren't any bits in dressing up the dregs. The Daimyo Governance would rather concentrate on creating new, high-profile projects like Albright Stadium. The bit-rich had already bought out front-row tickets at the newly renovated arena. Meanwhile, Murray could literally see through the crumbling wall of a building here in the dregs, where a lady was hopelessly attempting to hang her clothes to dry.

The two turned onto a street with a series of banners hung across it, water streaking the slick surfaces. Lifelike visages peered down at them—Grievar, each with their name boldly scrawled across a banner. *Kal Yang. Raymol Tarsis. Tullen Thurgood.*

Cego stopped and stared at the last banner, which was bigger than the rest and displayed a square-jawed man with fiery red hair, a gleaming belt hung across his muscled frame. Even within the image, the man's blazing eyes seemed to pierce the sheets of grey rain.

"Artemis Halberd." Cego whispered the name.

"They insist on hanging banners of the entire Knight team on streets across the Capital," Murray muttered. "Never saw how it did any good to have citizens staring up at my ugly mug every morning, though."

"Is he really as good as they say?" Cego asked.

"Halberd?" Murray looked at the banner above them. "Yeah.

Only one Artemis Halberd is born every few generations. He may be the best in recorded Grievar history. Undefeated to date, hasn't even been darkin' challenged in the Circle. He graduated from the Lyceum just when I was on my way out, though, never got a chance to fight alongside him."

"If Artemis is so good, why do I keep hearing you say Ezo is falling behind the other nations when you speak with Masa and Tachi?" Cego asked.

Murray shook his head. The kid was always listening, even about darkin' politiks. "Knight team is pretty much restin' on Halberd's shoulders at this point. But one Grievar can only do so much. Even Halberd needs to rest between fights, recover, take time to study opponents and learn new techniques. And that's when the other Knights need to step up. Come on, kid, let's keep moving."

As they approached the Courthouse, the sky continued to darken and the rain fell even harder. Cego peered from beneath his hood to survey the folk around them. Clumps of them hid in the shadows under the eaves of the surrounding buildings to shield themselves from the rain, and some attempted to keep warm by small bonfires.

Other folk stood openly in the elements, seemingly oblivious to the world around them. They were disoriented, stumbling around, shouting incoherently against the wind.

One lady with gnarled hair blocked their path, unaware they were standing right in front of her. She held a small metallic cylinder up to her eyeball and pressed the button on the back. A short blast of yellowlight pulsed from the cylinder directly into her eye. The lady fell back into the mud, her eyes rolling back into her head and her face going slack before an eerie grin spread across it.

"Cleavers," Murray explained dryly to Cego as they continued past the lady. "Those addicted to photocleaving—when you send a pulse of spectral light into your eye that feels like a real spectral swarm." The high only lasted about thirty minutes, and then the user would need another blast. Murray shook his head. Somewhere out there, Daimyo were making a bit-fortune off the mass of addicts in this city. "Not far from the stims Governance is pushing on our Knights...even some Lyceum students lately," Murray said. "All the stuff is darkin' addictive, just to get ahead to the next moment, forgetting everything about our past."

"Isn't it against the Codes?" Cego asked. "A Grievar needs neither tools nor technologies to enhance their physical prowess."

"You might have noticed the Codes isn't something too many are still holdin' to." Murray grimaced, though he was impressed at how the kid had taken to their nightly lessons.

The two continued through the wreckage of the dregs until they arrived at the very center of the city.

A sprawling domed building with a dirt yard rose above the surrounding dregs—the Courthouse. The Courthouse's marble dome had originally been a brilliant white. The grand set of stairs leading to the glimmering steel Courthouse doors had once been magnificent, symbols of the path to PublicJustice. Go through those doors, and no matter who you were, you had a chance to get justice.

Now the Courthouse façade was dull and streaked with darkness like the rest of the surrounding dregs. Half the stairs had completely eroded, and rust covered the great steel doors. More of the destitute congregated in front of the Courthouse steps.

"What are those folk waiting for?" Cego asked.

"Waiting their turn for processing," Murray said. "They've got grievances to file. Maybe their home's been bulldozed to plant a new buying center, maybe there's been a theft or murder too insignificant for the Enforcers to get involved. If they're heard, they'll be assigned a defender to represent them in the courts and a Grievar to represent them in the Circle. One who will fight for their justice."

Murray didn't tell Cego the rest of the story—the truth. The fact that PublicJustice was a darkin' lie, a veil the Daimyo Governance put up to keep the masses in check. These folk wouldn't find any justice behind the steel doors of the Courthouse. Those who didn't have a bribe on hand or a connection on the inside would be turned back to the streets with some Governance script telling them they'd have their justice at a future date, if they lived to see it.

Murray looked down at Cego, who was staring at the Courthouse steps with those wide eyes.

The kid didn't deserve Murray's truth.

* * *

High Commander Albion Jonquil Memnon briskly walked the corridors of the Citadel. He moved with a determined, long stride. Though far past his prime, Memnon was the epitome of a Grievar—tall, thick, and weathered from combat. Out of habit, he wore his second skin, the formfitting shirt that was still glistening from training this morning. He often didn't bother to switch into his more formal commander's uniform.

Memnon didn't slow as he jogged down the Knight Tower's spiral staircase, the same stairs he'd descended every day since he'd become high commander nearly a decade ago.

Though Memnon no longer fought in the Circle, as he had during his Knight service, he was meticulous with the upkeep of his body. Even on the busiest of days, he trained every morning. He was known to jump into the sparring sessions of his much younger Knights, both to ensure they were sharp and to test himself. He often left the bouts bruised and panting, though he never succumbed to the weariness until he was alone.

Memnon could show no weakness, not to his subordinates within the Citadel, nor to foreign nations that would seek to diminish Ezo's influence.

"Mornin', High Commander." A Grunt cook bowed his head low as Memnon passed the kitchen and servicer's quarters. His stomach grumbled as he smelled something savory on the sizzler, but he didn't slow his pace down the stairs.

Rain battered the windows on each floor as he descended. Memnon thought about his Knights running drills up Kalabasas Hill, their clothes soaked and boots soggy.

The Knight Tower was located at the center of the Citadel's walls, a cylindrical beacon that rose above the surrounding structures. The Tower served both as the living quarters of the Knights as well as the command center for all of the Capital's Grievar.

Memnon passed two of his newer cadets in the corridor, freshly graduated from the Lyceum. Both stood at attention and raised their arms in salute, followed with the cry of "O Toh!" Even for formalities like this, Memnon did not stop. He nodded as he passed but kept his brisk pace toward the Citadel's command center on the ground floor.

Memnon couldn't stop moving.

When he stopped, some Kirothian or Desovian commander kept moving, strategizing and improving their program, getting ahead in the arms race. When Memnon stopped, he failed his Knights, who were training at this very moment in one of the many combat centers in the building. When Memnon stopped, he let down all the citizens of Ezo—those who depended on his team winning to ensure they had food, shelter, medtech, or any other comforts in life. Though the nation's other cities had their own Knight teams, they were inferior and couldn't be depended on in the big international bouts, the fights with the highest stakes.

The only times Memnon slowed down were to sleep or to peer from the window of his room at the top floor of the Tower. Even then, gazing over the Citadel's grounds, Memnon's mind was racing. When his hard yellow eyes swept over each of the storied branches of the Citadel, he could only dwell on problems.

PublicJustice, led by Dakar Pugilio, was in dire need of talent and leadership. Despite being an old friend from service, Pugilio had become nearly uncontrollable, spending more time drinking than managing his team. The Lyceum, headed by the ancient

Commander Aon Farstead, had grown old in its customs and training methods. And the newest branch of the Citadel, the Scouts, was far too young and brash under the leadership of Callen Albright. Even Memnon's own domain, the Knights, had fallen in standing over the last decade, in a constant struggle to keep up with other nations. Memnon knew that without Artemis Halberd anchoring the team, they'd have become second runners to Kiroth long ago.

Memnon turned a corner and walked through a pair of sliding doors into the command center. The room was round, built in the exact dimensions of a Circle, ten meters in diameter. Shield windows looked out at the Citadel's grounds in every direction.

The remaining three commanders of the Citadel sat at a circular table in the center of the room. Aon Farstead, Dakar Pugilio, and Callen Albright. They stood and saluted Memnon, their forearms crossed high, before returning to their seats. Memnon did not sit. As usual, he paced the circumference of the room.

"Didn't even have time to change out of his second skin!" Dakar shouted in his boisterous manner. "Albion, you need to relax every once in a while." The commander of PublicJustice threw his legs up onto the table, leaning back in his chair. "I'm telling you, one hour at Lady Pompei's joint right off Central Square and that tension will be gone. I have just the girl in mind for you too. Real sweet lass..."

"Yes, because what we really need is for High Commander Memnon to relax. Perhaps we should all forgo our duties and take some time off. Why not take a jaunt to the Courtesan Houses? Perhaps then we could be more like you, Dakar, and this place would really fall apart." Callen sneered from his seat across the table.

Dakar stood. He looked like an angry walrus as he stared down at the wiry Scout commander, his cheeks bright red above his long, drooping mustache. Though he was taller than Memnon, Dakar Pugilio had not cared for his body or mind as the high commander had. His belly sagged from beneath his tunic, displaying the distorted edges of an old flux tattoo, and his shoulders hunched from many years of torpor.

"Why don't you stand up, worm, and I'll show you why this place is really fallin' apart. Because of bit-rich kids like you who don't know how to shoot a double, walking in here on Daddy's—"

"That's enough. Sit down, Dakar," Memnon said quietly as he continued to pace.

Dakar slowly sank back into his seat, muttering and staring at Callen as he did so.

"Provide me with your reports," Memnon said. "You start, Dakar."

Dakar attempted to straighten in his seat, but even then, he somehow looked slouched, as if his body had forgotten how to try.

"Yes, sir, Albion. Err, High Commander Memnon. Last several days, well... we won some, we lost some," Dakar said.

"Win percentage?" Memnon asked.

"Thirty percent," Dakar said in a low voice as he tugged at his mustache. "Let me tell you, though, some of the wins we had, they were great. Old Byron took out some hotshot merc—put the light of justice on him, all right. Just like the old days, Albion—remember Byron? How he'd always catch some poor sod off guard with that overhand right? Well, he's still got it. He threw—"

"Stop," Memnon said. The high commander sighed as he paced. He rubbed the long scar that ran across his eyelid and down to his square jaw. "I can't hear more of these stories, Dakar. The only stories I need to hear are those of an improved win percentage. We need to get back to tolerable levels. Balance the weight of Justice. What do we need to do that?"

"Yes, yes, I know," Dakar said. "We have good men on the team; it's just that—"

Callen cut in. "That's just the problem. He has so-called *good men*. They don't need good men in PublicJustice. What they need are more killers. That's who the companies and the Daimyo lords are hiring to represent their interests: killers. Any sane person with the bits to spend will hire the best that's out there. Why settle for less? I'd certainly do so if it were my head on the line."

"You wouldn't understand," Dakar said, his face getting red again. "Some of my Grievar have served Ezo for decades. They've given their entire lives to follow the path. I can't just throw them out on the street like pieces of trash."

"What choice do we have?" Callen retorted. "It's either get with the times and completely overhaul our team at PublicJustice or have the courts continue to rot, stinking as they have for years under your command. We're talking about Grievar who represent Ezo, our nation, in the courts of combat. Just as High Commander Memnon only seeks the best for his Knight team, I would expect the same from PublicJustice."

Dakar fumed. "Do you realize what you're saying, boy? Fresh on the job and you think you already can tell me how to lead my men?"

Memnon interjected before Dakar had a chance to get too heated. "We do need to make changes, Dakar. I understand that you don't want to put your men out of their path, but we can't keep going with the way things are."

"The Goliath has a one hundred percent win percentage," Dakar said. "He's a killer to the core. Is that what you want more of?"

"We both know the Goliath is not sustainable," Memnon responded. "He's uncontrollable, as likely to turn on us as he is to—"

"The Goliath is a freak," Callen interrupted. "But Dakar might have the right idea for once. Freaks or not, all we need are wins in PublicJustice. In particular, we need wins for some big upcoming cases, like the latest in *Ezo v. ArkTech Labs.* Ezo's Daimyo Prosecutors have already presented evidence against ArkTech in the courts and are likely to win arguments by end of week. Then it's up to your Grievar to close it out, Dakar. It will all be up to one of your old, broken men, standing across the Circle from one of ArkTech's best hired mercenaries."

Dakar began to speak again but closed his mouth as Memnon flashed his eyes at him.

"Start with the worst. The two defenders on your team with the lowest win percentages this cycle. I'm sorry, Dakar, but they are out," Memnon said. "We'll replace them with two of Callen's fresh recruits. Especially ahead of this ArkTech case, we need to do it. If PublicJustice takes too many more losses, Governance is likely to scrap the program completely. If that happens, Ezo's laws will lie solely within Daimyo discretion and their courts of trickery, babbling, and bribes. We Grievar will lose our voice entirely."

Dakar looked down at the table dejectedly.

"Callen, who have we got to spare that has experience from this cycle's take?" Memnon asked.

"Well. To start, I'd suggest the Falcon, Sit Fanyong, who we recently acquired. He has at least two years' experience as a Knight, and I believe he also served in the Desovian justice system for a year, as different as that is from our own," Callen said.

Dakar looked up from the table with wide eyes. "We're going to put a darkin' Desovian on my team? There's no way my boys will train with some sponge-eater!"

Memnon stared down at his old friend, his eyes suddenly blazing. "Dakar, your team will train with the Falcon, and they will do so diligently. *You* will make sure of it. You are Ezo's commander of PublicJustice. Your lightpath does not mean reliving your days of glory in the Citadel, bantering with your team of old-timers. Your path means putting together the best team possible. Your path means making sure the scales of justice are balanced not just for high-profile Governance cases but for those folk who don't have the bits to hire expensive mercenaries. And that will start with integrating Sit Fanyong into your team. We will reevaluate after the next report as to whether we need more transitions."

Dakar looked at Memnon with his mouth slightly open. He bowed his head in concession. "O Toh, High Commander."

Memnon continued to pace around the room, his frenetic steps matching the tempo he set in his command meetings. "On to the next. Commander Aon, are we ready for the Trials?" Memnon turned to the commander of the Lyceum, who had been silently observing the heated discussion.

Aon Farstead was ancient. Hunched over the command table, he looked diminutive, even next to Callen's lean frame. A few remaining wisps of white hair hung from Aon's bald, wrinkled scalp, and two massive cauliflowered ears hung by the sides of his head like Besaydian dragon fruit. Aon's eyes no longer had the yellow tinge of a Grievar. They were milky white. He'd been blind for nearly two decades.

Aon spoke in a slow, deliberate cadence, his voice a whisper that carried the strength of over a century of wisdom. "That we are, High Commander. One year to the next, the world changes around us, but the Trials remain the same. Like a stone lodged in a stream."

Memnon nodded respectfully at the venerated elder member of Command. "Aon, what do you see in store for this year's Trials?"

Aon chuckled. "High Commander, I *see* nothing in store." The old Grievar batted his eyelids playfully. "But I do have a strange feeling of late. The light has been stronger these past few months. I can feel its gravity tugging on these old bones of mine. I can't remember that sort of pull since... Well, it's been quite a while now."

"What could it mean?" Memnon asked. "Could it be a good sign for us? Perhaps one of the Trial-takers..."

Aon's milky eyes wandered as the hunched man took a deep breath. "The light often whispers. All Grievar can hear it if they stop to listen. Not just in the Circle or under the bright arrays. Even beyond the halls of combat, we all carry the light. Walking, sitting, sleeping, breathing; it is there, whispering to us."

From across the room, Callen let out an audible sigh as he rolled his eyes in disdain.

"Even you can hear the light, Callen Albright, though I sense you do not believe you can." Aon directed his voice at Callen's seat, causing the wiry Scout commander to stiffen in his chair.

Aon continued, unperturbed. "In these recent months, the pull I've felt—the light is no longer whispering; it is roaring. I do not know what it saying, but I do know it is speaking to us, to the Grievar who are forever intertwined with it."

Aon's words quieted the room. Dakar's face was no longer red with anger; he breathed evenly as he listened. Even Memnon had stopped pacing, pausing for a brief moment.

Callen broke the quiet. "That is all good and well, Commander Farstead, but bluntly, I don't hear anything beyond the sound of Ezo getting crushed under our competitors. Perhaps, in your considerable age, you are hearing things?"

Memnon's brow creased. He opened his mouth to reprimand Callen's blatant disrespect, but Aon lifted his frail hand to hold him off.

Aon smiled through his thin lips. "It is said that Grievar infants, fresh from the womb, can hear the light most ably. Infants are pure, untainted by the world around them, their eyes not yet formed to see the petty underpinnings of grown folk. Perhaps that is why I can also hear the light so clearly—my years put me closer to the end, or the beginning, and with that comes a purity that dispels all the distractions of this world. I can hear the light, Commander Callen, and it whispers no longer."

Callen had clearly stopped listening to Aon, his eyes shifting back and forth calculatingly. "Yes, yes. That's all great, Commander Farstead. But on the subject of strange myths, as you so often bring us in the direction of, I'd like to revisit a portion of the Trials. The Combat Codes."

Memnon spoke up. "Callen, we discussed this during our last Command meeting and decided it's better left as is, for this year at least."

"Yes, I know, High Commander, but I felt the need to bring it up again. The light told me I needed to." Callen smirked at Aon. "I just feel that of all the Trial protocol in place, the Codes are the part that is least applicable to getting Ezo where it needs to be. How does deciphering ancient Grievar texts, which really have no place in society today, have anything to do with bettering our teams? What good do some words have in making a better fighter in the Circle?"

Memnon shook his head. "Callen, I like what you bring to this team. A youthful perspective. We need that; we need to change things in order to get Ezo back to where it was. But change can't always happen as fast as you'd like. We're already making major overhauls. We need to take things one step at a time."

Callen replied, "Do you think the Kirothians are taking things one step at a time, spending valuable resources having their Knights recite old, forgotten texts? No, they are providing them with the newest neurotech and training them round the clock, making them into killers. When one of Ezo's Knights goes up against a Kirothian, he may well be able to recite some ancient text by heart, but then he'll get ground into the dirt by a better-trained Grievar. We can only rely on the strength of Artemis Halberd for so long."

Memnon was pacing around the room again. The Kirothians had forgone many of the Codes over a decade ago in favor of more modern training philosophies: neurostimulant cycling programs, simulation training, spectral acclimation chambers. They'd taken nearly 60 percent of the disputes against Ezo until Memnon had made the decision to start playing catch-up.

Aon seemed to sense how Callen's calculated words played on Memnon's paranoia. "The Combat Codes are a part of us, High Commander. Since the beginning. The Codes are as much of a Grievar's makeup as are our fists, elbows, and knees, or our techniques that have been learned and passed down from the Ancients."

Memnon stopped pacing again as he listened to Aon. "The Trials are an introduction, a test to those worthy Grievar who would become learned warriors within the halls of our Lyceum and, eventually, forces of justice to fight for the downtrodden in our courts or Knights to represent us in the world's arena. Each Trial is representative of Grievar skill and character. To remove the Codes from the Trials would mean removing a piece of ourselves," Aon said.

Memnon nodded. "Aon is right, Callen. We cannot remove the Codes from the Trials. Getting rid of them would mean reworking the whole process. They stay for now. However, I will consider giving the Codes less weight in overall scoring."

Callen leaned back into his chair, smirking.

"Command, thank you for coming today. You are dismissed." Memnon signaled with the Grievar Knight salute.

"O Toh," the three commanders replied in unison, raising their arms.

Aon creaked from his seat, slowly moving toward the doorway without the aid of vision. Dakar stood and walked beside Aon. "I'm headin' the same way you are, old friend; need a hand to get back to your classroom?"

Aon smiled as the doors slid open in front of him. "Thank you, Commander Pugilio, but no, this old Grievar can make do."

Callen remained seated after the other two had left, looking up at Memnon with his arresting yellow eyes.

"Don't you want to know where we are... with that other program of ours?" Callen asked.

Memnon shook his head, quieting Callen. "Do not speak of that here, Commander Albright."

Callen nodded. "All right. Well, things are going according to plan, if you'd like to know. You've made the right choice for your nation."

Memnon nodded and turned, exiting through the sliding doors.

The high commander walked briskly, his pace increasing as he distanced himself from the meeting room. He had to keep moving. The Desovians were moving, getting ahead. The Kirothians wouldn't stop, so he couldn't.

Memnon couldn't stop moving or the shadows would catch up to him.

CHAPTER 10

Voices in the Rain

When encountering an opponent for the second time, a Grievar must not consider the outcome of the previous match. Focusing on a past defeat will only hinder the mind in finding a new path to victory.

Passage Six, Seventy-Third Precept of the Combat Codes

The previous night, as he turned restlessly in his makeshift cot out by Violet's soft glow, Cego had replayed every possible scenario of the Trials in his head. He still wasn't ready. But today was the day.

He looked down the wet, cobbled road toward the Citadel, a cluster of sprawling stone structures surrounded by a deep trench. Despite the persistent rain, a thick fog rose from the ground, drifting around the ancient buildings and curling up the tall tower at the center. The Citadel was distinct from everything Cego had seen of the Capital so far: the gaudy glare and raucousness of the city were replaced by a faded, dense quiet here.

"These structures were standing long before the skyscrapers in the Tendrum." Murray spoke from beside Cego. "Solid stonework, some cracks in places, but sturdy as ever."

They walked across the trench on a wooden footbridge, and Cego peered over the edge at the dark river that ran beneath. On the other side of the bridge, a Grunt digging at the bank of the trench shouldered his shovel and stared at them from beneath his tattered hood.

The two weaved their way between buildings on the muddy road and past flickering lanterns hung on posts until they reached a set of structures that looked even older than the rest. Grey, pillared open-air walkways ran between vine-snared gazebos at the perimeter. Cego stared with wide eyes through the sheets of rain.

"The Lyceum," Murray said.

Two large rotundas anchored the Lyceum on either side, each capped with a moss-encrusted dome.

"The sister domes of the Lyceum." Murray nodded. "Trials are held in the Valkyrie, classes in the Harmony."

They stepped onto one of the stone walkways, this one with life-sized carved statues set between pillars. Cego's heart began to race as they climbed a short flight of cracked steps and neared the entrance to the Valkyrie. Even through the din of the heavy rain, he could hear voices echoing from within the majestic rotunda.

"You ready?" Murray put a hand on Cego's shoulder and looked him in the eye.

"Yes," Cego said as he stepped forward. "I'm done waiting."

Torches lit the enormous hall, casting shadows up and down the walls. Thick stone pillars circled the room, each engraved top to bottom with ancient sigils. There were hundreds of kids within the Valkyrie's round walls. Murray directed Cego to the base of one of the pillars.

"All right, kid, now just a bit more waiting. Old Aon should be out shortly for the commencement."

Cego nodded and glanced around him at the assortment of Grievar brood. They were all shapes and sizes. Some were stretching on the stone floor while others warmed up by jogging around the perimeter of the room.

Cego's eyes were immediately drawn to a massive blond boy, his cheeks rounded into a strange smile, who stood like a giant among his peers. Two mercs were stationed at either side of him.

"Who is that?" Cego whispered.

Murray was looking at the giant boy with a deep frown on his face. "Brood of the harvesters. Scouts nabbed him from the borderlands," Murray said. "Only ten years old. Most don't try to pick kids up so early. No better than Thaloo's slavers."

Cego continued to scan the room, trying to push down the butterflies that were swelling in the pit of his stomach.

A tight-knit pack of kids chatted noisily in the center of the rotunda, separated from the rest, who orbited the fringes. Cego noticed they wore pressed uniforms, many emblazoned with colorful emblems.

"Purelights from the Twelve." Murray must have noticed Cego staring at the kids. "The big Grievar houses that have been tied to the Citadel for centuries."

Cego watched the purelights as they pointed at the blond giant and laughed, their glowing yellow eyes unnaturally bright in the torchlight. They acted as if they owned the place already.

Cego's eyes moved away from the purelights and settled on a boy across the room. He was robed, sitting cross-legged under the shadow of a pillar. What caught Cego's attention was the steam that steadily billowed from the top of the boy's shaved head. His eyes were closed and he breathed deeply, quietly, even amid the commotion in the room.

Suddenly, the boy's eyes opened, directly meeting Cego's gaze. The two maintained their stare for several moments before the boy shut his eyes again and continued to breathe in silence, the steam rising from his scalp.

Cego was about to ask Murray about the boy when he noticed two others jog past him, running side by side. He stared at their backs. One boy was large, with thick, muscled shoulders, and the other was lean, with dark hair.

Something about the two piqued Cego's interest—the synchronized pace they fell into as they rounded the perimeter of the circular hall. Cego tracked them as they passed to the back side of the room.

The large boy playfully pushed his running partner, throwing him toward the center of the room. The smaller boy caught his balance with a hand on the floor, turning his face in Cego's direction as he did so. The boy grinned, highlighting a scar that ran across his jaw.

There was no mistaking him: it was Knees. He threw a playful elbow into the ribs of his large companion as they began to jog again—Dozer.

Cego shook with excitement. From the corner of his eye, he saw Murray raise an eyebrow. Dozer and Knees had made it out of the Underground. They'd escaped Thaloo's.

Cego could barely restrain himself from shouting from across the room but decided to wait until Dozer and Knees circled past him again. Cego smiled at Murray and slid behind the pillar.

Just as he saw Dozer's bulky shadow cross in front of him, Cego shot his foot across his path, a basic sweep that caught the big boy right on the ankle and sent him sprawling to the ground.

Cego stepped out from behind the pillar as Dozer flipped around, his face contorted in anger until he met Cego's eyes. Knees spun around, also looking ready to pick a fight with whoever had messed with his friend.

"Cego!" Dozer charged toward him and wrapped him in a crushing bear hug, only setting him down when Cego began to cough from the pressure.

"We thought we be findin' you here." Knees smiled and clasped Cego's wrist firmly.

"You told me I'd make it up here! Remember, Cego?" Dozer yelled.

"You don't know how good it is to see you two," Cego said. Amid the horde of strange kids crowded in the big hall, the constant rain pelting the ceiling, and the Trials ahead of him, it somehow felt all right now that Dozer and Knees were here with him.

"How—how did you—"

"You're not going to be likin' this..." Knees said.

"Any way you got here, I'll take it. What happened? Did you escape somehow?" Cego asked.

"No. We be comin' with *him*." Knees directed his gaze across the hall to the pack of purelights in the center.

Cego stared at the pack again. A haughty laugh came from within the group. The cackle dredged up a sharp pain in Cego's stomach. A boy stepped from their midst. Shiar.

Cego's anger ignited like oil-doused kindling at the memory of Weep on the ground, Shiar kicking the life out of him. Knees placed a hand on Cego's shoulder to steady him.

"How—how—" Cego growled.

"Few days after you left, some big-time Scout from Citadel comes to be watchin' us in the yard. He's especially interested in Shiar. Scout gets to talkin' with Tasker Ozark, negotiating on Shiar's patronage. Few days later, they hit on a deal. Ozark throws in the next two best from Crew Nine along with Shiar there, which be Dozer and me... We be packaged, the three of us," Knees said.

"Whole time we were riding up on the Lift, I wanted to take Shiar's head off," Dozer said. "But I also didn't want to muck my chance of making it to the Lyceum and meetin' up with you."

Cego let out a deep breath. If it took Shiar coming up here to get Dozer and Knees back, he'd take it. They would find a way to avenge Weep when the time came.

Murray stood several steps away, watching the reunion with a smile on his face before returning his attention to the balcony above.

"You two been practicing your techniques? Are you ready?" Cego asked, desperate to take his mind off Shiar.

"Yeah, we be practicin' the ones you showed us down below. Also, the Lyceum been runnin' some practices when we got Upworld two weeks ago. Even worked along with those inbreeds," Knees said, narrowing his eyes at the pack of purelights.

Murray chimed in. "That's the doing of Commander Aon Farstead. He believes in starting all Grievar on equal footing, though that's hardly possible with the advanced training most purelights from the Twelve get from birth."

Knees nodded. "Yeah, we be up against quite a field." The Venturian sat on the stone floor, stretching out his legs as he looked at the room of Trial-takers. "I hear purelights usually be takin' most of the placements. Last year, they say almost all the students that got through the doors came from the Twelve. Our chances be looking pretty dim right now."

"Purelight or not, it doesn't make a difference," Cego said confidently. "I've seen you two in the Circle. It should come down to skill, and I know you have what it takes."

Knees shook his head, always the pessimist. "I like to think so too. But I been doing some scoutin' of my own and we be up against some of the best. For starters, we got Shiar over there. We know what he be capable of when he wants to get ahead."

"He's just one kid, though, there are supposed to be twenty-four accepted each year," Cego said.

"Yeah. I know, I'm just gettin' started. And I'm thinkin' Shiar might be the least of our worries," Knees said. "They be sayin' Gryfin Thurgood is a shoo-in." Knees nodded to a tall, chiseled purelight with an athletic build at the center of the pack. "Thurgood House always got a kid in the Lyceum, one brother every few years."

Murray cut in again. "True. Even I had a Thurgood in my class. And there's one on the current Knight team—Tullen Thurgood. Darkin' good wrestler. Wouldn't be surprised if his brood had some of that skill."

Cego's heart sank again. Murray always had a way of boosting his spirits.

"Speakin' of famous names—over there with rest of the inbreeds, we got a Halberd kid goin' into the Trials with us," Knees said.

Cego's eyes widened. Artemis Halberd. The nation's most famed Grievar Knight and the current champion. Captain of the Knight team. The man who carried Ezo on his shoulders.

Cego looked among the pack of purelights for a boy who resembled the elder Halberd—a mane of red hair, sculpted jaw, thick, muscular shoulders, legs that looked like they could spring across a ravine. He didn't see anyone who matched the image in his head.

"Where is he?" Cego asked.

"*She*," Knees said. "Solara Halberd."

Knees nodded at one side of the pack of purelights. A thin girl stood straight-backed at the edge of the pack, a red braid of fiery hair falling across her shoulder. She gazed at the torches, her eyes giving off a determined amber glow.

"She hits hard," Dozer said, rubbing at one of his forearms. "Training two days ago, I got paired up with her. Just holding pads, she nearly kicked right through them. Fifty straight and she wasn't even breathing hard."

Though Cego believed his friend, he couldn't picture Solara slamming kicks into Dozer. She had a sharp nose to accent her almond-shaped eyes. He could see the slight resemblance to her father with the red braid of hair, though he guessed she must have taken after her mother with her more delicate features.

Just when Cego realized he'd been staring for several moments at the Halberd girl, she cast her eyes toward him. Cego looked at the floor.

"Uh...what about him?" Cego quickly turned his attention to the boy with the bald head sitting beneath the pillar. "Was he at training earlier?"

"Nope. Haven't seen him till today," Knees said. "Walked in by himself, drippin' wet. Kid didn't say nothing, just sits down and starts his breathing, steam comin' off his head like that. Hasn't moved in the three hours since we got here."

"Bet he's trained by the Kirothian Priest Knights!" Dozer whispered. "I heard they can hold their breath for over two hours and can expand their blood vessels to prevent getting choked!"

"You'd believe someone tellin' you the spirits of Ancients be real too, haunting these very halls." Knees jabbed at Dozer's stomach playfully.

Dozer raised a hefty forearm to block Knees's shot and followed with a pawing right of his own that the Venturian ducked. Cego had missed these two.

Just as he was about to ask them what they thought of the Surface, the torches around the room flared brighter, dispelling the shadows along the walls. New torches sprang to life on the balcony above, where Murray had been keeping his eyes throughout the wait.

Several figures stepped forward onto the balcony. At the front was Aon Farstead, commander of the Lyceum, and by far the oldest person Cego had ever seen. Aon leaned against the railing, hunched over and wrinkled, dwarfed by the three other men who stood behind him.

"Welcome to the Lyceum, Trial-takers!" Aon whispered, yet his voice echoed around the wide circular chamber.

Aon's milky-white eyes darted around the room, reflecting the dancing light from the torches as he spoke. "You hail from many roads. You hail from faraway lands that have never seen the famed domes or the ancient libraries of the Citadel. You hail from Deep caverns blanketed in myriad shades of light. You hail from houses rooted in Ezo's history." Cego glanced over at the group of purelights. He saw Shiar's chin raised proudly, as if he were born of the Twelve.

"You hail from the very minds and spirits of the Ancients, the Grievar who stood at the dawn of combat itself." For a moment,

Cego felt Aon's ghostlike eyes on him, as if staring directly through him, before continuing to dart around the room.

"You hail from many roads, but now you only have one that lies before you. This is the path of the Grievar. The Trials were built by the Ancients to distinguish those young Grievar worthy of acceptance into the Lyceum. Those students accepted will continue the tradition of learning techniques passed down for centuries. Those accepted will tread a lightpath all Grievar seek, yet very few follow.

"From the Lyceum, our Knights are born with the strength to protect Ezo and provide a beacon of light at the darkest hour." Commander Memnon stepped forward on cue, his broad shoulders stiff and his hard eyes scanning the room with authority.

"From the Lyceum, our Defenders are born with the spirit to guide the hand of PublicJustice and represent the downtrodden during their time of need." Commander Pugilio stepped forward, the tallest man on the podium, yet he seemed smaller than Memnon, with his sagging shoulders and drooping mustache.

"From the Lyceum, our Scouts are born with the sharp eyes to spot the tiniest glimmers of hope within the darkest corners of our lands." As Aon spoke, Commander Albright stepped forward, dressed in a collared uniform, his chin held high.

"The Lyceum's halls are sacred to all Grievar, even those outside the Capital, even those who live beyond Ezo's borders. Though many schools around the world have sought to replicate our process, none possess our collective technique and wisdom.

"That is why we must be discerning with our Trials. For those who enter the Lyceum's studies must represent Ezo's next generation—our leaders, our light, our honor. All Trial-takers that are gathered in this hall today are distinguished already, whether it be by blood, skill, or spirit. By day's end, as the Trials are finished, we shall be even more distinguished. Only a select few will enter the Lyceum. Twenty-four students total," Aon said.

The kids in the room looked around at each other, some appearing fearful at the sheer weight of the competition, while the purelights stood steadfast, whispering among each other, never even considering the thought of getting cut.

"I can see some of you stand confidently with the Trials looming before you. You do so rightfully. To your sides stand the strongest and most skilled Grievar brood of your generation. Many of you already have an extensive knowledge of techniques, conditioning, and combat strategy," Aon said. "However, the Trials are not made as a pure test of strength and skill. The Trials are made to test your potential to endure. Each of your Trials will be unique. The light within the Hall of Trials knows you already. How you move, what your strengths and weaknesses are. Where your pride and fear live. The light will exploit this; it will seek to unsettle the unstable stones in your walls of defense. You would be wise to tread warily—expect anything."

The crowd of Grievar kids hushed. Even the purelights quieted.

"Those students accepted into the Lyceum will not only be the best but the most enduring. They will be able to handle any situation in front of them, even during the darkest hours.

"The lightpath of the Citadelian is not an easy one. It is one filled with sacrifice. You will give up the luxuries, the love, the very trimmings of life that you may depend on. But you will gain something even more valuable: honor. We fight so the rest shall not have to." Aon whispered the mantra with reverence.

Aon lowered his head, his eyes closing as he took a deep, labored breath. He lifted his chin, quiet for several moments. He cocked his head as if listening to something before raising his fist to the air in salute.

"Today begin the Trials! May the best emerge from the darkness." Aon's closing remark was punctuated by the swish of a massive sliding door opening at one end of the hall.

CHAPTER 11

Trials and Tribulations

A Grievar must respect the dream as much as any waking moment. Shadows passing in the night may not emerge to be blood-starved wolves, and yet there is always a chance a shadow can bite with ferocity.

Passage Three, One Hundred Sixty-Third Precept of the Combat Codes

A blast of frigid air hit Cego.

The cold seemed to crystallize the air itself as shards of frost swirled across the tundra. The landscape was barren but for a few trees pushing through the hard ground like skeletal hands reaching from their graves.

Cego was wearing standard-issue trousers and a skin guard the Lyceum had provided him, but nothing had prepared him for this. His hands were already streaked with veins of frost, and he couldn't feel his feet through his vat-hide boots.

As he stepped forward, the cold sucked the air out of his lungs like a knee to the stomach. The cold of the tiny cell in Thaloo's dungeon was a warm bath compared to what Cego now faced.

In this place, the cold was an opponent about to lock on a choke; Cego had to deal with it, or he would die.

Another wave of frostbitten air swept across the tundra, blanketing Cego's vision with white crystals and bringing him to his knees.

How did I arrive here?

Cego had already taken some sort of test. It hadn't been what he'd expected.

He'd waited for several hours in the Lyceum's great hall until a grey-haired clerk had called for him. "Charge of Scout Murray Pearson! Number ninety-six."

Murray had grabbed Cego's shoulder to meet his eyes before he was escorted away.

The clerk had directed Cego into a small, sterile room with a single chair at the center. He'd taken the seat and the man had brought out a strange device, a lightdeck sprouting wires with metallic clips at each end. The clips had attached to the base of Cego's scalp, pinching at his skin. The clerk had then pricked Cego in the neck with a small needle.

"Provide brief responses to each of the questions," the man had said in a monotone as he swept his hand across the lightdeck.

"You find yourself in the aquatic markets of the Emerald Isles," the clerk started. "Two hawkers approach you, one speaking common tongue and the other babbling in ancient Tikretian, which you can't understand. The common-tongued hawker offers to sell you two pounds of water fruit for a clearly rotten price. The Tikretian speaker makes another offer, though you can't understand what it is." The grey-haired man paused. "Do you take the horrendous offer, or do you attempt to bargain with the man you don't understand?"

"Well, I guess that depends on the look of the man I don't understand. Does he look trustworthy?" Cego had asked.

"No questions, just answers," the clerk had replied.

"All right. Well, first, I'd make sure the two hawkers weren't working together to—"

"Choose one of the two options," the clerk had interrupted him.

Cego thought for several moments before going with his gut. "I'd take the bad offer."

The clerk hadn't provided any indication as to whether Cego had answered correctly; he swept his hand across his lightdeck and continued.

"You find yourself in the marshes of Swampskil, suddenly stricken with rotworm and utterly lost..." The clerk had asked similar questions for the better part of an hour.

Cego couldn't remember how the Trial had ended. He remembered a final question regarding the plight of the harvesters in the borderlands, and then suddenly he was here, forced to his knees on the ice, barely able to keep his eyes open as the frost accumulated on his lashes.

A quick flash of movement near one of the few trees sprouting from the tundra caught Cego's attention. Something was whipping around in the wind, attached to one of the tree's emaciated branches. From a distance, it looked like a flag.

Cego gritted his teeth and slowly pushed himself off the ground, taking a slow step forward against the wind. This was his Trial. They were watching him.

Cego closed in on the tree, peering out from beneath his heavy eyelids. A white piece of cloth jumped back and forth like a ghost dancing on the gusts of frigid air, strung to the branch with a thin rope.

He reached out and grabbed it. It wasn't a flag at all. It was made of a thick, rough, woven material—all too familiar to Cego after the past month of training in Murray's barracks. A gi jacket.

Cego didn't even hesitate; he needed the layer of warmth or he wouldn't last. He untethered the uniform from the rope and slipped into it. The gi fit perfectly, the sleeves reaching just to the end of his wrists.

To Cego's surprise, the inside of the gi wasn't laden with frost as he expected. The soft inner fabric felt warm to the touch. He felt heat surge through his veins, as if the gi were boiling the blood running through them. He took a deep breath—the air didn't burn his lungs any longer.

Cego looked at the gi in wonder. What sort of tech was this?

The wind softened along with the cold. Cego could suddenly see across the white-cast tundra, as if a blustery veil had been lifted.

Across the barren landscape, a solitary patch of green stood out in the distance. Could grass somehow be growing in this desolate climate?

Walking with more confidence in the newfound warmth of the gi, Cego made his way toward the green oasis.

As he got closer, Cego saw the patch of green was not grass but ice. An ice field, glimmering green—the source of its strange color was the glowing Circle planted dead at its center. Emeralyis.

A stocky figure stood within the Circle, unmoving. The figure was facing away, clad in a white gi jacket similar to his own.

"Professor?" Cego shouted over the wind as he neared. He assumed the man was one of the teachers at the Lyceum. "What would you have me do?"

The figure did not respond or turn to face him.

Cego stepped onto the sheet of ice and nearly lost his footing. It was as slippery as a wet moss-rock. He could remember the old master testing his balance on the rocks that dotted the island's tide pools. He'd stand across from Sam, and the two brothers would vigorously attempt to push each other into the water.

Cego slowly started to shuffle along the ice toward the pulsing green Circle ahead. Perhaps that would be the aim of this Trial—a test of his balance, fighting on this slick surface.

"Professor, I'm ready for your Trial," Cego said as he entered the Circle. He'd never trained in emeralyis before, but Murray had versed him on the effects of the alloy.

"Overly creative," Murray had told him. "Emeralyis will make you think you're a painter, creatin' new works across the Circle's canvas—techniques you've just now invented."

Cego didn't feel any more creative standing just past the steel frame on the ice. He could only concentrate on the man standing across from him.

The man creaked his head from side to side, his neck popping loudly each time. He turned around. His face was completely veiled in black fabric except for a small slit above his nose, where two burning yellow eyes were set on Cego. He was thick, nearly twice Cego's width.

The veiled man spoke in a whisper. "Take me down."

Cego understood and approached in a crouch. He'd practiced in the gi with Murray for the past several weeks. The uniforms would make this a game of grips. The fighter who established dominant grips on his opponent's gi uniform would have the control for a proper throw or takedown.

Cego feinted as if he were about to shoot low before taking a quick inside step and reaching for his opponent's lapel. Just as he expected, the man's arm fired out like a piston, reaching for his own lapel. Though Cego was able to secure a grip, the man mirrored it and grabbed on to his collar.

Now the real test began. Cego pulled with his grip, testing his opponent's reaction. The man was like a rock. He didn't waver. Cego tested him on both sides, seeing if he'd shuffle his feet, but again, he didn't react.

Cego knew he needed to take action fast or his opponent would. He yanked on the man's collar again, hard this time, looking for any reaction. The man's feet slid forward on the ice slightly.

It was enough of a sign for Cego. As his opponent's body moved toward him, he stepped between the man's legs with one foot and swiveled his other foot outward. He bent his knees while launching his hip into the man's waist, attempting to leverage him up and over in seoi nage. Cego had practiced the shoulder throw with Murray for the past several weeks.

His opponent countered expertly. As Cego pushed into him, the man arched his back, drove his hips forward, and lifted Cego into the air, heaving him up to eye level and letting him fall onto the ice with a thud. Urisho goshi. The air burst from Cego's lungs on impact, leaving him breathless on the ice.

His opponent stood above him, his eyes searing from beneath his veil. "Take me down," he repeated.

Cego got up slowly, a dull pain arcing down his back. He approached the man again. The man's hand shot out and grasped Cego's lapel. Cego countered with his own grip. They circled each other, matching sleeve grips on each side.

After attempting seoi nage, Cego knew he could never win that game. His opponent's reactions and stability were masterful. Cego's throws were not nearly good enough. Cego needed to go after the legs. He'd drilled single- and double-leg takedowns with Farmer since he could walk. That was Cego's game. Though the ice prevented him from initiating his attack from too far out, he knew there was an opportunity for a closer attempt.

The man was standing upright, stiff-backed, which seemed a prime opportunity. When Cego tested his reactions and lowered his base, though, he could feel the firm grips preventing him from getting any mobility. The man was like a statue, holding Cego in place. Cego needed to break a grip and get in close enough to clinch.

Cego released both of his grips and double-handed one of the man's wrists, jerking sharply at his sleeve to try to break his grasp. It didn't budge. The man's viselike fingers didn't even seem to strain as Cego tugged at them full force several times.

The man rushed forward, quick-stepping past Cego and sweeping his leg out from under him while throwing him toward the ground with his collar grip. Osoto gari. Cego's shoulder exploded against the ice, sending a blast of pain down his spine.

The man stepped back, repeating the words in a monotone. "Take me down."

Cego felt the doubt closing in on him, constricting his movements, making him second-guess his techniques. How would he ever get this man to the ground? He couldn't take a long-distance shot, because of the slippery ice. He couldn't match the man throw to throw. He was like a wall; he wouldn't budge. His grips were viselike. There was no way Cego could execute his takedowns without breaking them.

Cego stood again, grimacing. The man didn't move. Cego approached. They gripped up.

Cego stared into the man's glowing yellow eyes. They were completely expressionless, robotic.

Perhaps Cego wasn't meant for the Lyceum. Though he'd done well in the Underground, this was different. He didn't have the training or the genetics that the purelights did. It would be easy to give up. Call out to whoever was judging him that he'd forfeit.

Sometimes, we need to lose to win, Farmer's voice whispered. Cego wanted to yell back at the voice in his head, or wherever the old master lived in there. Hadn't he already lost? He'd tried every course of action, and all paths led to the same result: lying flat on his back on the ice.

Suddenly, it dawned on him.

The cold. He needed to lose something in order to gain something. That was it. Cego's mind raced as he charted a course of action.

He tugged at his opponent's gi to assure him he was still putting up a fight. As expected, the man barely reacted, keeping his posture straight and his grips on Cego's gi as tight as ever.

Cego yanked again, this time harder, looking for the slightest reaction. His opponent slid forward on the ice again. Just at that moment, Cego loosened his arms in his gi jacket and twisted his shoulders forward. His opponent's hands remained viselike on the gi, allowing Cego to slide out of the jacket and into the cold air.

The frost hit Cego again like a kick to the stomach, immediately stifling his breath. It felt as if his blood had stopped flowing, frozen within his veins. But he was free.

Cego shot forward with lightning speed, unencumbered and lithe without the uniform, and wrapped his arms around his opponent's waist, the man still grasping Cego's empty gi. Cego drove forward with every ounce of strength he had, wrapping his foot behind the man's knee as he pushed.

Caught off-balance, the man began to topple, his feet frantically attempting to grip the slippery ice.

Cego smiled slightly as he felt his opponent fall backward beneath him. He had sacrificed his gi, his only heat source, in order to get inside with enough speed. Just as he was congratulating himself on the crafty maneuver, Cego found himself suddenly head over heels in the air again. His opponent had framed his feet on Cego's hips while going down.

The man pushed out with his feet as he rolled over his shoulder, slamming Cego back onto the ice. Tomoe nage. He landed on top of Cego in mount.

Farmer's voice again echoed in Cego's head, scolding him. *Victory is sitting at home by the fire long after the fight.* He'd celebrated the takedown too early. He hadn't anticipated the counter roll.

This time, his opponent did not stand. He bore down from on top of Cego, squeezing him against the ice. The man's bulk blocked out the light above and his weight on Cego's chest restricted his breath. The little air he did inhale was icy frost, sending chills down his throat, paralyzing his innards.

Cego tried to escape from beneath the man's crushing mount, but there was no space. Nowhere to move. No air to breathe. No options.

* * *

Murray couldn't help but shiver as he watched Cego up on the lightboard. He'd seen too many fall to the ice over the years.

Murray was constantly surprised at the kid's ingenuity, though. Slipping out of the gi like that and actually bringing the Guardian to the ground—he'd only seen a handful of kids get their opponent to waver. Even the giant blond boy from the borderlands hadn't mounted any real offense like Cego had.

The first stage of these Trials—Ice, they called it—was all about each kid's reaction to adversity. When put up against a nearly immovable opponent and the frost, how would each respond? In addition, Ice tested the candidate's reaction to the emeralyis Circle. Would the greenlight goad them toward trying untested, inefficient techniques, or would it inspire true innovation?

Murray sat in a circular room full of Citadelians, mostly nervous Scouts who had their careers riding on the success of their talent in the Trials today. Even Command made a point of watching every year.

There were dozens of lightboards in the room, each tuned in to the Trial of a different taker. Some of the boards had gone dark for those who were out of the running already. Cego's board was still displaying the kid struggling beneath the Guardian's immovable form.

Many takers hadn't even made it to the Circle—they'd succumbed to the ice, shivering and curling up on the cold tundra grounds. Others had tried relentlessly to take the Guardian down. Even after getting slammed to the ice countless times, they'd never changed their strategy.

And then there were those who didn't know how to handle the greenlight at all. Murray had briefly watched a board displaying Cego's friend from the Underground, Dozer, to see the big kid attempting a flying wheel kick on the Guardian, which resulted in him getting rag-dolled to the ice.

But Cego had embraced the greenlight from the emeralyis Circle. He'd tried to stick to his game plan to start, but when it wasn't working, he'd opened up his mind. Murray found a smile creasing his face, thinking again about how Cego had slipped out of the gi like that. Darkin' smart kid.

Murray glanced over at Callen Albright, who was staring at Cego's lightboard with disgust. The man had expected Cego to fail from the start.

For some, like Dakar Pugilio, who had already polished off a cask of ale, the Trials were pure entertainment. The commander of PublicJustice slapped the side of his chair as he downed another glass, his eyes intently watching Cego struggling beneath the weight of the Guardian.

"You picked a good one this year, brother Murray," Dakar shouted. "Dark horse indeed!"

"The lacklight got lucky." Callen sneered. "Wasn't too smart, either, with his little maneuver there. In real combat, he'd freeze to death, crushed under his opponent."

"That's the point of the Trial." Dakar straightened his back in his chair as he glowered at Callen. "Murray's boy took a risk. He made a proper sacrifice to take the Guardian down. That's admirable."

"When Ezo's Knights are fighting for us in Circles around the world, do we want them to be admirable? Or do we want them to win? Perhaps they all should make the sacrifice of dignity like you've clearly done long ago, Pugilio," Callen retorted.

Dakar stood, red-faced. "You gutless worm, why don't we—"

"Enough," High Commander Memnon said from his seat in the center of the room. "We are here to watch the Trials, not participate in senseless arguments. Sit down, Dakar."

Dakar slowly sank back into his seat, glowering.

Memnon glanced up at the screen of a girl who'd just taken a vicious throw from the Guardian, rendering her unconscious against the ice. The girl's screen flickered before fading to black.

"Your boy has fared well in this Trial, Murray," Callen said from beside Memnon. "But we'll see how he does in the Arena." He was the type to always get in the last word.

Murray didn't respond, keeping his eyes on Cego's lightboard above. Cego was still pinned beneath the Guardian, struggling to escape from beneath the bulk of his opponent. His efforts would be fruitless, though; a Guardian was not just any other opponent.

The kid didn't know the truth about the Trials. That they were part of the Sim, Daimyo tech designed to replicate real combat in a variety of environments.

Not that the Trials didn't feel completely real. The Sim was seamless—the pain Cego was feeling right now, getting crushed against the ice by the Guardian on him, was real in his head. Though any physical wounds Cego sustained in the simulation would be gone when he woke, many kids were plagued for years with mental scars from their Trials. The Guardian was a part of the Sim. It was a near-perfect machine of combat, its only flaws purposeful parts of the code. The Guardian could appear in any number of forms—huge and immovable as a Desovian Juggernaut or wispy and untouchable as a Besaydian Vapoeria. Though the Guardian wasn't real, it felt real when it was breaking your arms or choking the life out of you.

Murray felt something gnawing at him as he watched Cego succumb to the crushing pressure and the frigid temperature. He'd grown attached to the kid over the past few months.

Murray had told himself he wouldn't do it again. Invest himself in one of these kids. Watch them go from scrawny, dirt-covered urchins to proud Grievar, filled with confidence and hopes of becoming a Knight someday. He'd trained countless kids in his barracks just as he'd trained Cego, watching them harness the techniques and teachings he had passed down.

They had all broken.

Of all the talent Murray had recruited over the past decade, one boy named Tarick had gotten the furthest in Trials. But he'd still broken.

Murray could vividly remember visiting Tarick in the medward for the next month, the boy feverishly screaming in his sleep. The kid hadn't been able to wake up. The Sim was too powerful—it could trap minds within those strange, foreign environments. Eventually, Tarick's body had given way.

After Tarick, Murray had sworn he wouldn't get attached again. He'd keep doing what the Citadel forced on him, but he wouldn't invest himself in their sick experiments. The whole thing—digging up kids from the Deep, building them up, and breaking them again during the Trials. Just to test them. To see if they had what it took to become a Knight.

The worst part of it was the Sim. Grievar using Daimyo tech. High Commander Memnon had worked with the Bit-Minders to develop the technology as another weapon to give Ezo's Grievar the edge. A way to keep their Knights training day and night without wearing out. A new tool to test his Knights in various environments from the comfort of the Citadel's walls.

They had expanded the Sim from training environments for the Knights to the Trials. The Citadel didn't want its newest and most promising students to be physically injured going into the Lyceum, so they were put through the Sim. Within the virtual environment, they could probe at every potential weakness a Trial-taker might have.

A few of the smaller nations still ran live Trials, but the Citadel had long advanced past those times. The last live Trials had been during Murray's schooling, when prospective students did sprints up Kalabasas Hill and took beatings from the upper-level students. But the Sim was more efficient and, in some ways, more brutal. It got inside the kids' heads.

Murray watched helplessly as another of his kids was broken. Cego was strong, but Tarick had also been strong. And Cego still could not escape the Guardian. Murray watched as the kid screamed voicelessly for space and air, his golden eyes bulging in his skull.

Why is Cego's Sim still running?

Nearly all the other screens had flicked off when the Guardian had smothered its opponent against the ice. Only one other Trial-taker was standing against the Guardian, the bald boy whose name, Murray had learned, was Shimo.

Murray swiveled his head to see Callen lean over and whisper something in the high commander's ear. They both were observing Cego's screen, unflinchingly watching the kid get brutalized beneath the Guardian.

"Why the dark isn't—" Murray stood and started to move toward the high commander, but suddenly Cego's lightboard wavered.

Murray met Memnon's eyes before he looked back toward Cego's fading screen.

It wasn't the screen itself that was shifting—the Sim was changing. The frosty tundra began to dissipate around Cego's inert body. The Guardian on top of Cego shimmered and faded as well, just another part of the Sim. Another illusion of the Bit-Minders. A theater of light and dark, particles playing their parts to simulate reality.

Soon, only Cego remained on the screen, a boy floating in a sea of darkness.

* * *

Cego's eyes fluttered open.

Instinctively, he thrust his hips backward, escaping from the immovable weight he believed to still be mounted on top of him. There was no resistance, though. His opponent was gone. He was alone in the darkness.

Cego stood gingerly, his body beaten and bruised from getting thrown against the ice so many times. He put his hand to his cheek. His skin was raw, ripped from the man's gi grinding against it.

Had he failed the Trials? Though Cego had initiated a takedown and thrown his opponent off-balance, he had ended up on the bottom. It had seemed he'd been stuck beneath that man for an eternity, unable to move or breathe. Perhaps this was where they transferred the kids who didn't pass the Trials, keeping them in the dark until the rest had finished.

Cego crept forward in the darkness, his eyes eagerly searching for the slightest prick of light, his ears perked for any sound beyond his own rapid breathing.

Though his senses had little to work with, he sought out every detail of the world around him. The floor was covered in thick cobwebs, like soft tufts of grass beneath Cego's naked feet. His vathide boots were gone.

Cego took a deep breath. He savored the air in his lungs. Warm, thick air. He certainly wasn't on the icy tundra any longer.

He listened to his heartbeat. It was heavier than usual—he felt the blood pumping in his arms, at the base of his skull.

As he focused, Cego began to see the darkness. Maybe it was in his mind—it certainly did not become lighter—yet he could see its form now, the empty corridor a flat plane in front of him.

Just as light has form, so does darkness, said Farmer.

Suddenly, the darkness was pierced by a glowing wisp igniting in front of Cego's eyes, casting shadows along the long stone walls. A spectral.

Though the wisp didn't look any different from the multitude floating across the Capital, Cego *knew* the spectral hovering in front of his face. It was the same spectral that had kept him company for so long in his little cell in the Deep. It was the same spectral that had appeared in Thaloo's yard on the day he'd faced off with Weep. This was *his* spectral. Cego could feel its light, like the warm embrace of an old friend.

The spectral slowly floated away from him, pulsing as if it were bidding him to follow.

"Where are you taking me, little one?" Cego whispered as he stepped forward. Speaking with the wisp again somehow felt right, and it certainly wasn't the strangest thing going on in the Trials.

As Cego moved farther down the corridor, he noticed a faint thumping. At first, he thought the rhythm was his own heightened heartbeat—he half expected some horror to leap from the shadows ahead. Cego realized the thumping wasn't coming from within, though. The webs along the wall were bouncing to the rhythm. The beat became louder as he continued; he felt the vibrations in the floor beneath him.

The little spectral stopped several meters ahead of Cego. The wisp cast its light on a dead end, a solid stone wall standing in his path. Was he trapped in here? Perhaps he'd missed some passage hidden by the thick cobwebs.

The spectral pulsed with urgency this time, getting brighter for a moment and then dimming as if it had exhausted its energy. The thumping was louder here. Cego felt the reverberations coming from beyond the wall. He stepped forward to stand beside the little wisp, placing his hand against the stone.

What he'd thought was a wall slid open with a sudden swish, showering Cego in light and noise.

Cego stepped forward as the spectral catapulted itself into the bright light. He watched as the wisp careened upward toward the blue above, joining thousands of other spectrals swirling across the sky like tufts of dandelion hair.

Cego lowered his gaze from the piercing blue sky and saw people everywhere, standing around him on elevated platforms, slamming their hands against the metal frames set in front of them.

Though the arena wasn't quite as big as Lampai, it was far louder. The sound was overbearing, as if the stadium itself had a heartbeat, a forceful pulse that Cego felt deep in his bones.

Cego peered into the stands, looking for any familiar faces. Was Murray up there somewhere, watching over him?

Cego directed his attention in front of him. A glistening steel Circle was planted at the center of the arena's dirt floor. It pulsed with a luminous blue glow. *Auralite alloy.*

A man, covered head to toe in a black second skin, stood at the center of the Circle.

The man's face was completely blanketed except for two yellow eyes burning from beneath his mask. Expressionless yet calculating. It was the same man Cego had faced moments ago in the gi. The same man who had crushed him against the ice.

Cego neared the Circle. Though he was familiar with auralite, this was different.

This Circle pulsed with the strength of a raging river, fed by the swarm of bluelight spectrals circling overhead. Even before he entered the Circle, Cego felt the pull of the crowd from around him, rhythmically slamming their hands against railings, urging him to spring forward and attack.

He stepped into the Circle, facing the man in black. It was hot, wherever he was. He could already feel beads of sweat forming on his brow.

"Strike me down," the man said in the same monotone voice.

Cego readied himself, his hands up by his chin. He shuffled toward his opponent across the Circle. The man raised his fists. He rotated slowly as Cego circled to his right and threw a few feinting jabs to gauge his reactions. Nothing. He didn't even flinch as the punches came within inches of his face.

Cego threw a low cross at the man's midsection, this time aiming to connect. His opponent shifted his hips back slightly to avoid it and followed with a lightning-fast counter jab. Cego barely turned his chin in time as the punch shaved his face, throwing him off-balance.

His opponent was a counterpuncher. He was baiting Cego's attack out and would respond with his own aggression. Farmer had played this same game. It was frustrating and required patience to overcome. Cego needed to attack, expect the counter, and then respond with a counter of his own. To succeed, he would need to be several steps ahead of his opponent.

"Strike me down," the man repeated.

Cego circled again, trying to look for some opening in the man's defense. He breathed out, steadying himself.

The rhythmic drumming of the crowd picked up pace. Cego attempted to ignore it, but the beat reverberated in his skull. He felt the impatience of the crowd, as if they were prodding him to move forward, to increase his tempo. Though he knew he shouldn't listen, he wanted to please them. He switched directions, circling to the man's left, then stopped and circled to the right. He shuffled his feet faster, moving back and forth, trying to catch the man off guard as he pivoted.

Cego jumped in and threw a quick inside leg kick, the same kick he had often employed against Masa during training. The man in black was lightning fast with his parry, bringing up his shin and angling his bone at Cego's own shin, pushing down right before impact. Cego felt an electric jolt shoot up his spine as their shins clashed. He stumbled backward and fell to one knee, his leg quivering. The man didn't even register the attack.

Cego knelt on the ground, trying to suck in a breath of the humid air. The beat of the crowd continued to heighten, getting louder and faster.

He got up and began to circle again. The man in black rotated, his defenses up. Cego desperately looked for an opening, his heart beating rapidly along with the crowd's clamor.

He threw a series of jabs again at the man, still not getting any reaction. He quick-stepped in and let a jab loose, following it with a cross. His opponent weaved his head, letting both punches slip by at the last moment. The man countered, a stiff jab of his own that smashed into Cego's nose with an explosion of white, then followed it with a roundhouse that clipped Cego's temple, sending him to the ground in a heap.

The arena spun around Cego, interspersed with flashes of light and the blur of the crowd.

Why was he here? To complete the Trials? To enter the Lyceum?

To become a Knight? The goals were distant now, like dreams fading in the sleepy seconds of waking.

Cego's vision steadied. His opponent stood before him, steadfast, unwavering, without any apparent chinks in his armor. The crowd got louder, as if they'd synced with the pulse of Cego's heart—every beat roared against the inside of his skull. Though he was beaten down and bloodied, he had to answer the crowd.

Cego slowly stood, his legs wavering.

It seemed impossible to even land one strike against such an opponent. The man's counterattacks were flawless. Every time Cego went on the offensive, the man retaliated with deadly precision.

Often, the fight is won before the first punch is thrown.

Farmer would emphasize that point before Cego's sparring sessions. He said that Cego's mindset going into a fight was as important as his physical conditioning or repertoire of techniques.

Before the first punch.

The crowd wanted him to attack. He felt it, as if he were a marionette dancing under their strings. Cego knew he must not listen to them. He needed to counter their influence and regain control of the situation. It was as much of a fight against the crowd as it was against the man standing across the Circle.

Cego stepped toward his opponent, his hands down at his side. He walked just out of the man's range and stopped in front of him. Cego stood completely still, staring at the man's blazing eyes. The crowd thundered around him, their rhythm urging him to move forward, to attack, and to win.

"Strike me down," the man said.

Cego breathed deeply, unmoving like his opponent. He focused on the spectral bluelight around him, soaking it in. He thought about Dozer and Knees—perhaps his two friends were facing the same unmovable opponent in their Trial. He thought about Murray, who truly believed in him, who had welcomed him into his home like family. He wouldn't let them down.

The crowd's roar quieted and the world around him dimmed. He saw only his opponent. Though the man did not move, Cego was mindful of every part of his body—ready to react to the slightest quiver.

Then, as if the man in black had snapped out of a deep slumber, he suddenly shot his leg forward into a push kick, aimed directly at Cego's midsection. Cego had forced the man to attack.

He couldn't completely evade the kick—it was far too fast—but he was able to suck in his stomach at the last moment to reduce the impact. He felt the ball of the man's foot blast into his lower rib cage. Something cracked.

Cego was the one ready to counter this time.

He wrapped the man's kicking foot up under one of his arms and dropped levels, hoisting the man's leg on top of his shoulder. Cego surged forward, throwing his opponent off-balance as he launched a cross at his face. The punch caught the man on the chin, though he barely registered it.

Cego let go of the leg and continued moving forward with a flurry of punches while he was inside the man's range. The man in black expertly bobbed and weaved, evading the punches easily.

Cego growled. If he couldn't hurt his opponent, he'd at least take something from him. He threw another jab, this time with an open hand. As the man weaved his head to the side, Cego grasped at the man's mask, getting ahold of the slick material and pulling his hand back. The mask came off.

Cego gasped, falling backward, away from the sight.

He didn't have time to get his hands up as the man moved in like a blur. A kick slammed into Cego's ribs, followed by a fist exploding against his temple. And then there was only darkness again.

* * *

Murray stared at the lightboard as Cego fell to the Guardian.

The look in the kid's eyes had been one of pure terror.

Now Cego needed to come to terms with the truth that the Trials weren't of this world—that he wasn't walking within the concrete walls of the Lyceum and battling flesh-and-blood opponents.

"Boy let curiosity get the best of 'im," Dakar slurred. "No one, 'specially not a kid, should have to come face-to-face with a Guardian."

"He needed better preparation. If he'd known about the true nature of the simulation, he could have readied himself for such an outcome," Callen said as he glanced smugly over at Murray from his seat.

"Each child needs a different sort of preparation, Commander Albright," Memnon interjected. "If Scout Pearson deemed it necessary to keep his talent in the dark on the true nature of the Trials, he must have had good reason to."

"Yes, yes. Of course, High Commander," Callen replied. "I was just saying that perhaps Murray's... talent was simply unprepared for the rigors that he would encounter in the Trials."

Murray couldn't hold out any longer. "Cego darkin' put his fist into the Guardian's face; did anyone else even see that? How many Trial-takers can you recall that did so?"

"Yes, and then he proceeded to completely let his defenses down, Scout Pearson. Your boy got picked apart like the swollen bit-purse of a nobleman wandering the hawkers' market." Callen spoke loudly enough for the entire room to hear. Scout Cydek snickered.

"Commander Farstead and the teachers of the Lyceum will be the judges of each child's performance. It is not for us to speculate upon," Memnon said with finality.

Murray fell back into silence, staring at the screen as the Arena simulation around Cego began to shimmer and fade. The screen was black for a moment before it lightened again, swelling to a hazy tangerine like the early moments of a dawning day.

Cego had scored highly enough to make it to the final stage of the Trials. The majority of the lightboards in the room were dark now; only a select group of kids had progressed this far.

Murray shivered as he thought about what was to come. The last stage of the Trials had broken many minds. Murray would never be able to dispel the image of Tarick's wide, empty eyes, the kid's body lying inert in the medward. Murray had done his best to prepare Cego for the Trial over the past month, but in the end, it would be the kid's own spirit that determined his success.

Murray had seen it in the Underground. He'd seen it during Cego's training in the barracks. Beyond the technique and endurance that were required of a Knight, the kid grasped something more—honor, sacrifice, spirit. The qualities the Codes emphasized, which were lacking in even some of the high-ranking Grievar around him.

Qualities that would desperately be needed in the days to come.

CHAPTER 12

Beneath the Surface

A Grievar shall make any worthy decision within the space of seven breaths. Indecision is the loose soil that stirs beneath the mountainous soul. It is better to take control of one's path decisively, without a mind fraught with the weakness of indecision.

Twentieth Precept of the Combat Codes

Cego floated in the inky darkness. There was nothing to see or grasp, no form or feeling to the empty space.

Perhaps he was dead. He could still remember the last Trial, though, the booming crowd, the man in black moving impossibly fast before Cego had ripped his mask off. What Cego had seen under that mask was burned into his mind: a void where a face should have been. Utter emptiness had stared back at him before that man, that creature, had struck out and sent the ground rushing up to meet him.

And then nothing. Cego had no idea how long he'd been in this darkness. Seconds or days—it didn't matter. Maybe this was death. Being left alone with your thoughts, forever drifting aimlessly.

But suddenly a familiar voice broke through the void, bringing Cego back. "I'm right here, can't you see me?"

Cego opened his eyes.

Clouds drifted lazily across cerulean skies. White flecks passed overhead. Birds.

Cego was lying on his back in the soft dirt. He held a hand to his forehead and winced as he touched a swelling hematoma, a reminder of the damage he'd taken in that noisy arena. It must have been just moments ago.

Another flock of birds passed above and Cego turned his head to track them, squinting into the bright sun. He breathed fresh, temperate air.

Cego didn't want to move. He wanted to stay flat on his back wherever he was, watching clouds and birds flying overhead. If he moved, he was afraid of what he would find in this new place, in this new Trial. He'd already been dragged from icy tundra to thundering arena and faced that terrifying man twice. Each time, the creature with blazing eyes had fought with a completely different style to dismantle Cego.

But Cego needed to move. They were watching. Murray was watching and Cego wouldn't let him down.

He slowly sat up, his entire body groaning with the effort. Green and brown surrounded him. Cego rubbed his eyes. He was in the center of a grove of trees, each planted only an inch or two apart, like bars on a cell.

These weren't just any trees, though. These were trees Cego was intimately familiar with: ironwoods. The Circle he'd trained in on the island had been made of ironwood. Every year, Farmer had instructed Cego and his brothers to cut several trees down from the forest, before smoothing, sanding, bending, and binding them together to form a new Circle.

And now, Cego seemed to be imprisoned within a tightly cropped thicket of ironwoods.

"Can't you see me?" A shadow abruptly flitted behind the trees. The same voice that had woken him to this place.

"Who's there?" Cego spun around in the dirt. It must have been the creature he'd fought in the previous two Trials. Except this time, his opponent wasn't out in the open, he was hidden.

Cego stood and walked in silence toward one side of the grove of ironwoods. He placed a hand against a tree, rubbing it up and down the smooth grain. He could smell the sour sap, amber streaks of it running down the trunk. He thought of the countless hours he'd spent kicking ironwoods with Sam and Silas on the island.

Your shins need to become as hard as these trees, Farmer had always said. *Iron sharpens iron.*

Though Sam would easily tire of the drills and drift off to watch the family of ferrcats that had made a nest in one of the canopies, Cego and Silas would compete to fell their ironwoods, repeatedly slamming kicks against them until one snapped.

Perhaps that was the goal of this Trial. Kick his way out of an ironwood prison.

He walked back to the center of the grove, standing on the mound of soft dirt and turning in a circle. These ironwoods were young, too smooth and flexible to climb. And they were planted too closely together to squeeze through. Knocking them down seemed the only option.

Cego certainly couldn't sit here and wait. This was his Trial and he was expected to take action.

Back on the island, Cego had the space to get the full force of a round kick. He'd swivel his hips and send his foot out in a wide arc, finding the same spot over and over to slowly weaken a tree, just as he'd been taught to break down an opponent's leg. But in this Trial, the trees were only inches apart, barely enough room to wedge his foot between.

Cego breathed out slowly before ripping a kick into one of

the trees. His foot found the target but slid across the trunk and scraped against two others, shearing a bit of bark off along with a swath of his skin. Cego winced, looking down at his bleeding foot. During training on the island, his feet and shins would often end up bloody messes. That hadn't stopped him then. He'd kept kicking until Silas won the contest.

Cego tried again with another round kick, this time successfully planting his foot between two of the trunks. But his aim was too good; his foot lodged in the gap and he felt his knee strain. Cego instinctively rolled forward with the momentum to remove his foot and prevent his knee from getting torqued. He landed on his back in the dirt.

He exhaled slowly, looking up at the sky again. Round kicks wouldn't work. Not enough room.

Cego stood and changed his strategy, this time aiming a front kick at the same ironwood with a scrape on its trunk. He hit the tree with the heel of his foot and felt the shock wave run up his leg. He tried again in the same spot. And again, this time kicking even harder and bouncing backward.

Though front kicks were powerful, the technique did little to snap the sinews of the sapling. The trees were so close together, and with their canopies entwined above, they seemed to absorb the impact jointly.

He stood back, breathing hard.

Cego felt frustration simmer in him. Though he knew he'd only attempted several tries so far, it already felt as if he'd been fighting these trees the entire day.

He craned his head toward the sun in the sky. It hadn't moved.

Cego needed to generate more force. He eyed the scraped spot on the tree before spinning on his heels and hurling a side kick into the trunk. He found his mark but bounced off again and landed in the dirt in a heap.

The tree hadn't taken the slightest damage. Cego knew what it felt like to make progress in breaking down an ironwood, and this wasn't it.

Exasperation began to well up in him. The creature he'd fought in the two other Trials was absent. And though Cego had been defeated so soundly, he now wished the thing were here with him. At least then, he'd have a physical opponent to take on instead of an empty grove of ironwoods.

"I'm right here." A voice came from the treetops, seeming to respond to his thoughts.

Cego wheeled around. He saw a shadow flicker behind the small gaps between the trees again.

"Who's there?" Cego yelled. "Show yourself!"

There was no response but the faraway squawk of another bird passing overhead.

Cego sat in the dirt, trying to calm himself. Whatever the point of this Trial was, he knew getting upset would do him no favors. And he knew this place was not normal. Cego had witnessed the void behind the creature's mask. He'd woken up in one strange environment after another without understanding how he got there. Cego didn't understand what the Trials were, but he knew they were watching him. The Lyceum administration would see his panic, his anger, his heart beating rapidly in his chest.

Cego assumed the cross-legged lotus position the old master had shown him to practice ki-breath. He would not show them his frustration, though he felt it festering. He would wait for his opponent to come to him in this Trial.

You will feel pain after sitting so long, Farmer had always said. *It will not be the pain of a well-placed strike to the chin, or a thudding knee to the ribs. No, the pain of sitting and waiting will be far worse. It will be the pain from not knowing what comes next.*

Cego sat with his eyes open, letting his gaze become unfocused, the ironwoods in front of him blurring as he heard Farmer's words echo in his mind.

But there is nothing to wait for. There is no future, no next moment. Those are creations within your mind. Here and now are your only reality.

Cego breathed deeply. He felt his diaphragm swell in and out, just as he'd practiced on the black sand beach for so many years. He followed his breath, tracing it up and down his spine. He felt every tingling sensation across his body, the pain searing his back from the throws to the ice and the sting of the punches he'd taken in the arena. But that pain was in Cego's mind, just like the next moment.

He could endure each single moment, stay afloat on each wave that passed beneath him. Cego knew it was the thought of the next moment and the suffering that was to come that would drown him. He would only be here and now.

As he breathed, he saw the sun rise high above him before it sank behind the ironwoods in a crimson swell. A glowing moon climbed into a darkened sky dotted with stars; then dawn broke and sent the sun streaking above Cego's head again.

* * *

Murray stared at Cego's lightboard in disbelief. Everyone else in the room was also watching his board, their eyes glued to Cego as he sat in the grove of ironwoods.

Murray had no idea how the kid was doing this. In this final Trial, time was the taker's enemy. Time, which won over everything in the end, was distorted in this simulation; it would seem to stop altogether or move incredibly fast. Days could pass in what seemed like moments, or single seconds could last for weeks. Most takers lost their minds almost immediately upon entering the Time Trial.

Callen Albright was looking over at Murray, his face contorted in anger. Murray knew what the Scout commander was thinking—that somehow, Murray and Cego had cheated.

That was impossible, though. Murray had no idea how Cego was doing this either. The kid was sitting calmly as hours and days flowed over him like a boulder lodged in a stream. As Murray looked at the boards across the room, he saw that most of the kids had already been carried away by that rushing stream of time.

The purelight from the Underground, Shiar, had found a rock in the dirt and hammered it into one of the ironwood trees for several seconds before falling to his knees and weeping uncontrollably. Dozer had charged the trees repeatedly until he dropped onto his back, laughing like a madman, unable to even stop and breathe. Knees had screamed in terror while trying to cover his face from some invisible attacker. Even Gryfin Thurgood, a purelight from the Twelve, had succumbed to the Time Trial in mere moments, curling into a ball in the dirt. It was only Cego and the bald boy, Shimo, who were sitting calmly, unaffected by the hallucinations that came with time distortion.

Murray shook his head again. It didn't make sense that Cego would know how to handle the blacklight. His mind raced. Luck was out of the question—there was no way Cego could chance upon such resistance techniques.

Even if the kid had somehow known about the Sim beforehand and studied intensely, he wouldn't have had this result. Some purelight families with the resources tried to prepare their kids with stories and details from the memories of those who had already gone through the Time Trial, but even then, the kids were equally as incompetent when faced with the real thing.

Murray continued to watch with wide eyes as Cego's chest rose and fell.

Callen Albright suddenly stood. High Commander Memnon was moving for the doorway, nodding for him to follow. Albright gave Murray another derisive look before following Memnon out of the viewing room.

They knew something.

Murray wanted to go after them, but he couldn't leave Cego alone. He stared back at the screen. No matter how the kid had managed to stay sane so far in this Trial, Murray knew it wouldn't last. In the end, time caught everyone.

* * *

Over and over, the sun rose and fell in the sky. Darkness dropped and dissipated again with each new day. The heavens swirled above Cego, and yet he sat, breathing, only living in each single moment. He didn't pay heed to the hunger pangs striking at his stomach or the amplified ache vibrating through his body. He sat for days, perhaps weeks, just breathing.

But finally, a small voice infiltrated Cego's mind despite his focus, like a thief breaking into an empty house.

"I'm right here, can't you hear me?"

Cego broke from his reverie with the moon directly overhead and the sky full of sparkling stars. The ironwoods stood steadfast in front of him.

"Why aren't you listening to me?" The voice came from behind the trees again. "I'm right here. Can't you come with me to catch the blue crabs by the water?"

Cego knew the voice now. It was unmistakable. His little brother, Sam.

He stood, his body creaking like an unused mech as he moved toward the ironwoods. Even in the darkness, he could see a deep shadow lingering behind the trees.

"Come with me just for a little bit," Sam's voice pleaded. "Farmer won't even know we're missing practice."

"Sam," Cego shouted. He grasped the trees and pressed his face against them. "Where are you?"

"I'm right here," Sam responded. Cego watched as a shadow slid up the tree trunk in front of him and wavered there, waiting. Cego reached out and touched it. The shadow felt warm, like a hand. Sam's hand.

"Why aren't you coming?" Sam asked as the shadow withdrew from Cego's grasp and fled back beyond the trees.

"I don't know where you are, Sam," Cego responded desperately. "I don't know how to get to you."

"I'm right in front of you..." Sam said, though his voice seemed more distant now. "I need your help, please."

"Sam!" Cego screamed. He needed to get through these trees.

Cego slammed his fist against the hard bark in front of him over and over, trying to break through the ironwood prison. Even when his skin had been sheared from his knuckles, Cego kept ripping punches into the tree trunk. Though he saw the white gleam of bone protruding from his hand, Cego didn't stop. When his arms finally gave way, Cego used his head, slamming the crown of his skull into the tree repeatedly until he staggered backward.

"Sam!" Cego wept, his tears melding with his blood in the dirt. He knew his brother was gone; the shadow behind the trees had disappeared along with the voice. Cego's body shuddered as he lay on his back beneath the stars. His breathing was no longer steady—each pull of air was a ragged effort. The weariness of sitting and fighting and being imprisoned in this place sank into Cego all at once.

He was nearly ready to give in when he felt something beneath his outstretched hand. A strange indentation beneath the dirt. Cego sat back up and began to dig on his hands and knees until he grasped on to a cold, metallic object. He brushed the dirt aside to reveal a sliver of black. Even in the darkness, the black thing he'd unearthed somehow shimmered.

Cego frantically dug at the object. He slowly uncovered a form, like excavating the bones of some ancient beast.

Finally, Cego stood and looked at what he'd found, surrounding him. A black Circle, glimmering like wet coal. Shadows seemed to rise and fall from the strange material and the starlight from above vanished into its inky surface.

Onyx. Cego knew the alloy, though he'd never seen it before, never fought in it, only heard it talked about in whispers. This entire Trial, he'd been within the bounds of an onyx Circle.

Cego glanced back at the ironwoods and saw the trees were changing. They were sickly now, withering and turning the color of rot in front of Cego's eyes. The shadows from the onyx were spreading like a mist through the ironwoods and pooling above Cego. The bright moon had disappeared, replaced by an impenetrable black blanket descending on him.

The darkness pulled at Cego and he screamed, but no sound emerged. Shadows slithered into his open mouth, filled his nostrils and ears, blotted out his eyes. And then, once again, there was nothing.

* * *

Murray stepped up to the door of High Commander Memnon's private office, unannounced. Not many in the Citadel would consider such a breach of protocol, but Murray didn't care. He needed to get some answers. He set his eye in front of the lightdeck planted in the door and let it scan him. The shouting inside the office quieted immediately.

After a few moments, the door swished open. Callen Albright was sitting in Memnon's office, as Murray had expected. The two looked like they'd been having a heated discussion—Memnon was standing over Callen, his eyes fiery. Albright flashed that smug grin that made Murray want to put his head through the adjacent shield window.

"Scout Pearson, I don't believe you had an appointment with the high commander," Callen said.

"Did you have an appointment, Commander Callen?" Murray retorted.

"No...but I am—"

Memnon cut Callen off. "Dark this appointment talk. Scout Pearson, your arrival is actually timely. We have some questions for you."

"Questions for *me*?" Murray asked incredulously. "I'm here because I have questions for you. What happened in the Sim?"

"What did happen in the Sim, Pearson? Something your commanders should be aware of perhaps?" Callen fished.

"I'm not here to play mind games with you, Commander Albright," Murray said. He turned away from the wiry Grievar and addressed Memnon directly. "Be straight with me, High Commander. I've only ever done such with you. I know something is going on—whatever happened with Cego in that Sim was not normal. The way he was able to endure the Time Trial, the way he took the blacklight from the onyx. It doesn't make sense."

Memnon met Murray's eyes. Murray could see the wear on the high commander's face. He looked tired, as if he'd aged a decade since Murray had last spoken with him.

Memnon and Coach had come up in the Citadel together. They'd been practically brothers, fighting on the same team throughout their Knight service. Coach had been offered the commander position first but turned it down, saying he wasn't a politik, he was a Grievar. Memnon had been second choice and found himself as high commander within five years. Coach stayed on as head trainer of the Knights.

At first, the two had worked well together, Coach coordinating his program to complement Memnon's vision: training a team of Knights that was well rounded, made of Grievar who could fight and win in any climate or Circle.

Soon, though, Murray could remember Coach muttering about Memnon getting in the way of him doing his job, saying the Citadel was heading down a path he didn't like. Part of the rift between the two had developed because of the neurostimulants circulating in the team—Coach couldn't get behind that. But there was more to it, something that drove the two friends even further apart.

Eventually, Coach wouldn't even mention Memnon's name, as if saying it out loud would sully the Codes. It wasn't too long afterward that Coach had disappeared.

"Scout Pearson. I understand your concern for your talent. But you dishonor us by implying that we know more about this situation than you do," Memnon said pointedly.

Dishonor? Murray had the mind to say a thing or two about darkin' honor right here in the high commander's office, but he held his tongue.

"We need you to answer some questions for us so that we can appropriately deal with this situation," Memnon said.

"What do you mean, *deal with*? Cego didn't do anything; he doesn't deserve any—"

"Don't worry. Your talent will remain safe at study in the Lyceum. As I said, though, to deal with this situation, we need you to answer a few questions." Memnon waved toward a chair in front of him.

Murray slowly slid into the seat. Callen stood next to Memnon. Somehow, this had turned into an interrogation.

"Go ahead, Callen, ask your questions." Memnon sighed.

Callen paced in front of Murray with his hands clasped behind his back. "Where did you first discover your talent, this boy... Cego?" he asked.

"Don't you already know the answer to that? It's all reported in my Scout's log."

"Perhaps you decided to leave out some integral details. After all, we all know you've never been the most fastidious Scout. You aren't known for your attention to detail," Callen said.

Murray let the insult slide by as if he were slipping a punch. "I saw him fighting in Thaloo Jakabar's Circle off Markspar Row, Underground," he answered.

"And what about this lacklight boy piqued your interest?"

"I may not be the most *detail-oriented* Scout, but I know fighting. I saw that Cego had potential. The way he moved, the way he handled the light. He also took to the Codes, something we don't see much of anymore in these halls," Murray said, looking directly into Memnon's eyes, searching for a reaction.

Was that a flash of anger? Or perhaps resentment? The high commander looked out the window.

"And perhaps you could refresh the high commander on how Cego came into your possession?" Callen asked as he continued to pace in front of Murray's seat.

"Thaloo would not grant me patron rights for the bit-purse I was allotted by the Scouts, so I decided I'd strike a deal to fight for him at Lampai. I won, and here we are," Murray said flatly.

"Ah. It all sounds so simple, doesn't it?" Callen cooed sarcastically. "What a miraculous story. You came upon this undervalued lacklight urchin fighting in the Deep, and you simply knew all of a sudden that you had a gem in your hands. So much so that you said, 'I'm going to come out of a decade-long retirement just to fight for him.'"

"You've got it," Murray said.

"You've got some nerve, coming into the high commander's office and lying—"

Murray stood up abruptly, his eyes flashing at the wiry Scout commander. Memnon stepped between the two.

"Now that I've answered your questions, answer mine. What the dark is going on here?" Murray growled.

Memnon looked Murray in the eye. "As with everything we do here, we're working for the good of the nation. We're trying to improve our Grievar program here at the Citadel, Scout Pearson," Memnon said.

"Trying to improve your Grievar again, Memnon?" Murray asked. "First it was neuros, then the Scouts, then the Sim. How could you possibly stray further from the Codes?"

"Scout Pearson, stand down," Memnon said.

Murray stayed on his feet, face-to-face with Memnon. His muscles were still tense. What was he going to do? Take a shot at the high commander of the Citadel? Coach certainly wanted to all those years ago. Perhaps he'd be doing his mentor a favor.

"What do you have to hide?" Murray asked, his face inches from Memnon's. "What new ways have you found to give in to the demands of the Daimyo, to further erode our honor? I want to hear it from you—not your yapping bayhound here."

Memnon didn't budge, eyes level with Murray's. The two men were roughly equal-sized. "Stand down, Scout Pearson," he said again.

"I've hit a nerve here, haven't I? Is this why Coach was so darkin' pissed all those years ago? Somethin' you politiks are cooking up here?"

"Stand down, Scout Pearson," Memnon growled.

"If I can't get answers from you, I'll get them my own way," Murray said. He turned and walked back through the sliding doors.

* * *

Murray strode briskly into the Lyceum's ample medward, the largest in the Citadel, which served the entire Grievar population.

Murray watched the clerics moving around the room with a mixture of fascination and disgust. Usually, they kept to the cover of their thick red cloaks outside, but here in the medward, they stood boldly, wearing sleeveless tunics and silken pants.

He could best describe the clerics as sickly. At least in his approximation—a healthy, robust Grievar was heavily muscled, thick-boned, with skin rough from wear like a suit of armor.

These Daimyo were quite the opposite. Their skin was paper-thin, the veins beneath clearly visible, streaking their faces, necks, and arms like spiderwebs. They looked like brittle sticks; Murray had no doubt he could snap one of them in half with little effort.

But they certainly got the job done. Murray had experienced the clerics' work at the Lyceum firsthand—he'd been badly injured numerous times along his lightpath. There were times when Murray was sure he was done, his path ended due to a shattered collarbone, a smashed kneecap, even a spinal injury that left him paralyzed for several weeks. The clerics had brought him back from that.

Though they were technically Daimyo by blood, the clerics were different from the gaudy nobles that Murray was used to seeing, parading like kings on the Underground's thoroughfares. The clerics oversaw their patients without emotion, their probing faces bathed in the light of nearby hovering spectrals. There was no cooing or soothing bedside manner with them. They determined the root of the problem and fixed it. If there was an injury or malady they could not fix, they moved on to the next patient with cool indifference.

Murray passed Lyceum students and Knights in various states of injury, ranging from torn ankle ligaments to Grievar near death. Murray shivered as he glanced over at a battered Knight floating in a vat of inky red liquid, his neck twisted at a strange angle. Murray had been there before; it wasn't pretty.

Murray examined the faces of each of the injured Grievar as he passed. He was here for Cego.

He recognized Scout Cydek's purelight talent—Shiar—sitting in a small cot with his arms crossed behind his head. "More water, and where is that omelet I asked for?" The little shit was shouting at the clerics who were attending him, as if the medward were some sort of luxury inn. Cego would be nearby.

Murray found Cego several cots down. The kid was sitting up against the wall, focused on the window across from him, where the rain was pattering against the glass.

"Seems like we've been here before, huh, kid?" Murray sat awkwardly in a small chair next to the cot.

Cego didn't respond; he continued to stare blankly out at the rain. Deep rings hung beneath his golden eyes.

Murray knew how it was. Having reality distorted. Thinking certain rules applied to the world around you and then having those rules broken—the world permanently altered. Cego's mind would need time to heal properly.

"I wanted to tell you about the Sim beforehand. But it wouldn't have done you any good in there," Murray said.

Cego didn't respond. Murray hadn't even seen the kid blink yet.

"I know things seem darked up right now. What's real and what's not. But I can tell you something that's real. You passed."

Cego's eyes focused, his pupils dilating. He looked toward Murray. "I passed?"

"I'd bet Violet on it that you did," Murray said. "Kid, your performance in there was...extraordinary."

Cego looked back out the window. The two sat for several minutes, the rain filling the silence.

Murray broke the silence. "I know you probably want to forget the entire darkin' thing, but I have to ask. How did you do it?"

Cego looked over at him, his eyes flashing back and forth. The kid knew something. He was deciding whether he could trust Murray.

"I understand. You can't trust everyone. Can't trust most modernday, even here in the Citadel. I'm on your side, though," Murray whispered.

Cego nodded slowly as he began to speak, his voice raspy. "It's hard to explain...I'm afraid I might sound crazy."

"I've seen and done some crazy things in my years, kid—don't worry," Murray said.

Cego breathed out, then whispered, "I heard him, Murray-Ku. My little brother, Sam. I heard him in there. He needed my help."

"You're not the first," Murray said. "That Trial does things to your mind. Makes you lose track of past and present, mushes it all together. I'm not surprised you heard your brother's voice."

"But..." Cego trailed off. "Sam was there. I felt him, he was so real."

"I know," Murray said. "Your brother was real to you. Just like the Guardian was real when you were facing him in each of the other Trials."

"The Guardian?" Cego asked. "You mean...that creature I fought?"

"Yes," Murray said. "You weren't supposed to see what was behind that mask. But they use the Guardian to test each taker's weaknesses. To see how someone stacks up against impossible odds. And you did things in there that I've never seen before, even after having watched over a decade of Trials."

"I just used what I learned," Cego said. "What you taught me."

Murray chuckled. "You're too darkin' nice, kid. Yeah, we had some good lessons in my barracks, but what you did in the Trials, you certainly didn't learn from me. In that last Trial, we haven't seen anyone able to take the blacklight like that... ever."

"The blacklight," Cego said softly. "You mean those shadows... coming off the onyx Circle."

"Right, those shadows were blacklight spectrals," Murray said. "And most of the other Trial-takers lasted about a full breath in there with them. You sat for nearly an hour."

"It seemed longer than an hour," Cego said. The kid looked tired, and he had a right to be.

"That's what the blacklight will do," Murray said. "But how did you learn how to handle it?"

Cego took a deep breath as he stared back out the window, watching the rain. Minutes passed and Murray worried he'd lost the kid again, but Cego suddenly started to speak. "Where I'm from, my home, I lived on an island with my two brothers. We were raised by an old man... He was our master. He taught us to fight, but he also taught us to sit and breathe. Sometimes for an entire day, we'd sit on the black sand beach, breathing with the waves as they rolled in and went back out to the sea."

It was the most Murray had heard Cego speak of his home.

"Sam was always terrible at ki-breath." A tired smile creased Cego's face. "He wouldn't be able to sit more than two minutes before he was running down the beach."

"I think I'd likely be doing the same," Murray muttered, having never had the patience for any sort of meditative practice.

"Silas, though, he could sit for the entire day." Cego's smile had disappeared. "Silas would even sit through the night when storms came to shore and battered him. He wouldn't move an inch."

"And you?" Murray asked.

"Silas was always better at everything. Fighting, hunting, swimming, ki-breath, it didn't matter. He'd always win," Cego said. "I could never find a path to beat him."

"Based on what I just saw during your Trial, I think you found your path just darkin' fine," Murray said. "Seems like you got some good training on this island."

Cego nodded, his eyelids fluttering with fatigue.

Murray's mind swirled. There were thousands of little isles floating in the Emerald Sea; the kid could have been raised and trained on any one of them. It wasn't unusual for ex-Knights or mercs to train Grievar brood with the hopes of selling them to the highest bidder. But that didn't answer the question of how he'd just handled the Trials so well.

"Cego," Murray said. "I haven't prodded, because I know our pasts can be shit. I certainly have much of my own I'd rather not speak of. And it's really none of my darkin' business where you come from. But I need to know one thing. How did you end up in the Underground? Who took you from your home?"

Cego slumped back into his cot. The kid was exhausted.

"I don't remember," Cego said.

"You don't remember who brought you there?" Murray asked.

"No…" Cego said. "I don't remember anything. There was my home on the island. And then there were the streets of the Underground. Everything between those two places…I can't remember. When I try to, it's like I'm grasping at a dream just after waking up, and it slips away."

Murray met Cego's eyes. He was straining to remember. He was telling the truth.

The rain fell harder outside the window.

"I'm sorry," Cego said. His breathing had grown deep, as if he were sleeping with his eyes open.

"Why should you be sorry?" Murray shook his head. "You've got nothing to apologize for. You did great in the Trials. I was proud."

The kid had much ahead of him. Though the Trials were complete, Cego was at the start of a long journey. He needed to focus on moving forward. He couldn't be bogged down by his past, whatever its nature.

"Don't worry about this stuff, kid," Murray said reassuringly. "I'll look into it. I'll figure this out for you, I promise. You just need to focus on where you're at. I'd bet my life you passed the Trials. You're to be one of a select few in Ezo to enter the Lyceum. You'll train to become a Knight. You need to focus on your studies. And you need to get some rest," Murray said.

Cego eyes fluttered closed. "Thank you, Murray-Ku."

CHAPTER 13

The Harmony and the Valkyrie

When attempting to finish the triangle choke, a Grievar can easily tire. With a finish at hand, one risks extinguishing their ki by utilizing weak adductor muscles to attack the neck of an opponent squarely in front of them. One must instead find the proper angle prior to attempting the finish, perpendicular to the opponent, while utilizing the far stronger gluteal muscles to constrict the exposed arteries.

Passage Four, Fifty-Third Technique of the Combat Codes

Cego spent four days in the medward. He mostly stared out the window, watching the rain. He tried not to think too much about the Trials or any of the confounding questions that had come from them. It hurt his head too much to do so.

One of the clerics, a lithe girl with inky pools for eyes and straight black hair, stopped by to check on Cego a few times per day. The girl never said anything. She only stared, her face awkwardly close to his at times. Cego saw the blood flowing beneath her translucent cheeks, traveling down her neck in narrow blue rivulets. Her breath was warm.

The girl examined him with cool indifference and took notes on the lightpad strapped to one of her wrists.

At first, Cego was amazed to see a small red spectral hovering just over the girl's shoulder. When the girl examined him, her little spectral would float across Cego's body, as if it were observing the spots she was concentrating on.

Every so often, a senior cleric would stop by to check on the girl's work—a man with a round, bald head with thick veins running atop it. The man would review her lightpad and then ask the girl several questions Cego didn't understand.

"Base photosensitivity?" he asked.

"No movement," she replied in a blank voice.

"Spectroscopy levels?"

"No signs of differentiation."

"Signs of neuropathic schizophrenia?"

"Rapid eye movement standardized during sleep; no emotive elevation during waking hours."

On his fourth day in the medward, Cego made an attempt to speak with the cleric girl. After his experience in the simulation, he felt the need to reassure himself that the world he occupied was the real thing. He'd spoken with Murray earlier, but that was different. Murray was somehow a part of it all—the Citadel, the Lyceum, the Trials, the Sim. He needed to speak with someone who wasn't a part of it.

The girl came by in the morning as she had done the previous four days, her little crimson spectral in tow just over her shoulder.

"Does... does he follow you everywhere you go?" Cego asked.

Though she didn't stop examining him, she replied. Her voice was monotone. "What makes you think it is a *he*?" she asked.

"Hmm. I'm really not sure," Cego responded. "He... er... *it* looked like a he to me."

"Typical Grievar," the girl said. "Always assigning emotional value to everything."

Cego considered her words. "Well, you seem pretty happy with the spectral yourself. You keep checking to see if he... or *it's* there."

"You mistake my vigilance for what you call happiness, Grievar," she said blandly. "I'm making sure my Observer is functioning properly."

"Observer? Isn't it a spectral?"

"Correct, it is a spectral, one born of the redlight. But more specifically it is an Observer, assigned to a neophyte such as myself for research aid. We clerics have further classified our spectrals beyond their base wavelengths to include function, reactivity, and life span, among other data points. In the medical science, classification and specification are integral," she said.

Cego gave her a confused look.

"Ah, yes, I forget I am speaking to a Grievar, where such knowl edge is void. How can I term it properly for your limited understanding?" Though the words coming out of the girl's mouth sounded insulting, she didn't have a hint of malice in her eyes.

"Specification and classification are as important to clerics as... punching and kicking are for Grievar. Was that the proper analog to your own lightpath?" she asked.

Cego chuckled. "Well, yes. Good enough. Don't forget that we Grievar also specify, just in different ways. You might think of punching and kicking broadly, but we're thinking about the details of the movement. Like a jab is a specific type of punch, and even within that classification, it can be broken down into more specifics—how to clench the fist properly, the twist of the feet, the hip movement, extending the arm fully and rotating the shoulder, pulling the second hand up for cover, snapping the fist back. Just for starters," Cego explained.

The girl nodded. "I see. Perhaps I should reconsider my base description of your... fighting techniques. Though I still do not see the need for such emotive assignment like your sexual classification of my Observer here," she said.

Cego laughed—was that supposed to be a joke? He found her blunt manner of speaking refreshing. With a Grievar, he'd have to look between the words for meaning. Read a person's eyes and body for emotion—whether it be anger, deception, or hostility. With this girl, it was all laid out in front of him.

"Agreed. It's an it," Cego said, watching the spectral's red, dancing light. He thought of his own spectral, the little wisp that had appeared to help him during his recent Trials. "How long have you had it?"

"My Observer has been with me for three months and five days now," she replied.

"How does it know to follow you around like that?" Cego asked with genuine curiosity.

"Observers are programmed to follow every neophyte cleric at the start of their fellowship," she stated.

"Fellowship?"

"This is the period where a cleric begins their live studies in a field of specialty. In my case, this field is Grievar orthopedic, muscular, and neurological reparation and rehabilitation."

Cego again gave her a confused look.

"How shall I say it for you to understand? Let us see. I am studying here to...fix...Grievar, like you, who have returned physically or neurologically damaged from combat. In your case, we are studying the potential adverse neurological effects of your time in the simulation."

"Have you fixed me yet?" Cego asked, half joking, though the girl took his question with a deathly seriousness.

"This medward at the Lyceum is one of the premier facilities in Ezo, if not on the planet. I am studying under High Cleric Azeeth Despithi, who is often considered to be the brightest mind in the field of Grievar...fixing. If you have any neurological damage that is within our abilities to diagnose and repair, it shall be done," she said with apparent pride, despite the lack of emotion in her voice.

Cego nodded. For some reason, he felt safe speaking his mind to this girl. "So, you're here for the same reason I am. I'm here at the Lyceum to study under the best Grievar in the world. To perfect my combat skills and become a Knight. And you're here to study under the best clerics in the world to perfect your healing skills."

She brought her face awkwardly close to Cego's again, her black eyes boring into his. "Yes, I see the analog you are making, Grievar. I would agree; we are here for similar reasons, though certainly not the same."

"Either way, it's good to know someone else is in the same boat I am," Cego said. "My name is Cego. Thank you for your help."

For a moment, the girl appeared surprised at Cego's gratitude, as if she'd never heard anything like it before. "It is my lightpath, not my choice, to help those such as you, Griev... Cego," she said the name awkwardly. "Though your thanks is well taken," she added.

"And your name is?" Cego asked.

"Xenalia," she replied briskly as she turned away. "I hope I do not see you here at the medward again, Cego. Though I highly doubt that will be the case. Here in the Citadel, Grievar always seem to find a way to damage themselves..."

Xenalia walked away, her little spectral trailing behind her.

* * *

It was the day of selection.

Murray met Cego first thing in the morning at the medward, located next to the base of the Knight Tower. The two walked back across the yard toward the Valkyrie, where the selection of the final twenty-four would take place. The rain had subsided momentarily and given way to a thick white fog that crept along the yard, clinging to the edges of the stone structures.

When they arrived, the Valkyrie's wide rotunda was not nearly as crowded as it had been before the Trials. Many of the kids from the commencement had been trimmed out, either because they had outright failed or because they were unable to attend the selection due to sustained neurological damage within the Sim.

There was a nervous energy within the room. Parents were boasting of their kids' performances to each other, and the Scouts in attendance were already chatting about what they'd do with the extra bit-purse they'd receive if one of their picks made it through.

Though Cego tried to separate himself from the buzz, he couldn't help but feel a nervous twinge in his stomach. He was worried about Dozer and Knees. Or maybe he was worried about himself. Since reuniting with his friends, he had pictured attending the Lyceum with them. Cego couldn't imagine entering alone, along with the group of purelights from the Twelve who would surely make it through.

Cego glanced around the room, looking for either of his friends. He saw the huge bulk of the boy from the borderlands, still escorted by two mercs. He caught sight of Shiar out of the corner of his eye, consorting with the same group of purelights he'd seen earlier during the Trial's commencement. Solara Halberd was standing by herself several paces from the purelight pack. Cego stared for a moment.

He noticed a big shadow by one of the pillars across the room. Cego told Murray he'd be back and walked toward the pillar. Broad shoulders swaying back and forth, a foot nervously drumming against the floor—it had to be Dozer.

Cego crept behind Dozer and slowly pushed his foot against the back of his friend's knee, lowering the big Grievar to arm level, and started to snake his wrist across Dozer's thick neck. Dozer quickly grabbed Cego's arm and swiveled around to face him.

Cego smiled and slapped his friend on the shoulder. "Nice choke defense!"

A wide smile creased Dozer's face, and he pulled Cego in for his standard bear hug.

"Nice to see a familiar...well, familiar *and* friendly face round here," Dozer said, looking warily over at the exclusive group congregated in the center of the room.

"Knees?" Cego asked, though he was afraid to know the answer.

Dozer looked at the floor, tapping his foot nervously. "I don't know...I heard he had it pretty rough in there. I asked about him and they said he was taken down to the medward in the Capital's dregs—the Lyceum's ward was full already."

Cego felt his face flush. He'd been given preference over his friends again, getting a spot at the nearby medward while Knees had to be taken outside the Citadel into the dregs. He was probably getting treated alongside all the cleaver addicts out there.

"He'll make it here," Cego said with determination. "He's made it this far; he wouldn't let anything stop him now."

"I hope so," Dozer said.

"How about you? Did you need any treatment afterward?" Cego asked, trying to get Dozer's mind off Knees.

The big Grievar smiled, showing his crooked yellow teeth. "Nope! Just been holed up in the Lyceum for three days now."

"What? How'd you do it—did you know it was all a Sim beforehand?" Cego asked.

"Didn't know anything," Dozer said proudly. "I mean, I got beat up pretty bad in there, but now I feel fine. Someone tried to explain it to me...but I had a hard time understanding 'em."

Cego was astonished. He couldn't help but chuckle at his large friend's complete lack of awareness, which in the end appeared to have saved him from any mental scarring. Dozer wasn't thinking about what was real, his purpose here, or anything that deep. Dozer was...Dozer. Cego could learn something from him.

The two boys returned to Murray's side.

Murray nodded at Dozer. "Glad to see you made it through, big guy."

"Thanks, Mighty...er, sir...Murray." Dozer fumbled with his attempts at formality.

A smile broke across Murray's face for the first time that day. "Just Murray will do."

"Murray," Dozer said affirmatively.

The three stood quietly for several moments as the hall continued to fill. It was almost time. Dozer stared at the entrance like a sad pup—still no Knees.

The room suddenly hushed as Commander Aon Farstead and several other Grievar stepped onto the balcony above. Murray whispered to the boys, "Those are the Lyceum's professors—and the judges of the Trials."

Commander Farstead pulled a long paper scroll from the podium and brushed his fingers across it.

Cego glanced back at the entrance and saw a solitary figure slowly walking in. Knees.

He tapped Dozer on the shoulder to get his attention, and the big boy nearly jumped into the air in excitement. Their enthusiasm quickly waned when they saw the state Knees was in.

Though he didn't appear to have any physical injuries—the Venturian boy might as well have been through a war. His face was pale and huge circles ringed his eyes. He walked toward them slowly, tenderly, as if his body were injured. Knees lacked the mischievous glint in his eyes and the crooked smile that Cego had become accustomed to.

Dozer pulled Knees into a hefty hug that he gingerly accepted. The Venturian pulled up next to Cego. Cego grasped his wrist and nodded—silently saying that he understood what Knees had been through. Knees nodded back at him blankly.

The three companions stood together, ready for the selection.

Aon Farstead's voice echoed off the tall chamber walls. "Greetings, Trial-takers, families, and all Citadelians in attendance," Aon said. "This year's Trials have completed, and we have chosen our class of twenty-four."

The room was deathly quiet. Even the purelights shut up in anticipation of the selection.

Aon continued. "This year's Trials were unique. Extraordinary, really. I truly believe this class to be the Citadel's best over the past several decades—and that includes classes with some our most notable Knights of recent times, with the likes of Derondal Markspar, Artemis Halberd, and Murray Pearson."

Cego looked at Murray, but the burly Grievar didn't blink.

"The scores of our top three were unparalleled this year." Aon spoke softer, though Cego could hear the commander's voice ringing in his eardrums. "I believe it is a sign. Of times to come."

Many of the Citadelians in the room took Aon's words as a rallying cry—they responded with a chorus of *O Toh* that echoed across the chamber. Aon held his hand up to silence them.

"Do not take my words lightly." Aon's blank eyes swept across the room. "In the times that approach the Citadel, we have two paths, one in the light and one in the shadows. Just as we choose our new class today, we must choose which path to take in the coming days. How we proceed and how this new class is shaped will determine the Citadel's future—Ezo's future."

Aon handed the scroll he had examined earlier to a Grievar standing beside him, a stocky man with thick shoulders.

Murray whispered in Cego's ear again. "That's Mack Tefo, the Lyceum's professor of striking."

Professor Tefo read from the scroll in a booming voice. "If your name is called, step forward into your designated slot at the front of the room."

Cego noticed twenty-four circular steel platforms lined up along the wall beneath the balcony.

"Our twentieth-fourth pick is Mateus Winterfowl, age fifteen, of the Capital's Fudai District."

A purelight with a sharp plume of blond hair jutting from his scalp stepped forward and onto the platform farthest to the right. The boy raised his hands into the air as the crew of purelights cheered and clapped together in unison. The platform Mateus stepped onto began to pulse. Cego craned his head forward for a better look. The platform was composed of some elemental alloy, just like the Circles. Answering the call of the alloy, the spectrals congregated in the hall's domed roof slowly began to float toward the ground, like feathers on a soft wind.

Several of the spectrals found their way to Mateus, bathing the boy in a victorious glow. As the light covered him, his image suddenly flared to life along one of the chamber walls. Beside Mateus's image, his biometric stats came to life on the wall.

Murray whispered to Cego again. "Class biometrics are now up for the public on SystemView, all day, every day."

Professor Tefo continued reading from the scroll with his booming voice. "Our twenty-third pick is Tegan Masterton, age fourteen, of the Capital's Fudai District." A purelight girl with tightly braided black hair stepped from the center of the room onto the next platform over, her image and biometrics also displayed on the wall.

Just as Cego expected, most of the picks were purelights, and the majority of those were from the Capital's Fudai District—an exclusive area of the city where the Twelve Houses were located.

A few lacklights were interspersed with the picks. Cego watched as the huge boy from the borderlands stepped onto the platform, that strange smile on his face. Cego had secretly been curious to see the boy's biometrics, and he wasn't disappointed. Joba Maglin, age ten, six-foot-three, two hundred eighty pounds. Someone in the crowd shouted, "Freak!" though the boy kept smiling.

A smaller, dark-skinned lacklight stepped onto the steel platform. "Our eighteenth pick is Abel Mohandar, age thirteen, of the Capital's Karsh District." Someone in the room yelled, "Sponge-eater!" Several others laughed as the Desovian boy stared out from his platform.

Cego wondered what the purelights would scream when he stood up there. *If* he stood up there. Perhaps Murray had too much confidence in him. Maybe his score wouldn't stack up against all the other seasoned fighters in this room.

"Our twelfth pick is Dozer, age fourteen, of the Underground."

Dozer was in. Cego quickly forgot about his worries when he saw the expression on his big friend's face—pure elation.

Dozer stepped forward onto the twelfth platform, his face frozen in a huge, toothy grin even as the purelights hissed and booed at him—"Deep scum! Dark slagger!" Cego didn't think Dozer's smile could get any bigger, but it did, as soon as the next name was called.

"Our eleventh pick is Knees, age thirteen, of the Underground."

Knees didn't share Dozer's elation as he stepped toward his platform. He walked unsteadily, as if he didn't know where he was. The spectrals that cast their light on Knees only served to illuminate the empty look on his face.

Cego proudly watched his two friends standing against the wall. Several months ago, they had been fighting for their lives in Thaloo's slave Circle. Now they'd just gained admission into the world's most prestigious combat school.

The next several picks were more purelights from Ezo's long-established Grievar bloodlines. Each one was met with louder roars of approval.

They were down to the final six spots and there were still over fifty kids in the room who hadn't been picked yet, including Cego. Murray placed his hand on Cego's shoulder reassuringly. Now that Knees and Dozer were up there, he wanted more than anything to gain entrance into this year's class.

"Our sixth pick is Marvin Stronglight, age fifteen, of the Capital's Fudai District."

A lanky boy with a long mane of tangled black hair stepped onto the sixth platform.

"Our fifth pick is Solara Halberd, age fourteen, of the Capital's Fudai District."

Though Solara was from the Twelve, and the daughter of the most famous Grievar in Ezo, the rest of the purelights quickly quieted as she took the fifth spot against the wall. "Our fourth pick is Shiar Shankspar, age thirteen, of the Capital's Fudai District."

Shiar's place of origin was not listed as the Underground. It was as if they'd erased that blotch from his past. Shiar stepped forward onto the platform, smirking as the purelights showered him with cheers.

"Our third pick is Gryfin Thurgood, age fifteen, of the Capital's Fudai District."

The chiseled Thurgood boy stepped forward onto the platform, smiling through his pearly white teeth. He looked like the epitome of a Grievar—the sort that Cego had seen in the ads up on SystemView. Several of the girls in the chamber cheered especially loudly as Gryfin waved at the crowd.

Cego breathed out forcefully, trying to steady his heartbeat.

Professor Tefo took his time, waiting dramatically to read the next name from the scroll. Finally, his voice boomed.

"Our second pick is Cego, age thirteen, of the Underground."

Murray clasped Cego's shoulders and prodded him forward. "Well done, kid. You were made for this place."

Cego nodded to Murray in thanks and stepped forward. As expected, the purelights in the room shouted various insults as Cego walked toward his spot against the wall. "Cave dweller! Deep scum!" Of course, Cego had become used to such derogatory terms after being confined with Shiar for so many months in the Underground.

Second pick. He'd made it. Just as Murray had said, he was nearly at the top of his class. Cego caught Solara Halberd's steely stare as he approached his spot. He took his place at the front of the room with his class as several spectrals slowly circled him.

Cego, age thirteen, of the Underground. Professor Tefo's words echoed in Cego's head as he stood on the platform, looking out into the chamber. *Of the Underground.* Those words were a lie.

Cego wasn't from the Underground. And neither was Knees; he'd been brought down from Venturi. It was as if they'd decided to erase their pasts once they'd been sold to the Deep.

Cego's mind wandered back to the Trials, to the sound of Sam's voice calling out for him. He clenched his fists, thinking of his little brother grasping his hand through the ironwood trees.

Cego nearly forgot there was one more name to be called. The top spot. Despite how long he'd lasted in each of the Trials, Cego hadn't gotten the top spot in this class. There was one ahead of him. Someone better.

"Our first and top pick for this year's Lyceum class is Kōri Shimo, age thirteen, from the Capital's Fudai District."

Another purelight. Of course, Cego thought. Who else but a purelight, bred for this sole purpose, would get the top spot?

The crowd parted as a figure at the back of the room stood and walked forward. Cego quickly recognized the bald head. It was the boy who had made steam rise from his scalp, the one sitting silently by the pillar during the Trial's commencement gathering.

Kōri Shimo didn't have the look of any of the other kids from the Twelve. He wore simple clothing, white trousers and a tunic, and not the expensive garments worn by so many of the purelights standing on the platforms.

Shimo certainly was athletic-looking—tall, with long arms and legs—though none of his features stood out. He wasn't a giant like Joba Maglin, or a chiseled statue like Gryfin Thurgood. In fact, he was fairly plain—average, even. Cego could probably say the same about himself.

Cego's confusion was mirrored by the rest of the purelights in the room. They didn't clap for Kōri as they had for the rest of their brethren. Many peered at him in confusion, trying to recognize one of their own who had taken the top spot.

Kōri paced to the front of the room and stood next to Cego on the first platform. He didn't appear to be happy or sad. He looked as if he had just gotten out of bed and was wondering what he'd have for breakfast.

Aon's whisper broke the silence. "I present the Lyceum's new class of Level Ones."

* * *

Within an hour, the crowd had filtered out of the Valkyrie's rotunda and only the twenty-four new Lyceum students and Professor Mack Tefo remained.

Murray had walked to Cego's side before he left, grasping his shoulder tightly. "I'll figure things out for you, kid. I promise," the burly Grievar had said. "Just concentrate on your studies."

Cego hadn't known how to reply to Murray. Part of him didn't want Murray to delve into his past—perhaps it would be easier to forget where he came from. He'd replied, "Thank you, Murray-Ku," as the man turned and walked from the hall.

Cego stood by a pillar with Dozer and Knees as they waited for something to happen. Dozer was having trouble containing his excitement in front of Knees, who was statuesque in his silence. Cego knew now was not the right time to prod his Venturian friend about what had happened within the Sim.

"Do ya think we'll get to bunk together? Just like in the Deep?" Dozer asked.

"Don't know," Cego replied. "Though I hope I don't end up with the lot of them."

Cego watched the pack of purelights who had stayed clumped together, chatting in excitement. Gryfin Thurgood stood tall and proud at the center of the pack. Shiar was at Gryfin's side, whispering to him. The jackal was already trying to form his alliances.

A few other kids were scattered around the room, like islands at the fringes of the mainland.

Solara Halberd stood apart from the rest of the purelights. She looked like she was ready to pick a fight; her fists were clenched and her jaw was tucked.

The smallest of the twenty-four, the dark-skinned Desovian named Abel, had made his way to the side of the biggest boy in the room, Joba. The two looked like a parent and child in size difference, though Cego knew Joba was the youngest kid in the class. Abel whispered something that widened Joba's strange, broad smile.

Kōri Shimo, the first pick, was sitting cross-legged by a pillar, just as he was when Cego had first seen him. His eyes were closed. Many of the kids in the room occasionally shot nervous glances at the boy.

"Shut up and line up! On the wall!" Professor Tefo suddenly called out in his booming voice.

The kids quickly scrambled to get in a line against the wall, the purelights jostling to keep together.

"I am Professor Mack Tefo." The man's voice softened now that he had their full attention. "As Commander Aon said, welcome to the Lyceum."

He stroked the rough stubble on his face as he paced in front of the kids. "I stood where you stand over three decades ago, in this very hall of the Valkyrie. I was eager, as I'm sure you brood are, to begin my studies. I can remember the day as if it were yesterday.

"I see many weary faces here." Tefo looked directly at Knees, who was nearly slumped against the wall. "You think you had it hard in the Trials? We didn't have the Sim when I went in. It was as real as a kick to the nethers. When I was in your place I had a fully shattered knee. Eviscerated by a Level Sixer with a love for taking the limbs of fresh Trial-takers. And you didn't hear a peep out of me, so I don't want to hear no griping about how the Sim gave you some headache now, all right?

"As I was saying... many things have remained the same at the Lyceum for centuries. Here are two things that won't be changing anytime soon. Number one. All students here stand on equal ground. I don't care whose son or daughter you are or what you've done before you got here—all students stand in the same Circles. You work hard, you learn, you improve. That's what matters here."

Some of the purelights shook their heads snidely.

"Two. I know that some of you are not used to taking orders." Professor Tefo eyeballed the purelights. "You'll soon find out that will not be the case in the Lyceum." Professor Tefo walked down the row of students, silently assessing them.

"Your first order will be to break into teams." Professor Tefo elaborated. "Here at the Lyceum, each incoming class of students is broken up into four teams of six. You will bunk with your team. You will take challenges with your team. You will feel the pain of your team. And, speaking of pain, you will get fluxed with your team today to start things off."

Dozer excitedly whispered to Cego, "Finally! I'm gonna get a proper flux tattoo, not just this stupid thing." He rubbed the top of his head where the brand from Thaloo's was now covered by his short-cropped brown hair.

"Top four Trial-takers. Get up here," Professor Tefo ordered.

Cego stepped away from the rest of the students, along with Kōri Shimo, Gryfin Thurgood, and Shiar.

"You four are our team captains," Tefo said. "You will each take turns picking your teammates."

Cego hadn't been prepared to make any decisions, let alone a huge one like picking the group of kids he would be bunking with and fighting alongside. Even worse, for his first pick, he'd need to choose between Dozer and Knees.

Kōri Shimo started off the team selection. In a barely audible whisper, he picked the largest purelight in the room, Wilhelm Bariston, a hulking boy who looked like he could already grow a full beard. Wilhelm confidently strode out from the line and took his place by Kōri's side.

It was Cego's turn. He stared at his two friends against the wall. Dozer was tapping his foot rapidly, clearly excited at the prospect of being here at the Lyceum, training with the great masters, getting his first flux tattoo. Knees didn't show any of Dozer's enthusiasm. The Venturian looked like a shadow of himself, his shoulders slumped and his eyes on the ground, as if he didn't care if Cego chose him or not.

Cego knew that Dozer would likely get picked first by the other teams—the thick-shouldered, heavily muscled boy looked more intimidating than the lanky Venturian. Knees had placed higher in the Trials, but he would run under the radar as he always did. Cego needed to choose strategically.

Cego looked Knees in the eyes. *Forgive me, my friend.*

"Dozer," Cego said. Dozer hooted and walked to Cego's side. Knees didn't seem to even register Cego's choice.

Gryfin Thurgood picked Marvin Stronglight next, the sixth-ranked student from the Trials.

It was Shiar's turn. The jackal stepped forward and slowly paced in front of the line, eyeing each kid, sniffing at the air and even grabbing Joba Maglin's huge forearm as if he were appraising the quality of a slab of meat.

Cego clenched his fists and held his breath as Shiar made his way down the line.

Don't pick Knees. Don't pick Knees.

Shiar stopped in front of Knees, looking curiously at his old bunkmate from Thaloo's.

"Knees." The jackal spat the name as he turned and locked eyes with Cego.

Shiar took his place back beside the other captains, Knees following behind him.

Cego couldn't concentrate on the rest of his picks after that. He wasn't thinking strategically anymore, so he picked up the leftovers, those kids he knew wouldn't be picked otherwise. He selected the huge lacklight, Joba, and his little Desovian friend, Abel. He picked the twenty-fourth-ranked Trial-taker, Mateus Winterfowl. He picked Solara Halberd, who, although ranked fifth overall, was still standing up there as the last round came to a close.

Solara squeezed her way into the spot next to Cego. She was just about as tall as him. She looked at him defensively, as if she expected Cego to tell her to get out of line.

"All right! Now that we have our four teams, let's move on," Professor Tefo said.

Tefo led the class out of the Valkyrie's rotunda and down a long, dim-lit corridor. Cego watched Knees walking ahead beside Shiar. His friend fell forward with each step, as if he could barely catch himself from sprawling to the ground.

He wanted to walk next to Knees and tell him he would have chosen him next. He wanted to tell his friend about his own experience in the Sim—maybe it would help Knees to know he wasn't alone.

The twenty-four emerged from the long corridor into another massive rotunda that extended several floors upward. The Harmony—sister tower to the Valkyrie, where the Lyceum's classes were held.

The hall's shape was similar to the Valkyrie's, with supporting pillars that ran the height of the structure. The Harmony wasn't full of echoes and flickering torches, though—this hall was bustling with brightness and movement.

Each floor above had a circular balustrade encrusted with spectrals, the wisps spiraling toward the domed ceiling far above. Students bustled along the walkways, disappearing behind sliding doors and stopping to chat along the railings. On the ground floor, students carefully watched several large lightboards tuned in to SystemView. Some were jotting down notes on handheld decks as they studied the Grievar on-screen. Off to one side of the room, there were several practice Circles laid out on the floor, where students were grappling casually, experimenting with techniques, or sitting and chatting on the rubber canvases.

"Welcome to Level Zero, also called common ground," Professor Tefo said. "This is where students of all levels can congregate, set up private meetings with professors, watch SystemView, or experiment with techniques within our Circles."

Professor Tefo led the class around the periphery of the common ground as he continued to speak.

"Each floor above is segmented by class levels. Because you have just gained admission to the Lyceum, all your classes will take place on Level One. We have six levels rank our students. At the end of the year, if you pass testing, you'll gain access to Level Two."

Cego peered up, looking toward the top floor. He didn't see any movement along the balcony up there.

Professor Tefo continued. "You all must believe you are an elite group now, after passing the Trials. However, by the end of your studies here at the Lyceum, you will be far fewer. Only a small percentage of our first-year students make it through to Level Six graduation. Look around you at your classmates—there's only a handful of you that'll make it through in total."

The twenty-four Level One students in the class sized each other up, some straightening their backs to make themselves appear bigger. Dozer whispered to Cego, "We'll be up there on Level Six. Knees, too, together by the end of it."

Cego nodded and glanced over at Knees. His friend looked out of place standing next to Shiar and his team of ornately clothed purelights.

"From the look of 'em, Mack, not sure if any of these whelps will even make it to Level Two." A young, thickly muscled Grievar with a well-trimmed beard pulled up next to Professor Tefo, appraising the new class. Several prominent flux tattoos ran along his arms, legs, and neck, swirling under the light.

"I think that you forget that you barely made it up there either, Kit," Professor Tefo said jovially to the Grievar. "Students, I'd like you to meet one of our Level Sixers, Kit. He'll likely be assisting some of your professors this year when he isn't off studying for his Knight test."

Kit's eyes twinkled as he took a superfluous bow. "Well met, whelps in training. You're in good hands here with Professor Tefo, believe me. Keep your eyes open and you might even learn something from him." He slapped Professor Tefo on the back as he walked off.

Cego watched Kit go. *Level Six.* He could only imagine how much Kit had learned during his time at the Lyceum. Cego wished he could access that knowledge now without having to go through six years of arduous training and testing first.

Professor Tefo led the class to the opposite end of the room, across from the training Circles, where several students sat chatting at the base of a stone staircase.

"This goes to each class floor. Sometimes, you'll be asked to go past floor one to help clean up a training room or bring down some equipment. Otherwise, don't go up past your own floor unless you're told to," Professor Tefo warned. "Head downstairs to get to the dining hall. All students share the same one," he added.

Cego saw Dozer's eyes light up at the mention of the dining hall. It was strange seeing so many amenities provided for the students after slaving away in Thaloo's Circles. Cego almost felt guilty that he had access to these resources when there were so many kids barely surviving in the Deep.

"All right, any questions?" Professor Tefo asked.

The class was silent, in awe of their new surroundings. But Dozer's fist shot up in the air. "Where do they keep the rocs?"

Professor Tefo chuckled and shook his head. "It's always someone... The Lyceum hasn't used birds for decades. The old roost down in the forest is empty."

Dozer frowned and looked like he was about to ask a follow-up question, but Cego prodded his friend in the ribs. This was Cego's team, and though he didn't feel like any sort of leader, he'd rather they didn't start off on the wrong foot with the professor of striking.

"All right, if that's all the questions, now that you are officially Level Ones, we need to get you properly fluxed," Tefo said.

Dozer let out a hoot and was quickly smiling again. He draped an arm around Cego. "First real darkin' flux, I knew this day would come."

The students followed Professor Tefo through a pair of sliding doors off the common ground and into a long room with a mirror set against the wall. A black cylindrical door spun around at the other end of the room.

An older student emerged from the spinning door, grinning as he looked down at a flux tattoo of a black ram running across his shoulder.

Professor Tefo spoke briefly with a heavily fluxed Grievar standing by a lightboard queue. She was covered head to toe in so many swirling patterns that her unmarked skin was the anomaly.

The four teams each claimed a corner as they waited to enter the darkroom. Though he was captain, Cego had no idea what to say to any of these strangers. Solara Halberd stood next to him in complete silence.

"Good to have you on the team," Cego stuttered. Solara didn't reply; she stared at the mirror across from them. Cego didn't know what else to say, so he paused awkwardly and shifted his feet.

The giant Joba sat with his back against the wall, that ever-present smile on his face, while Abel was barely visible sitting beside him. The little Desovian was quietly singing a tune in his own language.

"Shut it with that sponge-eater shit." Mateus Winterfowl glared down at Abel.

"It's song of my ancestors," Abel replied, not seeming offended. "It's about learning from great minds of old. I will teach to you if—"

"I don't want to learn your stupid foreign songs," Mateus growled, and stalked away.

"First darkin' flux," Dozer said again, grinning at himself in the mirror. The big kid seemed oblivious to the rest of his teammates. Cego took a deep breath as they waited their turn.

Kōri Shimo's team was the first to emerge from the darkroom. They each had a new flux tattoo on their neck, red and swollen. It wasn't difficult to make out the design—it was a praying mantis, holding its arms up as if in a puncher's stance.

Cego's team was called into the darkroom next. As they stepped into the rotating door, the light completely disappeared, and several glowing chairs came into view.

"Take a seat and the fluxer will do the rest," a voice said from the darkness.

Cego could barely make out a woman standing over a table, working intently on a large man lying facedown. The woman held up a small metal rod that glinted red. Cego could recognize the alloy even in the darkness—rubellium.

A spectral clung to the end of the rubellium rod. As the woman traced the metal along the man's back, the spectral followed along the tip, burning brightly and searing the man's skin. The large Grievar on the table writhed in pain.

Each of the six made their way into one of the fluorescent chairs. Cego sat in between Solara and Dozer, with Joba, Abel, and Mateus across from them.

As soon as Cego settled in the chair, a small spectral floated up in front of his eyes. An audio box built into his headrest emitted a robotic voice. "Level One, standard team flux protocol initiated. Maintain position until completion."

Cego tried to hold still, waiting for something to happen. The spectral drifted across his body as if examining him until it stopped above his left shoulder. Suddenly, the wisp became brighter, almost white. Cego felt the heat as it landed on his neck, searing into his skin. It felt like it was trying to burrow into the side of his throat. Cego gritted his teeth and exhaled deeply several times. He wouldn't scream.

Cego tried to look to the left without moving his head. He could see that Solara had a white-hot spectral branding her as well, moving down her neck onto her shoulder. She shifted her eyes toward Cego and smiled through her clenched white teeth. Cego smiled back.

The pain melded into the darkness like the whir of a fan. Cego almost enjoyed it. It prevented him from turning to the events of the past several days. The pain blurred the memories from the Sim, the sinking feeling he'd get whenever he thought of his brothers.

He stared across the room at the motley crew he was to call his team at the Lyceum. Joba's wide smile had not diminished as the branding spectral traveled down the length of his arm, burning the skin it touched. Abel was singing his Desovian song loudly, right into the ear of Mateus, who was gripping the chair's armrests with bloodless fingers, his eyes clamped shut. Dozer was laughing like a maniac beside Cego as the spectral twisted around his thick arm.

For a moment, even though most of these kids were still strangers, Cego felt connected to them through the darkness, through the pain.

And then the pain stopped. The world came back into focus around him, as clear as ever. Cego stood with the rest of his team as they made their way to the darkroom's exit. He caught Mateus discreetly trying to wipe the tears from his face.

His team went straight to the long mirror in the waiting room to examine their new flux tattoos.

At first, Cego thought something had gone wrong. He held his arm up and didn't see anything. The limb looked swollen and red, but unadorned otherwise. And then, suddenly, Cego caught a flicker of movement coming from the side of his neck. A serpentine head with little whiskers at the snout peeked out onto his shoulder.

A dragon. Well, not quite a dragon, just a whelp.

"Hello there." Cego reached gingerly toward his shoulder, as if he'd scare the thing away, though it was a part of him now.

The whelp flux appeared to respond, darting off Cego's shoulder and curling around and down his arm until it nested on his forearm, its little head perched at his wrist.

Now it made sense that the Level Sixer, Kit, had referred to them as *whelps* earlier—baby dragons that couldn't yet fly, or do much of anything. Cego remembered seeing a full-grown dragon fluxed on Murray's back, the biggest design the old Grievar had. It was hard to believe that Murray had once been a whelp too.

"I've got a darkin' flux!" Dozer was flexing his bicep in the mirror, his little dragon sitting on top of the muscle as if it were also showing off. Even Mateus was smiling as he tracked his new companion moving up and down his arm.

Shiar's team was called into the darkroom next. Cego and Dozer watched as Knees passed by, heading toward the revolving door. "Look, I've finally got one," Dozer said excitedly as he clapped his old friend on the shoulder.

Knees whirled around to knock Dozer's hand away, sudden anger contorting his face. "Why would I care?"

Dozer backed away from Knees in disbelief as the Venturian stared him down. It was the first time Cego had seen Dozer scared. The big kid's whelp flux had retreated to its home behind his neck.

"Knees?" Dozer said softly as his old friend turned and walked toward the darkroom.

Knees didn't look back.

* * *

It wasn't surprising that the other three teams, composed primarily of purelights with connections to the Twelve, claimed the newest of the Level One bunks. Even though Professor Tefo had said everyone was on equal standing here, those privileged kids still had some sway within the halls of the Lyceum.

Quarter D was the oldest of the dormitories in the Lyceum, a leftover from before the renovations several years back. The décor was a hodgepodge of furniture, carpeting, and drapes from a variety of times and places, as if they had thrown together all the unwanted items into one room.

The room was lavish to Cego's eyes, though. It had warm comfort mats in a spectrum of colors, a big shield window with a view of the Citadel's grounds, and even an old mechanical jogging machine to warm up before class. The wooden cots were old and creaky, but compared to Thaloo's prison, this room was a palace. It seemed fitting, too, that a room made of mismatched furniture and equipment would house Cego's eclectic group.

Though Cego was having a difficult time making connections, Dozer immediately befriended the others. Perhaps the big lacklight was distracting himself from his separation from Knees. He playfully sized himself up against Joba by standing on the tips of his toes and still only reached the giant boy's shoulders. "No words to describe the fear you feel facin' off with me?" Dozer asked Joba, who remained silent but appeared to be taking Dozer's friendly competitiveness in stride.

"Joba—he does not make words." Abel, the little Desovian, spoke up for his big friend. "We have one like him in Karsh, born without words. He can speak with eyes, though," Abel added.

Dozer nodded, looking up into Joba's big yellow eyes. "I see what you're saying. Yeah, I can see the words in his eyes right now. He's saying…this Dozer fella. He's sure to be the Citadel's next champion!"

Solara wasn't quite so jovial. Perhaps because she was the only girl in the bunk or among so many lacklights, Cego speculated. She only spoke in a brief *yes* or *no*, and Cego noticed she still had her fists clenched.

Within a few minutes of settling down, Dozer started grappling with Joba in the center of the room, where a natural circle formed between their cots. Dozer tried to hit a double-leg, and though

Joba's sprawl wasn't the most technical, the boy easily pushed Dozer to the ground and stood back up, smiling innocently.

"Wow. I'll needa get used to fighting bigger kids than me!" Dozer grinned and slapped Joba on the shoulder.

Cego was about to give Dozer a pointer on his form when Solara interjected. "For a larger opponent, you're better off scooping up a single or picking the ankle," she said in a steely voice.

Dozer looked at her curiously.

"Hmm... I think against someone that big, maybe tomoe nage would work—using their forward momentum against them," Cego quickly said as he thought back to his Trial on the ice. He actually agreed with Solara on the ankle pick, but he'd been thinking of a way to say something to her, and the words were already out of his mouth.

Solara eyed Cego, her brow furrowed. "You would say that, wouldn't you? Why don't we both try out our techniques on Joba here and see which works better?"

Joba gave the two a worried look.

"Um, I wasn't saying that your technique wouldn't work or anything... I was just saying maybe tomoe nage would be better," Cego said.

"Better?" Solara raised her voice. "Just because you placed ahead of me in the Trials, because you got to make picks for teams, you think you are already better at everything?"

"No—no. I'm not saying that—" Cego stuttered.

Dozer and Abel had taken a seat on the floor and were chuckling at the spectacle.

"Let's do it," Solara said. "Joba, let Cego try his technique on you. Do whatever you normally would do to prevent getting taken down."

Joba slowly nodded, though he seemed worried.

Looking at Solara's clenched jaw, Cego realized she wasn't going to have it any other way. "Okay... Joba, you ready?" Cego asked, staring up at the boy.

Joba nodded again.

Cego squared up with Joba. The boy really was huge.

Cego shot in for a quick double-leg, just as Dozer had done. He got in fairly deep, but he knew he wasn't going to hit it against someone so much larger. Joba sprawled his full weight on Cego's shoulders. Just as he felt Joba pressing forward, Cego rolled backward, pushing his feet against Joba's hips, attempting to throw the mountainous boy over his head. Unfortunately, one of Cego's feet slipped past Joba's hip, and the huge boy landed directly on top of him instead.

"Oomph." Cego's muffled voice came from beneath Joba's bulk.

By the end of it, even Mateus was keeling over with laughter, joining Dozer and Abel on the sidelines of the makeshift circle.

"My turn," Solara said as Cego slowly stood. Luckily, nothing but his pride had been damaged by the failed takedown. Solara squared up with Joba, flipping her red braid over her shoulder and tucking her elbows. Her eyes burned with intensity.

She shot in for a fluid single-leg, grasping around one of Joba's tree-trunk-sized thighs. Joba quickly dropped his weight onto her. It looked like Solara was about to get crushed, but she quickly swiveled between Joba's legs and around to his back. She crossed one of her legs behind both of Joba's feet and fell to the side while pulling him down by the thigh, making the massive boy topple over her.

Solara stood up with a satisfactory grin and blew a tuft of her hair out of her eyes, staring Cego down.

Cego shook his head. "But you didn't hit the single-leg! You ended up going for that back trip."

"Hopefully, you'll learn in one of our classes that it's important to reevaluate, even mid-technique," she replied matter-of-factly.

"But... if I had known I could go for a different tech—"

"Nice room you have here," Shiar said, standing at their entryway with two of his teammates. "A fitting junkyard for this team."

Dozer stood and tensed his shoulders, his eyes locked on Shiar. The quarter proctor, a Level Three student, had told them that combat without a formal challenge would not be tolerated. It was clearly what Shiar wanted—to get them in trouble right from the start.

He addressed Solara and Mateus, the two purelights on their team. "How sorry you two must be...stuck with this bunch of sponge-eating, Deep-spawned lacklights."

"I'm sure we're better off than any sorry team that has got to put up with you," Dozer growled.

Shiar turned to Dozer. "Dozer. It seems you've already grown attached to this group, so quick to defend them. In fact, the little dark sponge-eater here even reminds me of...what was his name again? Oh, yes. Weep."

Cego moved in front of Dozer. He could feel his friend breathing heavily, like a bull about to charge.

Luckily, Solara was suddenly up in Shiar's face. "Everyone knows your parents dumped you off in the Deep like most of the kids in this room. At least they have the guts to accept where they're from instead of pretending they're from the Twelve." She shoved Shiar backward.

Shiar's face turned red. He looked to his two companions, both of whom appeared equally baffled over how to deal with the fiery girl.

"What a disappointment you must have been," Shiar hissed. "Everyone expecting Artemis Halberd's brood to be Ezo's next savior...waiting on the edge of their seats. And then *you* popped out. Though, I must say, your dad has done quite a good job in trying to save face for his...mistake. He must have worked hard to make you into such a proper son."

Though Solara kept her face straight, Cego could tell Shiar had hit a soft spot.

"See you in class, son of Halberd," Shiar said as he turned and walked away with his teammates, laughing.

Solara stood quietly for a moment, straight-backed. Cego

approached her and placed his hand on her shoulder. "Thanks for standing up for us," he said.

"I wasn't standing up for you!" she snapped. "I saw trash in front of me and wanted it out of my new bunk."

Cego looked down at the floor, not knowing how to respond. "Uh, I know... but—"

"I'm sorry," Solara said, exhaling softly. "I've been dealing with people like him for my entire life. You'd think I'd be used to it by now."

"No one gets used to Shiar," Cego interjected. "If the Lyceum studied the techniques of verbal attacks, Shiar would be a Level Sixer by now."

Solara snorted. "I see. Well, we'll need to keep our eye on someone like that."

"Always," Cego replied. "And earlier... Solara, I wasn't trying to say your technique was wrong or anything. I was just saying there are other options."

"I know. I sort of just wanted to see you get smashed under Joba, though." Solara playfully shoved Cego. "And call me Sol," she said.

CHAPTER 14

The Whelps

Listen to the words of even the most neophyte Grievar. Though such a newly skilled combatant is unlikely to provide worthy advice to a veteran, one with stoppered ears and a shuttered mind will never find the path to mastery.

Passage Nine, Two Hundred First Precept of the Combat Codes

Cego looked at himself in the mirror set along the back wall of Quarter D.

He tried to flatten the matted black hair that stood puffed up on his head, a stark contrast to the bare scalp he'd shaved every day at Thaloo's.

Cego was wearing the new custom-fit second skin that the Lyceum had provided him. It was white to denote he was a Level One and clung tightly to his entire body from his neck down to his wrists and ankles. The strange, stretchy material lived up to its name: it literally felt like a second skin, and according to the proctors, it increased blood flow and decreased the chance of injury during practice.

"Level One second skins are white so that the blood shows up on 'em best. They get darker each time you level up," Mateus Winterfowl grimly told the rest of the team as they appraised their new skins.

Cego pulled down the nape of his skin to check out his new flux tattoo. Just as expected, the dragon whelp peeked out with its curious eyes before snaking back beneath the material. Cego had gotten in the habit of looking at the tattoo as a reminder to himself that he was actually a student at the Lyceum.

Mateus had interpreted the new tattoo as a jab at their relative inexperience compared to higher-level Lyceum students. They were all mere whelps compared to the bears, lions, and dragons that roamed these halls. Cego didn't take it that way, though. When he looked at his new flux, it reminded him to stay curious like the little whelp.

Cego doubled back to his cot and sat, checking his class schedule on his new lightdeck. He'd never actually owned anything before, and though he knew the Lyceum technically owned the equipment, it felt good to *have* something.

There were three mandatory classes that all Level Ones were required to take daily: Grappling Level One, Striking Level One, and Performance Augmentation. In addition, students were assigned one specialty class based on a skill the proctors thought they should focus on. Cego wasn't surprised to see that Circles and Alloys was listed on his schedule.

Each student also had two elective classes to fill out the rest of their schedule. Electives were cross-level courses open to all students within the Lyceum. By far the most popular elective was Stratagems and Maneuvers, taught by the famed ex-Knight Jos Dynari.

Dynari had been known for his crafty techniques in the Circle, which were tailor-made to dissect his opponent's games. Though he was never the strongest nor fastest of the Citadel's Knights, he'd been able to use his master grasp of strategy to attain one of the highest winning percentages in Ezo's history. Now Dynari served as one of the Citadel's top coaches, helping develop game plans for each Knight months in advance of their bouts. In his spare time, he taught a class at the Lyceum. Cego couldn't resist putting his name in the running for Stratagems and Maneuvers, though he doubted he'd be picked with students of all levels vying for a spot in the class. He also elected to take Commander Aon Farstead's class—the Combat Codes—which he figured would be easier to get into.

Cego's lightdeck flashed, indicating that Performance Augmentation was starting in thirty minutes. The Whelps—which his team had been aptly named, after their first flux tattoos—exited Quarter D together, heading down the main dormitory hall toward the common ground.

Abel had taken to teasing Dozer, filling a role Knees would usually take on. "Dozer. I think tailor fit your skin too small? Looks tight."

"This is just how I look," Dozer bragged, flexing his muscles beneath the second skin.

Sol joined in. "Yeah, I don't know, Dozer... Especially way back there, it does look a bit tight."

"What do you mean?" Dozer said with alarm as he spun around in a circle, trying to get a better view of his behind. The crew erupted with laughter.

Though it was great to see his team getting along, the good-natured teasing provided Cego with a stark reminder that his sharp-witted Venturian friend wasn't there with them.

They reached the common ground to find a throng of students surrounding a large lightboard on the wall. The names of various teams were flashing onto the board.

"Challenge board," someone said from behind Cego.

Cego turned to see Kit, the Level Sixer they'd met upon arriving.

Kit was wearing a bloodred second skin with black stripes etched along each arm.

Kit addressed several of the Level Ones who had gathered on the common ground to look at the board. "Professor Tefo told me to fill you guys in on what's going on, especially if I see you staring with those big, naïve whelp eyes, which is what I'm seeing now." The dark-haired Grievar flashed a smile beneath his well-trimmed beard.

"This board is where the team challenges are posted every week," Kit said. "Once a challenge is posted, the defending team has one full day to accept."

Kit continued his explanation, likely noticing the Level Ones' confused expressions. "Teams here at the Lyceum can challenge each other. A typical challenge is best of three fights—three members from each team matching up individually in our challenge Circles. Winner takes a chunk of the loser's total team score. At end of cycle, you'll not only be judged based on your individual class scores, but your team scores will decide how you rank. Most importantly, though, the lowest-scoring team gets held back from advancing to the next level. It's a way to weed out those who aren't performing."

Dozer gulped loudly next to Cego.

"Keep in mind, though, most challenges are interclass," Kit said. "You know, a Level One versus a Level One team, or a Level Three versus a Level Three. Challenging a team above or below your level involves more politiks, and the scoring system is a bit more complicated for that. Take a look at your *Guide to Challenges* before you Level Ones do anything too crazy. Needless to say, I wouldn't recommend challenging a Level Six team right off the bat." Kit winked.

"Why the challenges, you ask?" Kit posed the question in a mock announcer voice. "It's all to simulate reality out there. Most of us who graduate from the Lyceum will be doing just this—fighting over challenges. In the real world, they aren't called challenges, of course. It's called war. And it's not some silly score at stake. It's territories, resources, farmland, food, homes. Lives at stake." Kit spoke seriously.

"These challenges give our potential Knights prep for the world out there. To realize you aren't fighting just for yourself—your training, studies, and wins and losses make a difference to everyone around you."

Cego considered Kit's words. This wasn't like the Underground, where every kid was fighting for their own survival or to line the bit-purse of some Circle owner or patron. It was about a larger purpose.

"I expect to see some of you in one of our challenge Circles in no time," Kit said as he walked off. "Don't forget to get to class, though. Professors don't take kindly to late students."

* * *

Professor Kitaka was well into the second hour of his lecture and Cego saw it in the faces of his classmates. Cego had expected his performance augmentation class to be tiring, but not in this way. Half the class appeared to be on the verge of falling asleep.

"Every muscle fiber in your body is connected in some way, even if it is not immediately discernible. Though the muscles in your neck are nowhere near the muscles in your foot, they too are connected..."

Kitaka was an older, sturdy-looking Grievar. Though his bald head was small, he had two massive cauliflower ears and large, penetrating yellow eyes. Kitaka spoke in a steady tone, never changing his inflection.

The large classroom was filled with several unusual pieces of equipment—weights, pulleys, tracks, cycles, stairs, and other machines that Cego couldn't place. The initial excitement of first entering the classroom and seeing all the machines had long since faded as Professor Kitaka's lecture droned on.

"Breathing is something we do every day naturally. We never

think about it throughout the course of our day, saying to ourselves every moment—*now I will take a breath*. We simply breathe. In. And out again. In. And out again..."

Performance Augmentation was one of the mandatory Level One classes, so all twenty-four students were in attendance today, sitting cross-legged on the floor.

Knees was sitting with his own team, the Bayhounds, right next to Shiar. Cego had tried to catch his friend's eyes, but Knees wouldn't even glance over in his direction. Cego couldn't wrap his head around it. Though Knees had no choice in teaming up with the Bayhounds, how could he just sit there complacently next to Shiar as if the two didn't have any past? Had the Sim really scrambled Knees's brain so much that he couldn't remember those jackal eyes flashing in glee as Weep crumbled under Shiar's kicks?

Sol sat just ahead of Cego. Her red braid was thrown over one shoulder and Cego saw she was attentively taking notes on her lightdeck, even as the lecture droned into its second hour. Cego watched as Sol methodically swiped at her deck, recording clips of the lecture before moving them into meticulously labeled folders.

Cego had noticed that about Sol—she was organized in everything she did. The way she had carefully folded her sheets in Quarter D and stacked all her gear in a neat pile. Even her fighting technique appeared organized. The single-leg combo she'd used on Joba earlier had been by the book, as if it had been replicated directly from some SystemView instructional.

Cego glanced at Dozer sitting to his right and smiled at the contrast. His burly friend was out cold, his head folded over his lap, a pool of drool accumulating on the surface of his unused lightdeck.

Kitaka had stopped lecturing. He was staring over at Dozer. Cego stuck out his foot and prodded his friend, who snorted loudly as he woke.

Dozer stared up at Professor Kitaka, quickly muttering, "S-sorry, Professor, I didn't mean to—"

"Dozer," Kitaka cut him off, his voice without inflection. "When I first saw that name on my class registry, I pondered what it meant. Do you know that every Grievar name has an origin and meaning? For most of the purelights in the room, it is the blood name that holds the meaning. For example, take our friend Gryfin Thurgood here..." Kitaka nodded at Gryfin sitting up front, who flashed his trademark pearly white smile.

"Your brother Lior was in my class two years ago, and two years before that, I had Tycho. And of course, Tullen is now on our Knight team. Good students. Good, strong work ethic. I believe you must possess the same ethic, Gryfin. That strength comes from your blood name—Thurgood. Once, we Grievar rode large flightless birds called rocs to travel long distances. Instead of taking mech transport to arrive at our next challenge, we used the endurance of these mighty birds to get where we needed to go. Some of the finest rocs, which a man could truly rely on, were called thoroughbreds. That is where your name comes from, Gryfin—Thurgood. Your bloodline possesses the good strength of a thoroughbred roc. Which makes your team's name especially on point."

Gryfin puffed up with pride at Kitaka's compliments just as a feathered head with a hooked beak appeared on the boy's thick neck.

"Dozer," Professor Kitaka repeated. Dozer stiffened again. He appeared to have forgotten he was still in the hot seat after Professor Kitaka had gone off on the tangent about rocs. "Dozer, because you do not have a pure Grievar bloodline, you also do not have a blood name to carry meaning. Which is why many lacklights assign their meaning through their given name. So, when I saw your name on my registry, I wondered what Dozer meant. My first thought was perhaps that Dozer meant you were strong, as your biometrics clearly read. However, now I see that the true meaning of your name, Dozer, refers to your ability to sleep soundly even amid the most important parts of my lecture."

Dozer began to apologize again, but Professor Kitaka held a finger up to quiet him.

"Come up here, Dozer, and because you are clearly tired by my words, we shall do something more to your level of understanding."

Cego heard Shiar cackle in delight from the other side of the classroom.

Dozer looked at the floor as he walked to the front of the class and stood next to Professor Kitaka. Cego's friend was noticeably taller and thicker than Kitaka.

"Dozer, I want you to lift this weight above your head." Kitaka pointed to one of the heavier circular weights set along the wall of the classroom.

Dozer smiled and moved over to the stack of weights. Cego knew that smile; his friend was looking forward to showing off in front of the class—after all, lifting things over his head was one of Dozer's specialties.

Dozer took hold of the grips on the weight, lowered his knees, and heaved it over his head in one clean jerk movement.

"Hold there for a moment, Dozer," said Professor Kitaka, walking over to him. "Class, as you can see, our friend Dozer has easily lifted this heavy weight. As you can also see, part of Dozer's technique to lift the weight involved inhaling and holding his breath to create a strong base structure." Kitaka pointed to Dozer's expanded chest.

"Now, Dozer, can you do a quick jog around the room for us while holding that weight?" Kitaka asked.

Dozer, whose face was starting to turn red under the strain, started to jog around the room.

Kitaka continued to make his observations as Dozer ran. "As you can see, Dozer is still holding his breath to maintain his structure beneath the weight, but now that he is exerting cardiovascular strain on his lungs, his breath cannot hold."

As if on cue, Dozer exhaled sharply and began to breathe heavily.

"Continue to run for us, Dozer," Kitaka said. "As Dozer continues to exert more cardiovascular strain, you can see that the muscles that were holding up the weight can no longer provide the same support as they once did."

Just as Kitaka had observed, Dozer's arms shivered under the weight.

"In a relatively short period of time, Dozer simply cannot support the weight," Kitaka concluded, just as Dozer fell to his knees, clunking the big weight onto the floor.

Kitaka stood over Dozer, looking down at the boy as he took labored breaths. "Dozer did what came naturally to him. He was not wrong in thinking that holding his breath would help him lift the heavy weight over his head. However, he was not prepared for any continued exertion."

To demonstrate, Kitaka moved over to the same weight. The old professor bent his knees and jerked the weight over his head, much as Dozer had done. However, Cego noticed that Kitaka exhaled when lifting, and as soon as the weight was up and over, he slowly began to inhale.

Kitaka ran around the room with the weight, taking breaths in between speaking. "As... you can see... I am able to continue my pattern of breathing... while... exerting... cardiovascular strain."

Kitaka ran around the room for over a minute to demonstrate the effectiveness of the technique before calmly placing the weight back on the ground. He was breathing with hardly any difficulty.

"Now, obviously, everything we learn in this class relates back to combat. What Dozer has helped me demonstrate here is a principle of *exertion and conservation of energy*."

Dozer had taken his seat on the floor by Cego again, still breathing hard as Kitaka addressed the class.

"Any action taken in combat needs to be realized under pressure and likely will require continued exertion. Lifting an opponent over your head won't do anything by itself. One needs to be prepared for an initial action, or lift, and then continued exertion or energy expenditure after that action. For example, after you execute a successful takedown, you can't just stop and say you're done. You need to exert pressure on your opponent, pass to an advantageous position, and finish them. You cannot overexert yourself on the initial lift—otherwise, your opponent may take advantage of your depleted energy," Kitaka explained.

Dozer was nodding his head now. Cego had been afraid Kitaka's demonstration was made to embarrass Dozer in front of the class, a technique Tasker Ozark had been fond of. This wasn't the case. Dozer, and the entire class, had learned something from the demonstration.

Cego looked over again at Sol, still meticulously taking notes. He sheepishly slid his hand across his lightdeck to power it on and began to pay attention.

* * *

Murray sat at the kitchen table alone, tapping his foot nervously. His barracks were quiet without any of the kids around. Masa and Tachi were currently off on lease to PublicJustice. Though Murray didn't entirely approve of it, the twin Grievar had insisted that they take on contract work to help pay the bills.

The Jadeans had originally come to Murray in rough shape, right off the back of a greatstorm on their passage from the Emerald Sea. The two had attempted to make the crossing on a Grunt dinghy made for island hopping. They'd washed ashore on the Ezonian coast, clinging to scrap wood. The twins had been picked up by the Enforcers and primed for shipping to the borderlands when Murray had bought them on a tip from the inside. He wouldn't let that kind of darkin' talent get wasted on harvest work.

Usually, Murray appreciated the lack of Jadean chatter, but now the barracks just seemed empty. Murray's Scout work was on hiatus for the month after the Trials, so that left him without any clear objectives. Normally, drinking himself into a stupor every day would be on top of that list.

Something had changed.

Murray stood, paced around the kitchen, and walked briskly out to the barracks. He threw the cover off Violet and took out the wash bucket, kneeling as he started to apply another sheen of finish to his Circle's already-shining surface.

Murray couldn't get his mind off Cego. He couldn't stop thinking about the kid's experience in the Trials—in the Sim—and Command's reaction to his performance.

Memnon's words rang in Murray's head. *For the good of the nation.* Murray spat onto the dirt floor of the barracks. He could fill his gallon wash bucket with spittle for the number of times he'd heard some politik telling him it was all for the good of the nation. Memnon was a pawn of the Daimyo. Those were their words in the high commander's mouth. The Daimyo always needed more from the Grievar. They were never satisfied.

How had the high commander strayed so far?

Murray could still clearly recall Professor Albion Memnon's class at the Lyceum. When the man was still a lowly deputy commander, Memnon had taught Grievar History. He'd been a great lecturer. He reviewed the histories with a passion, drawing his students into a world long past.

For millennia, we Grievar-kin lived in isolation from our brethren. We lived in the darkness of the Underground, on the broken Emerald Isles, atop the icy peaks of Myrkos.

Murray was a Level Five when he took Memnon's class, still uninitiated in the grand scheme of things, but at that point, brash enough to think he was at the top of the fighting food chain. He could remember Memnon's deep baritone voice reverberating throughout the Dome, the Lyceum's largest lecture hall.

We kept to ourselves. Grievar lives were simple then. We gathered what food we needed, raised our families, and fought in the

Circles, honing our combat skills. Our Circles were the glue that kept us together. Disputes were resolved, resources distributed, and justice delivered—all within the bounds of our Circles.

Murray could see Professor Memnon pacing on the stage, the eyes of the entire class glued to the man.

Those simple lives couldn't last, though. While we Grievar lived peacefully, millions died around us. The Daimyo wars were fought with great numbers and devastating weapons, threatening total annihilation.

Though Murray had been distracted by the pretty blonde sitting two rows up, Memnon's sudden whisper had caught his attention.

We could have stayed in solitude. We could have kept to ourselves. We could have watched from afar as our brethren destroyed themselves. We could have stood still as the world around us crumbled.

Memnon had stopped pacing. He stared at the class of wide-eyed Lyceum students.

That's not what Grievar-kin do. We don't stand still. We fight.

Murray could still remember the end of Memnon's lecture with perfect clarity.

We came up from the Deep, we climbed down from the peaks, we sailed from the broken isles. We Grievar emerged from the darkness to stand before our Daimyo brethren in their time of need. We agreed to the Armistice—the pact signed between rival nations that stands to this day. We Grievar would provide the Daimyo a path away from their wars, and the Daimyo would provide us with a path to our destiny.

Memnon's voice rang out across the Dome.

The weapons would be sealed away. Nations would no longer raise arms for land or resources or pride. The bloodshed would stop. The inevitable annihilation would be held back. In the place of the ceaseless Daiymo wars, we Grievar would fight. They would build great arenas across the world, and we would stand in the luminous

Circles within them. Our fists would hold sway over the fate of nations. We would fight for the earth we stand upon. We would fight for honor. We would fight so the rest should not have to.

Memnon had said those words with such conviction, such passion that Murray had held them close to his heart for three decades.

Now those words meant nothing.

Now the Grievar were nothing more than a means to an end. Grievar fought for the Daimyo's petty political gains, for land or resources or slaves. The Grievar were their tools—things they could experiment on, weapons to warp to their purpose.

What bothered Murray most was the fact that the Citadel was complicit in the whole thing. Murray never expected the Daimyo to have any honor—but High Command? Memnon? How could someone who knew the Codes by heart treat their own kin like some sort of experiment?

What could Murray do, though? He was only a Scout. He'd already broken the rules once in the Underground, and he knew another instance of wrongdoing would mean his expulsion from the Citadel. He knew if he asked around too much, it would get back to the high commander or to Callen and his network of spies.

Murray slammed his fist into the dirt.

He'd given Cego his word. What was he worried about? Himself? His own path and future with the Citadel? How could he even consider thinking like some pathetic, self-preserving Daimyo?

Murray needed more information, and there was only one Grievar he could trust right now.

* * *

Cego's other two mandatory Level One classes were more of what he expected. Striking Level One and Grappling Level One reviewed many of the basic techniques Cego had already grasped firmly. Even so, he made sure to pay close attention and took Sol's lead by constantly pulling vid clips onto his lightdeck so that he could review them later.

Professor Tefo's first class began with an animated telling of his rise as a Knight.

"Back when I was a young Grievar, things weren't quite so cushy. Being a Knight didn't mean broadcasts up on SystemView, the adoration of fans, getting the best rooms when traveling, or spending all your time hobnobbing with noble folk. We did it all outside of the light. No one even knew who we were back then…"

Cego got the impression he was going to hear many more of these stories by the end of his semester with Tefo.

The rest of Professor Tefo's class consisted of a series of striking drills. Tefo, in his booming voice, called for his students to throw combinations of punches, kicks, knees, and elbows into the heavy bags that lined the classroom. Tefo would circle the room and examine each student's form, sometimes offering small corrections but more often just saying, "Hmm," which made most of the students nervous and more likely to throw a mistimed strike.

The Grappling Level One Professor, Sidney Sapao, was a young but experienced teacher. It had only been five years since he'd graduated from the Lyceum himself, but his lightpath as a Knight had been cut short due to a permanent neck injury. Sapao had shown such promise as a Knight that the Lyceum immediately picked him up as a professor.

Professor Sapao concentrated his entire first class on the concepts of base and posture. The Level Ones took turns maintaining their posture on their knees and standing, all while a partner tried to break them down.

Cego was surprised to see that many of his classmates were unaware of the most basic concepts in grappling. They were fast to show off the new, flashy techniques they'd seen on SystemView or moves they'd learned from an older sibling, but when asked the best way to break an opponent's closed guard, they were completely clueless.

Luckily, Farmer had stressed the basics throughout Cego's

training. Cego could remember the extreme frustration that came from practicing mundane concepts like posture for hours every day in the ironwood Circle. Now, watching some of his classmates struggle during class, he felt lucky to have had such a meticulous teacher.

Cego was amazed to see that all his professors assigned after-hours training assignments for students to review the techniques shown in the class.

"More class, even after class? What's with this place? I just hope they assign us a trip to the dining hall soon," Dozer said to Cego as they left Grappling Level One and headed downstairs toward the common ground.

Sol brushed past the two boys. "What'd you think? Knights were just magically made here without putting any hard work in?"

Compared to the complete lack of direction for what they called training at Thaloo's, the Lyceum's regimen was refreshing to Cego, though he was starting to worry about the workload already piling up on his shoulders.

Cego paused on the common ground with Dozer to take a deep breath between classes. A crowd of students had gathered to peer up at the large challenge lightboard. Rallying cries emerged from some teams as the challenges were posted. Matchups flickered across the board, starting with Level Six challenges at the top, all the way down to the Level Ones. Cego's eyes found the bottom of the board.

TEAM TUSKER (LV. 2) CHALLENGES TEAM WHELPS (LV. 1)

"Already?" Dozer exclaimed. "First week here and we've already got a darkin' challenge on our hands. And a Level Two team! What's with that?"

"I'm not sure," Cego replied. "I think we need to decide what to do now, though..."

"Didn't you blocks read through the Lyceum's *Guide to Challenges*?" Sol said from beside Cego as she gazed up at the lightboard. "It was part of our prescribed reading last night."

"Um... I was planning on getting to that," Cego said guiltily.

"Read?" Dozer responded. "I'm not gonna spend my night with my face in a lightdeck like some Daimyo clerk."

Sol rolled her eyes at the two boys. "Well, if you two had actually taken the time to go over the guide, you'd have a clue as to what is happening right now."

Both boys looked at Sol expectantly, waiting for an explanation.

"I see how this is going to be," Sol said. "This is the last time I'm explaining things to you just because you are too lazy to do the work."

The two boys nodded.

"We have to decide whether or not to accept the Tuskers' challenge by end of day today. Each of us individually votes on our lightdecks," Sol said as she swiped her device to show Cego and Dozer the voting screen.

"If we choose to accept the challenge, we'll be put in the Circle against them this coming study intermission, three days from now," Sol explained.

"But why would a Level Two team want to pick a fight with us?" Dozer asked. "I've never even heard of the Tuskers before."

"Well, lucky for you guys, I made it through the strategy section of the *Guide to Challenges* as well," Sol said with satisfaction. "Although they are not as common as intralevel challenges, there are advantages and disadvantages to challenging teams that are lower or higher level than your own. The most obvious reason the Tuskers challenged us is because they are looking for an easy way to boost their score. Even though we barely have any score to lose, they know we are fresh Level Ones and they think they can get an easy win off us."

Dozer growled, "They aren't gonna get no darkin' easy win off me..."

Sol continued. "However, there are built-in disadvantages to challenging lower-level teams. The first is that the lower-level team always gets to pick the matchups."

"You mean we get to pick who fights who?" Cego asked.

"Yes, if we accept, we pick three of our fighters to match up with any three from their team," Sol said. "It gets a bit more complicated depending on the level difference of the teams involved. For example, if a Level Four team were to challenge a Level One, they'd lose a Grievar, meaning one of the Level Fours would have to fight two bouts in a row. The handicaps dissuade the higher levels from bullying the lower levels all the time."

"How about a Level Sixer?" Dozer asked. "What prevents them from challenging us?"

"Well, nothing prevents them, but Level Sixers get the biggest handicaps. They'd need to take on three of us in a row with a single member of their team to win a challenge," Sol said.

"Wow," Dozer said, clearly amazed at the prospect of one Grievar taking on three fighters back-to-back.

"And what if we decline the Tuskers' challenge?" Cego asked, though he could tell by Dozer's determined expression that wouldn't be as simple as it sounded.

"Well, if you decline a challenge, your score takes a hit," Sol said. "Not as much as if you lose the challenge, though. It depends on how much risk the challenger is taking; a decline penalty gets bigger with the risk factor."

"If there are so many disadvantages and risks, why even make a challenge?" Cego asked.

"That's what challenges are all about," Sol said matter-of-factly. "Torm Ironhand, the Grievar who created the challenge system, famously stated: *Challenges are macroscopic versions of combat itself.*"

Dozer snorted. "You actually memorized the darkin' guidebook?"

Sol ignored him, continuing her recitation. *"In combat, one has to take calculated risk in order to open an opponent's defense. Eventually, one Grievar has to make the first move in combat, just as is the case in the challenge system."*

Sol added, "You're right, though, Cego. Some teams play the defensive game and wait for other teams to make the challenges."

Cego nodded as he listened to Sol's explanation. Fighting was all about taking risks. Playing it too safe with any worthy opponent gave them the opportunity to slowly pull apart your defenses. But counterattacking was a valid strategy as well, waiting for an opponent to show an opening and then capitalizing on it.

Cego gazed at the screen to see that some of the challenges had already been marked as accepted in emblazoned red text. In addition, a small *TC* insignia had appeared next to some of the challenges on the board.

"What's TC mean?" Cego asked Sol.

"Trade clause," Sol said. "That means the defending team has accepted the challenge, but they've invoked a trade clause. Only a defending team can do this, and only if their calculated risk in accepting the challenge is high enough. If they win, they get to make a trade for a select member of the attacking team."

Cego immediately thought about Knees. This was the answer he'd been looking for—a way to get Knees back.

"Is there any way to make a trade challenge directly?" Cego asked, trying to contain his excitement.

Sol shook her head. "You can't challenge another team for one of their members, like you could for a trophy. A trade clause can only be invoked as a response to a challenge... I don't like the sound of this. What are you thinking?"

"Well. I was just thinking about getting Knees back," Cego said.

Dozer's eyes lit up. "Yes. We need to make a challenge to get him back!"

"Didn't you just hear me, you big block?" Sol said. "We can't make a challenge for a trade."

"But if the Bayhounds were to challenge us... then we could invoke the trade clause," Cego pondered.

"Yes, but how would we get the Bayhounds to challenge us?" Sol asked.

"As you just said, Sol, this is all just a bigger version of a fight,"

Cego responded. "We need them to think our hands are down because we're too tired to keep them up. When they make their move, we counter at just the right moment."

"It's not as simple as that," Sol said. "Most challenges are attempts to bite into another team's score. Currently, as our score is hanging right near zero, there is no real reason for the Bayhounds to challenge us. Plus, the trade clause can only be invoked if the defender's calculated risk is very high. Ours is not."

Cego sighed. He knew Sol was right, which was starting to become a trend this week.

They would need to play the long game.

"All right. Well, then, we need to start building our score," Cego said as he swiped his lightdeck, voting in favor of accepting the Tuskers' challenge.

* * *

Luckily, the day before the Whelps' first challenge, Cego's class schedule wasn't as jam-packed. Cego was already painfully sore from the variety of grappling, striking, and endurance drills his professors had them running throughout that week, and he hoped to have some recovery time before getting into the Circle against a Level Two opponent.

After Cego had voted to accept the Tuskers' challenge, Dozer and Sol had followed suit. The only decline to the challenge had come from Mateus Winterfowl, who pretty much did everything in opposition to what the rest of the team decided.

Cego's final class of the week was Combat Codes with Professor Aon Farstead. Cego had received an alert on his lightdeck that told him he'd been accepted into the class. As expected, he'd been rejected from the more popular Stratagems and Maneuvers.

Unlike the rest of Cego's classes, which were on level one of the Harmony, Aon's class was on the other side of the Lyceum, in the Valkyrie. Cego walked the long hallway between the two buildings alone, watching the torches flicker along the walls. His heart had sunk when he'd received notice that Aon's class was located in the Valkyrie—he hadn't been back there since the Trials.

It was impossible to forget what had happened in there. Since the Trials, since he'd heard his brother Sam in that strange simulation, he couldn't shake the feeling that he was being watched. Even now, hearing his footsteps down the empty hallway, the hairs on the back of his neck prickled.

Cego was glad he hadn't been given much time to consider the past. There was enough to worry about here at the Lyceum—classes, training assignments, scores, and challenges. Getting Knees back.

"You go to Professor Farstead class too, Cego?" A voice sprang from behind him.

Cego spun around and barely muffled a surprised yelp. Abel. The little Desovian was alarmingly agile. "You scared me there, Abel," Cego said. "Yeah, I've got Combat Codes—you?"

"Yes... what privilege!" Abel said in near-breathless excitement. "My ancestors, in Desovi, still they speak of Aon Farstead in daily prayers. If only they could see Abel now."

"In their prayers?" Cego asked as they continued down the long hallway.

"Yes. In Desovi at evening prayer, Grievar pay respect to those who came before," Abel said. "Long list of famous Desovian Grievar. So long that Abel sometimes fall asleep. Aon Farstead on that list. In his young age, Professor Aon, he come to Desovi and teach our folk. He spread the Codes."

Cego had thought that the Codes were always there, since the beginning. Like the black sand beach or the emerald waters of his home.

"I hope to find seat in Professor Aon's class," Abel said as they began to climb the stairs toward the sixth floor of the Valkyrie.

"Why, do you think it will be crowded?" Cego asked.

"Of course," Abel replied. "How could whole Lyceum not be there to hear Professor Aon's wise words?"

Abel's jaw dropped when they opened the door to Professor Farstead's classroom. It was nearly empty. There were only a handful of students sitting in a small semicircle. The room was set up informally and had the feel of a study, with wall-to-wall shelves of books, just like the sort Murray had stacked in the corner of his bedroom.

Cego quickly recognized the red braid hanging off the back of one of the chairs—Sol. They took a seat next to their fellow Whelp, who gave them a surprised look, perhaps because the rest of the students in attendance looked to be from the higher levels.

"Wow. I didn't expect to see you two here," Sol whispered.

"Why not?" Cego asked. "Professor Aon is famous. He's even mentioned in daily prayers around the world." He wasn't quite sure why he'd added that detail, and he caught Abel smiling.

Sol gave Cego a quizzical look. "Well, I just didn't think the Deep Grievar gave much credence to the Codes any longer. Isn't it all about making a bit down there?"

"You're right. Most folk don't care about the Codes down there. But I'm not from the Deep," Cego replied.

Sol raised an eyebrow and was about to say something when Professor Aon entered the study.

From his long grey beard to his wispy robe, the old Grievar oozed wisdom. The class stood as he entered, but Aon motioned for everyone to sit as he took a seat in the center of the semicircle.

"That walk from the Tower is getting longer and longer every day." Aon chuckled as he straightened out the folds in his robe. Cego knew Aon was blind, but the old Grievar's white eyes had a life of their own, never staying on one point in the room.

"Eight this year, eh?" Aon said. "Every year, a few less. When I first started teaching this class at the Lyceum, five decades ago, we needed to hold this lecture in the Dome to fit all the students. Now my quaint little study does the trick."

Abel suddenly raised his hand.

Professor Aon cocked his head, somehow sensing Abel's outstretched arm. "Yes, young Grievar?"

"Professor Aon, I would like to express honor I have to attend your class, and for those who do not come, I feel sorrow that they cannot hear your wise words," Abel said stoically, as if he'd rehearsed the line.

"The honor is mine, young Grievar. And no matter how many students attend my class, I plan on being here, every year, until my body is more dust than bone," Aon said. "Is that an East Desovian accent I detect?"

Abel smiled widely. "Yes, my parents from Thirkarsh, not far from border."

"A wonderful place...and a wonderful people," Aon mused. "Some of the best years of my life I spent in Desovi. Even at my age, I think I'd shave a few years off the top for one of those fresh sponge cakes right now. *Throcksh mafalesta.*" Aon made a quick signal with his hands clasped together.

"*Threeksh mafalesta,*" Abel replied in Desovian, making the same solemn gesture.

"The young Desovian here brings us to a good starting point for today's lecture," Aon said. He paused for a moment, as if listening to the quiet in the room. "There are Grievar around the world right now, each fighting for a different nation, different people, and a different reason. Why do *we* fight?"

The room stayed silent. The question seemed so simple. Aon asked it again. "Why do we fight?"

One of the Level Sixers responded. "We fight so the rest shall not have to."

Aon nodded. "I'm glad you know the first precept of the Codes. Yet reciting directly from the Codes does not answer my question. Why do we fight?"

Cego thought about growing up on the island, which now seemed more a distant dream than ever before. Cego had sparred ferociously with his brothers, often so hard that his arms hung at his sides like sea slugs afterward. He fought then because he wanted Farmer's approval. He fought on the island because he wanted Sam to look up to him, because he wanted to finally beat Silas.

In the Underground, Cego had fought because Thaloo had forced him to line the bit-purse of patrons and mercs and other nefarious Deep folk. He considered his time on the Surface so far. He fought to enter the Lyceum, to get where he was now. To study, to become a Knight. And then... Cego hadn't really given much thought to what would happen after. He assumed that when he became a Knight, he would be fighting for his nation, for Ezo.

"We fight because we have to," Cego said.

Aon's ears perked up and he turned in Cego's direction. "Cego, is it?"

"Yes, Professor," Cego answered.

"Care to elaborate on that, Cego?" Aon asked.

"Um, well..." Cego didn't realize he'd be put on the spot. "I don't really know why we fight, to tell you the truth. Grievar fight. I was never given any choice about it. It's not like with the Daimyo, who choose their lightpath. They get to choose to be painters or politiks or merchants or makers. I just knew from the start, a Grievar fights. That's just the way it is," Cego said.

"That's just the way it is," Aon repeated Cego's words. "I've heard that many times before, young Grievar. Do you know what that usually means? It means that folk have forgotten why. That is the case here. Most have forgotten why we fight. We cannot forget, or all is lost," Aon warned.

Aon waved his hand around the classroom at the tall bookshelves surrounding them. "These books are why we fight, young Grievar. They are filled not only with the Combat Codes, but also with our history. The history of this world, from before your time and even my time, as hard as that might be to imagine for some of you. These books are filled with tales of strength and honor, deception and cowardice, love and sorrow. These books are why we fight," Aon repeated.

Cego swiveled his head around the room, taking in the shadows that the bookshelves cast in the dancing light.

"To truly answer the question—why do we fight?—you would need to read through every single word of every single book in this room. And then you would need to find every other book written by Grievar and Daimyo historians alike and read their words. After that, you would need to listen to every tale ever told, spoken from the crafty tongues of the Daimyo nobles to the pleading whispers of the Grievar slaves held in the deepest, darkest Underground cells.

"I do not say this to dissuade you from seeking the truth, my students," Aon said. "After all, it has been the sole purpose of my long years on this planet to answer that question, and I shall continue trying to do so until my last breath. I say this to tell you that the answer to why the Grievar fight is in the very history of this world. It is in the blood that runs through your veins and in the light that shines up on our walls."

Aon paused, as if examining each student's reaction to his words.

"That is the purpose of this class. Though it is called the Combat Codes and we will certainly be studying those very texts, we shall also keep in mind that we strive for greater purpose than simply reading a text. We each are seeking our own answer to that question: Why do we fight?"

* * *

The question—*why do we fight?*—was notably absent from Cego's mind as Gunnar Cavanaugh's shin skimmed the top of his head.

The Tuskers' team leader was bearing down on Cego, attacking him with a variety of strikes from unorthodox angles. Cego was defending ably enough, but he wasn't sure how much longer he'd be able to keep up the pace.

Cego sucked in his stomach, narrowly avoiding another blistering kick aimed at his liver. Gunnar didn't look like he was slowing down anytime soon—the Level Two's blue second skin was barely wet. Cego's white second skin had completely soaked through after the first ten minutes of the bout.

The Lyceum's challenge grounds were nowhere near as grand and looming as Lampai Stadium, yet somehow, Cego found this venue more intimidating. The room was utilitarian—unadorned walls, several rows of long wooden bleachers on each side, a canvas with three adjacent Circles planted at the center.

The intimidation stemmed from who was in this room: Cego's peers and teachers, not just random spectators. The audience was made of Lyceum students who were levels above Cego, Fives and Sixers who were on the verge of graduating and becoming Knights. His own professors were also likely watching him from somewhere up in those stands, judging his performance.

Well into minute twenty of the fray, Cego was short on ideas on how to beat Gunnar. For a lanky striker, his opponent was surprisingly agile, with solid takedown defense. Gunnar had stuffed most of Cego's shots and had easily returned to his feet after the rare takedown.

Though Gunnar's attacks had more than occupied Cego's attention, he had noticed Sol's quick win in the next Circle over. The daughter of Artemis Halberd had proven herself an able grappler. Cego had heard the familiar crunch of bone and ligament as Sol had torqued her opponent's knee to a vicious angle.

Mateus Winterfowl, who'd refused to join the Whelps during their strategy session, had lost his bout near minute five. Mateus had gone up against the Tuskers' resident brawler, who'd overwhelmed him with what Cego could only describe as an ugly but relentless show of striking.

With the score tied up, it was up to Cego to take this first win for the Whelps.

Gunnar leapt in with two quick jabs, one breaking through to bloody Cego's nose even as he tried to slip to the left.

Cego was fighting in rubellium, a familiar setting after the month of training in Murray-Ku's Circle. Though Violet was technically a hybrid of rubellium and auralite alloys, she still had prepared Cego adequately for the push he felt now. The Circle's red glow had urged him forward throughout the bout, but Cego had stayed calm, patiently waiting for his opening. He was still waiting.

He slipped another jab and tucked his hand against his jaw, taking Gunnar's high round kick to the forearm. He'd feel that one tomorrow.

Cego responded with a spinning back fist. He'd attempted the technique several times so far with little success. Gunnar stepped out of reach again.

The Tuskers' team leader was tall and corded, with short-cropped blond hair. Gunnar seemed confident in his every movement, not hesitating as he surged forward with another rapid combination.

Cego's brother, Silas, had fought with a similar style. "Every punch needs potential," Silas had said to Cego during one of their bouts in Farmer's ironwood Circle.

"How about a feint?" Cego had asked his older brother. "What if I'm just trying to get you to react?"

"Even a feint needs potential," Silas had replied. "Otherwise, your opponent knows it's a feint. It loses its purpose."

Silas had demonstrated his lesson on Cego firsthand, as he often did, throwing a series of quick combinations and breaking through with a cross that left Cego crumpled on the floor. "So, how do I win?" Cego had asked his older brother, holding a hand up to the gash under his eye.

"You don't win." Silas had flashed that mocking smile of his before walking away, leaving Cego alone in the Circle.

At the time, Cego had thought Silas was simply being arrogant. His elder brother had often treated him harshly, almost with disdain, not with the care he reserved for Sam.

Gunnar fought the same way Silas did, though—every attack he threw had the potential of causing damage. He didn't throw feints haphazardly. If Cego didn't get his hands up, he knew he'd pay for it. He was constantly defending, always one step behind Gunnar.

You don't win.

Cego was trying to defend every attack, win every series. He was wearing down, constantly on the defensive. Eventually, Gunnar would catch him standing.

Silas was right. He wouldn't win the standup game.

Cego took a deep breath as Gunnar threw a leaping cross, springing forward off his front foot, propelling his weight into the punch.

Cego kept his hands low as the blow caught him on the chin. He tried to turn away to lessen the impact, but the force still had him reeling to the canvas.

Gunnar was on him in an instant, taking the opportunity to pummel Cego on the floor. Though Cego was still spinning from the attack, he'd drilled the technique too many times to fail.

Every morning, under the island's tangerine light, Cego had practiced off his back. Shooting his hips up, throwing his legs open, catching an invisible opponent's neck, locking his foot in the crook of his knee, squeezing, and repeating the drill a thousand times more until Farmer's rare nod of approval.

Wherever the island was, wherever Farmer and Silas and Sam were, it didn't matter right now. Everything he'd learned from them was real—as real as the air he was breathing or the canvas he lay on. His body knew the technique. He was the technique.

Cego shot his hips up as Gunnar came in, latching the triangle choke around the boy's exposed neck while trapping his arm. He found the perfect angle, reaching under Gunnar's knee to turn his hips and thrust his leg forward. He locked on and squeezed.

As Gunnar went out, Cego saw his brother Silas standing over him, flashing his mocking smile.

CHAPTER 15

Why We Fight

Throwing opposite-side strikes in cadence surely is an effective way to utilize a Grievar's momentum to the fullest. Just as the pendulum swings back and forth, each strike can feed off the force of the previous. However, against an experienced opponent, a Grievar needs to consider switching cadence, attacking out of rhythm with multiple strikes focused to one side. Attacking out of cadence requires a greater expenditure of ki—a Grievar should practice doing so regularly.

Passage Six, Ninetieth Technique of the Combat Codes

Cego was tired and hungry—a trend at the Lyceum. Even as the semester approached its midpoint, he felt the constant strain of training.

As usual, the Whelps descended the stairs toward the dining hall together.

"Think there'll be real animals down there?" Dozer had asked the first time they'd gone down those stairs. "I'm beat. But not so beat that I won't be able to catch some dinner."

Sol had given Cego a look that said, *Is he for real?*

The Lyceum's dining hall was quite impressive, though Cego realized his primary frame of reference had been the cans of green slop they called food in the Underground. Of course, there were no animals, live or dead, as Dozer had hoped for, but there were several stations that served various forms of vat-protein and insta-carbs, along with dehydrated fruits and vegetables.

The other Level One teams sat along the same wooden table as the Whelps. For now, the lacklights and purelights coexisted without disturbance. Kōri Shimo sat alone at one end of the table, maintaining his trademark blank stare. Gryfin Thurgood confidently sat between two female students, regaling them with the tale of his first broken bone.

Even Knees sat at the far end of the table with the rest of the Bayhounds, though the Venturian had avoided eye contact with Cego or Dozer for several weeks now.

Professor Tefo had been speaking the truth at the start of the semester when he'd said that the boundaries of birthright and wealth would be broken down at the Lyceum. The intense class and challenge schedule had the effect of bringing everyone to the same baseline. Not to say that there wasn't any discrimination. Shiar and most of the other purelights still walked around like they were superior beings—they were just too worn down to do anything about it.

There was a whole new way to discriminate here at the Lyceum, though—Levels. Those wearing their brand-new white second skins—Level Ones—clumped together and wearily watched the sea of bigger fish swarm around them.

The Level Twos, who wore blue skins, sat congregated among their own kind, as did the Level Threes, who wore purple, the Level Fours, in brown, Level Fives, wearing black, and Level Sixes, all in red. Here and there, Cego noticed an outlier sitting apart from their own level, but overall, the tables in the dining hall reminded him of the various monochrome patches of berries that used to grow on the island.

The segregation around him made Cego feel all the more fortunate to be a Whelp. He felt at home with his team, though his prior conceptions of home had unraveled at this point.

Abel was always full of interesting tidbits of foreign knowledge. Today, he was attempting to enlighten Dozer on the nude fighting rituals of the Thanti folk, an indigenous Grievar tribe that had gone unnoticed by the rest of civilization for thousands of years.

"Completely darkin' naked?" Dozer exclaimed. "Wouldn't that be... dangerous for, you know. Delicate parts?"

Sol slapped Dozer on the shoulder. "Oh, manliest of Grievar, I was under the impression that one such as you did not have any delicate parts."

"You know what I mean," Dozer protested.

Abel proceeded to stand and mimic how the Thanti folk would tuck their delicate parts to keep them out of harm's way, eliciting raucous laughter from the rest of the team. Though he sometimes questioned the legitimacy of such tales, Cego had become fond of the way Abel told his stories.

Joba continued to stay silent, though Cego could sense the boy's steady presence. No matter what the circumstances, Joba had a broad smile spread across his face. Throughout the toughest workouts or during the most mundane lectures, the boy's smile remained steadfast. Cego often wondered if Joba was smiling because he was happy to be removed from whatever hardships he'd suffered in the borderlands.

Cego glanced at Sol from across the table. The daughter of Artemis Halberd was continuing to chide Dozer about his delicates, fluttering her sunflower eyes in what she called proper noble-lady fashion. Her braid swung across her back as she shook her head.

At this point, Sol seemed to accept her role as the team's resident fight librarian. Though she did roll her eyes on many occasions, Cego had come to find that Sol wasn't just a brain. She backed up her vast banks of martial information with flawless execution. In the individual Level One scoring sections, Sol was leading in every class with nearly perfect test scores.

Even Mateus Winterfowl appeared to have eased his reluctance in associating with the rest of the Whelps. At the start of the semester, Mateus would constantly complain about the great indignities he was suffering, sleeping amid a group of foreigners and lacklights. Now he mainly just grumbled, which Cego could more easily digest.

Part of Mateus's acceptance of the Whelps came from the indisputable fact that the team performed well together. Team scores were an essential portion of each student's total score, and the Whelps had been very successful so far. They currently stood second in the Level One standings, narrowly trailing the Bayhounds going into midterms.

The Whelps' primary advantage had been the full use of their six team members. Because each challenge only used three Grievar, many of the other teams had come to rely only on their best three while the rest remained unused. Though this strategy was strong to start, the top three were fast to wear down because of their increased fight load.

Though the Whelps had a solid top three—Cego, Sol, and Dozer—the true strength of their team came from spreading out their fights based on each member's strengths.

Abel's ability to rapidly move in and out of striking distance made him the perfect matchup for slow-moving, heavy-hitting Grievar he could wear down. Joba was the best match against lanky strikers—the boy had the uncanny ability to absorb a barrage of strikes before bearing down on his opponent.

Unlike most of the cocky purelights on the other teams, the Whelps also found strength in their admission of weakness. They weren't afraid to know where each member was lacking. Dozer was baffled by plotting opponents—those smart Grievar who came in with a bout-long game plan. He always fared better in slugfests.

Sol performed fantastically against those same intelligent opponents. Somehow, she could always out-strategize them, thinking one step ahead for each of their moves.

Despite the Whelps' current standing, Cego had not lost sight of his plan from the start of the semester. He glanced down the long table toward Knees, who had that same blank stare on his face as he slowly picked at his food.

Cego had attempted to reach out to his friend several times this semester so far; after all, they were in three of the same classes and it was difficult to avoid any Level Ones at such close quarters. Each time, Knees had responded to Cego with those bleary eyes, as if he didn't recognize who he was.

Even if the Whelps did somehow pull the plan off—convincing the Bayhounds to challenge them at a huge risk and invoking the trade clause for Knees, not to mention winning the challenge against the leading Level One team—what then? That didn't mean Cego would be able to help his friend with what he was going through. Even if Knees was on the Whelps, they couldn't get inside his brain.

One step forward is one step where you are not standing still. Farmer's voice cut through the surrounding clamor of the dining hall.

The old master was right, as usual. Even if Cego didn't know how to help Knees, getting him onto their team and away from Shiar's Bayhounds would be a step forward.

Like preparing for a fight, the Whelps needed to be methodical in their research and execution. He'd already discovered that Shiar and the rest of the Bayhounds had been sniffing around to evaluate the strength of the other teams.

Currently, though, there was too much at stake for the Bayhounds to challenge the Whelps. Shiar's team could lose their coveted first-place spot going into the end of the semester. The Bayhounds needed more incentive—they needed to smell blood.

That's just what Cego planned to give them.

* * *

On first attending Circles and Alloys, Cego had expected to walk into a large classroom; after all, how would they train within the wide variety of Circles without having access to each of them?

He'd been surprised to enter a tiny room, barely the size of Murray's barracks, with a single Circle set at the center. Almost more surprising than the classroom was his teacher—he'd nearly gasped at the sight of Professor Adrienne Larkspur. She was the size of Murray-Ku in both height and breadth, her blond topknot collecting dust from the ceiling during her lectures.

Professor Larkspur's size wasn't her defining feature, though.

Larkspur had a gargantuan memory for all things relating to the Circles. With terrific clarity, she could recall every mixture of alloys, every set of engraved sigils, and every sort of clasp and gear that had ever composed a Circle. She knew the minutiae of every significant fight that had occurred in the last century—the nations the Grievar hailed from; each combatant's biometrics, strengths, and weaknesses; every punch, kick, knee, or elbow that had landed during the bouts.

Though at times she could overwhelm her students with the sheer weight of data, Professor Larkspur wasn't boring. She recounted famous fights with vigor—setting up each Grievar's backstory, building the suspense, and finally drawing her students into the Circles as if they were actually participating in the bout.

Today, Larkspur was finishing her week's review of emeralyis alloy by recounting a recent battle between Artemis Halberd and Yongl Floree, a Besaydian Knight.

"Artemis saw his opportunity—any Knight of his caliber would see the same. Though Floree's limbs were intact, though his heart rate hadn't fluctuated, though he wasn't winded, Artemis could see something else was wrong with his opponent." Larkspur flashed her eyes back and forth at the class.

Professor Larkspur stood at the center of the mimicry Circle, which was now glowing with the green hue of emeralyis. Cego's question about the tiny classroom had been answered on the first day of class when he'd seen the mimicry Circle in action.

Though it wasn't as powerful as a Circle built of a single alloy, the mimicry Circle could imitate nearly any of the other elements. Created from a low-level mixture of the entire spectrum of alloys, a Grievar could simply speak of a fight that had taken place in a specific alloy to will the mimicry Circle to assume its properties.

"Artemis had been watching Floree's footwork," Larkspur continued. "The Besaydian was a southpaw. He always circled to his right, away from Artemis's power. Floree had already tried to pepper Artemis with jabs, as southpaws tend to do, though so far, they hadn't amounted to much. That's when Floree started to doubt himself. He started to let the emeralyis influence him. The Circle beckoned him to do something new, something creative to break Artemis's defenses."

There were only five students this semester in Circles and Alloys, each taking a ringside seat for Larkspur's lecture: Cego, Mateus Winterfowl, Wilhelm Bariston, Tegan Masterton, and Kōri Shimo. Four of the five were enraptured by Professor Larkspur's story. Kōri Shimo was staring out the window—the strange boy couldn't seem to care less about the lesson.

"Floree suddenly decided to change directions. The Besaydian circled to his left this time. He surely knew he was moving toward Artemis's power side, but he did it anyway. The emeralyis had convinced him it was a good idea." Larkspur's words were accentuated as several green spectrals lifted from the edge of the mimicry Circle's glowing frame.

"We all know what happened next. You just don't circle toward Artemis Halberd's power." Larkspur feigned a massive right-handed roundhouse. "Yongl Floree's lightpath ended right there."

Cego felt the need for an *O Toh* after Larkspur's rousing lecture, but he refrained.

"Any questions before we wrap up?" Larkspur asked.

Tegan Masterton raised her fist in the air and Larkspur nodded at her. "I know you've covered lots of historical fights and the sort of Circles they took place in, but I'm just wondering about the spectrals. They're always there, flying around the Circles, giving off different sorts of light. But what are they?"

"By the expression on all of your faces, I can see this is a good question." Larkspur raised an eyebrow. "So...does anyone have any idea what the spectrals are?"

Mateus Winterfowl spoke up. "I hear they are spirits. Sent down to watch over us from the gods."

The statement elicited a laugh from another student, but Larkspur frowned. "Mateus is not naïve to think this. In fact, many Grievar around the world believe that the spectrals are some sort of otherworldly spirit."

"But it's not true, is it?" Tegan Masterton shook her head in disbelief. "There's no such thing as spirits, no one's watching us, right?"

"Well..." Larkspur trailed off, seeming to consider Tegan's question. "There are many mysteries that do surround the spectrals, and much even I don't know, though I've studied Circles for the entirety of my life. But let's start with what we do know. Where do they come from?"

"From the alloys," Cego said. He knew for certain that each type of spectral was directly related to the type of alloy it was attracted to.

"Indeed," Larkspur said. "We believe the spectrals are created in the reaction that occurs when the alloys are extracted. For example, when rubellium is smelted from ore to its base form, red-light spectrals are born. Those spectrals are continually attracted to rubellium, which is why we see them flocking around a Circle created from that alloy. The purer the Circle, absent of any other metallic mixtures, the greater the attraction."

Cego thought about Murray's Circle, Violet, a hybrid of two alloys that attracted the strange indigo spectrals. Cego hadn't heard from Murray since the start of semester, but he could imagine the man still habitually polished Violet every morning.

"But weren't the spectrals here before the Circles?" Tegan asked. "I've heard stories of the Ancients fighting in stone rings, and still there was light shining onto them."

"Yes, yes," Larkspur said. "It's debatable how accurate those stories are. But some say the spectrals have existed since the beginning, that they were created from natural alloy reactions deep beneath the earth and in the ocean trenches."

Cego was starting to notice a trend here at the Lyceum. Somehow, the more he learned about any subject, the less he realized he knew. He'd thought he was finally starting to understand the Circles, but he wasn't so confident anymore. Cego looked across the class to Kōri Shimo to see if he was as intrigued about these revelations, but, like clockwork, the boy was staring off into another world.

"Looks like our time is nearly up. We can continue this discussion next class," Larkspur said.

Cego stood with the rest of the class to receive their assignments via lightdeck.

"As always, we'll be moving on to a new alloy next week," Professor Larkspur said. "Onyx is one you've likely had little experience with, for good reason."

Cego's ears perked up. Ever since he'd discovered the onyx Circle in his Trial and felt the blacklight, he'd wondered if Larkspur would be covering the mysterious alloy in her class.

"Onyx compresses time," Larkspur explained. "Your past, your present, your future—a strong onyx Circle can bind them together."

Cego's mind drifted to the Time Trial, when he sat in the ironwood grove for what seemed like weeks on end, though he'd discovered afterward he'd lasted less than an hour.

"I only fought in onyx twice during my path," Larkspur continued. "I don't remember much—that's one of the effects of time compression. Some Knights come out of onyx not even remembering their own names."

As Professor Larkspur spoke, the room seemed to darken, as if the shadows were growing like vines along the close walls. The green hue of the emeralyis had diffused, giving way to a strange new light. Cego couldn't quite describe it. It almost appeared to be the absence of light, as if the glow from the mimicry Circle was sucking away at any external sources of brightness.

"Blacklight. An onyx Circle's blacklight can do many things to a Grievar," Larkspur said quietly. Her voice was getting softer. "Loss of memory, heightened memory, confusion, anger, insanity—we've had cases of nearly every ailment over the... In some cases, onyx has even..."

Larkspur's words faded in and out, though Cego could still see her mouth moving. Darkness crowded the edge of his vision.

Cego could see himself then, wavering at the edge of the mimicry Circle. There was a smudge of blood staining the back of his white second skin.

He was looking in from the outside, pressed up against the window, peering through the thick glass into the classroom.

He saw Professor Larkspur waving her hands, commanding the attention of the class. He saw the mimicry Circle glimmering like wet coal. He saw dark spectrals rising from its frame like fleeing shadows.

The spectrals were hovering over his head. He saw tendrils of darkness reaching from the wisps, pulling at him. Cego wanted to bang on the window. He wanted to warn himself, but he couldn't move, couldn't speak.

Suddenly, two eyes met his, burning yellow embers staring directly back out at him through the window. Kōri Shimo.

Cego panicked; he was losing control. He was getting pulled

away from the window. Why was he here? What choice did he have?

Cego breathed in deeply. He released the breath. *Rolling like a wave.*

He inhaled again, just as Farmer had showed him. He exhaled.

The darkness faded. The noise and light crept back toward him.

Cego was back in his body, standing at the edge of the Circle in Professor Larkspur's tiny classroom.

"—so I'll expect you to be ready for your end-of-semester test by that point, and as always, feel free to stop by for any extra help before then," Larkspur concluded.

The others began to filter out of the room. Mateus was muttering about being late to the dining hall.

Cego turned toward Kōri Shimo. The boy was still looking out the window.

* * *

Murray made sure to remain unseen as he climbed the stairs of the Valkyrie toward Commander Aon Farstead's study. Even under the guise of a harmless visit to one of his old mentors, Murray didn't want to raise any notes of suspicion.

Aon's door was open when Murray arrived at the end of the sixth-floor hallway.

"Commander Farstead?" Murray said as he entered. He scanned the room, which had remained exactly the same for the past few decades, still full of musty old bookshelves. Aon Farstead was nowhere to be seen.

"Murray Pearson, I thought you'd be paying me a visit sometime soon." A voice suddenly fell from above Murray.

Murray peered up and saw the ancient Grievar perched at the top of a ladder set against one of the tall bookshelves. Aon had a small sack hanging off his shoulders. He carefully pulled a book from the sack and deposited it in an empty section on one of the shelves.

"No matter how much we think we know, there's always some empty space up there," Aon mused as he set another book in place.

"Commander, shouldn't you be careful? I mean, let me help you..." Murray walked to the base of the ladder to make sure it was steady. A fall from that height would certainly kill the frail man.

Aon chuckled. "While I appreciate your worries, Knight Pearson, I can't help but think I should be insulted by your lack of faith in my climbing abilities."

"No, no. I wasn't saying you can't...I was just—" Murray stuttered.

"—just helping out an old Grievar." Aon finished his sentence. "Yes, yes, I know. And I appreciate it, my friend," Aon said as he began to climb slowly down the ladder.

Murray watched tentatively as Aon finally made it to the bottom rungs.

"Helping me more often than not involves stowing me in some corner where I can't be a bother," Aon said as he accepted Murray's hand and stepped off the ladder. The old Grievar shuffled over to his chair across the room and fell back into it, breathing hard from the exertion.

"And they're probably right. I'm more of a nuisance than anything now, always getting in the way. And yet I'm not really willing to stop," Aon noted.

"Nor do I think you should stop, Commander," Murray said, standing at attention in front of the old Grievar's chair.

"You know better than to call me Commander, Knight Pearson." Aon motioned for Murray to sit across from him.

Murray took his seat. "And you know better than to call me Knight a decade past my service."

"Once a Knight, always a Knight. Even those Ancients buried beneath wet earth and dry leaves are still Knights, though they've certainly seen better days," Aon exclaimed. "That's where I'll be soon, no doubt. I'm hoping at least I'll take some honor to the grave."

Murray nodded.

"In fact, Pearson, though you're no longer active, and despite that stunt you pulled down at Lampai, you're more of a Knight than most of those who walk the Tower's halls today," Aon said.

"That's actually what I came to talk to you about," Murray said.

"And that's why I've always liked you, Pearson. You're to the point. Direct. Not like these Command meetings I'm forced to sit through, wasting away my final hours," Aon said.

"It's about the Knight program. The way things are being run," Murray continued. He wasn't sure how he should broach the subject. "I know I'm just a Scout, but..."

"I don't entirely agree with the Scout program, particularly with that fool Callen, but don't use that to diminish your own self-worth, my boy. We both know that you are far more than a Scout," Aon said. "And I sense that your visit here isn't about you. It's about someone else."

"Yes, it is about someone else," Murray said. "The talent I scouted this cycle. His name is Cego."

Aon's white eyes shimmered under the light. "Yes, I know the boy. He's in my Codes class. Very perceptive for his years."

A smile crossed Murray's face. He hadn't realized that Cego had applied to be in Aon's class. Perhaps those late-night talks in his barracks had meant something.

"Yeah. Cego is different," Murray said. "I'm not sure if you're aware... or if the rest of Command has looped you in about what happened during his Trial?" Murray didn't want to underestimate Aon's position as commander of the Lyceum.

"Ah, yes, the Trials. Quite an anomaly that was. Your boy did exceptionally. The way he was able to sit through the Time Trial was quite a feat. Not the only anomaly during these Trials, though. And no, Callen and Memnon made a point of keeping any pertinent information from my ears, though I suspect they are keener than they look," Aon said with a sly grin as he pulled on one of his bulbous, cauliflowered lobes.

"Not the only anomaly?" Murray asked curiously. "You mean Cego wasn't the only one who was able to handle the Trials like that?"

"Yes. There was another. He didn't get through the same way that Cego did—with such finesse in navigating each stage. The other one had more of a...brute-force technique for getting through the Trials," Aon said forebodingly.

"Who was the other?" Murray couldn't help but ask.

"As you said, you are here for one Grievar, and that is Cego. I don't want your attention to be diverted."

"You're right. I am here for Cego," Murray affirmed. "I wanted to see if you knew anything. I saw it with my own eyes, Aon. Cego was able to sit for nearly an hour in the Time Trial. This is a kid I dug up from the slave Circles. I think he was shipped in from the Isles, but he doesn't have any memory of how he got to the Underground. It doesn't make any darkin' sense..."

"These are strange times, Pearson," Aon whispered. "As I said after the Trials commenced, the Citadel is at a crossroads. There is a choice coming. A path in the light or a path in the shadows."

"Yes. And I'm thinking whatever's going on here stinks like the dark. Smells of Daimyo Governance pushing on the Citadel. I paid a visit to Memnon and Callen—they're gone. It's all about winning for them, for *the good of the nation*," Murray said with spite. "Cego isn't a part of all that, though. He's different. He lives by the Codes."

"Yes, I know he does. I've seen so much in my class already. He is already familiar with the way of the Grievar—he yearns to follow the path. And yet Cego has emerged from the shadows. He does not only fight in the Circle—he is battling something within. You need to help him find his path," Aon said.

"How?" Murray asked, hoping that the wise man could provide him with a straightforward answer.

"Unfortunately, Pearson, my age does have its limits. Whatever darkness is at work here, it is not from my time. It is the machination of the new age. An age that I'm not so certain an old Grievar like me should still be living in," Aon said.

Murray looked at the floor and sighed. This was the man who had taught Murray's own Codes class decades ago. Aon had instructed Murray on honor and loyalty; he'd given him a path forward. He was one of the only people in this darkin' world Murray could truly trust. If Aon Farstead didn't know anything, Murray was lost.

"Do not lose hope," Aon said, accurately reading Murray's thoughts again. "Though I can't tell you what to do, I believe I can provide some insight."

Murray looked up. Anything would help.

"The Codes are like a blanket."

Murray shook his head in confusion. "Not sure I understand how that helps, Commander..."

Aon chuckled and squinted his eyes, just like Murray remembered the man doing in his class so long ago. "You are someone who follows the Combat Codes rigidly, Murray. You've tried to live a life that complies with the words the Ancients wrote so long ago."

Murray nodded, attempting to follow the old man.

"But you and I must admit, times have changed," Aon said. "Look around the Lyceum. Students swiping into lightdecks in their classes, watching SystemView feeds up on boards. Though of course, we know tools and technologies were not to be a part of Grievar life, according to the Codes."

"Yes, but they still can't carry weapons—" Murray began.

"I'm not saying it is a bad thing," Aon explained. "Sometimes what was written long ago needs to be interpreted for a new day. The Codes should not be rigid like a board, ready to break when the pressure of time is applied to them. The Codes should be like a blanket, changing shape over the time they cover."

Murray thought for a moment about Aon's words. "So... you're saying I should change the Codes? That will somehow help me figure out what's going on with Cego?"

Aon chuckled again. "Murray, even when you were young, you tended to meet your problems head-on. Like how you came directly to me today. You asked me straightforward what was on your mind, which I certainly appreciated."

"How else would I do it?" Murray shrugged.

"Sometimes, Murray, you need to apply the Codes to the day you live in," Aon said. "And today, you need answers. Ones that I cannot give you. But there are those in the Citadel that know more than an old man like me, those that are still active in their service, those that you won't be able to ask straightforward questions."

"You think I need to lie?" Murray shook his head. "Like some street hawker? Or like the way that coward Callen Albright follows his path, always slinking in the shadows?"

"I think you know your own path well enough, Murray," Aon said. "It is with the boy, Cego. You are to help him find his place in this world. And to follow that path you'll need the Codes with you. But you cannot use the Codes like a board, you must use them like a blanket."

"Like a blanket," Murray repeated softly.

CHAPTER 16

Weakness

A Grievar should contemplate the end of all things. Attachments, whether friendship, loyalty, or love, must be viewed as impermanent truths, otherwise they are destined to become crutches.

Passage Five, One Hundred Ninth Precept of the Combat Codes

Cego shifted uncomfortably on the floor, trying to find a position where he didn't feel so sore. After a full day of classes and training, he hadn't been looking forward to sitting through another one of Kitaka's lectures this evening.

Dozer however, who sat beside Cego, had his eyes glued to the diminutive professor as he paced the room. Just last week, the big Grievar had proclaimed Kitaka was his favorite teacher, which seemed strange given how his semester had started with the man.

"Now, surely, you've all heard of Nonrespar Arena?" Kitaka said. "One of the oldest and greatest stadiums that borders Kiroth and Desovi. It sits at an elevation of thirty thousand feet above sea level."

"Is that pretty high?" Dozer whispered to Cego, who kept quiet.

"Yes, that is pretty high, Dozer." Kitaka pulled at one of his large ears and smiled. "It's so high that one of the primary problems with fighting within Nonrespar is breathing."

Kitaka took a deep breath through his nose and paused for several moments, staring at the class in silence.

"We've worked on many breathing techniques thus far this semester," the professor said. "Unfortunately, in a place like Nonrespar, even expert breathing technique will not compensate for the lack of oxygen at that altitude. If you could last ten minutes at a high pace here in the Citadel, you'd only last a single minute at the same pace in Nonrespar."

Cego watched as Sol jotted down the ratio on her lightpad. He held his own pad up for a moment before sighing and placing it back in his lap. He'd get the notes from Sol later.

"Or perhaps you might fight on the ice flats of Myrkos," Kitaka continued. "There's been many an unprepared Knight who has traveled north to fight against a Grievar from the Ice Tribes and succumbed to the cold before the first punch could even be thrown. In fact, the extreme cold is one of the primary reasons the Kirothian Empire has not been successful in conquering Myrkos after so many centuries.

"Now, on top of our standard breathing and conditioning practice, you will be prepared at the Lyceum in a variety of ways for fighting in extreme environments." Kitaka paced in front of the students. "As Level Twos, you will begin to run Kalabasas Hill several times per week. As Level Threes, you will spend hours at a time in the frost containers. As Level Fours, you will gain access to the air deprivation chambers. As Level Fives, you will use rubellium-lined hot rooms. These environments will all help acclimate you for what is to come so that when you step into the Circle on foreign lands, representing Ezo, you will at least have a chance to use the combat skills you've spent so much time honing."

Abel raised his fist and Kitaka nodded at him. "Professor, what else can we practice now to prepare, before we gain access to these places?"

"This is what I like to see, Abel," Kitaka said. "Initiative. And we think alike, because today we'll be practicing something that will prepare you for all these extreme environments."

Cego looked around the room. There wasn't any new equipment beside the weights, bars, and pulleys that lined the classroom.

"Dozer," Kitaka said, and Dozer leapt to his feet, smiling. The professor had taken to choosing the big kid as his aide since semester start.

The grin left Dozer's face as Kitaka called out another name. "Knees, if you might help us demonstrate as well."

Knees stood across from Dozer, the two glaring at each other as if they might start throwing punches in front of the class. Luckily, Kitaka stepped between the two.

"Though using targeted environments is helpful, I find there is nothing better than another body when training for single combat." Kitaka held his hands out toward Dozer and Knees.

"I'm guessing many of you are familiar with sloth carries," Kitaka said. Both Dozer and Knees tensed, and Cego felt the soreness in his body amplify at the thought of the endless carries Crew Nine had done under the menacing eye of Tasker Ozark.

"We must've spent half our time in the slave Circles doing sloth carries." Dozer shook his head.

"Yes, and though some of the methodologies of the Taskers below are both brutal and senseless, there is some merit to it," Kitaka said. "However, here at the Lyceum, we always keep an eye on tactics. And so, you won't be practicing standard sloth carries. The person being carried will not be a useless sack of meat. They will be a participant in the exercise. In fact, they will be an active hindrance to the runner."

"Hindrance?" Dozer stared past Kitaka at Knees.

"Yes," Kitaka said. "Knees, climb on Dozer's back."

Cego saw the hesitation in Knees's eyes. The Venturian didn't want to be near Dozer, let alone cling to the boy's back. But he nodded and lifted himself adeptly onto Dozer, slinging one arm above the boy's shoulder and the other under his armpit in a standard belt grip.

"Now, when we practice as a class, this will be a race. Dozer will try to get across the room and back five times to complete the course, with Knees on his back. But—"

Kitaka paused with emphasis and took a deep breath through his nose. Cego could feel impatience building in the class as they waited for the rest of the instructions.

"Knees will be allowed to emulate an inhospitable environment. He can cover Dozer's mouth or nose, so that he may find great difficulty breathing. He can sag his body toward the ground to make each of Dozer's steps heavier or to off-balance him from a straight path. Knees, why don't you show the class what I mean."

Dozer grunted and began to jog across the classroom. Knees immediately clamped a hand in front of Dozer's mouth. When Dozer reached up to strip the hand off, Knees grabbed his arm and yanked it to the side, sending Dozer teetering to the ground.

"Darkin' piece of..." Dozer growled as he stood again and jabbed backward with a quick elbow, catching Knees in the rib cage. Dozer reached the other end of the class and turned back. Cego saw Knees's eyes narrow before the Venturian swiftly wrapped his arm around Dozer's neck in a tight choke.

"Hey," Dozer said, his voice high pitched against the pressure on his neck. "He's not allowed to..."

Before Dozer could finish his sentence, he was falling forward with Knees still on his back. Dozer's eyes rolled into his head as his arms stayed straight by his side. He slammed face-first into the ground.

Knees slipped off Dozer's back and walked away. A muffled snore escaped from the boy while he was still facedown.

"Let's refrain from strangles in this exercise, to prevent injuries," Kitaka said as he casually rolled Dozer over onto this back. The big kid's nose was a bloody mess from the impact. "But always a good idea to protect your neck, even when you're not in the Circles."

"Hey, that's my roc!" Dozer mumbled as he woke with a snort. He slowly sat up, touching a hand to his bloody face and looking around the class in confusion. Dozer's eyes finally fell on Knees and his face turned bright red as he realized what had happened.

"All right, class," Professor Kitaka said quickly. "Let's pair up."

Sol put her hand on Cego's shoulder and smiled. "I've been wanting to get a chance to get on your back for a choke."

"You heard the professor, no strangles." Cego smiled back. His heart was suddenly beating faster. "But...I think I need to pair with someone else for this round."

Sol looked hurt until she saw Cego making a straight line toward Knees, who hadn't made any attempt to find a new partner yet.

"Need someone to work with?" Cego asked.

Knees responded with a silent nod.

Cego offered his back to start and found Knees attempting the same aggressive techniques he'd used against Dozer, first muffling Cego's breathing with an open hand across the mouth, before disregarding Kitaka's instructions and going for the choke again.

Cego was ready for the offensive onslaught and protected himself ably enough. He'd spent countless hours defending himself against his brother Silas, who used to go after Cego's neck like a blood-starved wolf.

When it came time for Knees to walk across the classroom, Cego took his opportunity. Not to get revenge, but to talk to the boy. Cego secured a tight grip and lodged his face up against the Venturian's shoulder.

"Why are you doing this?" Cego whispered.

"It be the professor's instructions," Knees replied as he suddenly jerked forward. "Create an inhospitable environment."

"No," Cego said as he switched his grip to prevent Knees from bucking him off. "Why are you…acting like you hate us?"

Knees was silent as he struggled across the room, but finally, he breathed a single word.

"Trials."

Knees spun around to make the second trip.

"I was in there too," Cego whispered. "I can't shake it either."

"You don't know…" Knees grunted and was suddenly stumbling to the ground. Cego rolled off the boy's back and sat across from him while the other students kept moving past them.

"You don't know what it be like," Knees panted. "In the third Trial, I was back in Venturi with my sis. With my uncle again."

Cego shook his head. It had hurt to see his brother Sam in the Trial, to feel the presence of someone he'd missed so much. But Cego couldn't imagine being sent back to someone you hated.

"I was weak again," Knees's voice trembled as he looked at the ground. "I was weak for so long in that place. I was helpless. I couldn't help my sis, couldn't prevent that monster from hurting us again."

Knees's eyes were shimmering with wetness.

"When I came out of the Trials, I swore I'd never be weak again."

"You can be strong without being against us," Cego said. "We've got a plan to get you away from Shiar. We're your friends, Knees. We want you back with us."

"Shiar be strong," Knees said as he stood and turned away. "In this place…I don't need friends. I only want to be strong."

The drill timer rang, and Knees walked away.

* * *

"What's going on?" Dozer shook his head in confusion as a stampede of students passed them on the stairs down to the common ground. The big kid had just come from the medward to reset his broken nose, though Cego noticed it was still a bit crooked.

"Not sure." Cego shrugged. "New challenges get posted?"

But Cego realized no matchups would cause this sort of

excitement. A Level Two student stumbled three steps past the crew and nearly did a front roll on the platform before continuing to descend the stairs.

Cego and Dozer looked at Sol expectantly. The girl was usually up-to-date on current events around the school. "Sol, what's going on?"

"Just a fight," Sol said stoically. "On the big lightboard."

"Who?" Dozer exclaimed as the three Whelps reached the ground floor and saw a crowd of students pushing forward to try to get a view of the large display. "They haven't had many fights up this semester. Must be a big one... it must be..."

Cego heard the SystemView announcer's voice bouncing off the walls of the common ground. "And fighting for the nation of Ezo... the greatest of warriors, with an undefeated record... The Fist of Songs, the Paladin of the People, the Shining Knight himself, Artemis Halberd!"

The students surrounding the board erupted in a hail of applause as Halberd's familiar face came on-screen: chiseled jaw, well-trimmed beard, and sunflower-yellow eyes set atop a statuesque body carved for combat.

Cego glanced at Sol. She was expressionless watching her father on the board and hearing nearly the entire Lyceum student body cheering for him. She looked as if she might want to turn from the room. Cego was going to ask if she'd rather leave when Dozer grabbed her shoulder.

"Sol!" Dozer shouted as they pushed their way through the crowd to find a suitable viewing spot. "There's your da!"

Cego shook his head. As if the girl didn't know that, and unfortunately Dozer's loud voice seemed to attract unwanted attention, as usual. He saw Shiar, standing beside Knees and Gryfin Thurgood, several feet away, sneering back at him.

Cego focused on the screen to see Artemis squaring up with a Desovian Knight. Though they were a smaller nation, Cego had heard that Desovi had won a disproportionate share of fights due to their fierce training regimens. This Knight—Yassif Galot—seemed to mirror that ferocity; a series of long, snaking scars were carved across his shoulders, running up his neck and etched into his face.

"Over here!" Cego heard Abel's voice and turned to see the small boy sitting high atop Joba's shoulders to get a better view. Dozer, Cego, and Sol pushed their way through the crowd to stand next to their fellow Whelps.

The common ground went from clamor to complete silence as Artemis lifted his hands in his Knight salute, slamming his forearms together in a cross above his head. The Desovian Knight responded with an open hand to beckon Artemis forward.

"Counterpuncher," Abel whispered from his perch atop Joba's shoulder. "Yassif is one of Desovi's best. He will wait for Artemis to make first move."

Artemis obliged the Desovian by launching a front kick that seemed impossibly fast for a man of his size. Yassif barely was able to lift a hand to parry and stumbled back against the force of the kick.

Cego blinked and Artemis was already somehow inside Yassif's guard, landing two thudding body shots that reverberated on the common ground's audio system, followed by an inside trip to bring the Desovian to the ground.

A cheer erupted from the Lyceum students as they sensed a quick finish. Cego lowered his eyes from the screen to see Knees looking directly back at him from across the floor. Cego nodded, even let a smile crease his face, but the Venturian did not return the gesture, only looked back at the screen. After hearing about Knees's Trial experience, Cego finally understood why the boy had become so distant, so angry. Knees had been forced to relive the worst part of his childhood over and over within that sadistic simulation.

Another loud cheer brought Cego's eyes back to the screen. Yassif had somehow returned to his feet and was attempting to hold off Artemis's onslaught of attacks.

It truly seemed like every student in the Lyceum was packed

onto the common ground, along with most of the faculty on the outskirts of the crowd. Cego saw Professor Tefo bobbing his head as he watched Artemis dodge a series of punches and Professor Kitaka with his arms crossed, performing his breathing exercises as always. Professor Larkspur was easy to pick out across the room, a head above most, her eyes likely focused on the brilliant auralite Circle the two Knights were fighting in, bluelight spectrals dancing between punches and kicks.

"Get him!" Dozer yelled, his fist pumping the air as Artemis connected with a solid cross to his opponent's chin, sending him stumbling backward.

Cego's eyes fell back to the crowd. He found himself looking for Kōri Shimo. Of course, the strange boy wasn't here. Though Shimo attended Circles class, Cego had heard he skipped nearly all his other classes. If not for Shimo's extraordinary performance in his sparring exhibitions and challenge matches, Cego doubted the boy could muster the score to graduate.

Another cheer erupted from the students and Cego saw Artemis straddling the Desovian in mount position, raining down a hail of blows to the man's body. When Yassif attempted to cover up, Artemis switched to devastating head shots. One punch found Yassif's chin, and Cego watched as the Desovian Knight's eyes rolled to the back of his head.

But the lights still shined down on the Circle. The feeds still glowed on the boards around the great stadium they fought in, beckoning the Ezonian champion for more violence. Artemis raised his fist over his inert opponent.

Cego glanced at Sol and saw the girl looking down at the floor, away from her father, away from the arena across the world, away from the greatest living Knight as he drove his fist into the skull of his opponent in an explosion of blood.

The common ground was silent again, the student's jaws agape at the display of raw strength, skill, and brutality they'd just witnessed. A chant began to bud across the common ground, just several low voices in unison before the cheer spread and erupted around the entire floor. "Halberd! Halberd! Halberd!"

"Halberd." Shiar appeared from the cluster of students in front of them. "Halberd, Halberd, Halberd." The boy clapped his hands lightly and stared at Sol, who was still looking at the floor. "If not for the name, I don't think a person in this school would think you come from the same line as that man up there."

Cego put himself between Sol and Shiar. They couldn't risk getting docked points for fights out of the Circle, and though Solara Halberd could be the picture of calmness, he could sense she was not herself right now.

"Shut up, you piece of roc dung." Dozer shouldered his way in front of Sol as well. "Sol's got her da's instincts. And his jab. If you ever stand across from her, you'll find that out quick."

Cego swelled with pride watching Dozer, who had once been a bully in the Deep, now standing up for his friends against Shiar.

But Sol didn't seem to need her teammate's support. She pushed past Dozer and came within inches of Shiar's hooked face, staring into his eyes. "Why don't you take a shot and see if I have anything in common with my father. I wouldn't mind putting you down like the dog you are."

Shiar cackled and raised his hands. "Wow. Finally, some real anger from the girl. Seems I hit a nerve. Or maybe it wasn't me. Maybe it was watching your father win another massive fight for Ezo, knowing you'll never live up to it. Knowing you'll always be... just his little bitch."

Before Cego knew it, Sol had sliced a cutting elbow across Shiar's jaw, sending him stumbling to the ground.

"You're crazy!" Shiar growled from the floor, holding a hand to his mouth. "You knocked a tooth out!"

Behind a steady stream of blood, Cego saw a large gap where the boy's front tooth had been.

"Oh shit!" Dozer hooted and clapped Sol on the shoulder.

Shiar stood slowly, clutching his face, just as Cego saw a professor stalking toward them through the crowd.

"Just because you pitiful lacklights are a lost cause this semester, bound to not graduate, doesn't mean I'll fall into your trap." Shiar sneered.

Knees was at Shiar's side, facing off with Dozer and Cego.

"How can you stand with this piece of shit?" Dozer growled at Knees. The big kid brought a hand up to his recently broken nose. "I thought I knew you."

"You never knew me." Knees shook his head, meeting Dozer's stare. "Not the real me."

Just as Professor Tefo arrived, Shiar and Knees turned and shuffled through the crowd.

"What's the commotion here... Thought I heard unauthorized fighting." Tefo looked to Sol and saw the pool of blood on the floor beside her. "You know I love to see punches thrown as much as anyone else, but I can't have the chaos that comes with fighting outside our Circles."

Sol looked like she was about to admit to the act, but Cego interrupted her. "Nothing's going on, Professor. I was just trying a technique we saw Artemis Halberd throw on-screen. And I messed it up."

Professor Tefo looked at Cego skeptically before a grin spread across his face. "Did you see how Artemis handled that Desovian's counterattack game? Simply incredible. We'll need to work on it in class tomorrow."

"Right." Cego nodded in relief.

"I'd be proud to have a father like that," Tefo said as he walked off.

Cego looked at Sol. By the look in her eyes, he doubted she agreed.

CHAPTER 17

Sweat and Research

The experienced Grievar recognizes the body's chain of structures. In order to attack any part of the chain, a fighter must focus on first stabilizing the larger structure. To attack the elbow, the shoulder must be fully controlled. To attack the wrist, the elbow must be controlled. To attack the foot, a Grievar must first control the knee. Undue focus on a goal will prove less successful when the variables surrounding it are not controlled.

Passage Six, Eighteenth Technique of the Combat Codes

Murray trudged up the long stair of the Knight Tower.

Though he no longer had official access to the Citadel's prime training facility, he hadn't forgotten that the back entrance by the thicket of thornbushes was often left ajar. Murray had received a few suspicious glances from the Grunt servicers but had made it to the staircase without a fuss.

The quarters were quiet now. At dusk, most Knights would be resting their bodies between sessions. Memnon would have them moving again in an hour or so, sprinting up these very stairs to get to evening Circle training.

Murray felt a tweak in his back as he climbed, starting with a jolt at the base of his neck and ending in electric nerve pain spreading across his buttocks.

Darkin' Dragoon. Though Murray had won that fight, he'd pay for it for the rest of his life.

He looked down at the same cracked stairs he'd climbed so many times as a younger, fitter man, the same knotted doors leading to the Knight quarters at each level, the same soiled stone landings, blotched with spilled ale from drunken revelries and bloodstains from open wounds. Though he was sure nearly everything had gone to shit in this place, it was comforting to know a few things remained the same.

Murray heard footfalls approaching from above. He pulled his cowl forward, attempting to sink into the shadows despite his considerable girth.

"Then she says I got to bring her flowers e'ry day, just because I gone and done a nice thing for her this once." A lanky Grievar walked toward Murray, another thickset one at his side.

"That's your decision, Fegar," the thick one replied. "Never should be spoiling yer gals, sets expectations too high."

The two Knights passed Murray without a second glance as he continued up the stairs. Another thing that hadn't changed. Knights had their minds on fighting or their next conquest and not much else. Murray shook his head as he passed a floor of dormitories.

He remembered these halls well: the friendly banter beneath torchlight, the buzz after a good training session, being so hungry that you could finish five sizzler's servings in the mess hall. He could nearly hear Anderson and Leyna's voices echoing off the dense walls, the three of them talking about what sort of crazy practice Coach had in front of them, feeling that familiar excitement creeping up in his stomach.

Now Murray felt only the longing for a drink in his gut. He patted his vest and growled as he realized he'd left his flask back at the barracks.

Murray nearly passed the floor he intended to visit. He stepped back and slowly walked beneath a stone arch with a rusted plaque atop it, letters etched on the metal plate.

TRAIN IN THE DEPTHS OF HELL AND THE REAL FIGHT WILL BE ON A TIMID SPRING DAY.

The Knights living here likely thought the words were from the Codes, like most of the inscriptions across the Citadel's walls. But Murray remembered when this plaque was placed at the top of the training quarter entryway. He'd watched Coach hammer at the frame with a nail clenched between his teeth. Those were Coach's words above his head.

Murray listened carefully for a moment, heard nothing, and moved into a long hallway with tall windows running along each side. The large rooms beyond were dark and quiet.

Murray knew these rooms would normally be frenetic with activity: wrestling practice in the padded room, striking drills on the wood across the way. Circles of every alloy to train in. He passed a stocked weight room he remembered being full of Knights trying to best each other's lifts and a track for sprinting around when Coach didn't have them climbing Kalabasas Hill in the cold.

Murray had come at this hour because he didn't want to attract attention. He couldn't have all these Knights telling Memnon—or worse yet, the coward Albright—that Murray Pearson had come by asking questions.

But there was one place where he knew there'd still be some Knights milling around, even at rest hour. A place where men weren't afraid to wag their tongues. Because some things didn't change.

Murray stopped at the end of the hall in front of a thick oak door with a fogged window on top. He heard muffled voices coming from within, the echo of a dull laugh.

Murray took a deep breath, expelled it, and gritted his teeth as he prepared himself.

"Dark it, let's do this," the old Grievar growled as he untied his cloak, letting it drop to the floor. He lifted the vest from his shoulders and pulled his shirt over his head. Murray took his boots off, unbuckled his belt, and let his trousers drop to the ground before removing his undershorts.

He felt cold air cross between his legs, making the hair on his arse stand on end. Murray savored that breeze, breathed in again, and opened the door.

A blast of hot, dry air hit Murray in the face. He stepped with bare feet onto the wood planks of the room and winced as his flesh burned.

The room was about the size of his barracks at home. Small red spectrals flitted from the cracks between the cedar planks beneath his feet, seeming to languish in the extreme heat as they drifted toward the ceiling. Murray's eyeball dried out and he felt the pores of his skin preparing for perspiration.

Murray darkin' hated the hot room. Even when he'd been a Knight, he'd hated sweating until his body looked like a withered prune. Murray remembered feeling like a husk of a man in this hot room.

But there were always those that enjoyed it. Three Knights sat on a bench across the way, their bodies hazy behind the heat waves coming off the floor. One Knight was laughing, his thickly muscled shoulders bouncing up and down as another told a story from beside him. All three stopped as Murray entered, casting their eyes on the newcomer to the hot room.

"You get lost, old-timer?" the Knight with a razor shark flux swimming across his chest asked. "The histories museum is on the other side of the Citadel. I hear it's popular with retired folk like you."

Murray didn't speak. He stepped forward and focused on not grimacing visibly as the floor continued to scorch the bottoms of his feet. As a Knight, he'd built up calluses from visiting the hot room regularly, but those were long gone. Sweat began to bead atop his brow, little droplets forecasting the great flood that would leave his body in another few minutes. Murray watched another

Knight with a serpent flux wrapped around his shoulders look up at him in recognition.

"Yang, you darkin' idiot, this isn't no normal retiree coming for a visit of glory days," the man said.

"Huh?" the Knight named Yang responded, squinting his eyes to peer across the hot room at Murray. Yang suddenly sat a bit taller, his muscled form tensing.

"That's Murray Pearson," the serpent-fluxed Knight said as Murray slid onto the bench across from them. He exhaled as the burning hot plank scorched his backside. Though Murray knew he wasn't going to outlast these Knights in the hot room, he had to at least get enough time to hear what he needed.

"Well, I'll be," the bald Knight on the other side of the bench said. "The man himself. Mighty Murray. What the dark are you doing here in our hot room? Thought you'd gone and become a Scout for that worm Callen, last I heard."

"You heard right," Murray wiped sweat off his brow and attempted to set his breath to last in the heat. Three quick exhales and one long draw. Talk in between.

The Knight with the serpent flux stood unabashedly and offered a hand to Murray, which he grasped wrist to wrist. "Whatever reason you've come, it's an honor to meet you. My pops used to have you on SystemView every fight. One of the reasons I got into the service. Raymol Tarsis."

Murray nodded. "Well met, Raymol. Heard you're next in line for the captain's belt."

"Ray only has a shot at the belt because he's been licking Memnon's boots on the regular," the bald Knight said with a smirk as he also leaned forward to shake Murray's wrist.

"Go dark yourself, Jora," Ray responded. "You want the belt just as bad as I do. But neither of us has any chance with Halberd on the tear."

Murray let a smile cross his face as he took another measured breath. His entire body was glistening with sweat, and he could feel his heartbeat pulsing against his skull.

"I'll catch Halberd soon enough." The Knight named Yang flexed his muscled body, letting the razor shark dive across it. Yang did not appear to give Murray the same deference as his two companions. The man stayed seated with his arms crossed, frowning. "Lot of balls you got coming back here, after the way you left the service."

"Shut up, Yang," Ray said.

"Why should I?" Yang raised his voice and leaned toward Murray. "'Cause of this darkin' man, people I know starved. Didn't have carbs on the table because he decided he was done with the service all of a sudden. Because he couldn't handle a loss."

"It was his choice." Jora put a hand on Yang's shoulder to steady him. "It's all our choice to say when we want out."

"Yeah, it's a choice to leave," Yang said. "But most aren't cowards enough to do it like this one."

Murray felt a familiar nausea rise in him as sweat streamed from his body. He wanted to ask his questions right away. He wanted to get out of this hellhole. But he knew he had to sweat with these men before he could get what he wanted from them: the truth. And to get the truth, you needed to give the truth.

"You're right. I hurt folk by leaving." Murray met Yang's fiery stare. "I let my team down, my best friends, I made them pick up my slack, take my fights, risk their lives when they couldn't handle the load. It was my fault Ezo didn't pull the season's shipments over the border that year. It was my fault some Ezonians starved on the streets."

The three young Knights stared at Murray. He'd spoken the truth and he had their attention. Now he just had to make sure he didn't pass out.

"Good thing you can own up to it," Yang said as he stood. The man was a wall of muscle. He threw several quick punches, sweat flying from his corded arms. "So, what then? You here to see if you can still hang with the best? Heard you put the Dragoon down. But I'm no second-grade Deep merc. I'm Kal Yang."

Murray stood to meet Yang's eyes, but more to gauge his stance. Back leg planted, front leg light, ready to throw that head kick Murray had seen the man use so many times up on SystemView. Murray knew he'd lose this fight. He was too slow, too broken to handle a top-shelf specimen like Yang. But that didn't matter. Sometimes you had to take one on the chin to get what you needed. And he'd promised Cego he'd figure things out.

"Hold on." Ray stepped between Yang and Murray, his arms spread wide. "Do you realize what Memnon would do if he heard there was a scuffle in the hot room, let alone with Murray Pearson? And if you got injured before the tournament up in Venturi?"

Murray watched Yang's front foot slowly bear weight as he backed down. "I wouldn't break a sweat against this old-timer, but you're right." The Knight slid back onto the bench.

Murray breathed a sigh of relief that he wouldn't have to fight in this forsaken place. But the adrenaline had cut his nausea and helped him stave off passing out. Like he'd taken a shot to the chin and was still standing.

"I'm not here to fight either," Murray said. "I'm here for... information about Knight enhancement programs."

"Why not just go to the high commander himself?" Jora asked. "I hear you two go way back."

"We do." Murray nodded. "But that's the problem."

"Memnon and the old Knight commander had a falling-out back in the day," Ray explained. "And some held their loyalties."

"Yeah," Murray said. "Coach and Memnon couldn't see eye to eye. Coach left and the Knight program started changing. They were pushing some stuff hard I didn't want any part of... at the time."

"You mean stims?" Jora smirked. "So that's when it all started. Bet you'd like to see the sort of stuff we're getting now, eh? Makes those old-school stims feel like crunch candy."

Murray nodded. Now he needed to tell his first lie in this hot room. Like some hawker trying to sell a shiny rock in place of a lightdeck. Codes be damned, he'd made Cego a promise and he meant to keep it. *Not like a board, like a blanket.* Murray heard Old Aon's advice echoing in his head.

"Since I fought the Dragoon, my back's been a mess. I've been on the decline, can't seem to catch my wind. I heard the new sort of stims circulating might help me get back into the Circle. Something to turn back time a bit..."

"Don't know why you'd even want to get back in a Circle." Yang shook his head. "Know when to call it quits. Your day is over, old man."

Murray set his jaw and let the feint roll off his tongue. "Please, I need it."

Ray looked at Murray with pity. It was well known that many retired Grievar could never leave the light gracefully.

"Everything we're using here requires a full cycle," Ray said. "Whatever I could give you from my personal stash wouldn't help fix things for you."

"I don't expect to get anything out of you," Murray said as he wiped more sweat off his face. "Just need information on who can give me with what I need."

"From the outside?" Ray shook his head. "You're only going to find bad mixes on the street. Garbage cut with Kirothian tar. Sort of stuff you'll take for a fix, but you'll end up with an extra finger or two."

"Definitely don't need more fingers, maybe a new eye, though..." Murray trailed off. "Is there any new stuff out there that helps take the light better?"

There it was: the actual punch planted behind his feint. He eyed the men to see if any had caught on.

"There's something for everything now, old-timer," Yang said. "But we're Grievar Knights, not Daimyo makers. Don't think you're in the right place."

"Give the man a break, Yang," Ray said. "Try to see in front of your own ugly nose for once. Imagine when your career is over. When you've got nothing to live for. Wouldn't you want someone to help you out?"

"Thanks...I guess." Murray raised an eyebrow as little white stars started to spark at the edge of his vision. He tried to steady his breath. He wouldn't last much longer in this heat.

"Even if I wanted to help him, we don't have what he's needing." Yang shook his head. "Some miracle stim to help him turn back the years on that blasted body of his?"

"There's someone who used to work closely with Memnon when I first joined up," Ray offered. "High commander went to him for all recommendations on stim mixtures, dosage, any other training tech we've used outside the light. He'd know for sure..."

"Who?" Murray felt the room closing in on him, the waves of heat fluttering across his face.

"In fact," Ray said, "think the man came up with you. Strange fellow. Knew his stuff, though. Jezar D'lysien was his name."

"Shit," Murray heard himself say as he tried to get to his feet.

"You two didn't get along, eh?" Ray looked up at Murray. "Seems to be a trend with you."

Murray moved toward the door, no longer worried about looking weak or a fool. All he cared about was making it out of this hellish heat. He stumbled the last few steps and planted a hand against the cedar door before he turned back to the men.

"Where..." Murray tried to breathe. "Where's Jezar?"

"You didn't hear?" Ray's voice sounded distant, from another world. "D'lysien screwed the Citadel. He was selling half the stims he procured for the team to the black market and pocketing the bits for himself."

"Where is he?"

"Memnon threw him in a cell," Ray said. "Jezar D'lysien is a prisoner at PublicJustice."

Murray burst out the wooden door, using the last of his strength to close it. He slumped against the wall beside his pile of discarded clothes.

* * *

Cego stopped by the medward first thing in the morning before classes began. He craned his neck to peer over the curtains as he walked down the wide ward hallway. There were always so many injured Grievar in here. Cego passed by laid-out Knights, Defenders, even several Lyceum students that he vaguely recognized.

Toward the end of the hallway, he stopped abruptly.

He stood in front of a large glass vat, staring into it. *Marvin Stronglight.* The sixth pick in the class of Level Ones.

Marvin was suspended within the vat, floating in a red-tinged viscous liquid. Bubbles swarmed around the boy like feeding fish, and small tubes ran from his head to a control panel outside the glass vat.

Marvin had met Kōri Shimo in last week's challenge. Shimo had relentlessly battered Stronglight, even after he was down, even after the light had faded from the Circle. It had taken three of Shimo's own teammates to pull him off his opponent—his entire body had been covered in blood as they'd dragged him from Marvin's motionless form.

Cego would never forget the look in Kōri Shimo's burning yellow eyes. They'd been blank, as if the boy hadn't even been standing there in the Circle. Shimo hadn't savored beating on his opponent as a jackal like Shiar did. Shimo had done it as if he'd had no other choice.

Cego stared at Marvin's suspended form, pressing his hands against the glass vat. The boy's eyes were closed and he appeared completely lifeless. He almost seemed peaceful to Cego, floating there, suspended in time, between life and death.

The boy's eyes burst open. Cego fell away from the glass in surprise. Marvin stared directly at Cego with alarmingly wide eyes as his body twitched violently. The nearby panel started to beep before it shut off within a few seconds. The boy's eyes closed and his body relaxed again, floating peacefully as if nothing had happened.

"Neuroplasmic reaction to the solution," a little voice chimed from behind the control panel.

Cego was holding his breath.

"Sorry, I didn't mean to do anything…" Cego stuttered.

Xenalia, the Daimyo cleric, emerged from behind the panel, straight-lipped as usual.

"As I said, what caused the patient's reaction was a neuroplasmic reaction to the solution he is suspended in. It was not you, Cego, who caused the reaction," Xenalia said.

"Xenalia!" Cego was glad it was her and not some senior cleric who had caught him. "I was actually just looking for you, and then I saw Marvin…"

"Curiosity is one of the hallmarks of scientific inquiry, so I do not fault yours; however, I would warn you against wandering the medward like so, as the senior clerics are very protective of their patients and maintain a zero-interference environment here."

"Yes, I understand," Cego said, inadvertently keeping an eye on the floating Grievar beside him. "A neuroplastic… What did you say again happened?"

"Oh, yes. I forget from our previous conversation I need to speak in simpler terms for your kind to understand me," Xenalia said with no hint of condescension in her voice. "A neuroplasmic reaction is the Grievar's nervous system reacting to the chemical solution he is suspended in—aminolyte solution, to be specific."

"Oh… What's he doing in this vat?" Cego asked.

"Well, technically, he is not doing anything—which is exactly the point. After such a grievous injury—that *is* why they call you the Grievar, is it not—his body needs to be doing nothing at all, even without the force of gravity acting on it, to promote its full internal healing capabilities. The aminolyte solution provides the perfect in vitro environment for this promotion of non-activity, while also containing compounds to stimulate the Grievar's symbiot reaction."

A hundred questions ran through Cego's mind. He'd never given any thought to why Grievar were called Grievar, or what was going on inside his body.

"Symbiot reaction?" Cego asked, embarrassed that though he was a Grievar, he appeared to know so little about himself.

"I am...glad for you to ask this, Cego." Xenalia's eyes glinted and her thin lips curved upward, though she didn't quite smile. "My neophyte doctorate was actually written on the intricacies of Grievar neurophysiology. Grievar have the most wonderful internal mechanisms that have evolved over thousands of years."

The little cleric began to speak rapidly, making it even more difficult for Cego to follow.

"Obviously, the foremost mechanisms of Grievar physiology—the plurality of fast-twitch muscle fibers and the density of the skeletal structure—have evolved to cause injury to others. However, amazingly, the Grievar has also evolved a completely compatible healing system, a thoroughfare of blood vessels and dendritic nerve bundles, to counteract the injuries regularly sustained. This is what we call the Grievar symbiot reaction."

"I see..." said Cego, trying to appear thoughtful. "So, the aminolyte solution Marvin is floating in is helping his symbiot reaction function better. It's healing him?"

"Yes! Perhaps I have underestimated the capabilities of a Grievar mind. If you can grasp these basic concepts...Wayland's theory of Grievar neurodegenerative cognition may still be proven wrong."

Xenalia quickly jotted down some notes on her lightdeck. Her little red spectral had floated over during the conversation to hover above the cleric's shoulder.

"So, he is healing on his own, pretty much?" Cego asked.

"No. That is where a Grievar's internal healing capabilities lose touch with the actual damage inflicted on their body. I believe this one..." Xenalia swiped her lightdeck. "Marvin's top several vertebrae were severed, rendering him completely paralyzed. Though his symbiot reaction has kicked into gear, currently the main preventive factor from a full recovery is his mind."

Cego stayed silent. *Completely paralyzed. Why didn't Kōri Shimo stop?*

"The Grievar brain hasn't caught up to the Grievar body's ability to sustain extreme trauma. When this boy was injured, his brain shut down as a natural defense mechanism. So, while his spine is repairing adequately through his natural healing process, his mind is still in a state of extreme trauma. Without our intervention, his brain would certainly have shut down and instructed the rest of his body to do the same."

"Intervention?" Cego asked.

Xenalia nodded to the tubes running to the Grievar's head. "We have a Sim running into his lower anterior neocortex. It is the only way to keep his brain active. Essentially, the Sim is tricking his brain into thinking everything is okay. It is fooling his body into thinking it has not actually sustained the trauma that it has. Without the Sim, his brain would shut down completely. He would die."

Cego immediately thought about Knees. And himself.

"The Sim you are running in his brain...is it like the Sim used for the Trials?" Cego asked slowly.

"Good question," Xenalia said. "Though I'm no Bit-Minder...I believe the two are programmed off the same base code architecture. Although the Sim running here is primarily targeted to stimulate the cerebellum—base brain function—whereas the Trial Sim targets the cerebral cortex—the higher-functioning part of the brain. Our Sim code at the ward is purely developed for the long-term objective of maintaining base level stimulation. There's no need for the more complex code that the Trials use." Xenalia paused, staring into Cego's eyes.

For a moment, Cego could sense something in Xenalia he hadn't noticed before—she was worried about him.

"Speaking of the Trials, Cego, how are you doing? I've always been a proponent of having new Lyceum students come back to the ward for checkups, though my suggestion is turned down every year due to lack of resources. And I don't see any apparent physical injury to you currently."

"Oh, no... It's not that. I mean, that's not why I'm here. I'm fine," Cego said, quickly deflecting the subject. "I'm actually here to ask you a few other questions. Incidentally relating to the subject of the Grievar symbiot reaction and its potential healing capabilities..."

Xenalia perked up. "Of course. I have several minutes prior to my next patient check-in. Ask me your questions, Cego."

* * *

After the final class of the evening, Cego relayed his medward findings to the Whelps in the hopes of kicking off their covert campaign to recover Knees. They gathered in Quarter D, sitting atop mismatched pieces of furniture with the moon bright in the room's single window.

Cego tried to explain it simply to the Whelps. "The first part of the plan is all about perceived weakness. Each team here is always vying for the precise opening to challenge other teams. They're looking for the right time to strike. We need to give them that opening."

There were constant reconnaissance efforts at the Lyceum to see which teams might be in weakened states. If someone was hurt or got sick during training, it did not go unnoticed. The last challenge the Bayhounds had made occurred exactly one day after Damon Heartstead of the Rocs had shattered his collarbone. They were forced to fight without one of their top members and ended up losing the challenge to Shiar's team.

"We have to make this seem believable, though," Cego said. "If we all appear weak at once, the other teams will sense something's wrong."

Trickery like this had certainly happened before and would

happen again—it was a part of the gamesmanship at the Lyceum. The Whelps needed their weakness to seem genuine.

"Our natural symbiot healing reactions, in combination with planned visits to Xenalia in the medward, will keep us in the game," Cego said. "We can't be damaged so badly that we're unable to finish the last stretch of the semester and make a run at the final challenges."

Sol raised her eyebrow, clearly impressed. "You really have been doing your research for once. It's a big risk, but it just might work."

"It's for Knees," Cego said as he looked at the crew. "We all need to be in this together to pull it off."

Though Abel had never spoken to Knees, the Desovian boy was eager to help him out after Cego mentioned his friend had originally come from Venturi.

"Ah, my ancestors traveled over border to great desert of Venturi. Very hot, very big. But I heard good people there. They welcomed my family, gave us water," Abel said.

As usual, Joba just smiled broadly and nodded in response to the plan. If he did understand what was going on, the boy was game for pretty much anything.

Mateus Winterfowl surprisingly did not dissent. Cego made sure to make this fair—even a stuck-up boy like Mateus deserved to have a say. After all, if the plan was successful, Mateus would be their concession trade for Knees. Even though the pug-nosed purelight had relaxed over the course of the semester, he still made it clear that he wanted to be back with his group of peers.

"So, you'd rather be on a team that didn't even want you in the first place, just because they are purelights like you, than be with these folk, who picked you up and have tried their hardest to accept you?" Sol asked Mateus angrily, not expecting an answer.

It was the teammate who was usually most willing to rush headfirst into any endeavor that was the only dissenting opinion. Dozer.

"Why should we stick our necks out for him?" Dozer stood away from the rest of the crew with his arms crossed. "He wouldn't do it for us."

"Knees isn't himself," Cego tried to explain. "The Trials really scrambled his brain. He saw things from his past…that no one should have to relive."

Dozer didn't appear moved. "We all went through the same Trials. Don't see why that gives him the right to start acting like a piece of shit."

Cego saw the stubbornness in Dozer's face. The big kid was truly hurt that Knees had abandoned him. The two had been practically inseparable before the Trials.

Sol patted Dozer on the shoulder. "Listen, if we can pull this off, if we can get Knees, we'll at least be giving him a chance to recover. But as long as he's staying beside Shiar, seeing the way that coward thinks, Knees won't have a chance."

Dozer's chest heaved as he turned away from his team. Cego could see the boy was clearly conflicted.

"Dark that," Dozer growled before stalking out of the dorm. "I'm going to get myself second dinner."

"Not a bad idea," Mateus said as he followed Dozer. The rest of the crew dispersed for the evening. Abel continued the story he'd been telling Joba for the past several nights. The giant lay across two cots with his hands behind his head, smiling as the Desovian enthusiastically told his tale.

Cego had made a habit of going to the abandoned second-floor training room to work the heavy bag at this time, but tonight he didn't have the energy. He felt restless, though, so he paced across the floor, trying to breathe and quiet his thoughts.

"Dozer will come around," Sol said as she organized her training gear in neat piles beside her cot, just as she did every evening.

"I hope so." Cego stopped pacing. "I don't think he understands what Knees went through in there."

"Do you understand?" Sol asked, looking up from her folding.

The sudden thought crossed Cego's mind to tell Sol about his entire experience in the Trials. He'd largely avoided the subject and certainly hadn't told anyone but Murray about seeing his brother Sam in there.

"No," Cego said. "I went through my own experience. But it wasn't the same as his. So I don't know."

"But you still care," Sol said. "Knees has done everything possible to turn us against him but you still want to help him."

"Even though he's not asking for help, I'd like to think someone would notice and do the same for me," Cego said. He thought of Murray and his parting words, how the man had made a promise to help figure things out. Murray didn't have to help him. The man could have just gotten on with his life.

"Maybe we don't know it when we need help the most," Sol said.

Cego thought of watching Sol's father fight on the common ground's big board, how the fiery girl had put Shiar on his back.

"Do you... need help?" Cego asked.

"Help folding my gear?" Sol avoided the question. "I think you're better off looking after your own stuff, or Dozer's, better yet." The girl glanced in disgust over to Dozer's corner, where sweaty gear and leftover food were strewn about.

"Not with the gear," Cego pressed. "With... what happened after your father's fight the other night."

"I think I did a decent job of putting Shiar in his place." Sol clenched her jaw.

"But it's not like you to give in like that. He was looking for a reaction from you," Cego said.

Sol looked at the floor. "You're right, I shouldn't have done that. I risked our team getting docked points. It was selfish."

"I don't care about the points." Cego sat on the cot beside her. "I care about... what you're going through. With your father. You don't need to talk about it, I just thought—"

"It's why I keep my gear organized like this," Sol said.

"Because of your father?"

"My mother died in childbirth." Sol turned to the moonlit window. "It was just me and Father when I was growing up. When I was little, he made sure to teach me techniques every day."

"Not a bad teacher to have," Cego said. "Best fighter in the world."

"Sometimes, he'd let me do crawl-arounds." The corner of Sol's mouth curved up. "It was so hard to climb up on his shoulders and get all the way around, though. I'd fall off over and over. But still, he stood in place like a statue for hours at a time, just to let me work."

Cego smiled. "No wonder you've got such good back takes."

"Yeah," Sol said. "But... eventually, the team demanded more from him. He had to travel for fights. The nation was depending on him. He wasn't around much and so I made sure to keep up the work on my own. I needed to stay sharp. I studied technique on SystemView, drilled with my mechanical dummy, ran around the estate for cardio every day.

"Last time I saw him, he was heading out to Karstock." Sol's voice became quiet. "He told me he'd bring me along on the next trip so I could come help him train and watch him fight. I made sure to keep all my gear organized, neat and folded, so I'd be ready to travel when he came back."

Wetness shimmered in Sol's eyes. "He never came back."

Cego wanted to pull her close, but his hands remained at his sides awkwardly. "I know what it's like. To have someone by your side all the time. Then one day, they're just gone."

Sol sniffed before she shook her head and turned away. "Best we get some rest. If Dozer's in, and we're going to pull this plan of yours off, we'll be needing it."

CHAPTER 18

The Path Back

A Grievar shall become neither arrogant in victory nor broken in defeat. This is the path to complacency. A Grievar's opponent is their greatest teacher; one learns more walking the path of defeat than one does on the road to victory. Such a balanced spirit will give a Grievar the continued purpose to strive for combat mastery.

Fourth Precept of the Combat Codes

Cego opened his eyes to a glowing sheet of white.

He heard Dozer snoring loudly, so he knew he was still in Quarter D with the rest of the Whelps, and yet he couldn't see a thing. He felt a familiar warmth spreading across his face.

Only when the brightness began to dissipate could he see a glowing form floating just beyond the tip of his nose. His spectral had returned.

"Hello again," Cego whispered. He reached out and felt the spectral's warmth on his hand as it playfully flitted between his fingers. He sat up in his cot to check if anyone else was awake just as the spectral flew across the dark room. It stopped and hovered in front of the door.

"Not again..." Cego mumbled, wiping the sleep from his eyes. He knew this spectral, and somehow, it knew him. It had stuck with him from the little cell in the Underground to his first year at the Lyceum.

He thought about waking one of the crew. Sol certainly might be helpful in a pinch, depending on where the little thing decided to lead him this time. But Cego decided against it. The spectral didn't seem to show itself when anyone else was awake or watching. It would likely disappear as soon as he tried to alert his team.

Cego pulled up his drawstring pants and padded out of the room into the long hall that connected most of the dormitories. He heard chatter coming from the Rocs' door, likely Gryfin Thurgood entertaining visitors, and the grunts of bag work from the Bayhounds' dorm, where the team was likely getting in a late-night training session.

Cego passed Tefo's classroom, absent of the daily thud of shins against pads. The grappling mats of Sapao's class were also empty, the moonlight reflecting on their freshly swept surface.

"Where are you taking me?" Cego whispered.

Finally, the spectral stopped and hovered in front of a familiar doorway with a ring symbol on the front. Professor Larkspur's Circles classroom. The spectral slid through the crack in the doorframe.

"You know, I can't get through there like you," Cego complained. "How do you suppose I'll—"

The door slowly creaked open. Cego shook his head. Had it already been ajar? The hairs on his neck stood as he slid into the darkened classroom.

He half expected to see Professor Larkspur inside, studying some history book or watching old fight footage, but the room was completely empty. Even the spectral that had led him here had conveniently disappeared.

The mimicry Circle was flat on the ground at the center of the class. They'd trained in its auralite form just earlier today. Two students had stood at the center and the rest of the class around the edge, yelling, hissing, and booing. To the class's amazement, the more energized the spectators were, the more bluelight spectrals had formed above the Circle, goading the students within to attack each other.

Cego and Shimo had been the only students able to resist the auralite effect and hold their punches. Cego shivered thinking about staring into that strange boy's eyes for five minutes straight. Next time, he'd rather take a punch to the face.

Cego stepped over the flat edge of the Circle and felt nothing. No spectrals rose. The alloy didn't take on any specific form without Larkspur there to activate it.

"Why am I here?" Cego whispered, searching for the spectral that had brought him. He knew if he was caught sneaking into any classroom during unauthorized hours, the Whelps would face severe penalties, lowering their chance of climbing the scoreboard and graduating as Level Twos.

Cego was about to turn and leave when he noticed one of the closets in the classroom was ajar. Larkspur normally kept all the closets locked. He'd once seen the tall lady lean into the storage space to pull out a musty stack of books about fight history. Treasures, she'd called them.

Cego crept to the closet door where a diffuse light shone from the crack. He peered in and found his spectral hovering in the middle of the space, which was far wider than Cego had imagined, nearly an entirely different room. The spectral pulsed, as if saying *What took you so long?* before it drifted toward the floor. The wisp landed on an object raised off the floor. A pitch-black ring. A Circle of onyx.

Cego stumbled backward in surprise, as if he'd just intruded on a stranger. He tripped and slammed his head against the closet wall before pressing his back up against it. He caught his breath and stared at the glistening, dark surface, his heart pounding in his chest. The spectral had led him to this onyx Circle.

Cego put a hand to the back of his head and brought back blood, but he barely noticed. He couldn't pull his eyes off the onyx. He caught a subtle movement on the surface of the ring. Shadows were rising off it. Cego knew the name for those shadows now. Blacklight.

He suddenly found it very difficult to breathe. His body spasmed—it felt like the calf cramps he got after practice, but this time, every one of his muscles clenched up. Cego didn't want to move, but he was on his hands and knees, crawling toward the onyx.

And then he was sitting in the middle of the Circle, watching the curved shadows on the walls around him shifting slowly, beautifully at first, before they picked up their pace, becoming jagged and frantic as they raced around the closet. Cego tried to shut his eyes as the whirlwind of shadows tore around him, shrinking in, suffocating him. But he couldn't close his eyes. He needed to see.

* * *

A wet, cold object pressed against his face. Cego lashed out with his hand defensively and felt something soft—fur.

He turned and looked into two dark eyes, a shaggy grey face behind them. Arry. She licked him with her warm tongue. He was here again. Home. Arry curled up against him. Sunlight streamed through the wooden shutters of the loft. The wind chimes played their melody outside the door. Just as it always happened, it would be seconds before Cego woke. He wanted to make the most of it.

Cego smiled and pushed his face against Arry's, nuzzling her. She yelped happily and he wrestled her down, letting her lick his face and head. When the pup drew back, Cego noticed her snout was red. He felt a sudden pain at the back of his skull and reached there to feel wetness in his matted hair.

Cego drew his hand away. It was covered in blood. How could he be bleeding like this? Here, in the safety of the loft—in his dream?

The memory flooded back to him. Following the little spectral to Professor Larkspur's classroom. Finding the open closet. Falling and bashing his head when he saw the onyx Circle.

Cego slowly stood, patting Arry's head as she cocked it curiously at him. He was a student at the Lyceum, studying to become a Knight. He lived in Quarter D with the Whelps. And yet he was also here, in the loft with Arry curled up next to him.

Cego's breathing became faster.

He ran toward the loft door, holding his breath as he pushed it open.

The world exploded into view around Cego, a sudden burst of color and light. The blue sky above him. The stark emerald waters retreating toward the horizon. The dune sloping down to the black sand of the beach below. Everything looked so crisp, so beautiful—just as he remembered. As if the previous world he'd inhabited had been a dull, faded canvas, while here, the world was painted in vivid color.

The ocean air was salty and tinged with the pungent odor of fish drying in the sun. The sweet scent of freshly bloomed calendulas greeted Cego, bringing back the memory of every morning that he'd opened the loft doors to slide down the dune onto the beach. Cego couldn't help but breathe deeply, feeling the air settle in his lungs.

How can this be?

He was home; that was certain. He was on the island again in all its bright, vibrant texture. And yet he was not dreaming. He could remember every detail of his time at the Lyceum. How he and his team had just formulated a plan to save Knees. How it had felt to sit beside Sol last night as she told him about her father.

Cego's mind raced as he stood atop the dune. Everything certainly felt real—the throb at the back of his head, the air that he was breathing, Arry nuzzling up against his legs.

He steadied himself as he gazed across the lush landscape. *It can't be real.* Somehow, the onyx Circle had transported him to the island, this place in his memory. It was like the Trials, when he'd spoken to Sam in the ironwood grove, except here, he saw no sign of his brothers.

He walked across the cobbled pathway toward Farmer's compound. It looked exactly as he remembered. The yellow beach grass gave way to smooth pebbles and seashells raked flat around the main house. A base of chiseled boulders bearing dark wooden planks made up the home's frame. The gracefully curved stone shingle roof glinted in the sunlight. Cego walked past the rock garden out front with its carefully manicured miniature trees and the slow trickle of the waterspout. He saw the translucent walls of the back room where the old master practiced ki-breath.

Cego felt his mind shearing in two directions.

He was sitting in the onyx Circle in the closet, the blacklight engulfing him. He remembered every event that had led him to this place. The darkness of the Underground, Tasker Ozark's grating commands, Weep's death, the constant cold, grey rain that fell on the Capital, Murray-Ku's gruff voice reminding him to practice Codes every evening. He remembered the pain of the Trials, the awe of learning at the Lyceum, the warmth of being near his new friends.

But he also saw the crisp blue skies above, the slow, rolling waves on the emerald waters. He could only focus on the next breath of fresh air and the intoxicating scent of the flowers in bloom. It was as if he'd woken from a dream and was now back where he belonged—on the island, home again.

Cego went around the back side of the house as he usually did, toward the Circle. He didn't know what to expect as he slid the thin wood door open, but part of him knew *he'd* be there.

Farmer.

The old master sat cross-legged in the middle of the Circle, facing away from Cego. His grey hair was tied into a topknot, strands falling onto his shoulders, and his tattered grey robe pooled around him. His arm flowed back and forth with a brush in hand, painting black curves onto parchment set in front of him. An inkstone and pile of loose scrolls lay at his side. It was just how Cego remembered the old master, always writing when he wasn't teaching.

"Master, I'm home." The words left Cego's mouth without thinking. It was what he always said.

Farmer slowly set the brush down beside the inkstone. His shoulders heaved up and down in a deep breath. As if speaking from a very distant place, the old master whispered, "A boy dreams for a thousand days and nights that he flies among the constellations. The boy rides atop icy meteors; he warms himself on the surface of the sun; he dives deep into the watery depths of aqueous worlds; and he falls asleep on the crook of the moon. His home is in the stars."

Farmer paused, as he often did, letting the silence that followed his words speak to Cego. The translucent walls of the room grew darker as clouds covered the sun outside. Rain started to patter on the roof.

"Suddenly, the boy wakes. The world he opens his eyes to is different. He no longer can fly among the stars. He stands on the cold, hard earth. The boy feels things he does not remember—pain, exhaustion, despair."

Thunder cracked above as the room grew darker still and the rain began to fall in earnest.

"The boy tries to live his life. He follows a path, he becomes a man, he finds a wife, he bears a family. Every day, though, the man remembers his dream in the stars and is saddened by his loss. He remembers what it felt like to ride a meteor."

Cego listened to the story in silence. Atop Farmer's voice, he could hear the ocean swells growing with the storm outside, crashing against the seaside cliffs.

"Late in his life, as he becomes old and feeble, the man sits outside and looks at the sky. He grieves, remembering his dream in the stars. Out of sadness, the man does not eat, drink, or even move. His family shouts at him, jostles him, cries for him as he continuously stares at the sky. Soon, the man becomes dust, and the wind carries him away."

Cego knew the question was coming.

"Was the boy dreaming of his time among the stars, or was it the man who dreamed of his time on earth?" Farmer asked, just as a heavy crash of thunder shook the ground beneath them.

Cego understood there was no answer to this question. Just as the storm rolling into the island had no purpose, the old master's words were not to be solved or puzzled out.

Farmer suddenly stood, his robe straightening around him. A gust of wind broke into the room, whipping Farmer's grey hair up and tossing scrolls across the floor.

Cego knew what was next. He'd fought the old master a thousand times, and this time would be no different.

Farmer turned around and Cego's heart fluttered. In the place of the old master's wrinkled face was an emptiness full of writhing shadows. A void where a face should be. Just as when Cego had unmasked the Guardian in the Trials—this was no man who stood in front of him. This was not Farmer.

And yet, the faceless creature bowed from across the Circle, just as the old master would always do.

Cego returned the bow; he'd done so a thousand times before. He had no choice.

"Who are you?" Cego asked as the room lit up with a bright flash of lightning.

"I am who I have always been," the creature responded along with the deep rumble of thunder. It approached Cego slowly in a crouch, elbows tight to its body. It had Farmer's fighting posture.

The creature shot in, its body moving with the unrivaled swiftness and fluidity that Cego remembered of the old master. Cego sprawled back, but its hands were already clasped around his legs, putting him down on his back.

Cego quickly got to his knees, but the creature pressed into him. It fished a hand beneath Cego's armpit and slid it across to the other side of his neck. Cego tried to turn away from the choke, but the creature tracked him with unyielding pressure and pushed him back to the floor.

Cego sensed his opponent shifting its weight, so he quickly rolled over his shoulder and wrapped his legs around the creature's torso. He caught an arm and tried to break it, but the thing was always one step ahead, driving Cego onto his neck and swiveling around his body.

The creature popped up and pressed its knee into Cego's sternum, pulling his neck at the same time and forcing the air out of his lungs. Cego turned his body for a split second to relieve the pressure, and somehow, the creature was already on his back, as if it had teleported there.

Even in the compromised position, Cego smiled. Though this creature didn't have Farmer's face, he now knew it was the same old master who had trained him for so many years. This fight was their conversation. Cego asked his questions with quick escapes and arm bar attempts, and the old master answered with stifling pressure and chokes. He recognized the way the old master moved—at one moment, as light as a feather, and at the next, as heavy as a boulder.

Cego fought Farmer's hands, each seeming to have a will of its own when snaking across his throat. He twisted his hips to the side, trying to free himself from the man's hooks. He knew his last efforts were fruitless. He'd been entangled in this web before and there was no escape.

Farmer's arm tightened across his neck. The edges of Cego's vision blurred. For a moment, he felt warm as the cocoon of darkness closed in on him. Cego remembered the warmth like the embrace of an old friend.

"Wake up, Cego," the old master whispered just as the world went dark again.

* * *

"Wake up, Cego."

Cego gasped and tried to pull Farmer's arms from his neck.

But the old master wasn't there. Cego was in Larkspur's closet again, lying just outside the onyx Circle. Shadows were smoldering at the ring's surface.

Cego was covered in sweat but uninjured except for a splitting headache. He tried to take a deep breath, but it caught in his chest. He'd been back home to the island. It was just as he remembered, in such vivid detail. Everything had been in its right place except for his absent brothers and Farmer's face.

Cego's mind raced with a whirlwind of questions. How could the onyx know his memory so distinctly? How could it transport him back to his home?

"You woke up."

Cego whirled around, expecting to see Larkspur's towering form, ready to reprimand him for his intrusion. But it was no professor standing there. It was Kōri Shimo. And to Cego's recollection, those words might have been the first he'd ever heard the strange boy speak. In fact, he couldn't recall hearing Shimo's monotone voice before.

"How long have you been there...?" Cego wiped at the sweat on his forehead.

"Long enough," Shimo said.

Cego thought back to the potential penalty he'd face for being caught in this classroom. Shimo was on a rival team and could easily turn him in to Larkspur. "The door to the classroom was open...I just—"

"I don't care that you are here," Shimo said. "What did you see in there?"

Cego's stomach fluttered. Though it didn't seem the boy would turn him in, trying to describe what he'd just experienced seemed a whole different obstacle.

"It's just a big closet, there's a Circle in there. It looks like Larkspur keeps it in storage. I hit my head and..."

"Where did the onyx take you?" Shimo asked flatly, ignoring Cego's rambling.

"I...I saw...my home," Cego said. It felt good to say the words out loud, even to a stranger like Shimo. "Was it...was it your voice I heard calling me back?" Cego asked.

"I woke you up," Shimo stated without emotion.

"You knew what I was seeing in there, then," Cego said. "You knew what I was fighting."

"No," Shimo said. "But I know what the blacklight does. The toll it can take."

"The blacklight." Cego whispered the word as if the Circle across the room might hear him. "How does it know? How can it know what's in my mind like that?"

Shimo shrugged and turned to leave.

"Wait!" Cego put a hand on Shimo's shoulder. Lightning quick, the boy clasped Cego's hand and whipped around to apply a wrist lock. Cego defended the technique by shoving Shimo backward with his other hand.

"Fast..." The boy stared at Cego. He'd made the attack simply to gauge the reaction.

Cego met Shimo's eyes and remembered seeing Marvin Stronglight floating lifelessly in the vat. He remembered how Shimo had relentlessly battered the defenseless boy.

"You've been in this onyx Circle too, haven't you?" Cego asked. "Where does it take you?"

"The blacklight always leads to the same place," Shimo said before he turned and walked from the classroom, back into the shadows of the hallway.

Cego stood silently for a moment until he noticed his hands

were shaking. He suddenly felt incredibly tired, not with the fatigue that came from a single night up, but a lingering weariness deep in his bones.

He turned to see the door to the closet still ajar. Shadows were pooling around the onyx and slithering onto the floor. Despite what he'd just been through, though Cego felt like he could close his eyes and be asleep in an instant, he had a strong urge to step back into the closet, to sit again within the ring of blacklight.

Instead, he shut the closet door quickly and exited the classroom into the silent Lyceum halls. As Cego walked back toward Quarter D, he couldn't help but feel he was leaving something important behind.

CHAPTER 19

A Step Forward

A Grievar does not strive to reach old age. One may be inclined to prolong life span, to seek health and prosperity, to watch brood grow and carry on a bloodline. This is a spirit that will perish before the heart stops beating. The Grievar should fondly watch death, fully expecting to embrace darkness at every moment, never vainly seeking the next breath.

Passage Three, Sixty-Sixth Precept of the Combat Codes

Murray climbed the broken steps of PublicJustice, pushing past the throngs of waiting Grievar. If you could even call them Grievar; they were addicts, broken-down things that looked like they'd crumple just setting foot in a Circle.

He reached the front entry, where a thick, neckless man stood behind a steel barrier.

"Wait yer turn just like the rest," the guard growled. "Don't make me set the Enforcers on you."

"Dakar sent for me," Murray lied, something he'd been getting accustomed to lately. Though he certainly could have asked the commander of PublicJustice for a favor, he still needed to keep away from prying ears.

"Has he?" The guard looked at Murray warily. "And who're you to know Commander Pugilio?"

Murray sighed. He hated announcing himself, yet he seemed to be doing it every other day now, using his name to get ahead like some spineless Daimyo.

"Murray Pearson."

The guard looked Murray over, as if trying to recount the last time he'd seen him on SystemView.

"It is you, isn't it?" The guard smiled through his broken teeth. "Well, I'll be. Darkin' Mighty Murray in the flesh. You know, wasn't only a week ago I was watching one of yer old bouts with my nephew. Who was the body you put down in Karstock? The Kirothian missing the ear—"

Murray tried to hide his impatience. "Hugo Vladshar."

"Yeah, Vladshar!" The man clapped. "Darkin' deadly spinning elbow you threw to put 'em down too, don't see that one too often—"

"If you don't mind," Murray interrupted, "I'm in a bit of a hurry to see the commander."

"Right, right." The guard nodded before he turned to the crowd at Murray's back and screamed, "Stay back, you scum, or you'll be blasted to high hell before you get a chance at yer darkin' justice!"

The man set his hand on a lever by his side to raise the steel gate. A red pulse of light flashed across Murray's eye.

"You'll be good to go all the way to the commander's offices, you remember where—"

"Yeah, I remember," Murray said.

"Course you do," the guard said as the portal lifted in front of Murray.

Murray stepped through into the gargantuan lobby of PublicJustice. Though the old building was in sore need of renovation, it still set Murray's head spinning to see its grandeur: tall stained-glass shield windows and monolithic statues surrounded him. The sculptures were carved in the likeness of the ancient Ezonians who had written the Codes of Justice. They looked down at Murray with colorless grey eyes, surely disgusted over what their system had become.

"Processing, case five eighty-two," a robotic voice announced on the overhead speakers as a pack of cloaked Daimyo scuttled by toward the courtrooms across the lobby. The Prosecutors whispered in hushed tones and glared at anyone who might be listening in.

"Leave me be!" Murray turned to see a prisoner getting dragged forward by a chain around his neck, saliva dribbling from his mouth as he attempted to keep himself planted on the floor. "I didn't do nothing!"

The prisoner was ripped from the ground with such force that Murray was surprised the man's head stayed attached. The creature on the other end of the chain was nine feet of rippling steel.

Murray shook his head. *Enforcer.*

The Enforcer grasped the prisoner's chain with a taloned claw while swinging its other arm menacingly, a glowing red cylinder at its end. A small window was visible at the mech's center, where Murray could make out a blue-veined head within. Black, pupilless eyes stared out from where the Daimyo pilot sat inside the cockpit. The brains behind the mech.

Murray couldn't help but shiver at the abomination. Even from this distance, and though the Enforcer's pulse cannon wasn't fully charged, Murray could feel its lethality. He'd seen firsthand how an Enforcer's cannon could reduce a stone floor to a smoking crater, how it could incinerate flesh and bone in mere seconds. It didn't matter how strong or skilled you were; that beast was the great equalizer. The Enforcers were the reason so many Grievar and Grunt revolts over the centuries had been quashed with mass casualties.

Murray kept his eyes on the floor as he walked through the hall, not wanting to be spotted. Callen's men were everywhere. One little bird flitting back to that man, and Murray's chance would be gone. Cego's chance would be gone.

Murray passed the lift to the commander's offices, where he guessed Dakar was most likely out cold at his desk. Instead, Murray turned down an adjacent hallway, passing a servicer who nodded at him before stepping up to another thick steel gate. He stood in place and stared at a viewport above, shifting his hips to relieve the pain that had started to flood up his spine.

Finally, a voice reverberated from the box beside the viewport. "State your purpose."

"Here to see a prisoner in holding," Murray said.

The voice on the other end was silent for several moments and Murray dreaded the notion of having to use his name to get through another door. Instead, a red light flashed across him, checking his security access.

"Who are you here to see?" the voice asked.

Murray shook his head, as if he couldn't believe he'd be saying the man's name. "Jezar D'lysien."

After another pause, the steel slab slid to the side, revealing a long flickering hall beyond.

"Block fifteen," a gangly guard said as he stepped from his booth and looked Murray up and down. "I'll need to come along."

The hall was lightless but for the yellow spectrals that floated up and down between vents on either side of the rusted walkway.

"Cytrine," Murray muttered as he peered through the yellowlight into one of the dark cells beyond.

"Then I swung on 'em, ducked his charge, and put the slagger flat on his back!" The light illuminated the bony face of a prisoner within, his rib cage nearly bursting from his emaciated chest. Despite his sorry state, the man was smiling, a wide, toothless grin spread ear to ear.

"Prepare yourself! Cower in the face of the great Uni Yaharan!" Murray turned to see another prisoner, nearly as emaciated, this one missing both his ears, also smiling as he swung his frail arm through the air against some invisible enemy.

Murray himself felt the pulse of the yellowlight, the quickening of his heartbeat, the need to suddenly tell the guard beside him of the greatest feats of his career, to show him what techniques had won him fame in the arena.

Instead, Murray growled, "What in the dark are you doing to these men?"

"Men?" The guard chuckled. "There are no men within these cells. Holdups only."

Murray was all too familiar with the term. Holdups were Public-Justice prisoners who were awaiting trial. But Governance often found it convenient to keep them here longer than the maximum legal month any Griever was allowed be kept in captivity prior to their court date.

"Why the cytrine?" Murray said as they walked by another pair of cells, each holding a man living out some fight fantasy.

"You know how it is, boss," the guard said. "Grievar ain't meant to be kept in holding. They go mad, gnaw their very bones off rather than stay in one place. With the yellowlight, they can at least be happy, thinking they're off somewhere else, fighting in the Circles or whatnot..."

"This is wrong." Murray shuddered as he met the eyes of another prisoner, who was smiling as he slammed his fists into the stone wall of his cell. The skin had completely come off the man's hands, and the bones beneath had dug a small trench into the stone.

"Some don't take to it as well as others..." The guard shook his head and pulled a stool away from the wall. "Anyhow, here we are at block fifteen. Make sure you keep your hands away from the bars. These men were no good to start, and now... well, now they're less than no good. Especially this one here."

Murray sat on the little stool and stared into the darkness. This cell lacked the cytrine hue of the rest, without any spectrals surrounding it. Still, Murray could make out a shadow deep within.

"Jezar." Murray said the name unwillingly, as if his tongue would rather speak some other word.

Something clattered to the floor and the shadow shifted.

"Jezar." Murray said the name again, louder this time over the screams from across the hall.

"Could it be?" A whisper from the cell. "Could the light have finally got me?"

A lanky man with ashen skin and long, tangled hair stepped forward. He was bare-chested and wearing nothing but a loincloth.

"Of all the people I'd expect to pay me a visit, you'd have been the last on the list, Murray Pearson." The man crouched to pick a wooden ladle off the floor. He spooned some gruel into his mouth before holding it out to Murray. "What sort of host would I be if I didn't offer some sustenance to an honored visitor?"

Murray shook his head, keeping his gaze on the man's dull mustard eyes.

"No?" Jezar helped himself to another spoonful of the slop. "Well, then, mind my manners, please, we only have such a treat every other day here in holding."

Jezar straightened his back and looked Murray up and down. "Why, you've let yourself go, Murray. I remember that once, you looked to be the proudest Grievar the Citadel could conjure up, without a slouched vertebra in your spine. Now…you appear tired. Or perhaps defeated is the proper word?"

"I'm not here to talk about me," Murray said.

"Oh, no? So different from the old days? I remember a time when you only talked about yourself. Always told the rest of the Knights how they should compose themselves, just like you. Proper. With honor. Abiding by the Codes. Was that how you used to say it? Are you here to tell me more about the Codes, Murray?"

Murray breathed deeply, trying to let the tension drain from his neck and shoulders. "I'm here to ask you some questions, Jezar."

"Ah! Much has changed, then. The state of the world outside these stone walls must indeed be dire if Murray Pearson is asking questions all of a sudden instead of giving orders. Instead of flashing your captain's belt like some glorious beacon given by the gods."

Murray ignored the man. "I spoke with some of the Knights in service. I wanted to know about current... training methods at the Citadel. Your name was mentioned."

"Was it, now?" Jezar smiled as he tugged at one of his frayed earlobes. Murray remembered that ear being full of glinting metal once. "Good to know my name is still spoken in those halls. Hopefully not all bad talk. And training methods, you say? Why wouldn't you just go to your ally, the man at the top, our old friend Memnon?"

Murray shook his head. "It's not so simple. Memnon... He's part of it, somehow."

Jezar's smile grew wider. "My, my, Murray Pearson. Finally seeing the world for what it is. Not black-and-white, as you used to see. Honor or dishonor. Good or evil. Right or wrong. No, it's all a spectrum, isn't it? And our old friend Memnon isn't the great force for good you once believed? And perhaps, if that's true... Perhaps it might be said that I, your old comrade, fellow Knight, might not be so bad either?"

"Dark that," Murray growled. "You broke every Code in the darkin' book during our service. You nearly made a laughingstock of our entire team and brought down all that we'd worked for—"

"Oh, was it really so bad?" Jezar's eyes twinkled. "A little fun, some dalliances on the road, a Code broken here and there, I never hurt any—"

"You darkin' brought a blade into the Circle and stabbed a Grievar in the eye."

"Well, yes, there was that." Jezar shrugged. "But he surely deserved it, and I was able to disguise the attack. No one even knew the difference."

"You bedded an opponent the night before your fight with him," Murray said.

"Right, yes! Oh, another great memory...and besides being a fantastic romp, he was an easy win the next day. Did I not achieve victory for the team, oh great captain?"

Murray took a deep breath. "I'm not here to reminisce, Jezar. I need to know about the newest in training tech. They said you were handling procurement of stim supplies for Citadel, before you tried to rip them off."

"Tried?" Jezar set his wooden bowl down and paced the cell. Though the man had clearly degenerated during his years in holding, Murray could see Jezar had somehow maintained some muscle mass. "What makes you think I'm not storing those bits I rightfully earned somewhere safe for a sunny day?"

"Doesn't matter to me," Murray said. "I just want to know about the newest stuff Citadel has been buying. Something that might help the Knights handle the light better."

"Even though you always chose to ignore their delightful effects, there have long been stims that could alleviate the pull of the various alloys," Jezar said. "Doesn't sound like something you'd come all this way to visit little old me for."

"There's something new," Murray said. "Maybe it's not stims, but some tech Citadel's been using. I'm not sure what it is, but I know it's big. Something that could make a lacklight boy I pulled from the slave Circles somehow perform better in Trials than any in the last decade. I tried to get it out of Memnon but he was tight-lipped, so it must still be in development."

Jezar suddenly went silent. His eyes darted to the side, and then back to Murray. The man knew something.

"You know what I'm talking about." Murray stood and pressed

against the bars, gripping them with white knuckles. He could smell Jezar's breath, somehow tinged with sweetness despite being in this shithole.

"Let's say I did know something," Jezar said. "Why would I tell you? You, honored captain, who forced me off the team? You, Murray Pearson, who still hates me as much as you once did long ago?"

"Because I've got this." Murray reached into his vest pocket and pulled out a bundled cloth. He unwrapped it to reveal several small metal cylinders, each with a glinting lens at the end.

Jezar's eyes fixed on Murray's open hand. "Murray Pearson. He who could do no wrong, who could never break a Code, is now standing in front of me holding a pile of cleavers?" Jezar lifted his head and laughed until tears poured from the corners of his eyes. "Oh... things truly must be dire on the outside."

"Do you want them or not?" Murray looked over his shoulder toward the guard, who would likely be coming back shortly.

"Oh... yes." Jezar licked his lips. "I want them very much. How I've thought about taking a hit through the years I've been stuck in holding. Getting that rush, suddenly all the pains, the worries of life, flowing away like silt in a river. Yes, I would like them very much."

"Give me what I need," Murray said. "And you'll be able to get a hit off before the guard gets back."

"Let me ask you a question for a turn, Murray," Jezar said. "Do you know why there are no yellowlight spectrals outside my cell? Do you know why the little wisps don't shine their oh-so-very-happy light down on me?"

Murray shook his head. "You cut a deal with the guards. Told them of some treasure you might provide them on the outside if they spared you. Or maybe one of your associates has their family in a bind."

"You know me well, don't you?" Jezar laughed. "Alas, this time it was not through bribery or blackmail that I got my way."

"How, then?"

"You see, I've found the spectrals like to see the fruits of their labor," Jezar said. "They love to see men bask in their glow with budding smiles. They want to hear the shouts of glee, the praise, the awe. And so... when I gave them nothing of the sort, when I sat beneath the yellowlight with nothing but a boring stare for a year straight, the little things simply grew tired of me and floated off to frolic with someone else."

Murray heard the footsteps of the guard approaching from down the hall.

"I am not as weak-willed as you think," Jezar said as he stepped up to the bars of the cell. "Codes and honor are not all that is required to be strong. Have you found that out yet?"

Murray looked the man in the eye. "Yes."

"All right, then." Jezar flipped the hair from his face. "I've gotten what I want from you, after all these years. I'll tell you what you need."

"You don't want the cleavers?"

"Oh yes, I'll take those too." Jezar's hand shot out like a piston and lifted the cylinders from Murray's hand. The man immediately raised one of the cleavers to his eyeball and set off the switch, resulting in a great burst of light.

Jezar's head lolled back, and a deep smile etched his face as he slumped against the stone wall. "Oh... that was very, very nice indeed."

"Jezar!" Murray hissed. "You gave me your word. Tell me..."

"My word?" Jezar cocked his head, as if listening to some echo Murray couldn't hear. "My word?"

"Tell me about the new tech! What is Memnon hiding?" Murray heard the guard getting even closer, humming some tune amid the screams from the nearby cells.

"Memnon's always hiding something..." Jezar drifted off. "But, I believe, to find what you're really looking for, you'll need to go to them."

"Them?" Murray growled. "Who the dark is *them*?"

"Them... who is it ever? Who is the only them? Them that watches from the shadows. Them that buzzes in our ears, in our brains. Them that are everywhere and nowhere..."

"Them..." Murray whispered. "The—"

"Bit-Minders." Jezar spoke the word as his head lolled to the side, a giant smile still etched into his face.

Murray stood from the stool; his stomach clenched. The guard was looking at him. "Say anything interesting, this one?"

"No." Murray was already walking back down the long corridor, listening to the shouts of the prisoners along the way.

* * *

Cego's body shuddered against the cold glass of the shield window.

The empty training room on the second floor of the Harmony was where he often found refuge. There was a state-of-the-art facility beside the common ground where most of the students trained during off-hours, so Cego rarely encountered anyone in this outdated room. Though he practiced here, hitting one of the old heavy bags or drilling on the frayed mat space, Cego mostly came for the solitude.

After what he'd encountered in Professor Larkspur's closet, Cego needed it. He couldn't shake the experience he'd had in the onyx Circle. Seeing his island home again in such vivid detail brought him no comfort. Though he'd relished the flow state of sparring with the old master, now that he was on the outside, everything felt cold and colorless.

Cego put a hand to his head and massaged his temple. He should be focused on getting Knees back. The Whelps needed to launch into action tomorrow for the plan to work. But Cego could only focus on himself. On his past.

He thought of Murray-Ku's parting promise again. *I'll figure things out for you, kid.*

Perhaps the old Grievar had abandoned him. Cego wouldn't

blame the man for giving up. After all, Cego was just another lack-light boy he'd picked up from the Deep. Murray-Ku had brought kids up year after year. How was he any different?

Cego looked up to the training room's entrance and saw a thick-shouldered shadow hovering in the doorway. *Murray-Ku?*

Joba emerged into the dim-lit space, the ever-present smile adorning the big boy's face as he lumbered toward Cego.

Cego turned as if to look out the window and wiped a hand across his wet cheek. He needed to be strong for his team. If they saw his weakness, they would become weak too.

Joba sat beside him on the bench, the wood creaking beneath the boy's massive frame. Cego looked up at his smiling friend.

"How are you, Joba?"

Joba gently put his hand on Cego's shoulder, meeting his eyes.

"Right..." Cego looked away, embarrassed. "I'm guessing you were watching me for some time, then?"

Joba nodded.

Though Cego had grown accustomed to Joba during their semester at the Lyceum together, Abel was almost always beside the giant, the little Desovian speaking in his place. Cego often forgot that Joba was only ten years old, a prized specimen the Scouts had captured from Ezo's borderlands. Cego couldn't even recall the number of insults he'd heard slung at Joba over the past year, most of the barbs labeling his friend a freak of nature. Though Joba could hear just fine, the insults seemed to pass by him like water over a heavy boulder.

"Sometimes it's all too much," Cego said as he stared out the window. "Everything happening here at the Lyceum, everything that's happened in the past, I don't know how to sort it all out."

Cego felt he could speak freely with Joba. Looking at the boy's wide, smiling face, he saw wisdom beyond a mere ten years of age.

"I've made good friends here," Cego said. "But I miss my brothers. I miss my home."

Joba nodded understandingly.

"And Murray-Ku left," Cego said. "I relied on him for guidance. Whenever I wasn't sure about something, I could ask him. And now he's not here."

Cego felt his face flush, but Joba did not judge him. He simply stared back with that smile.

"I feel alone." Cego shivered. "Like I don't belong here."

Joba nodded slowly.

"There's other things too, Joba," Cego said. "Other reasons why it feels like I can never catch my breath. My past—there's just so much I don't understand. Like I'm always trying to grasp at sand falling between my fingers."

Cego stood and turned away from his friend, trying to take a deep breath.

He felt Joba's strong hand on his shoulder again. He turned and looked up to meet the boy's eyes. Joba nodded, stepped back, then suddenly grabbed the white second skin he was wearing and lifted it over his head.

Cego stared at his friend's shirtless torso. Jagged scars covered nearly every inch of the boy's body, running from his navel up to his shoulder blades. Joba turned to show Cego that his back was even worse. Chunks of flesh seemed to have been ripped from his shoulders, the deep wounds now crusted over in brown, scaly patches.

"Oh, Joba..." Cego trailed off. He realized he'd never seen Joba without his second skin on before. The giant would always change his clothes in some corner, away from prying eyes. He'd always known Joba had a rough brooding, put to slave labor among the harvesters, but the sight of his friend's scars brought tears to Cego's eyes.

Joba looked down and brushed his hand across Cego's face to wipe away the tears. The boy touched the scars on his own chest, and then pointed up to his face. He was smiling still, just like he always was.

"You…you've gone through so much," Cego said, as if he were Abel translating for the giant. "You've dealt with terrible things in your past, and yet here you are, standing in front of me and smiling."

Joba nodded, seemingly satisfied with Cego's translation.

"I understand," Cego said. "That's all we can do, right? Smile and take the next step forward."

Joba nodded and took a long stride away from the window toward the door. Cego took another deep breath and followed his friend.

CHAPTER 20

Operation Recovery

A Grievar who perishes in the Circle has fulfilled their path. If this is the manner of death, it should not be celebrated or mourned. Death should be viewed as the passage of seasons, as the summer's last warmth gives way to the chill of frost.

Passage Two, Seventeenth Precept of the Combat Codes

Dozer was the first cog of Operation Recovery, as it ironically came to be known. It was either that or Operation Self-Damage, which Cego thought had too much of an ominous ring to it. And though the big kid hadn't agreed to help Knees yet, Cego could only hope that Dozer would come to his senses in the moment.

Cego and Sol had mapped out every possibility and combination of fights that needed to occur for Operation Recovery to work, and unfortunately, the plan first required Dozer to take a fall during Professor Tefo's striking class.

Cego knew he'd have to actually hurt his friend, as Dozer certainly wasn't known for his acting abilities. He just had to make sure he didn't hurt him too badly. Dozer would need to make a full recovery by the time the Bayhounds issued their challenge.

Tefo had the class hitting pads to start, as usual, and Cego paired up with Dozer. Though his mind still felt hazy after coming out of the onyx Circle, Cego's encounter with Joba had given him a renewed vigor to take on the task. If Joba could be so steady in the face of pain and hatred, then Cego could be a leader.

"You know what we need to do." He stood in front of Dozer, circling his hips in preparation for the drill.

Dozer's brow furrowed as he strapped a kick pad onto his forearm. "I know the plan. Doesn't mean I like it."

"Look at him." Cego gestured across the room at Knees, who was paired up with Shiar. The jackal was holding his arms out like some noble lord, waiting for Knees to strap him up.

"It's too tight, idiot," Shiar complained to Knees as the Venturian refastened the straps.

"Don't think you're due a squire until you graduate as a Knight," Professor Tefo said with a frown as he passed the pair.

Cego turned back to Dozer. The stubbornness in the boy's face had fled, replaced with a look of grim determination.

"Let's do this," Dozer growled.

Cego nodded. "For Knees."

"For Knees," Dozer said as he clenched his jaw and held the large kick pad up. It was time for builders. Cego would slowly build the number of kicks he landed, each subsequent strike aimed with increased power.

Tefo bellowed, "Go!" and the sound of shins slapping against the rubber pads echoed across the classroom.

Dozer was crouched over the pad in the proper position, with his face tucked behind it to prevent any errant kicks. One. Cego slammed his shin into the pad. Two. He kicked the pad twice in rapid succession, harder this time. Three. Three kicks in a row, with even more force. Four. Cego slammed his shin into the pad four times, almost as hard as he could.

Five. Cego saw out of the corner of his eye Dozer had raised his face above the top of the pad. His eyes were closed—he was bracing himself. Cego didn't want to do this.

Cego threw four full-force kicks directly into the center of the pad. On his fifth kick, he aimed toward the top of the pad. His shin slid along and off the edge, slamming into Dozer's exposed chin and knocking his friend flat to the ground like a toppled tree.

Cego knelt over Dozer, wincing as he saw the awkward angle his jaw was hanging at. Dozer opened his eyes and looked up at Cego. He tried to smile but grimaced in pain instead. Cego had done it—Dozer's jaw was certainly broken.

"Sorry," Cego whispered before Tefo arrived at their side. "Let one get away from you there, eh, Cego?" Professor Tefo asked.

"Yeah . . . I don't know what happened," Cego said. Some of the class had come to stand in a circle around Dozer, who was lying inert on the floor.

"I guess I'm just tired from all the extra classes." Cego made sure to say that part loud enough for Shiar to hear, who, as expected, was among the group standing around Dozer. He was smiling as he looked down at the fallen boy.

"Looks like these lacklights will end up knocking each other out of the running. No need for any of us to help out," Shiar said sarcastically.

"Mistimed kick. Happens to the best of us," Professor Tefo said, defending Cego. "Why, I can remember when I was at the Lyceum, we had a fella in class by the name of Tamarind Kormary, immigrant from Besayd. Huge—with thighs like tree trunks. I ended up holding pads for him, don't know how it ended up like that, maybe I drew the short end of the straw, but anyways . . ."

"Professor, don't you think we should get Dozer to the medward?" Cego interrupted Tefo's story, knowing the professor wouldn't approach the end of it anytime soon.

"Oh, yes, yes, of course." Tefo helped Dozer off the ground. "I've seen my share of broken jaws. Looking at this one, it'll be at least two days to get that jaw wired and set. Definitely not the worst that I've seen, though. Class, keep up with the builders!"

Cego caught Shiar eyeing Dozer as he slowly walked away with Professor Tefo's aid. The jackal had caught the scent of blood.

* * *

Joba was the next piece to put into play for Operation Recovery. Though he was young, the other teams had already seen the great strength the boy possessed. A healthy Joba would be a huge disincentive for the Bayhounds to make their challenge.

Abel excused himself from Professor Aon's lecture early, leaving Cego and Sol sitting in the musty study.

"I believe Abel has the right idea, students. If you'll excuse me momentarily as well, a Grievar of my age needs to use the toilet more often than I'd like to admit." Aon chuckled as he slowly made his way out the door.

Cego and Sol sat quietly for a minute before Sol spoke up.

"Do you really think this plan will work?" she asked. "What makes you think Shiar will actually take the bait? I mean, if it were me, I'd have made the challenge right off the bat if I thought I could beat your team."

"Yes. But you have honor, Sol. Shiar does not. The reason I know this plan will work is because Shiar goes after weakness. That's how he works. It was the same in the Deep. He knew Weep was injured, literally fighting with his last breath. And he took that opportunity to attack him. This time...we'll be ready for him," Cego said as he clenched his fists.

Sol regarded him silently. "Weep. You and Dozer mention him all the time. He must have been quite a Grievar to have made such an impression on you guys."

"Yes. He was. Not in the way you'd think, though," Cego said. "He wasn't stronger or faster, or even more skilled than anyone. In fact, he was the weakest of our crew. But he overcame that weakness and he kept fighting. He kept wanting to become better. I think that's what being a Grievar is about. Not strength, or speed, or even skill, but wanting to become better."

Sol nodded. "My father used to tell me something like that. *We learn more in defeat than we do in victory.*"

Cego had heard the famous saying before. Farmer had repeated it on regular occasion as well. "Will your father be back from his fight in Kiroth soon?" Cego asked. He knew there was fanfare whenever Ezo's champion returned home, victorious.

Sol looked down. "I don't know. And even if he's back training at the Knight Tower, I won't be expecting a visit."

"I'm sorry," Cego said. "I didn't mean to—"

"Don't be," Sol said with sudden fire. "I've had more opportunity than most Grievar out there. And my father's absence has made me stronger. I've had to figure things out for myself."

Cego could tell Sol wanted to leave the conversation at that, so he stayed quiet until Professor Aon returned.

After Aon's lecture, Sol and Cego returned to Quarter D, where Abel was hunched over a desk with several half-full canisters of liquid set around him. The little Grievar was singing a Desovian tune as he worked, his hands expertly distributing the liquids into a glass bottle.

He turned as they moved forward to examine his work. "Ah—my friends! How was rest of lecture? I can take notes I miss?" Abel asked Cego.

"I think you'd be better off with Sol's notes," Cego said. "But tell us about your work here. Is it ready?"

"Yes, yes. Is ready." Abel held up the bottle of liquid in front of his eyes and swished it around. "Was difficult to find right ingredients. Abel looks in dining hall, cleaning supply, everywhere. But I make work. Will work."

"How did you learn how to do this, by the way?" Sol asked Abel.

"Old Desovian recipe," he replied. "I have many sisters at home. Use recipe for... how do you say, make man friend sick. Then sister take care him when he sick. He very happy, stay, make baby."

Sol and Cego looked at each other, quiet for a moment, and then broke out in laughter.

"What so funny?" Abel asked. "This not how baby made here in Ezo?"

Cego tried to calm himself. "Well, I'm not an expert on the subject... but I don't think so."

"Let's hope Joba doesn't run into any problems like that!" Sol added.

The rest of the crew, except for Dozer, who was at the medward, soon returned after their classes. Abel patted Joba on the back and handed him the bottle of liquid. Joba looked at it, shrugged, and downed it in one huge gulp.

"Okay." Cego reached up and gripped Joba's shoulder. The giant boy had given Cego strength when he needed it most and now Joba was sacrificing his own strength for the team. "Let's get to the dining hall in time. We'll need to make sure the Bayhounds are there for this."

The dining hall was completely full, but Cego directed his team to sit beside the Bayhounds. Shiar was bragging loudly about how he'd knocked someone out in striking class that day.

The Whelps sat silently. They were all waiting, their eyes occasionally flitting to Joba, who sat with an unperturbed smile on his face as he downed another glass of insta-carbs. Cego needed his crew to appear natural.

"Mateus, pretty great that you are taking Stratagems and Maneuvers. Mind telling us how the class is going so far?" Cego asked Mateus, who was sitting across from him.

Mateus appeared to be put off by the question at first, but as he caught Cego staring at him intensely, he took the hint. "Oh, yes... yes. Professor Dynari is truly a genius," he said loudly. "He showed us this one strategy today. It was amazing. Completely designed to make your opponent think you're hurt when really you're just waiting to throw the counter. In fact, *ooof*—"

Sol had elbowed Mateus under the table. "What the? Why'd you—" Mateus suddenly realized what he'd been saying. Cego glared at him. Luckily, Shiar didn't seem to be paying attention.

Cego checked on Joba and had to double-take as he stared at the giant boy. Joba's face had gone ghost white. He looked panicked.

"Um...you all right there, Joba?" Cego asked, though he knew his friend was not all right.

Joba shook his head and stood up in a hurry, shaking the whole table with his bulk. The neighboring teams were looking at the boy now, Shiar's included.

Joba tried to cup his hands around his mouth, but it was useless. With a noise that sounded to Cego like a bullfrog in labor, Joba jerked his head forward violently as waterfalls of vomit poured from his hands. The poor boy tried to wipe his hands on his shirt, just as the next eruption burst from his mouth, splashing onto the table in front of him and, to Cego's amazement, onto Mateus Winterfowl's head, which happened to be perfectly positioned in Joba's zone of havoc.

The whole dining hall was watching the spectacle. Even the seasoned Level Sixers had expressions on their faces that said they'd never seen anything like it before. The smell was already pungent, and many of the students started to filter out of the hall rapidly.

Joba fell to his knees, his hands back over his mouth, trying to stop the next eruption unsuccessfully. Cego caught Shiar's gaze as he evacuated with the rest of the nearby students. The jackal's eyes were wide in amusement, watching the big kid hurl his last few meals across the floor.

The job was done. Now his friend needed some attention. "Someone get a cleric in here! My friend is sick!" Cego yelled.

There would be nothing to do at this point but wait. Cego stood above Joba as he lay on the floor like a fallen beast, taking deep breaths between his bouts of sickness. "You did good, my friend," Cego said, putting a hand on Joba's back.

Hopefully, Joba would recover in time—they would need him. Abel had said that the sickness should last for only one day, but looking at Joba's chest rise and fall fitfully, Cego wasn't so sure.

Cego nodded to Sol, who was smiling for some reason. He took one look at Mateus Winterfowl, covered in Joba's handiwork, and Cego smiled too.

* * *

With both Dozer and Joba out at the medward, Cego was ready to put the final piece of Operation Recovery into play—himself.

He looked into the bunk mirror prior to heading down to Grappling Level One. Between his recent bout in the blacklight, training every day, studying for his Codes test, and the late nights planning Operation Recovery, he felt weaker than ever.

Cego had dark circles beneath his eyes, and a bruise was swelling on his cheek from an errant knee during training yesterday. He ran his hand through his hair—it was getting quite long and unruly at this point. Cego's back was stiff and his neck felt like a vise was clamping down on it. He was starting to understand what Murray-Ku was complaining about all the time—the constant aches and pains that wore his body down.

As was his habit every day before he left Quarter D, Cego rolled down the nape of his second skin and checked on the flux tattoo. He watched the little dragon's snout poke out first before its serpentine body emerged onto his neck.

"Wow, doesn't look like you'll need to do much to convince Shiar that you're beat up," Sol said from behind him, looking into the mirror.

"That's what I was thinking," Cego replied. "Walking around like this, I'm surprised the challenge hasn't come already."

"Ah, I wouldn't worry about it," Sol said. "You still look better than any of those prissy purelight boys, always making sure their hair is combed."

Cego felt warmth flush his cheeks as he stuttered, "Uh... yeah.

What's with that, anyways? Who combs their hair before getting in a fight?"

"I think it's another custom they picked up from the Daimyo," she replied, turning her face in disgust. "Father used to bring me to Daimyo gatherings along with the Grievar from the rest of the Twelve. Before we could sit with them, a servicer would comb my hair and put makeup on my face. I hated it."

"Makeup?" Cego asked.

"Yes... It's a set of powders and creams that Daimyo use to cover up bruises and scars on their faces. Both the men and women, they put it on whenever they leave their homes."

"Why would anyone want to cover up their scars? What strange creatures..."

"Strange...and weak. Yet they control us," Sol said grimly before changing the subject. "Guess who wears it here, though?"

Cego shrugged. He couldn't fathom doing something like that.

"Mateus," Sol whispered. "I saw him putting some powder on in this very mirror to cover up a bump on his cheek."

Cego shook his head in disbelief. "No!"

"Yes!" Sol smiled as they both tried to contain their laughter.

Cego hurried over to Grappling Level One with the rest of his team. He was still thinking about his conversation with Sol, but he needed to concentrate on the task at hand. He needed to isolate Shiar and convince the Bayhounds to make their challenge. This was the final touch. If he didn't pull this off, Operation Recovery would be stopped in its tracks.

The class began as usual—Professor Sapao leading warm-ups and then showing a series of basic techniques for the class to drill. Though Cego usually enjoyed the drilling, he couldn't focus today. He was looking ahead to the free-rolling period of the class.

During free rolling, the students paired up and grappled for ten-minute rounds, with the goal of submitting their partner as many times as possible during that period. After each round, the students would switch partners. There were five rounds total, so Cego needed to make sure the Whelps timed this right.

Cego started off the period with members of his own team—Abel, Sol, and Mateus. He kept it relaxed with Abel, letting the small boy gain top position to hunt for submissions. With Sol, Cego fought harder. He'd never submitted her, though he'd tried to some extent. Her defense was excellent. With Mateus, Cego loved to attack—he really didn't feel so bad about taking the pure-light's arms and legs at will. As the end of the round neared, Cego pushed off Mateus's chest and swung around to attack his exposed arm. Mateus wisely tapped as Cego cranked on his elbow.

The bell sounded and the students began to search for new partners for the fourth round. Sol, Mateus, and Cego headed directly for the clump of Bayhounds nearby.

Cego needed to get on the mat with Shiar.

Sol and Mateus successfully initiated rolls with two of the Bayhounds. Though it was a student's choice to accept or decline a roll, it would be seen as a sign of weakness to turn someone from an opposing team down.

Cego sought Shiar's eyes but the boy had already partnered up with a member of his own team. Instead, Knees stood directly in front of Cego.

"Let's be doing this," Knees said, his face expressionless. Cego hadn't even thought about the possibility of rolling with Knees. Though Operation Recovery was entirely for the Venturian, Cego had nearly forgotten the reality that his old friend was a member of the Bayhounds, standing right in front of his face.

"Knees… Thanks for the roll," Cego managed to say, though he was caught off guard.

Knees and Cego squared off.

The Venturian attacked with a ferocity Cego had never seen before—his expressionless demeanor shattered the second the buzzer sounded. Knees leapt at Cego, growling like a beast, trying to pass his guard in every direction. Cego tried to stay calm, but it was difficult with the frantic pace. This wasn't part of the plan.

Cego wanted to tell his friend about the details of Operation Recovery, about all they were doing to get him back. He wanted to tell Knees they hadn't abandoned him—he wasn't alone. But he couldn't say anything. It was too dangerous. He didn't know how indoctrinated Knees was as a member of the Bayhounds.

Though striking was prohibited during free rolling, Knees caught Cego with several cutting elbows to the face as he tried to smash past his guard. Cego didn't want to believe the strikes were on purpose—but looking into Knees's wild eyes, he wasn't so sure.

Cego panted on the floor after the roll was over. Knees didn't meet his eyes or clasp his hand; he got up and looked for his next partner.

Shiar. Cego had completely forgotten why he was here, rolling on Bayhound mat turf. He looked around desperately. If Shiar already had a partner for the fifth and final round, the plan would fall apart.

Luckily, Sol, Mateus, and Abel had intercepted and taken some of Shiar's potential picks. Shiar was about to match up with Andrew Antonius from the Rocs.

"Shiar!" Cego shouted from his spot on the ground.

Shiar swiveled and met Cego's eyes. The jackal smirked when he saw Cego on the floor, panting from his heated bout with Knees. Cego didn't need to pretend he was tired at this point.

"Looking for someone to put you out of your misery, lacklight?" Shiar said as he walked over to stand above Cego.

Cego didn't say anything. He couldn't look into the boy's eyes without seeing Weep in their reflection. The two did not bump fists as the round began.

Shiar attacked furiously from the top, switching side to side to pass Cego's guard just as Knees had done. He tried to take hold of Cego's foot and yank it upward into a leg drag, but Cego swiveled his leg to break the grip, recovering his defense.

Shiar drove in for a double-under pass, attempting to stack both Cego's legs onto his shoulders, but Cego pushed backward to recover with his feet hooked in the crooks of Shiar's knees. Cego shoved one of Shiar's knees out from under him and looped his hand around his neck, attacking with the guillotine choke.

Cego felt it immediately—he had just the right angle, the blade of his hand was just deep enough, he could finish Shiar right now. He could tighten the guillotine, and even as Shiar tapped in submission, he could keep squeezing until those jackal eyes were shut for good. Why shouldn't he?

The jackal had been yapping and gnawing at Cego since they were in the Deep. The boy only looked out for himself here at the Lyceum. The entire school would be better served if he weren't here. Shiar had killed Weep.

As Cego felt rage build in him, as his choke tightened on Shiar's neck, he saw Knees across the training room, fighting from the ground. He heard the words Knees had whispered to him about the Trials.

I was weak for so long in that place. I was helpless.

Cego breathed out steadily. This fight wasn't about his revenge. Or even about avenging Weep. This was about helping Knees. Cego needed to do something far more difficult than showing strength or fighting through the fatigue. He needed to show weakness. He needed to let Shiar win.

Cego loosened his grip on the choke, barely—he couldn't let Shiar know he wasn't going for the finish. The jackal now had just enough room to get his fingers beneath his chin and push his head to the ground. Taking the opportunity for survival, Shiar threw his legs over Cego's guard and passed to his side.

Snarling and savoring his newfound advantageous position, Shiar glanced over to make sure Professor Sapao wasn't watching, and then drove two quick knees into Cego's rib cage. He ground the point of his elbow into Cego's face, forcing him to turn away, and then sharply rode his knee along Cego's ribs as he swung his foot over into mount. Cego looked up into Shiar's eyes. The jackal was out for blood.

Shiar squeezed down from mount, applying pressure as he slid an arm beneath Cego's head. Even though he was weary, Cego could predict Shiar's moves several steps ahead. The jackal was going for an arm triangle, and when Cego defended it, he would pivot to an arm bar.

Just as expected, Shiar started using his head to push Cego's arm across his face. Cego gave him adequate resistance. Shiar didn't like that. The jackal snaked one hand over Cego's face and started to dig his thumb into his eye socket. Cego immediately protected his eye as he thought of the gruesome injury Murray had taken at Lampai. Cego shoved Shiar's hand away from his face. The jackal took the opportunity—swinging around into the arm bar.

Cego tapped quickly; the lock was tight. Shiar didn't stop, though; he thrust his hips forward into the elbow joint. Cego heard several loud pops, and then numbness slithered up his arm.

* * *

The Whelps met on the common ground after their last class of the day, their eyes glued to the big lightboard in the center of the room. Any challenges would be posted on the board in the next few minutes, and they were all eager to see if their plan had worked.

The team really did look broken. Even if Xenalia had been accurate in her predictions on each of their recovery times, his crew's current state worried Cego.

Joba sat hunched forward in his chair, the rest of the Whelps giving him a wide berth after the mess in the dining hall. The normal color had returned to his face, though the boy still didn't look quite right, as if he were making an effort to make sure everything stayed down.

Cego had taken a quick trip to the medward after Shiar had broken his arm. Xenalia had muttered something about her job being pointless and Grievar always re-breaking themselves as she stuck a needle into Cego's arm. Whatever it was, it had numbed the pain, but Cego knew that his left arm would be useless for a few days.

Dozer was in good spirits after returning from his med-ward stay. He kept reassuring the team that he was okay, though whenever he tried to speak, it was nearly indecipherable. Cego couldn't tell if it was due to Dozer's jaw or the meds they'd pumped into him.

"Awl I know is dat darkin' dackal...eel be oming fer us soon," Dozer slurred, wincing in pain as his jaw cracked.

"What did you say, Dozer?" Mateus asked, smiling slyly. "I couldn't quite hear you."

"Dat darkin' dackal Shiar! Ee'll be oming for us—soon!" Dozer tried to raise his voice.

"Stop messing with him." Sol glared at Mateus. "You're trying too hard. And look, it's smudged your makeup."

Mateus inadvertently placed a hand up to his face and then glared back at Sol as the rest of the Whelps laughed at him.

"Hahah-agh!" Dozer tried valiantly to join in the laughter.

A crowd of students had gathered around the challenge light-board, chattering about the new matchups that had just been posted. The Whelps hurried over.

Cego scanned the screen, looking past the higher-level challenges to the bottom of the board. There were three Level One challenges posted:

TEAM JAB MANTIS (LV. 1) CHALLENGES TEAM WHELP (LV. 1)
TEAM ROC (LV 1) CHALLENGES TEAM WHELP (LV. 1)
TEAM BAYHOUND (LV. 1) CHALLENGES TEAM WHELP (LV. 1)

Cego's stomach sank. All three Level One teams had challenged them. Their plan had worked—they'd appeared weak and Shiar's Bayhounds had taken the bait. But so had the rest of the class.

* * *

Cego paced Quarter D, shaking his left elbow out as if it would somehow magically heal within the next forty-eight hours.

"I ay we akem all on! Bring em!" Dozer was attempting to shout as he boxed the air emphatically.

"The odds are formidable," Sol said, levelheaded as always. "Accepting all the challenges means nine fights in one day, back-to-back. We do have the option of just accepting the Bayhounds' challenge—isn't that the point of this whole plan?"

"Yes, it is," Cego said. "Though if we decline the other two challenges, it will hurt our score. Even if we do pull it off against the Bayhounds, we'll be near to last place. We wouldn't have time to recover from that by end of cycle."

Sol nodded, swiping at her lightdeck to check on Cego's calculations.

"You're right. But we wouldn't be in last place. We'd be solidly in the third spot. Which means we'd be safe from getting held back," Sol said.

Mateus chimed in, "That settles it, then. Stick to the plan. We decline the first two challenges, accept Team Bayhound's, win your boy back, and I get traded back to some more cultured Grievar for the next cycle."

"This is very good for you, no, Mateus?" Abel said. "We win, you be trade to Bayhounds, and then you in first-place team. But we drop down, third place for us."

"Er…no. That's not what I was saying," Mateus said defensively. "I'm just saying we can't take the risk of fighting more than one team. That's lunacy. We're broken as it is."

"As much as I hate to agree with him," Sol said. "Mateus is right. We are broken. Look at us. We hardly have three fully healthy Whelps right now."

Cego nodded slowly in agreement.

"Joba, what do you think?" Cego asked. He wanted everyone to have their say before the team made a decision.

Joba smiled good-naturedly and shrugged his big shoulders. Cego looked to Abel for translation.

"Joba say he in for whatever," Abel replied quickly, smiling up at his huge friend.

Cego nodded. "Okay, then, let's take it to a vote. I don't want to make the decision for everybody else. We're part of a team here. We need to make decisions as a team."

"Wait," Sol said, eyeing Cego suspiciously. "You haven't said what you thought yet. Don't think we can take a vote before hearing what *everyone* thinks."

"I don't know if people want to hear what I think," Cego replied softly.

"Well, I do," Sol said emphatically. "In fact, I'm not voting until I hear it."

"Ee too!" Dozer yelled.

"Now we're in for it..." Mateus sighed.

Cego took a deep breath. "I think what you've said is completely true. Our goal was to get Knees back and accept the Bayhounds' challenge. And it's true that if we decline the first two challenges, we take far less risk—we'll be in better shape for our challenge against the Bayhounds and we also won't risk last place and getting held back.

"But if we decline the first two challenges, we've lost it all anyways," Cego said. "Yes, we might get Knees back onto our team—but what sort of team will it be? We'll have that mark on us forever—backing down from those challenges. Without honor. Knees will be forced onto a team of cowards. If it were me in Knees's place, I'd rather stay where I was, despite the horrible company."

"But—but—" Mateus started to interject, but Cego continued, his voice strong and steady.

"From where I stand, that's what separates us from them. From Shiar and the Bayhounds. From the Daimyo. From everyone trying to use the Grievar for their own selfish purposes." Cego thought about the many innocent kids just like Weep, still fighting for their lives in the Deep.

"It's not even about winning. It's about following the Codes. The other teams think we're cowering and ready to be crushed. If we decline their challenges, we're agreeing with them. We're telling them that we're afraid, that we don't have what it takes to stand in front of them. We're telling them that we have no choice but to concede."

Cego was silent for a moment as his team waited for his conclusion.

"If it were my choice alone—and I know it isn't—I'd accept all three challenges. I'd have us decisively win the first two, then I'd stare Shiar in the eyes and watch *him* cower as we take the third challenge. I'd have Knees back on a team with honor. A team in first place."

Dozer bellowed, "Ats what I've been sayin' da ole time! I'm in!"

Sol stared into Cego's eyes. He did not avert his gaze this time. Cego meant everything he'd said. Farmer would do the same. Murray would do the same.

"I'm in," Sol said quietly.

"Oh, blasted lacklights," Mateus screamed. "I can't believe you fools are actually—"

"In Desovi, we Grievar say something," Abel interrupted the furious purelight boy. "If you need to cross field, and step in arnyx dung, no use in trying to clean off. Better to continue to step in dung until you cross field. Clean off later."

The team looked at Abel with wide eyes. "I in too," Abel said as he looked up to Joba, who was smiling as usual and nodding. "And Joba in. Joba likes Cego's plan."

CHAPTER 21

Into the Darkness

A Grievar shall not burden themselves with the society around them. Whether the squawks of merchants, the goading of politicians, or the coos of sirens, a Grievar must stand apart. In doing so, one can enter the Circle with a clear mind.

Sixteenth Precept of the Combat Codes

Murray always got stares when he entered the Daimyo districts. He hated it. Not only was he at least two heads taller than most Daimyo, which naturally drew their gaze to him, but some still recognized Murray from his fighting days. Though combat was a Grievar lightpath, spectating fights was a Daimyo pastime—cheering and jeering, betting, criticizing, sitting idly, and watching SystemView.

Already, two of them had stopped Murray on the street, one trying to hire him for merc work and the other berating him for a fight he'd lost twenty years ago.

Murray walked beneath the shadows of towering skyscrapers in the Capital's Tendrum District—Daimyo territory. Not many traveled the lower street levels anymore, mostly Grunts and sweepers set on picking up refuse. The Daimyo preferred mech transport, most having forgone walking or any sort of physical activity long ago.

Murray glanced up as one of the transports briefly hovered above him. Images flashed across the pod's translucent windshield, giving the operator access to various information feeds, probably displaying Murray's complete history on the glassy surface.

Murray shook his head in disgust.

Transports sped back and forth between the tall buildings that surrounded Murray, crisscrossing lanes of aerial traffic and merging with docks set along each floor of the skyscrapers. The Daimyo were always speeding from one place to another to do so-called business, making goods, products, and tools to enhance their lives. They were never happy with what they already had.

Another broke from the aerial traffic to get a better look at Murray, gazing down from its mech like a floating deity. It was rare for a Grievar to enter the Tendrum, dangerous even, but Murray had business to handle.

Murray stopped at an intersection as a wide-mouthed sweeper methodically sucked up the debris on the street, picking up piles of refuse cast from the pod traffic above. Daimyo weren't all bad folk, naturally—Murray knew that. Coach had taught him to keep an open mind. The Codes called for it.

Murray crossed the intersection just as an Enforcer rounded the corner. Nine feet of rippling steel stomped purposefully toward Murray. Of course they would know he was here—a Grievar couldn't walk into a Daimyo district without having security called on him.

The Enforcer was imposing coming from a distance, its pulse cannon radiating with charge, the mech's frame looking like an impenetrable wall of metal. But as the beast closed in, Murray saw the little Daimyo pilot hiding in the cockpit.

He met the Daimyo's pupilless black eyes and wondered whether he could plant a punch through the layer of reinforced glass to crush the creature's skull.

"Grievar, state your purpose here in the Capital's Tendrum, designated Daimyo housing and mercantile district," the little man said with authority through the mech's speaker.

Murray brought out his Citadel badge. Though it certainly didn't give him free rein in the Daimyo district, it would at least assure the man he was here on official business.

"Citadel Scout Murray Pearson," Murray growled under his breath.

"Scout, you say? Aren't you a bit far from Citadel grounds?" the Enforcer asked suspiciously.

"I'm on assignment. I have a meeting at the Codex."

The Daimyo lifted his eyebrow. "A Grievar with a meeting at the Codex? What business do you have with the Bit-Minders?"

"What darkin' business is it of yours?" Murray growled.

"You're no longer within the Citadel's walls or in one of your slums, beast," the Daimyo spat. "It is my business to ask you whatever I want."

Murray felt his blood vessels constricting and expanding, the adrenaline pumping into his veins. These creatures believed themselves to be protected by the layers they put in front of them. Steel and glass and cloth. A mere illusion that Murray might dispel with a well-placed fist.

That's not what he was here for, though. He was here for Cego. Murray exhaled quickly to steady himself.

"Citadel Commander Callen gave me direct orders to report to the Codex," Murray said. "If you want to check back with him, go ahead. Course, I'll need to tell him you've held me back here."

At the mention of Callen, the Enforcer backed down. The Scout commander had a direct line to Ezo's Daimyo Governance.

"No need for that," the Enforcer said. "Just make sure you stay off these main streets. You're making the citizens uneasy."

Murray nodded. "I'll be sure to do that. Wouldn't want the citizens to get uneasy," he said.

Murray continued on his way, turning off the main thoroughfare into a side alley between two of the massive buildings. He passed several neon signs with stairs that led to lower-level establishments—stores hawking goods and products of some sort, more useless items that these creatures collected.

Though Murray had only come this way once before, he remembered the path to the Capital's Codex clearly. He'd visited the place when he was under Coach's tutelage. Out on a learning mission, as Coach called them—exploring the city with his team to see what and who they were fighting for.

As a young Grievar Knight, fresh out of the Lyceum, Murray had tried to keep an open mind. Seeing the makers at ArkTech, the hawkers in the mercantile districts, the clerics in the medwards—Murray could rationalize how those Daimyo had a place in the world. They made medicines, sold goods, created foods. Even if he didn't agree with how the Daimyo lived their lives, he had a basic understanding of why they were necessary in society.

When Coach had the team visit the Codex, though, Murray hadn't been able to fathom why they needed those... things.

Though Bit-Minders were Daimyo by breed, they were the farthest on the spectrum from the Grievar. Which is why Murray despised them.

The Bit-Minders had no allegiance to any nation. They sold their technology to the highest bidder, feeding off the ongoing Grievar arms race. They had a Codex planted in nearly every major city around the world, where they programmed the transports, the sweepers, biometrics, arrays, lightboards, SystemView. And the Sim. The Bit-Minders had created the Sim.

Murray emerged from the alley and crossed another major intersection, keeping his hood down. There it was across the street—a short, flat building, out of place in comparison to the towering skyscrapers around it. The Codex looked like a structure that had been chopped down to a stump.

In a sense, the Codex was as tall as the surrounding skyscrapers, but most of its floors were belowground. A network of System nodes grew beneath the earth like a maze of roots.

Murray shivered as he walked into the Codex through the steel sliding doors, emerging into a square, sterile room of polished black-metal walls. The room clearly was not built for a Grievar—Murray needed to duck his head to avoid brushing against the ceiling.

In fact, the room didn't seem like it was made to welcome any sort of visitor. It was empty, as if he'd entered an abandoned building. No receptionist for greeting or even security forces—just a large lightboard up against the wall in front of him, staring at him in silence. He knew they were watching him.

Murray took a deep breath and stepped up to the board, placing his head in front of the display panel to let it scan him. Light flashed in front of Murray's eyes, flickering back and forth. A previously invisible elliptical door swished open across the room from him.

Murray entered a brightly lit hallway with no doors or windows, made of the same obsidian metal. With no direction, he began to head down the corridor, listen to the echoing of his own footsteps.

Murray realized he was sweating. He'd barely broken a sweat before his fight at Lampai—and yet here, with no discernible threat, Murray felt his heart rate increasing, his palms getting clammy.

Another previously invisible door gaped open as if it had been ready for him. He was being herded, like some rat in a maze. Murray ducked into the doorway, entering a tiny room, the ceiling so low that he was forced into a crouch.

The room suddenly dropped, Murray's stomach dropping along with it as he braced his hands against the ceiling to steady himself.

He could feel the transporter twisting rapidly in different directions, moving through the intricate network of the Codex. He imagined himself like a piece of food being digested, sent through the inner tract of some gargantuan beast. Finally, the transporter stopped and the door opened.

He exited to another unmarked, sterile hallway, completely silent. Sweat was pouring off his brow. Murray stopped and steadied himself, trying to take a few breaths. He walked for several minutes down the blank hallway before another little door opened to his right, goading him to enter. There was nowhere else to go.

Murray ducked into a circular room, this one with no perceptible light beyond a soft glow at one end.

"Murray Pearson, Grievar brood," a monotone voice said. "Controlled birth, year eight twenty-one, Underground, Zone Three medward. Purelight heritage, father Mirko Pearson, mother Samelia," the voice continued.

Murray walked toward the glow.

"Age, fifty-two. Height, six feet, ten inches. Weight, three hundred fifteen pounds. Heart rate, one hundred ninety-seven beats per minute. Blood pressure—"

"Stop!" Murray yelled. "Stop with this darkin' blather." The voice stopped.

"Blather? I merely speak the truth, Murray Pearson. Data. Every moment we live in this world, the data reveals the truth." Murray shivered as the creature came into view. It floated within a glowing tube, staring out at him with two tiny black eyes.

It looked like a deformed baby, with tiny vestigial arms and legs and a massive bald head. The creature's head made up the majority of its body mass, a pulsing bundle of veins and nerves. "Blood pressure, two hundred over one hundred fifty-two...Do I scare you, Grievar?" the Bit-Minder asked Murray, its mouth not moving but its voice reverberating through audio boxes planted around the room. "I am so small compared to you. Three hundred fifteen pounds of muscle, built to rend limbs and crush bones. Why would *you* be scared of *me*?"

"Not scared. I just don't... can't believe something like you actually exists," Murray admitted. To a Grievar, a body was a sacred tool, a sword to be sharpened throughout life. A Grievar's physical prowess was their link to the world around them—how they communicated with it, how they stacked up in society. Bit-Minders didn't even use their bodies. They were nearly mechs. How could Bit-Minders be trusted if they had no physical stake, no roots planted in the earth?

"Exists. What a strange word," the Bit-Minder said. "Do you exist more than me because you have a body that does as you tell it? You tell your body to walk, to punch, to kick, to eat, to defecate, and you think, with your simple mind, that you have control. That you are free to do as you wish. And yet I, floating here, trapped in this space, who cannot walk the ground that you walk, have no control, no freedom to follow a lightpath. Is that what you think, Grievar?"

"I don't think any of that," Murray said. "I'm here because I've been told you can help me."

"Yes. I know this already, of course. Help. You, with your fine-tuned body and your fists, you need help from me—floating here so helplessly. Why is that?" the Bit-Minder asked. "Perhaps what you think of as control is not really so. Perhaps your actions, where and when you move your body, are not entirely your own idea. After all, like everyone on this planet, you follow the light. And where does that light come from—who determines where that light shines?"

"I control my own actions," Murray growled, knowing what the creature was suggesting. "Just like how I can decide to plant my fist through this tube of yours."

"The path is already set for you, Murray Pearson," the thing said. "You might think of me as small, weak. But you are the insect, following a trail of crumbs that we have set for you. You will not deviate from that path; you will not harm me as your kind typically threatens to do. You need to follow your path, eat up your little crumbs, and keep moving forward. Is that not so?"

Murray wanted to prove the Bit-Minder wrong. He forcefully steadied his hand.

"You're right," Murray said. "Whatever you say."

"As long as we know which side of the glass each of us is on, Murray Pearson, I can help you," the Bit-Minder said. "We are not so different, as strange as it seems for me to say so. I know your kind thinks of all Bit-Minders as the same, one indistinguishable from another, but just like you, we have designations. My real name is a list of numbers too complicated for your simple Grievar brain...but you can refer to as me Zero."

"Zero it is," Murray said.

"I have been informed you are interested in a particular point of System activity within the Citadel, is that so? That is why you are in the Codex, where I can see you are clearly uncomfortable, as you have already lost seven-point-three ounces of water weight since entering our doors," Zero said with precision.

Murray wiped the sweat pouring off his brow. "How did you know what I was here for?"

"We see everywhere the light shines," Zero replied. "We are everywhere and nowhere."

"That's comforting," Murray said. "And yes, I want to know what's going on with the Sim. How did a Trial-taker, my kid Cego...How did he perform so well? How did he resist the blacklight in the Time Trial for so long?"

"The Sim. It has been an asset to Ezo's Grievar program over the past decade; is that not so?" Zero asked.

Murray wished this brain in a jar would just answer his questions. He knew he needed to play its game, though. "The Training Sim lets our Knights practice more often without getting hurt. I'll give you that much. But the Trial Sim is different. I've seen it break kids. Too many times, I've seen a kid come out of that thing and there just isn't anything left. Like they've been burned from the inside."

"Some Grievar minds, especially those still developing, are not strong enough to recover from an immersed Sim experience. An unfortunate side effect," Zero said dismissively. "But for the good of the nation, the Sim has improved Ezo's winning percentage. Is that not what the Grievar at the Citadel wanted?"

Murray shook his head warily. *For the good of the nation*, again with that. "Yes...that is what the Citadel wanted. But we both know the Citadel is being run by Governance at this point, so really we're talkin' what you Daimyo wanted."

"Semantics. Grievar fighting for Daimyo. Daimyo working for the Grievar. Though technically we are Daimyo, we Bit-Minders choose not to participate in such senseless politiks," Zero said. "It is beside the point. We designed the Sim programming to improve Ezo's win percentage, and that is exactly what it did."

Murray was growing tired of this runaround. "Your point?"

"You grow tired of me?" Zero said, as if reading Murray's mind. "Your heart rate has slowed by four percent while your pupils have diminished in size by two millimeters. Perhaps we should end this meeting."

"No, no." Murray backtracked. "I just want to know what happened to Cego."

"As I was telling you. The first Sim, the Trainer, was designed to improve the Knights. The second Sim, the Trials, was made to test Grievar brood entering the Lyceum. The programs were certainly helpful, but they were not enough. Though Ezo became more competitive, they did not dominate as they set out to do. That is why there was a third Sim being tested simultaneously."

Murray looked at Zero's tiny black eyes. He felt his heart getting faster again. "Third Sim?"

"Yes. Something that would change the game entirely, not push a nation forward inches at a time like the other two programs. Something that would give a nation the clear advantage, making their Grievar second to none. We called it the Cradle."

Murray couldn't help himself. "You Daimyo are always trying to make the Grievar better. Breeding programs, stims, and now the darkin' Cradle. Call it what you will. When will you learn that it's not some fancy new technology that makes a champion? It's hard work, a warrior's spirit, honor. Artemis Halberd, probably the greatest that has ever lived, he was born without training in any of your Sims," Murray stated.

"Yes. Exactly the point, Murray Pearson. Artemis Halberd was born without any of the Sims. But he is a rarity. For every Artemis Halberd the Citadel produces, there are thousands of Grievar who are not champions. Ezo's wasted bits, resources, opportunities," Zero said.

"Wasted?" Murray yelled, his face up against the tube. "Do you know the kind of work our Grievar put in? The blood and sweat that soak the training mats every day? How the dark could you even understand?"

Zero was silent for a moment, staring at Murray as his breath steamed up the tube's glass. "Now, there, does that feel better? Heart rate two hundred twenty, two hundred nineteen, two hundred eighteen...I find it so strange how you beasts need to revert to fits of rage. Like some sort of pressure valve release. Are you ready for me to continue again?"

"Yes," Murray said blankly. He was already so sick of this creature. He had to get what he needed and get out.

"As I was detailing before your tantrum," Zero said, "that was the problem with the first two Sim programs. They were already too late. The Trials were designed to test young students entering the Lyceum. The Trainer was made to test Knights before they entered the Circle. But both were too late. They did not reach the

Grievar until after the formative processes in their brains had already solidified—the wiring and chemistry that determine the difference between a run-of-the-mill Grievar Knight and a true champion. The Third Sim, the Cradle—it overcomes this deficiency. It starts its work at the very beginning. It will make every Grievar who goes through it a champion."

"That's impossible," Murray said. "Distinct body types, multiple strengths and weaknesses, quality of the opposition—every Grievar is different."

"Not impossible, Murray Pearson," Zero said. "Statistically improbable, correct. However, with the Cradle, we cut out that statistical improbability."

"Clearly, it's not working," Murray responded. "You say the program started over a decade ago? Kiroth's still ahead of us. I don't see champions being churned out of the Citadel in the droves..."

"Do you not see?" Zero asked. "Of course you do not. Your kind never sees what is truly in front of them. Grievar are always living second by second, getting thrown helplessly down the rapids of time. We Bit-Minders are able to step out of that stream of time and truly see cause and effect. Which is what the Cradle is—an experiment in time. It enables the Citadel to truly use time to their advantage—without any wasted years. But it requires patience. Just about thirteen years, in fact."

"Thirteen years. Why does that...?" Murray's eyes widened.

"Cego was one of the Cradle's first subjects. Birthed and raised from childhood within the Sim, within the blacklight," Zero said without inflection.

Somehow, in the back of his mind, Murray had known it. It all made sense now. Everything about Cego made sense. But that didn't mean the words weren't shocking to hear. How could the Citadel knowingly be part of a program like this?

"*How.* Tell me how they do it," Murray said, his voice like ice. "Where do they keep the kids... the babies?"

"You were badly injured twenty-two years ago, Murray Pearson," Zero said. "Severed vertebrae—you spent almost a year in the medward. You were in stasis. Do you remember that time?"

"No. What does that have to do with this?" Murray growled.

"The Cradle uses a similar protocol that the clerics use to put Grievar in stasis. Except the clerics run very base code to keep the brain occupied and working for such long periods of time while the body repairs. The Cradle is far more complex—it not only keeps the brain occupied, it enhances the wiring. The Cradle exposes the subject to blacklight from birth, allows them to experience decades of training in mere months."

Murray thought about the Knight suspended in the gelatinous liquid in the medward. In a tube, much like Zero was floating in, right in front of his eyes. "You mean to say there are tubes of Grievar babies floating somewhere? You're growing them like that?"

"Put in very simple terms that you can understand...yes," Zero said.

Murray's body trembled. How had it gotten to this? How could the very folk that he had fought for, given his lightpath for, be a part of something like this?

"Where...where are they kept?" Murray asked, trying to keep his voice steady.

"Unfortunately, I cannot disclose that particular bit of information, Murray Pearson," Zero said. "Our assets are very valuable. Many nations have a vested interest in their proper development."

"If Cego was one of the first...why'd I end up finding him clawing his way through some slave Circle in the Deep? Why wasn't he being pampered at the Citadel, getting groomed to be Ezo's next champ?"

"Ah. And that is how we have arrived at the present," Zero said. "Cego was an anomaly. He was birthed into the Cradle before some newer modifications were made to the Sim code. There were certain...conditions included in the program that were determined to be superfluous to winning, which have since been cut out. Because of that, Cego's lightpath was to be terminated, as we determined it was statistically improbable he would become a champion."

"Terminated? Don't darkin' tell me you're saying..." Murray growled.

"It is all data, Murray Pearson; why can you not see that? Whereas you see lives, we see numbers, statistics. Nothing more. In fact, a large percentage of our Cradle subjects are terminated before fruition."

Murray was speechless. He couldn't believe what he was hearing.

"As I said—the Cradle is only made to produce champions. The perfect Grievar. Those subjects that are determined to have imperfection... Well, they cannot be simply released into the world. They need to be wiped clean."

"Why is Cego alive, then?" Murray heard himself ask. He felt like he could hear his voice from afar, a distant echo, as if he were floating in the vat beside the Bit-Minder.

"There was a glitch. The first version of the Cradle—it had some bad code, which we have since eradicated. Somehow, it shut itself down. It released Cego into the world. The real world. One he was never meant to live in."

"And, as smart as you Bit-Minders here at the Codex think you are, as smart as the Governance and the Citadel thinks they are... none of you knew what happened to Cego, your *glitch*, until he walked right back into the doors of the Lyceum and took the Trials?" Murray asked.

"Yes," Zero said.

Murray felt a knot form in his stomach. He'd brought Cego back to them. To the very folk who were planning on *terminating* the kid because he was some failed experiment. And now they knew. Memnon and Callen and the Governance politiks they were working for, they knew that their failed experiment had returned.

Murray had to get back to the Lyceum. Fast.

* * *

Dozer was holding pads for Cego, warming him up for his upcoming fight.

The Rocs were the first team the Whelps would need to get through, and Cego was going up against their captain, Gryfin Thurgood. Those who had faced Gryfin described it as akin to going up against an enraged Jadean bull, strong as the dark with an initial charge meant to take your head off.

Cego tried to throw a quick one-two combination, ducking under a looping roundhouse and following up with a swift body shot into Dozer's padding. His left arm screamed with pain as his fist made impact.

Out of the corner of his eye, Cego checked on the prep work of the other two Whelps set to fight in the first round.

Abel was warming up with Joba, leaping in to fire a series of quick punches and kicks and then springing back out of range. They'd selected the little Desovian to go up against Mos Aberdome, the Rocs' resident power puncher known for his notoriously thick skull. Abel's game plan had been meticulously mapped out, just like the Whelps had done for every other upcoming fight today. He'd use his superior speed to jump in and out of Aberdome's striking range while peppering him with leg kicks to sap his punching power.

Mateus Winterfowl was practicing quick sprawls as Sol shot in on him.

"That the best you got?" the purelight said as he threw his legs backward to fend off Sol's double-leg takedown attempt. Sol smiled and deftly swooped in again, this time transitioning to a quick single-leg and putting Mateus on his back.

The Whelps had selected Mateus to go up against the Rocs' weakest member—Jozlyn Fritz. Fritz was known for her highly technical grappling ability, but the girl had shown holes throughout the semester in her standing game. If Mateus could prevent the takedown, he'd be able to pick Fritz apart on the feet. Cego had warned Mateus about being too cocky, though—underestimating any opponent today would be a serious misstep.

Just as Cego threw another combo, he noticed a familiar blocky form emerge from around the corner of the prep room. Murray-Ku.

Murray smiled as he took the pads from Dozer and continued with Cego's warm-up, just as he'd done numerous times in the barracks. Murray turned the pads to face the ground as Cego responded with a series of uppercuts.

"Thurgood. He's going to bring you into a clinch war. You know that, right?" Murray asked Cego, as if the man hadn't been missing a single day over these past months.

"Yeah. I suspected as much," Cego said. "I've seen him do it to other kids."

"Use your dirty boxing, like this," Murray instructed as he yanked Cego's neck in and held one pad on the inside. Cego threw a series of uppercuts and body shots into the pad, grimacing as his left elbow buckled again.

"You all right?" Murray asked.

"Yeah... just a little stiff," Cego lied. He couldn't worry about his injury going into this challenge. He couldn't worry about the many questions he had for Murray-Ku after his long absence.

"You'll want to go for a takedown after he wears you down in the clinch. Get the fight to where you feel comfortable. Don't do that," Murray said.

Cego looked at Murray quizzically.

"You need to show him you're fine in the clinch because that's his best weapon. Once you take that away from him, he won't have anything left for you. Then you can break him," Murray said.

Cego nodded. Classic Circle strategy. Fire with fire.

"Don't forget your inside knees too," Murray said, prompting Cego to throw sharp knees into the pad.

"Speaking of knees," Murray said as he swiveled Cego around.

"Is that who you're doing this for? Either that or you've taken too many hits to the head... Three challenges in one darkin' day."

Cego stayed silent as he continued to mix in body punches and knees.

Murray nodded. "That's good," he said. "They'll keep telling you not to do things like that. After all, it's not in the interest of your lightpath. You're taking a risk."

Cego pushed Murray out and launched a quick front kick into the pad before shooting in for a single-leg. Murray half sprawled, letting Cego stand before pulling him back into the clinch.

"They'll tell you not to take those risks. They'll tell you to do things for the *greater good*. They'll have you forsake the Codes." The old Grievar said the last part with spite, tossing Cego backward.

"What I'm saying is... you're doing it right. Fight for what you believe in, kid."

Cego nodded; he didn't know what to say. Murray was giving him a strange look.

"I got something to talk to you about, but it can wait until after your fights," Murray said. "I don't want your mind wandering when you got a job to do in the Circle. Never helps."

Had Murray found what he was looking for? Cego couldn't wait. "I need to know—"

"It doesn't matter," Murray said, stopping Cego. "You think finding out will fix everything. It won't."

Cego looked at the floor.

"Whatever I tell you, it won't change anything. You will still be Cego. The same dirt-encrusted kid I met down in the Deep. The same kid who fought for the weak in the slave Circles. The kid who busted through the Trials like butter and is here now prepping to fight again for what's right. Not for the bits or for a nation—for what's right. For the Codes."

Murray placed his hand on Cego's shoulder and squeezed. "We fight so the rest shall not have to."

Cego thought about what Aon Farstead had asked in his class at the start of the semester. Why was he fighting? Not for Ezo. Not for the Daimyo. Not even for Grievar-kin.

He was fighting for Knees. For the Whelps. For Murray.

For Farmer and his brothers, wherever they were.

"We fight so the rest shall not have to," Cego repeated.

* * *

Cego stood on the sidelines, trying to shake out his throbbing arm. He was already sweating beneath his bleached-white second skin. A student announcer was breaking down the challenges for the audience, laying out what was at stake in the upcoming fights. Cego wasn't listening.

If the plan failed, his entire team would be held back from advancing to Level Two. Everything they'd worked for this semester would be for nothing. If the plan failed, Knees would be left with Shiar and the Bayhounds—the trade clause they'd invoked would be repealed. All because of *Cego's* plan, his need to do things the honorable way.

His arms and legs felt heavy, his breath shallow. He looked across the grounds at the three gleaming Circles laid side by side on the tan canvas. Each Circle shone with a distinct elemental hue: the noble blue cast of auralite, the fiery glint of rubellium, and the hollow blacklight of onyx.

Cego couldn't peel his eyes from the onyx Circle. It wasn't supposed to be here. At the last minute, the Lyceum administration had replaced the standard emeralyis alloy typically used for Level One challenges. When Murray-Ku had seen the onyx Circle dragged onto the canvas, he'd been furious.

"What's that darkin' coward Callen up to?" Murray-Ku had growled under his breath. "Onyx hasn't been used in lower-level challenges for decades." The man had stormed into the stands, leaving Cego with his team to warm up on the sidelines.

Abel and Mateus stretched out beside Cego. Abel was bouncing up and down on his toes, an unending ball of energy. Cego wondered how the Desovian ever managed to sleep. Mateus looked nervous, a frown etched onto his thin face.

Cego tried to loosen his shoulders, bending over and dropping his hands to his feet in a long stretch. He took a deep breath as he slowly stood upright, closing his eyes and trying to flush out the chatter of the crowd around him.

Accept it. Cego took another deep breath. He was already here fighting. There was no other path forward. He needed to accept the crushing pressure, the judging eyes of the crowd, the fate of his teammates and friends.

But the trepidation wouldn't leave him. It hung on him like a hostile partner during sloth carries. His eyes kept returning to the onyx Circle. He would be fighting in that ring of blacklight in moments. Because the Whelps had gotten their pick of matchups, the Rocs had their choice of Circles. Gryfin Thurgood has chosen the infamous dark alloy in a heartbeat, likely thinking he'd have a future story to impress the ladies with.

"Cego!"

The announcer's voice cut through the chatter like a razor. The crowd hushed.

Though he was only a Level One, Cego had built quite a reputation for himself during his first semester at the Lyceum. He wasn't leading his class scores, but that was due to the singular way in which he'd finished all his opponents during challenges so far. Submissions. As always, he'd rather put someone out with a choke than beat them bloody.

Abel and Mateus were also called forward to their Circles. Cego nodded at the two and stepped onto the canvas, the floor cold against his bare feet. He jogged over to the onyx, keeping his gaze straight, not daring to peer into the crowd to see familiar faces.

He paused before entering the Circle. Shadows were slithering off the onyx surface and pooling around Cego's feet. The blacklight was reaching for him already. He had no idea how he'd react within that black ring.

Cego thought about turning around. He could bring Dozer in from the sidelines as a replacement. Or he could call over the cleric in attendance to check on his broken arm. His mind began to churn out excuses, looking for every way to avoid the next step forward. But Cego knew there was no other path.

One step forward is one step where you are not standing still. Farmer's voice whispered to Cego as he stepped over the onyx threshold to stand at the center of the Circle. The blacklight shadows swarmed toward him like razor sharks on fresh meat.

Cego expected to see the auditorium dissipate around him. He expected to wake up in some other place or time, as he'd experienced within the onyx in Professor Larkspur's classroom. But nothing of the sort happened. The crowd still cheered from the stands. His teammates still awaited their opponents in their own Circles.

"Gryfin Thurgood!" The audio boxes around the room reverberated with his opponent's name.

Gryfin jogged to his side of the Circle and stood across from Cego. He looked larger than Cego remembered, his thickly muscled shoulders rippling beneath his second skin. He ran his hand through his golden hair and cracked his neck left, then right, keeping his eyes directly on Cego. He smiled broadly, and some adoring girls in the stands screeched his name.

Cego didn't have anything against Gryfin personally. In fact, of all the purelights in the class, Thurgood was among the better ones. He'd never taunted Cego or any of the lacklights like Shiar would.

Gryfin was complicit, though. He was the product of centuries of purelight breeding—the Thurgood family was the elite of the elite; only the best in their line were ever given permission to produce offspring. Each of Gryfin's distinct features—his chiseled jaw, his broad shoulders, his blocklike fists, his tree-trunk thighs—was artificially selected. All for one sole purpose: winning.

Why should Thurgood get all the glory when there were lacklights living in the dregs, fighting fruitlessly in the slave Circles?

Cego felt the hairs on his neck rising up. A tingling sensation crept up his arms and legs, as if a line of ants had found their way into his second skin. The strange buzz spread through his body, settling in his gut and vibrating at the top of his skull.

Cego was suddenly watching from the stands. He could see himself: the rings under his eyes, his limp arm hanging by his side, the blacklight emanating from the onyx Circle surrounding him. He saw Abel and Mateus to either side of him in their own Circles, standing across from their opponents in tense anticipation.

The tone rang out, a high-pitched buzzer that transformed the coiled combatants into creatures of action, and Cego snapped back into his body.

Gryfin morphed as he charged across the Circle. All his niceties fell aside—his polite manner, his charming smile. The boy's eyes blazed with purposeful rage. This was what Gryfin was born for, centuries of purelight breeding—for this very purpose. He was put in this Circle to destroy Cego.

Cego brought his hands up just as the Thurgood boy was about to crash into him. He swiveled to the side, dodging a barrage of lightning-fast punches. Gryfin followed, a torrent of energy, sending more punches at Cego, one grazing his brow and snapping his head to the side. Another elbow followed, catching Cego's shoulder and sliding up his collar to slam into his neck. A knee slipped through, blasting into Cego's midsection.

Gryfin's attack was seamless, without any moment for Cego to counter, think, or even breathe. Cego had no choice but to step inside and clinch up with his opponent, hunkering into him with the hope of slowing down the barrage. But the clinch was where Gryfin thrived.

Gryfin pulled Cego in violently with a plum clinch, yanking his head forward into waiting knees. Traditional strategy told Cego to battle for the plum, to drive his hands inward to gain the controlling points at the back of his opponent's skull. Cego knew that fight was already lost, though—Gryfin was a master of the clinch. He'd seen the boy in class. Thurgood was an expert at regaining the hold to throw devastating knees and elbows during the transitions.

Cego let Gryfin have the clinch. He wouldn't fight the current; he'd go along with it. It wouldn't be easy, though. The boy had freakish strength. Every inch of his body felt as if it were hammered from stone.

Gryfin followed another knee to the body with a quick elbow that sliced across Cego's face, gashing him just below the eye and throwing his head to the side. Cego instinctively shot in for the takedown, but Gryfin easily stiff-armed him.

The current was taking Cego away. He needed to do something.

Cego slammed his forehead into Gryfin's chest, creating some space, and followed up with two quick body shots, his left elbow buckling on impact. Gryfin grunted and threw two alternating knees. One skimmed off Cego's elbow and into his ribs again with a thud. Cego couldn't take many more of those. The two traded body shots and knees, rounding the onyx Circle as Gryfin yanked Cego forward and then pushed him backward into the range of snapping elbows. Though Cego kept his hands up and angled his body to avoid the knees, several more broke through into his stomach and ribs. He felt his organs groaning with the sustained damage.

Cego slammed the crown of his head against Gryfin's chest again, blocking a knee and then following up with an uppercut through the middle that caught Gryfin under the nose. A stream of blood gushed down onto Cego's matted hair. Gryfin still held on to the clinch.

Cego would make him pay for being a purelight. For having it so easy—for getting his path handed to him on a silver platter.

He stomped Gryfin's foot with his heel, smashing down on

the thin bones in the boy's toes. He slammed his head repeatedly into Gryfin's chest, aiming to shatter the boy's sternum. He threw more shots into Gryfin's ribs and uppercuts to blast through into his chin. Gryfin responded every step of the way, continuing to hold Cego in the clinch, countering with a steady stream of battering knees and elbows.

Soon, Cego didn't know whether it was Gryfin's blood or his own covering his shoulders, the slick ichor painting his second skin red, as if he had suddenly become a Level Sixer. Cego slammed another shot into Gryfin's body. He felt a rib crack. Gryfin groaned but kept his clinch tight.

As blood blurred his field of vision, Cego forgot why he was here. He forgot about Abel and Mateus battling in the Circles beside him. He forgot about Sol, Dozer, and Joba coaching from the sidelines. He forgot about Murray and his professors watching from the crowd and the rest of the Lyceum students appraising his performance. He forgot about Professor Aon's question: *Why do we fight?* Cego even forgot about Knees.

Cego spat blood from his mouth and slammed the ball of his heel into Gryfin's foot again. For some reason, Cego listened for the crackling of bones, as if he could hear each individual bone shatter. He threw more rapid body shots. He felt like he was working a heavy bag now, smiling through his bloody teeth as he slammed his fists into the hunk of meat in front of him, digging his knuckles in to soften up the boy's innards.

Cego felt something rising within him, trying to escape. Something forgotten but vivid, like the pungent smell of calendula flowers from the island or the memory of scraping his knee against the slippery tidal rocks.

He heard Gryfin gasping for breath. Cego savored his own breath, taking a deep one through his nose to let the boy hear it before slamming his fist into his solar plexus. He would suck the life from his opponent.

Cego continued to pound at Gryfin's body, ignoring the knees that desperately came in response, letting them openly smash into his own torso. The two traded blow for blow. Gryfin was a purelight, bred for fighting, trained to become a champion. He was fighting for his bloodline, for his prestige, perhaps even for his nation.

But Cego had become whole in this whirlwind of violence, as if the many shattered parts of him had suddenly stitched together. Cego wasn't born for combat like Gryfin—he *was* combat. This was his purpose, his path on this planet.

Gryfin was falling then. The boy was on his back and Cego was following, continuing to pound his fists into him. Gryfin was lying there, completely still, and Cego was on top of him, his fists digging into his body, now a bloody mass of flesh staining the canvas. Cego heard the buzzer ring; he noticed the light dying. But he felt the tendrils of darkness seeking a path out of him, reaching to consume Gryfin's body.

Hands were grabbing at Cego, pulling him off the lifeless boy. He looked up and saw Sol's face, her sunflower eyes staring at him like he was some sort of animal.

Cego felt his lips curl up. He was smiling.

* * *

Cego floated in the inky waters again.

He struggled with all his might against the weight of the water bearing down on him. His eyes bulged as if they would burst, water straining behind them into his skull.

He clawed his way upward, slowly climbing a pillar of bubbles, rising until he could touch the light, reaching with his outstretched arms, bursting through to the world above.

Cego's hands slammed into a cold, hard surface. He traced his fingers along an invisible wall surrounding him, trapping him within. He could see outside his prison—the wisp of light was hovering out there, peering in at him and illuminating the craggy grey walls behind it.

He needed to get out.

Cego dashed toward one end of the invisible wall, slamming his shoulder against it. The entire world shook around him. He propelled himself backward, bouncing off the other side of the barrier, creating another shock wave, a vibration deep in his bones.

Cego thrust himself forward again, and with a final explosive push, his world was suddenly tipping over. He felt the ground rush up to meet him amid an explosion of invisible shards, gnashing at his skin like a swarm of angry hornets.

* * *

"Cego." A voice cut through the void, reaching out to him.

Farmer?

"Cego," the voice was louder this time. Someone grabbed his wrist.

Murray was standing over him.

"We really got to get out of this habit, kid," Murray said gruffly.

The medward again? No. Cego was back in the practice room. He could hear the cheers from beyond the walls, the challenges ongoing.

He sat up from the flat bench he was lying on. A lightboard across the room was displaying the ongoing fights. He could see Sol, Dozer, and Joba on the screen. They were up against the second round of opponents from team Jab Mantis. Joba was fighting Kōri Shimo. Cego should have been in there, coaching him.

"What... what happened? Did we win?" Cego asked. He remembered entering the Circle, squaring up with Gryfin in the last round of challenges. After that, his memory was blank.

"Yeah. You won," Murray said quietly. "But... at a cost."

Cego put his hand to his face. He could feel the bruises along his cheek and a large hematoma on his forehead, though he couldn't feel any open wounds. He gingerly slid off the bench and stood. His legs were in working order, but his upper body felt tattered, like it was barely holding together at the seams.

"Your Daimyo friend...the little cleric. She stopped by," Murray said. "She helped fix you up. You were far worse for wear when I carried you from the Circle."

Xenalia. Cego smiled, thinking about the disapproving frown Xenalia must have worn when she saw his battered body.

Grievar, breaking themselves over and over.

Murray did not smile along with him.

"Compared to Gryfin, though...you were in great shape," Murray said.

"What...what do you mean?" Cego asked. "What happened in there?"

"You really don't remember anything, kid? The whole fight?"

"No...I just remember standing in the onyx Circle. Then nothing else. Darkness."

Murray was silent, staring at Cego with those piercing yellow eyes, as if he were trying to look through him.

"You...you won," Murray said again.

Cego knew something was dreadfully wrong then. Murray didn't sound like himself. He was talking to Cego like he was a stranger.

"Murray-Ku. Tell me what's going on," Cego said. Murray lifted his chest in a heaving, bearlike sigh but stayed stubbornly silent.

Cego suddenly saw himself on the lightboard above. SystemView was showing a replay from the last round. He was standing over Gryfin—both boys were covered head to toe in blood. Gryfin was out, his eyes were closed, and yet Cego was slamming his fist into him over and over.

Murray quickly switched the feed off. Cego stared at the blank screen.

"You were different in there. Something happened to you. Even after the bell sounded...You couldn't stop. I think it must have been the onyx. The blacklight."

Cego's stomach sank. Gryfin.

"Do you mean...? It can't be," Cego said. The words came out as a whimper. "Is he dead?"

"No. Nearly, though," Murray whispered. "They have him in a tube at the medward. Keeping his brain steady to see if he can repair."

Cego closed his eyes. He didn't want to open them again. His worst fear had been realized. He was no better than Shiar now. He was as heartless as Kōri Shimo.

A memory flashed across the surface of Cego's mind. Sol looking down at him like he was some sort of beast.

He was. He couldn't control himself.

Murray grasped Cego's shoulder and shook him until he opened his eyes. Tears were streaming out of them.

"It's not your fault, kid," Murray said.

"How can it not be my fault?" Cego yelled. "You saw it! I didn't stop! He was out, and I kept attacking!"

"It's not your fault," Murray repeated quietly. "You were made to do that. All this time... you've been holding back."

Cego stopped in his tracks. *Made?*

"What do you mean... made...?"

"I got some answers for you, kid, like I said I would," the big Grievar started. "You need to know that it won't change anything, though; you're still the same—"

"Tell me," Cego said.

"The reason you performed so well during the Trials. The way you sat in the Sim's blacklight for so long. It's because you were made in there. You were born of the blacklight," Murray said.

"It can't be... I was born on the island..." Cego's heart fluttered.

"They call it the Cradle. The Daimyo... Their Bit-Minders created it as a program to develop Grievar from birth in a simulated environment. They isolated Grievar brood, grew them, wired them into the Sim so that they could program them and make them into the perfect fighters."

Somehow, Cego had known. When he'd seen Marvin floating in the vat in the medward, he'd felt it. Cego had been the one floating in there.

Maybe he'd known even before that. Clawing his way across the Underground's streets, blinded by the unfamiliar light, his muscles weak from years of inactivity. Grown in a vat.

Had he just blocked out the memories this whole time? Or was he *made* to not know? Programmed like some mech to perform his specific function. To win. To kill.

"Far—The old master. He was all part of the Sim too? He doesn't really exist?"

"I'm afraid not," Murray said.

"And . . . my brothers. Silas and Sam. They grew up on the island with me . . ." Cego trailed off.

Murray shook his head slowly.

The room outside suddenly shook with a roar of applause as the buzzer sounded. Murray flicked the feed back on. The second round of fights had already finished—Sol and Dozer were done; he saw them standing in their Circles. Joba was on the ground with Kōri Shimo standing over him.

Cego didn't meet Murray's eyes as he moved toward the exit for the challenge grounds.

"What are you going to do?" Murray asked.

"What I was made for," Cego replied.

CHAPTER 22

Home

Autumn's hurried bustle breaks for the frigid stillness of winter. The yawning spring wind becomes the hot breath of summer. Though a Grievar remembers each season by its embellishments, this is an illusion. The truth is constant transition, change without memory.

Passage One, Fifty-Fifth Precept of the Combat Codes

Murray returned to the stands, taking his seat beside Dakar Pugilio.

"Drink, Pearson?" Dakar was slurring his words already as he held a frothy glass out.

"I need more than a drink." Murray shook his head.

Pugilio slumped back into his seat, propping his feet atop the shoulders of the spectator in front of him. The Level Five turned around with a frown, which quickly disappeared when he saw the commander of PublicJustice staring back at him.

"Always worryin' now, Pearson. Look, your beard's almost completely grey." Dakar stroked his long mustache. "Whatever happened to that grin I remember flashin' on SystemView? Not a care in the world back then..."

Murray was silent as he watched Cego standing on the sidelines, preparing himself for the next challenge.

The kid was a few inches taller and had put on about thirty pounds of muscle since Murray had first seen him in the slave Circles. His black hair had grown out, falling across his eyes. He still had that same straight-backed posture, though; his arms were down by his sides like he wasn't quite ready for a fight.

Cego would never be the same. Murray knew that.

No more looking out at the world with those curious eyes, asking why he was fighting. The kid knew why he was fighting now.

He was a part of the system. A part of the corruption, the politiks, the cowardice. A part of Callen Albright and Scout Cydek's game of deception, a part of Commander Memnon's blind devotion to the nation, a part of the never-ending Daimyo scheme to warp the world to their liking.

Cego was deeper in it than anyone—he had been created for this. And yet the kid was innocent. He didn't deserve this; he had no choice but to take the path he was on. Cego was a pawn in this game just as Murray had been a pawn.

Murray frowned, recalling his own days in the Circle. Fighting as a Knight for Ezo's glory. Actually thinking he'd made a darkin' difference.

We fight so the rest shall not have to.

They fought so the Daimyo could continue their senseless traditions—business, trade, diplomacy, culture. They fought so men like Thaloo could line their pockets and subjugate the helpless. They fought so the arms race would continue its vicious cycle—nations constantly trying to outdo each other and pushing their Grievar to the brink.

We fight because they force us to. We fight because they scream and spit, demanding our blood. How was a Grievar Knight fighting for thousands of cheering fans different from a street urchin getting pushed into the rusty bounds of a slave Circle?

A tone rang out, quieting the chatter of the crowd and signaling the fighters to take their Circles. Cego stepped onto the canvas, his stare blank. All eyes were on the six Grievar students at the center of the arena. Solara Halberd stood across from Tegan Masterton. Dozer faced off with Knees. Cego was taking on Shiar, again encircled by the onyx frame.

Murray glanced at Dakar, who was now slumped over in his seat, snoring loudly. The spectrals rose off the Circles, shedding their light on every corner of the arena.

Murray thought back to Old Aon's words in the study. *There is a choice coming. A path in the light or a path in the shadows.*

Perhaps it was better to walk the path of shadows to stay away from the light.

Perhaps Cego would have been better off if Murray had left him in those slave Circles. The kid wouldn't be standing here in the blacklight with shadows slowly enveloping him. He wouldn't be under the watchful eye of those who wanted to use him for their own motives. He wouldn't be fighting his friends or his demons.

Perhaps Murray should have kept to the shadowed path as well. What if he'd never fought for Cego under the lights of Lampai? What if he'd kept his cowl drawn, kept to himself as he'd been doing for the past ten years? He'd be back to his standard: going Deep to buy broken kids, returning empty-handed, drinking himself to sleep every night, and then repeating it all over again.

That didn't sound so bad anymore.

* * *

Cego stared across the onyx Circle at Shiar.

The jackal tossed his brown hair and played to the crowd, throwing combinations, switching stances, whipping out a fancy wheel kick. Some of his comrades cheered.

Shiar hadn't changed since Cego had met him in the slave Circles. He was the same arrogant, ruthless boy with a thirst for tormenting the weak. He still believed honor and humility had no place on a Grievar's path. He believed the Codes were dead. It was all about winning.

He still had that same smirk on his face, that same carnivorous grin he'd flashed at Cego while kicking the life out of Weep on the yard's red dirt.

Cego knew he should hate Shiar for what he'd done. He didn't hate him, though. Cego didn't care who stood across the Circle from him anymore.

He could already feel the blacklight deep in his bones, pulsing from the sinews of his muscles, writhing from his organs, seething from his skeleton. The light pulsated from every inch of his body, a body that had spent more time growing in some vat than walking on the hard earth.

Cego saw himself from the stands again—straight-backed, swaying slightly, staring blankly across the canvas at Shiar.

The boy was just another vessel, a body. Another sack carrying blood and bones and entrails, stuffed full of lies like honor and happiness, hate and love.

Another body to be broken.

Cego felt the light reach its height. By then he was already moving across the Circle, careening toward Shiar a split second before the buzzer rang. The crowd around them didn't notice the preemptive start; it was too fast. Shiar noticed, though.

The jackal raised his hands defensively as Cego ripped into him.

Cego slammed the ball of his foot into Shiar's knee, listening for the crackling of ligaments as the joint buckled. He threw two quick jabs and whipped around with a spinning backfist that found its home in the side of Shiar's skull.

Cego followed his prey to the ground, ramming two quick knees into Shiar's body to soften him up. He took mount, squeezing down from on top of Shiar, driving his fist into the boy's throat as he attempted to catch a quick breath.

Shiar abandoned technique to fend off the whirlwind of violence, frantically shoving at any part of Cego he could reach.

Cego seized the opportunity, swiveling around for an arm bar, not slowing as he heard the boy's elbow snap.

His prey was trying to escape. Shiar was squirming out from beneath Cego, getting to his feet, doing whatever he could to put distance between them.

He won't escape.

Cego hooked his feet around Shiar's ankle, sweeping him back to the ground. He found the boy's heel, wrapped it in the crook of his arm, and wrenched it, not stopping as he felt the boy's knee tear apart, ligaments and tendons writhing like sliced worms. Shiar screamed, a piercing wail that cut through the cheering crowd.

Cego didn't hear Shiar's scream. The sound was commonplace, the inevitable gasp a hound released as the wolf found its throat.

Cego didn't see the crowd around him, staring at him with both reverence and disgust. He didn't see Murray grimace from the stands and cover his face with his hands. He didn't see Callen Albright smiling from his box, watching the fight from high above.

Cego didn't see Sol and Tegan Masterton in the next Circle over, the two engaged in a strategic match, carefully circling, launching jabs and long kicks, fending off and precisely timing their takedowns, knowing that one mistake could be the decisive factor.

Cego didn't see Dozer and Knees trading blows at a frenetic pace, the two well versed in each other's games but unfamiliar with fighting with such heightened emotion, Dozer wincing every time his fist rattled Knees's skull, Knees attacking Dozer with a ferocity that forgot everything the two had gone through together in the Deep.

Cego didn't see anything but Shiar, his prey—more limbs to be torn, more flesh to bludgeon, more arteries to constrict. Everything else around Cego dimmed as darkness found its way to the edges of his vision.

He could hear Shiar's beating heart pulsing with the darkness that closed around him. He found the quickest path to that beating heart by wrapping his arm across Shiar's throat, feeling the arteries on either side, cutting off the blood flow to the boy's brain. He could feel the pulse slow, the boy's heart straining as it desperately tried to pump more sustenance through sealed pathways.

He needed to stop that beating heart. Only when it stopped could Cego rest.

* * *

"Feel that?"

The voice dropped into the darkness around him like a stone tossed into a still pool, sending ripples in all directions.

"Feel how the edges of your vision start to go fuzzy? That's how I know it's on."

It was his own voice. He sounded different—younger. "Now you try it on me. I'll let you know when you have it right."

He was small. Only a child.

"Did I do it right?" Another voice. Sam.

Little Sam was clinging to Cego's back, practicing a simple technique—Mata Leon.

"You're squeezing the front of my throat—that's an air choke. You want to squeeze here and here." Cego showed Sam where the arteries ran along the sides of his neck.

Sam, barely five years old, wrapped his arm around Cego's neck and squeezed until his brother slapped his shoulder.

"Tap, tap!" Cego coughed as his little brother released the choke. "That was perfect, Sam."

The two stood on the black sand beach, looking at the emerald waters. Arry sat beside the brothers, wagging her tail and trying to discern what they were staring at.

"Think he'll bring anything back?" Sam asked.

"Knowing Silas, yeah, he'll bring back a big one," Cego replied, watching the figure in the distance swimming toward shore.

"The big fish are the tastiest." Sam licked his lips. "Let's get some crabs too!"

Before Cego could stop the little boy, Sam began to sprint across the beach toward the tide pools, Arry making a valiant effort to keep at his heels.

Cego kept his eyes on the sea, watching his older brother get closer to shore. The sun dipped low in the sky, and he could see the faint outline of the Path emerging from the deep.

"You'd best be careful, showing Sam too much," the old master said, suddenly standing beside Cego on the beach. "He'll be nipping at your heels before long."

"It's okay," Cego replied. "My opponent is my teacher. Besides, it'll be good to have someone else to train with besides Silas. Someone a little bit easier…"

Farmer nodded, his grey topknot bristling in the wind. The two were silent, watching the sinking sun. Cego could hear Farmer breathing. He knew the old master's chest was rising and falling with the tide.

Silas was soon nearing shore and the sun painted the sky with wide swaths of reds and yellows. The Path was almost fully visible now, the stark green trailing its way to the horizon like a serpent.

"Where does it go?" Cego asked, staring at the luminescent water.

"It goes home," Farmer replied.

"I thought this is home," Cego said. "The island."

"This is home too," Farmer said. "We have many homes."

"How can we have more than one home?"

The old master pointed to the sinking sun. "The sun leaves home every morning, rising over the ironwood forest to the east. It travels the same path every day, reaching its height in the sky before sinking over the sea to the west. There, it finds another home at night."

Cego kept his eyes on the sun as it began to slink beneath the horizon.

"The next day, the sun rises over the ironwoods again. But this

day, it is different. The sun has arced through the sky and looked down on the world. It has seen every smile and frown, every old building crumbling, and every new framework set in the earth. The sun has watched screaming births and lives slipping away.

"Though it seems like the same sun that rises the next day, every next day, it is different each time. It changes and so does the world beneath it."

The sun flashed brightly in Cego's eyes as it fell beneath the horizon.

* * *

He could still see it in the dark. Was that the sun, rising again so soon?

It was bright, painful to look at. It was arcing toward him, pushing away the darkness around the edges of his vision. Cego had his hand wrapped around Shiar's neck, squeezing, waiting for the beating heart to stop.

He saw the onyx Circle around him glimmering like wet coal. He saw the neighboring Circles, Sol feinting in and out like a dancer, Dozer and Knees trading a frenzy of punches.

The crowd materialized around him. Students and professors. Parents and siblings in the stands. They were silent, staring at the grounds, some standing and pointing.

They saw the light too. It came from above him, a burning star descending on the melee, making the swarms of spectrals flying around the Circles seem paltry, mere flickering candles in comparison to the newly formed radiant body.

The light burned as it had when Cego had first emerged in the Underground and hid in the shadows of the looming buildings. It seared his eyes as it had in his cell so long ago when the little wisp had hovered amid the cobwebs. Though it wasn't little any longer—its light enveloped the entire arena. He knew this was his spectral.

The spectral descended toward Cego—he could feel its blistering heat as it neared. The onyx Circle around him dulled against the spectral's brilliance. Cego kept his eyes open and focused on the light until everything became a blinding, sterile white.

He felt the tendrils of light, one reaching through his open eyes, the other wrapping around his arm, getting hotter, urging him to release his choke on Shiar.

He let the jackal drop to the floor.

The light didn't leave him, though. Electric energy coursed through his arm. The pain was all-encompassing. He was screaming. He could smell his singed flesh.

In the haze of pain and light, Cego heard him. The baritone voice he'd grown up listening to. The man who had taught him nearly every technique he knew. The man who spoke the Codes. Farmer.

"You are home."

Cego stood on the canvas, looking up, staring into the heart of the light, reaching his burning arm toward it. The old master was up there. It had always been Farmer—the little wisp hovering in his cell, giving him strength in Thaloo's yard, showing him the way during the Trials, leading him to the onyx Circle. And now, shining like a radiant star here on the challenge grounds.

"Where are you?" Cego screamed at the light. Murray had told him the truth. The old master couldn't be real. Farmer was a part of the Sim, the Cradle—a programmed figment. How could he be here?

The spectral pulsed in response, a brilliant flash of white light that dispelled every shadow in the arena, found every watching eye.

And then it was gone. He was gone. Somehow, Cego knew he wouldn't hear Farmer's voice again.

Cego stared at the ceiling and then around him. The crowd was silent, many jaws hanging open.

Sol stood above Tegan Masterton, her face flushed and bruised, her opponent clutching her limp arm on the canvas. She met Cego's eyes.

Dozer and Knees had stopped fighting. They lay side by side on the canvas, breathing heavily, their eyes on the ceiling where the light had disappeared.

Cego looked at his arm. The sleeve of his second skin was seared away and a serpentine form was wrapped around his forearm. It was his whelp flux, but it had grown considerably and now pulsed with an array of bright colors. The dragon's curious eyes, set on the back of Cego's hand, had become smoldering embers.

Cego's gaze dropped to the floor. Shiar lay at his feet on the canvas, the jackal's chest rising and falling with shallow breath.

The challenge was over. The Whelps had won.

CHAPTER 23

Echoes from the Past

One might be inclined to pay attention to the peak of the wave as it breaks, the frothing white head, but it is what lies below the wave, the dragging darkness, that should be of concern.

Passage Two, Eighty-Third Precept of the Combat Codes

Cego rolled up the sleeve of his second skin, running his hand along his arm and examining himself in the Quarter D mirror. Even three weeks later, the skin was still raw where the spectral had burned him.

None of the professors at the Lyceum had seen anything like it before. "Darkin' strange workings" was all Murray-Ku had been able to say after the fight as he stared at Cego's arm.

Although some flux tattoos were intricate, they always followed a fixed rhythm and color pattern. The evolved brand on Cego's arm seemed to follow no such design. The dragon had a life of its own. He clenched his fist and the creature curled up his arm, pulsing a radiant blue as if some strange energy was building within it. He threw a jab and the serpentine flux coursed back across his arm, a green-scaled ripple that started in his shoulder, its open maw sparking yellow as it flowed down through his elbow before exploding in a crimson fireball at his knuckles.

"Now, that be something to get used to."

Cego turned to see Knees. He'd thought the Venturian was down at the common ground with the rest of the team to watch the fight.

Though Knees was still bruised from his bout with Dozer, he looked different. The glimmer had returned to his eyes since that day on the challenge grounds. The day the light had dispelled the shadows. The last day Cego had heard Farmer's voice.

"Yeah. I'm not really sure what to make of it yet," Cego said as he practiced a roundhouse, watching his flux whip its sinuous tail across his arm.

"Make of it?" Knees asked incredulously. "You'll make the best of it! Walk down there and throw a few feints in front of those inbreeds, why don't you? They'll be deepshittin' it!"

Cego chuckled. Though it would be interesting to see how the purelights would react to him showing off a one-of-a-kind flux tattoo—if it could even be called a flux. Cego had been wary of attracting too much attention since the incident. He'd even been avoiding the common ground and had Abel bring his meals up to Quarter D.

"How…how're you doing?" Cego asked. Knees had only recently left Xenalia's care in the medward. The cleric had given the Venturian extra attention at Cego's request.

"Good," Knees said as he began to spin for a kick, only to fall forward with a grimace.

"Well, maybe not good, but I be all right," Knees said sincerely this time, looking Cego in the eyes.

"It's good to have you back," Cego said.

"Erm…Cego. I been meaning to tell you something," Knees mumbled, as he had the habit of doing whenever he needed to speak seriously. "Heard everything the crew did for me. All these months, tryin' to get me back here. Meanwhile, I been off in my own world the whole time, not sayin' nothing but spit to you all and acting like a shit."

"Don't apologize. I understand. I know what it's like," Cego said.

"Yeah, I know. But still, it needs sayin'. You watched my back. You be knowin' I always got yours," Knees said as he extended his hand.

Cego grasped the Venturian's wrist firmly.

"Guys!" Dozer came huffing through the entryway to the dorm, his face nearly as red as it had been in his fight against Knees. "You gotta get down to the common ground, quick!"

"What, you be pickin' fights again and need our help?" Knees punched Dozer in the shoulder playfully.

"No, no—it's the Spine—the Knights—the fight," Dozer could barely get the words out between breaths.

One of the biggest fights of the decade between Ezo and Kiroth was happening today. The Auralite Spine, on the border of the two nations, was up for grabs again. This time, the winner was to take nearly 30 percent of the land, which was more than had been distributed over the past century.

Ezo could put only one Grievar in the Circle for a fight of this profile, with so much at risk. Artemis Halberd.

"Well, what be happening?" Knees prodded Dozer as they sprinted out of the room toward the common ground.

"It's—he—he lost," Dozer said breathlessly as they ran down the stairs.

"Artemis lost?" Cego asked in disbelief. Ezo's champion hadn't lost one fight since the very start of his path, when he was a Grievar fresh out of the Lyceum. Artemis Halberd losing was akin to Murray Pearson suddenly adopting the latest in Daimyo fashion trends. It just didn't happen.

Dozer shook his head emphatically as they turned the corner and burst onto the common ground.

The room swelled with students and professors, just as it had for Halberd's last fight. It seemed like the entire Lyceum was piled onto the rotunda's ground level, watching the big board with SystemView blaring. No one was speaking. It was deathly silent.

The feed panned across the massive Kirothian stadium, showing a crowd that was equally stunned. Though some spectators had their arms raised in victory, others were quiet, looking toward the center of the stadium. The feed followed their eyes to the Circle, where spectrals were cooling along the edge of the steel frame like flames that had been recently doused.

There were two Grievar in the Circle. One standing and one lying inert on the ground.

"Not just lost," Dozer said as the three stared at the screen along with the rest of the Lyceum. "Artemis Halberd is dead."

* * *

Cego saw her right away, the red braid stark against her white second skin. Sol stood apart from the crowd in front of the big lightboard, off at the edge of one of the practice Circles.

Cego carefully put his hand on her shoulder, which tensed abruptly but relaxed as she turned to see him. He didn't know what to say. Her father was dead, the feed still hovering over his lifeless body.

"I... I'm sorry," Cego whispered. It's all he could say. He could tell Sol he knew what it was like to have someone raise you, only to have them suddenly ripped away as if they'd never really been there. He could tell her he knew how it felt to be completely alone, without a home or family to return to. But that wouldn't do her any good right now.

Sol looked up at Cego, her eyes fierce, with no sign of sadness in them. She looked like she had three weeks ago, stepping into the Circle against Tegan Masterton, ready to give herself to combat. Blocking out any external stimuli, concentrating only on the task at hand.

"It's okay," Cego said. "It's okay... to be sad."

Though Sol had tried to distance herself from her family name, Cego remembered when she'd spoken about her childhood, about how her father used to let her climb around his giant body. When students whispered to each other as the daughter of Artemis Halberd passed them in the hallways, Sol would look at the floor, but Cego knew she was proud.

"I... Why should I be sad? I haven't seen him in over four years," Sol said. The feed was still tight on his body, as if the broadcasters expected Artemis to suddenly stand again.

"He was your father," Cego said. As if she didn't know that already. *Stupid.*

"He was Ezo's champion. Their tool. Governance and the Citadel used him to get what they wanted. I didn't even know him anymore." Sol turned her back to the screen.

Their tool. Her words caught Cego in the gut like a body shot. He hadn't told any of the Whelps. Not even Dozer or Knees. He couldn't bring himself to do it. Though the entire Lyceum was still buzzing about what had happened to him during the final challenge, they didn't know the truth about him. Only Murray and Command knew the truth.

"No," Cego said firmly. He had to believe it; otherwise, he would fall apart again. "He fought for Ezo. But he fought because it was his choice. He fought for what he believed in. Your father fought for you."

Sol turned her back to him, her body shuddering. She knew it was true. Though Artemis Halberd was a familiar name chanted on the Capital's streets like a rallying cry, a bright face on the boards that cast away the grey skies for many, he was more than that to her. He was her father.

Cego moved to place his hand on Sol's shoulder, which was shivering now as she crouched on the ground. He stopped. Something caught his eye on the board above.

The feed was panning from the body toward the man that stood across the Circle. The Grievar who had killed Artemis Halberd.

Cego hadn't even considered Artemis's opponent. The shock of the champion's death had turned his thoughts from the bout itself. How had he lost? How had a Grievar so seemingly invincible been defeated and killed? Who had such power?

The feed moved at a crawl toward the figure standing across the Circle. The man was blanketed in shadows, but Cego saw him as he turned toward the smoldering spectral light.

Cego fell onto the floor beside Sol with wide eyes on the screen.

It's impossible. How—how can it be? Murray said none of them were real.

There was no mistaking him, though. The man had a wry smile on his face, as if he were in on a joke nobody else could hear. Cego stared at the screen in disbelief.

The man standing across from Artemis Halberd's lifeless body was Cego's brother. Silas.

CHAPTER 24

Sacrifice

A Grievar must fully commit to the present moment. Weighed down by events of the past or too feather-footed in anticipation of the future, a Grievar will be unable to find the rhythm of combat. A wave rolling to shore and receding to sea knows neither purpose nor path; it has no awareness of time passing. So must it be with a Grievar's every breath: rolling like a wave and fully in the present.

Passage Three, Twenty-Seventh Precept of the Combat Codes

On a rare bright day in the Capital, Murray Pearson climbed the long staircase of the Knight Tower. The sun peeked through the lone shield window on each floor, casting light onto drab stone walls.

Murray trudged upward, spiraling past the central kitchen, the equipment room, the Circle study, the Knight quarters. He drew a heavy breath as he neared the highest floor. It was no surprise High Commander Memnon had maintained his body so well, making this climb every evening just to rest his eyes.

The stairs ended and Murray stopped in front of an oaken door—Memnon's quarters. He placed his hand against the door, feeling the thickness of the solid wood, the fissures that ran against the grain, the craters from decades of visitors rapping against it.

Murray curled his hand into a fist and hammered it against the oak.

"It's open." A muffled voice came through the thick wood.

Murray had never set eyes on the quarters before, but he'd certainly heard rumors of what the room contained. A torture chamber where the high commander strung up failed Knights on his walls. A resplendent auralite Circle that haunted Memnon with the whispers of some phantom crowd. A set of bubbling vats serving as a laboratory for growing Grievar brood.

Murray had always dismissed the rumors as crazy, but now he half expected to see every one of those things as he entered Memnon's private quarters.

No torture chambers. No Circles or vats. No paintings on the walls. No decorative carpets. None of the fineries found in so many of the Citadel's buildings modernday. Only a sleeping pallet on the floor, a frayed heavy bag hanging from a corner, and a tatami spread across the back side of the room.

Memnon's quarters were unadorned, spartan, as any Grievar habitation should be.

Memnon stood at the window against the far wall, his hands clasped behind his back. The high commander stared at the Capital, the city bathed in rare sunshine.

"It's strange how we live through such darkness just for these few bright days," Memnon muttered.

Murray walked to the window. Every time he saw Memnon, the man looked older, the rings under his eyes deeper.

"Yeah," Murray said. "It is strange."

The two stood side by side in silence, watching over the Capital. Much had changed over the years. Murray had once looked up to

Memnon with nearly the same admiration he held for Coach. The man was a living legend.

"What happened?" Murray broke the silence. He was truly confused. How had they strayed so far?

"We need to make sacrifices for the good of the nation." Memnon said the words wearily, as if he were as tired of hearing them as Murray was.

Murray shook his head. "Was one of those sacrifices our honor?"

"Honor." Memnon repeated the word. "Is it honorable for me to continue to shut down arrays across Ezo because we don't have the alloys to keep them running? Is it honorable to blanket more of our nation in darkness? Is it honorable to let our citizens starve because we can't win the resources to feed them?"

"The hand that feeds can also be the hand that fights," Murray responded with a line from the Codes. "We don't need to give up our ideals just to keep up. It wasn't always this way."

"Always with the Combat Codes." Memnon sighed. "You're just like him. He'd always take the easy path too. It's simple that way—strictly adhering to the Codes—letting the more complex problems wash over you like the tide. Never having to consider a nation in need, a changing world around us. Just holding on to that simple point of view. The Codes, honor. I always envied him for that."

"Coach stuck to the Codes because they were right," Murray said firmly. "If you'd done the same, we wouldn't be where we are right now. Living in dishonor. Artemis Halberd, dead."

"Where we are?" Memnon asked. "We stand on new ground, finally, with a light on the horizon that will let us defeat our rivals."

"Light on the horizon..." Murray felt his blood pumping. "Light on the horizon? Your light is a stain! You're darkin' growing kids in vats, exterminating them if they don't fit your mold!"

Memnon turned to Murray. Even now, as Murray stood red-faced in his quarters, the high commander seemed tired. As if the man had been through this argument a thousand times before.

"I understand your position, Pearson, but it takes more than honor to run the Citadel. Sacrifices need to be made."

"You choose your sacrifices, Memnon. Those kids you're growing, experimenting with, they're innocent. They have no choice."

"As high commander of the Citadel, I don't have a choice either. I need to do what's best for Ezo."

"That's why we're different," Murray said. "That's why Coach was different from you. That's why he left. There's always a choice."

"Always back to Coach with you," Memnon replied. "Coach, your shining beacon of honor. The man who could do no wrong."

"He deserves my respect," Murray growled. "He didn't forsake his beliefs like so many others."

Memnon looked Murray in the eye. "Coach wasn't what you thought he was."

Murray shook his head. More mind games.

"Don't believe me?" Memnon asked. "Where do you think Coach really went?"

The question caught Murray off guard. "I... He never told me."

"Why do you think he never told you where he was going? What he was doing? You were his star pupil, practically his son. You deserved to know."

Murray stayed silent.

"You think Coach left you. But he didn't. He never left."

"Never left?" Murray raised his voice. "No one has seen the man for over a decade!"

"Just as it is with the Codes, things aren't as simple as they often seem," Memnon said.

Murray wanted to leave right then. Coach was all he had left. Everything else he believed in this darkin' city had gone to shit.

"Yes, Coach and I had our disagreements." Memnon returned his gaze to the city. "But making sure Ezo stayed on top wasn't one of them. Coach understood we needed to make sacrifices too."

"He would never sacrifice the Codes," Murray said.

Memnon breathed out. "I miss him too, Pearson. He was a solid ear to sound off to, a fist always at your back. I understand."

"First you're saying he never left, now you're saying you miss him. What games are you playing at?"

"You think I've made sacrifices?" Memnon asked. "You think I've given up on honor, on the Codes? Coach made the greatest sacrifice of all."

Murray grabbed Memnon's shoulder, bringing the high commander's gaze back to him. "What the dark are you talking about?"

"He went in," Memnon whispered.

Murray stared into the high commander's eyes. The man spoke as if he inhabited another world.

"At first, he was against it. Against it like he was against anything that countered the Codes. *No tools, no tech.* He fought me every step of the way on the neurostimulants and the new experimental Trials... and it was no different with this. He threatened to leave the second I told him of our plans to access the Cradle."

"I remember," Murray said. "He wouldn't say what was bothering him that day, but I can clearly remember the day when Coach lost all faith in the Citadel."

"He was on his way out," Memnon said. "He'd already packed up. He walked into the command center and saw the feed I had pulled up on the board. It was the prototype they... the Bit-Minders were showing me. Selling me their product. Vats... Dozens of them lined up somewhere in the Deep. The brood were inside... babies... all of them floating..."

Murray's body trembled, just as it had when Zero had described the Cradle to him.

"He saw the feed and fell to his knees, right there in the command center," Memnon said. "The strongest Grievar I've ever met, sobbing on the floor."

Murray felt like falling to his knees himself.

"The Bit-Minders. They picked up on his weakness," Memnon

said, speaking faster now, as if he wanted to finally rid himself of the story. "They'd been running the Cradle for several years already... selling the rights to the brood they were growing to the highest bidders. But the Bit-Minders said the program needed improvement. The Guardians they were using within the Sim weren't providing the long-term... nurture... they were looking for. They needed a guide, a mentor inside the Cradle."

Murray was holding his breath. *It can't be.*

"They told him he could still help," Memnon said. "The Bit-Minders told him that instead of leaving, he could be a part of it all. He could go in."

Murray repeated the words hollowly. "Go in..." He closed his eyes, trying to take a deep breath. "Coach... went in...?"

"He accepted. He saw it as a way he could still fix things. A way he could teach those kids the Combat Codes from inside the Cradle," Memnon said.

Murray was on his knees.

"He went Deep to their Codex the following day... followed their instructions. They hooked him up. Just like the brood they were growing, they stuck him in a vat to keep his body in stasis."

"He... he's still down there?" Murray whispered. "Inside... the Cradle? On that island?"

"He never left us," Memnon said. "Farmer never left us."

* * *

Cego felt the warm sunlight against his eyelids.

The breeze gently rustled his hair, bringing with it the distant fragrance of blooming flowers.

Just a few minutes more.

He lay flat against the soft ground. He imagined he could sink into the earth. His arms and legs, fingers and toes, sinews and entrails would become roots burrowing into the dirt, his blood pumping toward some source deep below. Part of the earth. Living down in the cool darkness.

Just a few minutes—

"How the dark can you be sleepin' on a day like this?"

Cego's eyes fluttered open. Dozer was standing above him, offering a hand, a wide grin across the hefty boy's face.

"He be right for once," Knees said from nearby. "Rare that we be seeing blue skies like these."

Cego grasped Dozer's outstretched hand and was catapulted off the ground, suspended in the air for a moment, the sunlight and sky streaking his vision. He landed, falling forward, tucking into a front roll and springing back to his feet.

Sol stood inches away from Cego, her arms crossed, her eyes sparkling in the sunshine. "Show-off," she said.

The Citadel's grounds looked different today. The Lyceum's ancient grey walls stood in stark contrast to the blue skies above. Tufts of grass peppered the yard in front of the curved face of the Harmony, and the surrounding trees had begun to sprout buds. "I'll show you how to do a proper roll," Sol said, turning away from Cego. "Joba, stay just where you are."

Joba lay on the grass with his hands behind his head like a giant boulder in the yard, looking at the sky. Abel, who had been propped up against the huge boy, sprang to his feet.

"Rolling contest?" Abel said excitedly. "In Desovi, we jump over rivers for practice. Wider and wider makes bigger jumps, and Abel stay dry longer than most!"

Cego chuckled. "Maybe we should check with Joba before we use him as a hurdle?"

Abel looked down at Joba, who just smiled and continued to stare at the sky. "Joba in. Joba like the plan."

"I don't aim to be missing out on this one," Knees said as he lined up next to Cego. "Semester break's only a few days more, then we be back to training... Need all the fun we can get."

"Level Two training!" Dozer raised his fist into the air triumphantly. He was already wearing the blue second skin the team had been awarded at semester's end. "The Whelps are gonna take Level Two by storm!"

"Not so sure about that..." Knees said cautiously. "Other teams are regrouped now. Shiar, Gryfin, Kōri Shimo...they be healed up and wantin' revenge. And they say the Scouts be bringing in new Grievar next semester from all over the world. Besayd, Desovi, Kiroth, Myrkos, maybe even some other Venturians..."

"We'll be all right!" Cego said, louder than he'd meant to.

Sol met his eyes before breaking into a sprint directly toward Joba's hulking form laid out on the grass, her fiery braid trailing her. She launched into the air over the smiling boy, diving headfirst and landing in a graceful front roll before popping back to her feet. She propped her hands on her hips, looking back at Cego across the yard.

"Let's see how all right you are trying to match that one!" Sol grinned.

Cego took a deep breath. He stepped forward and started to run.

The story continues in . . .

Grievar's Blood

Book Two of The Combat Codes

Keep reading for a sneak peek!

ACKNOWLEDGMENTS

The Combat Codes has been a decade in the making. Since I first drafted the concept, I've moved across coasts, started a family, watched the world change drastically and myself along with it.

But the seed of *The Combat Codes,* the sprout of an idea that has grown in me for ten years, has remained the same. A world where martial artists fight in single combat for the glory of their nations, where students attend sprawling academies to learn a variety of combat techniques, where friendship and loyalty are constantly put to the test—my childlike fascination with this idea has remained steadfast.

But I would never have had the opportunity to work for a decade on a single idea without fortune, luck, and support. We fight (and write) alone in the ring, but it is those on the outside who carry us. There are so many who have carried *The Combat Codes.* Authors, artists, agents, bloggers, editors, podcasters, booktubers, narrators, beta readers, friends, family.

I'd like to thank my entire family for their unending support. Katie for listening to my many impromptu (and inopportune) brainstorms. My girls, Natalie and Jane and even little Claire, for showing me what true creativity looks like every day. Mom and Dad, I appreciate both of you for instilling in me a drive to read and learn. And thank you to Mike and Kathy for the many celebratory cakes and hugs at each milestone.

To my wonderful agent, Ed Wilson, who realized my potential and put up with my pestering (so far!). To Hillary Sames, who first championed the book when she was at Orbit, and my editor, Bradley Englert, who firmly held my hand through the entire process. And thank you to the entire superstar team at Orbit Books—editing, art, design, marketing, PR, production.

Finally, I'd like to give thanks to those in the Brazilian jiu jitsu and martial arts communities who have supported *The Combat Codes* so enthusiastically along the way. You were the spark that lit the fire and have continued to provide me with inspiration in my training and writing every day.

Alexander Darwin, 2022, Boston

extras

orbit

meet the author

Jeanette Fuller

Alexander Darwin is an author living near Boston with his wife and three daughters. Outside of writing, he teaches and trains in martial arts (Brazilian jiu jitsu). He's inspired by old-school Hong Kong action flicks, JRPGs, underdog stories, and bibimbap bowls.

Find out more about Alexander Darwin and other Orbit authors by registering for the free monthly newsletter at orbitbooks.net.

interview

What was the first book that made you fall in love with genre fiction?

I was really big on Dragonlance as a kid, in particular the opening to the series, *Dragons of Autumn Twilight* by Margaret Weis and Tracy Hickman. Most of my writing (and D&D campaigns) back then was essentially Dragonlance fanfic.

Where did the initial idea for* The Combat Codes *come from and how did the story begin to take shape?

The Combat Codes started with the worldbuilding, in particular asking the question: What if, instead of large-scale wars, nations resolved their problems with single combat? From that question I developed the Grievar, the Codes, the social structure, and the politics revolving around combat. But I still needed an inflection point in the established system to create a convincing story. That inflection point was Cego.

***What was the most challenging moment of writing* The Combat Codes?**

The Combat Codes is my debut novel, and so the most challenging moment was learning to scrap entire portions of my early drafts in service of a better story. It's so tough to let go of so many scenes and characters you have spent countless hours working on.

For the Whelps, the journey from the Underground to the Lyceum is arduous, but it's a thrill to watch their triumphs. If you had to pick, who would you say is your favorite of the team? Who was the most difficult to write?

I really loved writing Solara Halberd. Though we've all seen studious, hardworking types like Sol before, she has so many layers beneath the polish. Her father is the most famous Grievar in the world, but in the end it's not about her father, it's about Sol and her growth.

Murray is a character who's seeking to prove himself in a world that believes he's long past his prime. What was it like writing his character? How did his relationship with Cego develop as you wrote the novel?

Murray was a darkin' blast to write. As an aging martial artist myself, I can empathize with his body breaking down, not being able to perform like he could in his heyday. Though at first it seems like Murray is the one helping Cego, guiding him as a mentor, their relationship turns out to be very symbiotic. Murray needs Cego to keep his own head above water.

Without giving too much away, could you give us a hint of what happens in the next novel?

The world and scope really expand quite a bit in the next installment. The first book focuses primarily on the nation of Ezo and the events within the Lyceum, but the second book will take readers on a journey to new lands and cultures, with the stakes set far higher in the Circles.

Who are some of your favorite authors and how have they influenced your writing?

Though I was certainly influenced by many authors I read when I was younger, I'm most swayed by contemporary authors who I've read recently. Fonda Lee, Evan Winter, Pierce Brown, Joe Abercrombie, Brian Staveley, Anthony Ryan, M. L. Wang; when I read their books, I don't even remember I'm an author. I'm just a fan having a fantastic time.

Finally, if you were to get fluxed, what would yours look like?

Well...I'm seriously thinking about getting Cego's Whelp flux done as my first tattoo, so we'll have to see! You can't go wrong with a dragon, right?

if you enjoyed
THE COMBAT CODES
look out for
GRIEVAR'S BLOOD
The Combat Codes: Book Two
by
Alexander Darwin

In a world where single combat determines the fate of nations, the Grievar fight in the Circles so that the rest can remain at peace. But given the stakes, things are never so simple. The Daimyo govern from the shadows and plot to gain an edge by unnaturally enhancing their Grievar Knights.

Cego and his team are entering year two at the world's most prestigious combat school, the Lyceum. Though he'd like to focus on his martial studies, Cego feels the pull of his mysterious past and two missing brothers.

Solara Halberd and Murray Pearson also grapple with their pasts, each embarking on a journey to bury ghosts that are determined to stay alive.

In the end, all their paths must converge in the Circles, where the future of the world will be determined.

Chapter 1
The Name Choice

The Grievar who does not serve will be lost. All martial prowess shall be acquired for the purpose of serving the greater good of society, standing in the Circle in the stead of Lord or Nation. The Grievar who strays from the path of servitude will quickly find themselves stumbling in the thicket, tripped up by vice and lure.

Passage One, Ninth Precept of the Combat Codes

The beat of the drums reverberated in Cego's skull as he stood on his toes to get a better view.

"They be coming," Knees said from beside him, the Venturian at least a head taller than Cego and able to peer over the crowd.

Cego felt a strong hand on his shoulder. Joba, his behemoth

of a friend, was peering down at him. Joba pointed to his own shoulder, where Abel was serenely perched.

"Cego, come here," little Abel yelled over the din of the crowd in his enthusiastic manner. "I see it all from here; wonderful!"

"Umm... are you sure, Joba?" Cego asked sheepishly. "I don't want to weigh you down or anything."

The huge boy smiled silently and reached down with one hand to scoop Cego up with ease, plopping him up on his other shoulder across from Abel and well above the crowd.

From his new vantage, Cego could see the Myrkonians marching.

Throngs of the long-bearded Grievar passed over the entry bridge of the Citadel, striding to the beat of their fight drums. They were stout, proud, and nearly naked despite the chill in the air. The Northmen chanted to match the percussion of the drums, their deep baritone voices carrying through the outer grounds.

Cego looked toward the center of the formation, where several men hefted a platform on their shoulders with a pair of wide drums set atop it. Two boys stood in front of the drums and landed punches, elbows, kicks, and even headbutts against the leathery skins in a percussive rhythm.

"Wonderful!" Abel exclaimed again from Joba's other shoulder.

Cego couldn't help but smile. Abel was right to be amazed. The way the two boys moved congruously, fighting the drums in front of them, was a feat of precision and timing.

The formation of near two hundred Myrkonians approached Cego's perch. He saw they were all heavily fluxed, even the boys, swirling tattoos moving across their bodies with the rhythm of the march.

"Dozer would be enjoying this," Knees shouted from below. "The drums, people hitting things, naked folk all around him..."

Cego chuckled. His friend Dozer had some unfortunate disciplinary troubles at the end of last semester; the big kid got caught red-handed in the professors' meal quarters, halfway through feasting on their rations for the entire week. As punishment, Dozer had been cut from coming out today to watch the march.

"Sol also would have enjoyed," Abel said with a frown on his face.

Cego's thoughts drifted to his other missing teammate: Solara Halberd. The fiery-haired girl likely would have been citing a plethora of facts about the Myrkonians. Cego felt the pit in his stomach and shook his head.

He turned his attention back to the procession. Across the throng of Myrkonians, he could see the high stands set up for the Citadel's faculty and council. He could make out the high commander's broad, straight-backed figure, and though he couldn't see Memnon's face, Cego was dead sure the man wasn't smiling.

Beside the Grievar council, set higher up, were the ceremonial chairs of Ezo's Daimyo Governance. Some of the ornate thrones were empty, but at least a few of the Daimyo representation had come to welcome the Myrkonians to the Citadel.

Cego was jarred from his thoughts as silence enveloped the grounds. The drums suddenly stopped, along with the procession. The Northmen now stood directly below the Citadel's council members.

A thickly muscled giant of a Grievar, his red beard tied in tassels, stepped out of formation. Tattoos swirled across his naked body, icy blues and blacks coursing over his arms and legs, as if one could see his arteries pumping blood.

"He be as wide as I am tall," Knees muttered from below.

"Agh!" the man bellowed as he struck his bare chest several times. The entire contingent of Myrkonians behind him followed suit, screaming in unison.

The man advanced toward the council stand, keeping his blue eyes locked on to Commander Memnon. He lifted a hand in front of his face, displaying it as he removed several black rings from his fingers.

The Northman suddenly grabbed his middle finger with his opposite hand and wrenched it violently backward, cracking it at the joint. The man then proceeded to snap each of the fingers on one of his hands, followed by two fingers on his second hand.

Commander Memnon stood from his chair as he watched the bizarre spectacle.

The Northman finally spoke, his accent thick and his voice booming. "Ye Ezonians have welcomed us here, to your home. I give ye seven of me fingers. For ye be taking seven of me boys under your wing."

From within the Myrkonian procession, seven boys came forward to stand beside the giant man. Cego recognized two of the boys as those who had been striking the drums during the march.

"My name is Tharsis Bertoth," the man continued. "But where we hail from, names are not important. We Myrkonians are all of the ice blood, born from the Frost Mother. My boys standing here, they'll eat your foods, sleep up high in your wooden beds, and hear your fancy southern words. My boys, they'll fight and bleed for ye in the Circle. But they'll not bend the knee to ye. Or to your Daimyo lords up there. None of us will, ever."

Tharsis directed his icy stare toward the Daimyo politiks in the high stands.

Commander Memnon waited for Tharsis to pause before responding. "Tharsis Bertoth, you and your people are welcome within our Citadel's walls. We embrace you fighting men of the North as our brothers and your brood as our own. I can assure you we'll treat your boys with honor and respect and teach them our ways to become better fighters before their return to their northern home."

The response seemed to satisfy the giant man. A smile cut

across his bearded face. "Now that the arse-kissing be done, let's have some fun, eh?"

Memnon looked down at the man, wariness in his eyes. "What have you in mind, Tharsis?"

"Well, we'll be needing some fists flying to get things started. And my men need their bellies full of drink."

"Of course," Memnon responded, obviously prepared. He waved his hand and several Grunt servicers moved into sight from below the partitions, each pulling a wagon full of barrels. The Grunts unloaded the barrels in front of the Myrkonians and screwed a spout into the top of each.

"Enough of our famed Highwinder Ale to fill all your men three times over," Memnon said. "And, as far as combat, we have one of our Knights ready to face your champion of choice."

Tharsis lifted a barrel over his head and took a long swig, dark froth covering his beard. He wiped his face with his broken hand, the fingers dangling. "Eh... but we all be here for the brood. That's what this be about, growing the next of blood to be right-standing Grievar. I say we put one of each of our boys up in the Circle."

Memnon seemed surprised. "I understand your sentiment, but we really haven't prepared any of our students for combat right here, right now."

"You're saying here, at Ezo's famed Lyceum, no boy be ready to stand and fight? What're they doing all this time, knitting scarves for their matties?"

The chorus of Northmen laughed loudly.

"Enough." Cego had heard Memnon like this before: put to a challenge and unlikely to back down. "I was simply saying we'd prepared a Grievar Knight from our team on this occasion. As is the practice for any exhibition bout when we have visiting dignitaries. But of course, our students are more than ready for any of your boys."

"Ah, that's what I like to hear!" the big Myrkonian yelled. "Now I'll show ye how we in the North choose which of our boys be takin' to the Circle!"

Tharsis turned to his fellow Northmen and raised his hands to the air. "We from the frost are one. We from the frost choose as one. Raise your voices and let the Frost Mother's wish be heard!"

The contingent of Myrkonians bellowed all at once—but different names. To Cego, it sounded like a chaotic chorus, indecipherable what name anyone was screaming. The Myrkonians came to a crescendo, each man trying to bellow his name choice as loud as possible, before the chaos receded. Cego could now make out only two names being called, a back-and-forth volley between two groups of Myrkonians. Finally, all the Northmen were yelling one name in unison, a deep rumbling that seemed to shake the ground.

"Rhodan Bertoth!"

One of the drumming boys stepped forward from his companions. He bore a striking resemblance to Tharsis Bertoth. Though the boy didn't have a beard yet like his father, his hair hung in long tassels down his back, and the majority of his body was already fluxed with tattoos.

"I take to the Circle with the Frost Mother beneath me!" the boy shouted, meeting his father's eyes.

Memnon turned to Callen Albright, the Scout commander at his side, and whispered something in his ear. The two appeared to be in discussion for several moments.

"I wouldn't be the one wanting to fight that boy, on these grounds in front of the entire Lyceum," Knees said. "Though if Dozer were here, no doubt he'd be running up there right now to take it."

"It would be great honor to be chosen to represent our whole school," Abel chimed in from Joba's other shoulder, to which the giant boy nodded in agreement.

Chatter began to spread throughout the crowd of Lyceum students, wondering who would be chosen to fight Rhodan Bertoth.

Commander Memnon held his hand to the air, and the chatter died. "In respect for our guests from the North, we've decided to honor their own custom of name choice. We've brought them here, to the Citadel, and their boys will be taking on many of our customs during the next semester, so it only seems right that we do the same."

The crowd buzzed again.

Memnon held his hand up. "And we'll be choosing only from our pool of Level One to Level Four students, who are of similar age to Rhodan. It would be unfair if one of our older, more experienced students stood in against him."

Cego saw Tharsis snort at that mention as a wry smile rose on the younger Bertoth's lips.

"So, let's get this going," Memnon said to the students in attendance. "On my mark, raise your voice with your name choice to represent the Lyceum on this day."

Cego's mind flashed with possibilities. Of course, a Level Three or Level Four student would be preferable, given Level Ones were too young and inexperienced, and anyone from his own Level Two class didn't likely stand a chance against the burly Myrkonian boy. Cego looked to his teammates, and they all seemed to be doing the same calculations.

Memnon raised his hand and a chorus of student voices took to the air.

But unlike the Myrkonians' name choice, there was nearly no discord among the Lyceum students. They had already reached the same pitch. The same name. A name that rang loudly across the Citadel's grounds, like a bell being struck.

Cego.

if you enjoyed
THE COMBAT CODES
look out for
THE BLIGHTED STARS
The Devoured Worlds: Book One
by
Megan E. O'Keefe

Dead worlds, revolutionary spies, and a deadly secret propel this gorgeous space opera, perfect for fans of Children of Time *and* Ancillary Justice.

She's a revolutionary. Humanity is running out of options. Habitable planets are being destroyed as quickly as they're found, and Naira Sharp thinks she knows the reason why. The all-powerful Mercator family has been controlling the exploration of the universe for decades and exploiting any materials they find along the way under the guise of helping humanity's expansion. But Naira knows the truth, and she plans to bring the whole family down from the inside.

He's the heir to the dynasty. *Tarquin Mercator never wanted to run a galaxy-spanning business empire. He just wanted to study geology and read books. But Tarquin's father has tasked him with monitoring the settlement of a new planet, and he doesn't really have a choice in the matter.*

Disguised as Tarquin's new bodyguard, Naira plans to destroy the settlement ship before they make land. But neither of them expects to end up stranded on a dead planet. To survive and keep her secret, Naira will have to join forces with the man she's sworn to hate. And together they will uncover a plot that's bigger than both of them.

One

Tarquin

The Amaranth

Tarquin Mercator stood on the command bridge of the finest spaceship his father had ever built and hoped he wasn't about to make a fool of himself. Serious people crewed the console podiums all around him, wrist-deep in holos that managed systems Tarquin was reasonably certain he could *name*, but there ended the extent of his knowledge. The intricate inner workings of a state-of-the-art spaceship were hardly topics covered during his geology studies.

Despite Tarquin's lack of expertise, being Acaelus Mercator's son placed him as second-in-command. Below Acaelus, and above the remarkably more qualified mission captain, a stern woman named Paison.

That captain was looking at him now—expectant, deferential. Thin, golden pathways resembling circuitry glittered on her skin, printed into her current body to aid her as a pilot. Sweat beaded between Tarquin's shoulder blades.

"My liege," Captain Paison said, all practiced obeisance, and while he desperately wished that she was addressing his father, her light grey eyes didn't move from Tarquin. "We are approximately an hour's flight from the prearranged landing site. Would you like to release the orbital survey drone network?"

Tarquin hoped his relief didn't show. Scouting the planet for deposits of relkatite was the one job for which he felt firmly footed.

"Yes, Captain. Do we have visual on the planet?"

"Not yet, my liege." She expanded a vast holographic display from her console, revealing the cloud-draped world below. "The weather is against us, but the drone network should be able to punch through it in the next few hours."

"Hold off on landing until I can confirm our preliminary survey data. We wouldn't want to put the ship down too far from a viable mining site."

Polite chuckles all around. Tarquin forced a smile at their faux camaraderie and pulled up a holo from his own console, reviewing the data the survey drones had retrieved before the mining ships *Amaranth* and *Einkorn* had taken flight for the tedious eight-month voyage to Sixth Cradle.

Not that he'd been awake for that journey. His mind and the minds of the entire crew had been safely stored away in the ship's databases, automated systems in place to print key personnel when they drew within range of low-planet orbit. When food was so expensive, there was no point in feeding people who weren't needed to work during the trip.

Tarquin's father put a hand on his shoulder and gave him a friendly shake. "Excited to see a cradle world?"

"I can't wait," he said honestly. When he'd been a child, Tarquin's mother had taken him to Second Cradle shortly before its collapse. Those memories of that rare, Earthlike world were vague. Tarquin smiled up into eyes a slightly darker shade of hazel than his own.

At nearly 160 years old, Acaelus chose to strike an imposing figure with his prints—tall, solidly built, a shock of pure white hair that hinted at his advanced age. It was difficult to look into that face and see anything but the father he'd known as a child—stern but kind. A man who'd fought to have Tarquin's mind mapped as early as possible so that he could be printed into a body that better suited him after the one he'd been born into hadn't quite fit.

Hard to see through that, to the man whose iron will and vast fortune leashed thousands to his command.

"My liege," Captain Paison said, a wary edge to her voice, "I apologize, but it appears there was an error in the system. The survey drones have been released already, or perhaps were never loaded into place."

"What?" Tarquin accessed those systems via his own console. Sure enough, the drone bays were empty. "How could that have happened?"

"I—I can't say, my liege," Paison said.

The fear in her voice soured Tarquin's stomach. Before he could assure her that it wasn't her fault, Acaelus took over.

"This is unacceptable," his father said. The crew turned as one to duck their heads to him. Acaelus's scowl cut through them all, and he pointed to an engineer. "You. Go, scour the ship for the drones and load them properly. I expect completion within the hour, and an accounting of whose failure led to this."

"Yes, my liege." The engineer tucked into a deep bow and then turned on their heel, whole body taut with nervous energy. Tarquin suspected that as soon as they were on the other side of the door, they'd break into a sprint.

"It was just a mistake," Tarquin said.

"Mercator employees do not make mistakes of this magnitude," Acaelus said, loud enough for everyone to hear. "Whoever is responsible will lose their cuffs, and if I catch anyone covering for the responsible party, they will lose theirs, too."

"That's unnecessary," Tarquin said, and immediately regretted it as his father turned his icy stare upon him. Acaelus clutched his shoulder, this time without the friendly intent, fingers digging into Tarquin's muscle.

"Leave the running of Mercator to me, my boy," he said, softly enough not to be overheard but with the same firm inflection.

Tarquin nodded, ashamed to be cowed so quickly but unable to help it. His father was a colossus, an institution unto himself, a force of nature. Tarquin was just a scholar. The running of the family wasn't his burden to carry. Acaelus released his shoulder and set to barking further orders with the brisk efficiency of long years of rule.

He gripped the edges of his console podium, staring at the

bands printed around his wrists in Mercator green. Relkatite green. The cuffs meant you worked for Mercator's interests, and Mercator's alone. And while the work was grueling, it guaranteed regular meals. Medical care. Housing. Your phoenix fees paid, if your print was destroyed. The other ruling corporate families—who collectively called themselves MERIT—had their own colored cuffs. A rainbow of fealty.

Working for the families of MERIT kept people safe, in all the ways that mattered. While his father could be brusque, and at times even cruel, Acaelus did these things only out of a desire to ensure that safety.

The cuffs around Tarquin's wrists came with more than the promise of safety. Mercator's crest flowed up from those bands to wrap over the backs of his hands and twist between his fingers. The family gloves marked him as a blooded Mercator. Not a mere employee, but in the direct line of succession. Someone to be obeyed. Feared. His knuckles paled.

"Straighten up," Acaelus said.

Tarquin peeled his hands away from the console and regained his composure, slipping the aristocratic mask of indifference back on, then set to work reviewing the data the ship had collected since entering Sixth Cradle's orbit.

Alarms blared on the bridge. Tarquin jerked his head up, startled by the flashing red lights and the sharp squeal of a siren. On the largest display, the one that'd previously shown a dreamy landscape of fluffy clouds under the brush of golden morning light, the words TARGET LOCKED glared in crimson text.

That wasn't possible. There wasn't supposed to be anyone here except the *Amaranth* and its twin, the *Einkorn*. Of the five ruling corporate families, none but Mercator could even build ships capable of beating them here.

"Evade and report," Acaelus ordered.

Captain Paison flung her arms out, tossing holo screens to the copilots flanking her, and the peaceful clouds were replaced with shield reports, weapons systems, and evasion programs. There was no enemy ship that he could see. A firestorm of activity kicked off, and while Tarquin knew, logically, that they'd rolled, the ship suppressed any sensation of motion.

"It's the *Einkorn*, my liege." The captain's voice was strained from her effort.

"Who's awake over there?" Acaelus demanded.

"No one should be, my liege," the *Amaranth*'s medical officer said. Their freckled face was pale.

"Someone over there doesn't like us," the woman to Paison's right said between gritted teeth. "Conservators?"

"It's not their MO," said a broad-chested man in the grey uniform of the Human Collective Army. "But it's possible. Should I check on the security around the warpcore?"

"I iced Ex. Sharp," Acaelus said. "Without her to guide them, the Conservators are nothing but flies to be swatted. Captain, continue evasion and hail the *Einkorn*."

Tarquin cast a sideways glance at Ex. Kearns, Acaelus's current bodyguard and constant shadow. The exemplar had the face of a shovel, as broad and intimidating as the rest of him, and he didn't react to the mention of his ex-partner, Ex. Sharp. It had to sting, having the woman he'd worked side by side with turn against them all and start bombing Mercator's ships and warehouses.

The fact that Naira Sharp had been captured and her neural map locked away didn't erase the specter of the threat she posed. Her conspirators, the Conservators, were still out there, and Tarquin found Acaelus's quick dismissal of the possibility of their involvement odd.

The HCA soldier was right. They really should send someone

down to check on the warpcore. Overloading the cores was the Conservators' primary method of destruction. Tarquin rallied himself to say as much, but Paison spoke first.

"My liege," she said, "the *Einkorn*'s assault may be a malfunction. The *Amaranth*'s controls aren't responding properly. I can't—"

Metal shrieked. The floor quaked. Ex. Kearns surged in front of them and shoved Tarquin dead center in the chest. The world tipped and Tarquin's feet flew out from under him. He struck the ground on his side. Something slammed into him from above, stealing his half-voiced shout.

Tarquin blinked, head buzzing, a painful throb radiating from his hips where a piece of the console podium he'd been working at seconds before had landed. Red and yellow lights strobed, warning of the damage done, but no breach alarms sounded.

Groaning, he shook his head to clear it. The impact had pitched people up against the walls. Seats and bits of console podiums scattered the ground. Across the room, Paison and another woman helped each other back to their feet.

"Son!" Acaelus dropped to his knees beside him. Tarquin was astonished to see a cut mar his father's forehead, dripping blood. "Are you all right?"

Tarquin moved experimentally, and though his side throbbed, his health pathways were already healing the damage and supplying him with painkillers. "Just bruised. What happened?"

"A direct hit." Acaelus took Tarquin's face in his hands, examining him, then looked over his shoulder and shouted, "Kearns!"

Kearns removed the piece of podium from Tarquin's side and helped him to his feet. Tarquin brushed dust off his clothes and tried to get ahold of himself while, all around him, chaos brewed. Kearns limped, his left leg dragging, and Tarquin grimaced. Exemplars were loaded with pathways keyed to combat. For one of them to show pain, the wound had to be bad.

Tarquin nudged a broken chunk of the console podium with the toe of his boot. A piece of the ceiling had come down, crushing the podiums, and it would have crushed Acaelus and Tarquin both if Kearns hadn't intervened, taking the brunt of the hit on his own legs.

A knot formed in his throat as he recognized the damage Kearns had taken on their behalf. Tarquin had never been in anything like real danger before, and he desperately missed his primary exemplar, Caldweller, but that man's neural map was still in storage. Acaelus had deemed Kearns enough to cover both of them until they reached the planet.

None of them could have accounted for this.

"My liege," Kearns said in tones that didn't invite argument, "I suggest we move to a more secure location immediately."

"Agreed," Acaelus said. "Captain, what's the damage?"

"Uhhh..." Paison squinted at one of the few consoles that'd survived the impact. "The *Einkorn*'s rail guns tore through the stabilization column. This ship won't hold together much longer."

Brittle silence followed that announcement, the roughed-up crew exchanging looks or otherwise staring at the damaged bridge like they could wind back time. Tarquin studied his father, trying to read anything in the mask Acaelus wore in crisis, and saw nothing but grim resolve wash over him. Acaelus grabbed Tarquin's arm and turned him around.

"Very well. With me, all of you, we're evacuating this ship."

Tarquin stumbled along beside his father, half in a daze. Kearns assumed smooth control of the situation, sliding into his place at the top of security's chain of command. Merc-Sec and the HCA soldiers organized under Kearns's barked orders, forming a defensive column around the rest. Paison threw a brief, longing glance at her command post before falling in with the others. Tarquin found himself in the center of a crush of people, not entirely certain how he'd gotten there.

How had they gone from looking at fluffy clouds to fleeing for their lives in less than ten minutes?

The HCA soldier next to him, the one who'd said this wasn't the Conservators' MO, caught his eye and gave him a quick, reassuring smile. Tarquin mustered up the ability to smile back and read the man's name badge—DAWD, REGAR. That meager kindness reminded him that there was more at stake than his worries. These people had put their lives in the hands of Mercator.

If they died here, they could be reprinted later, but every death increased one's chance of one's neural map cracking the next time it was printed. Neural maps were never perfect; they degraded over time. Traumatic deaths sped the process exponentially, as even the best-shielded backups were never entirely disentangled from the active map.

As if there were fine threads of connection between all backups and the living mind, and sufficient trauma could reverberate out to them all.

Some people came up screaming, and never stopped. Some got caught in time loops, unsure which moment of their lives they were really living through. Neither state was survivable.

Tarquin summoned the scraps of his courage and stood straighter. He had no business in a crisis, but the employees looked to him for assurance. His terror no doubt added to their anxiety, and that was selfish of him.

Something metal groaned in the walls, taunting his ability

to hold it together. Tarquin cast an irritated glance at the complaining ship. If only ships would fall in line as easily as people.

Acaelus pulled up a holo from his forearm, but whatever he saw there was blurred by his privacy filters. The information carved a scowl into his face. He slowed and swiped his ID pathway over the door to a lab, unlocking it.

"Everyone, in here," he said.

They hesitated. Paison said, "My liege, the shuttle isn't far from here."

"I'm aware of the layout of my own ship, Captain. Get in, all of you, and wait. I've just received notice that Ex. Lockhart's print order went through. I won't allow my exemplar to awaken to a dying ship. You will go into this lab, and you will wait for my return."

That wasn't right. The secondary printing round wasn't automated; it needed to be initiated. Tarquin frowned, watching the crew shift uncomfortably. Every one of them knew Acaelus was telling a half-truth at best, but none of them were willing to say it.

There was a slim possibility that whatever was causing the other errors had triggered this, but making all these people wait while Acaelus collected one person was a waste of time.

"My liege." Paison stepped forward, squaring off her shoulders. "I can't guarantee this ship will last that long, and we require your command keys to open the hangar airlock."

"I am aware, and you are delaying. Get in the lab."

They shuffled inside without another word, though they were all watching Acaelus warily. The terror of offending their boss was greater than the fear of being left behind to die. You could come back from death. You could never re-cuff for Mercator after being fired. The door shut, leaving Tarquin and his father alone with Kearns. Tarquin's head pounded.

"What are you doing?" he demanded in a soft hiss. "Ex. Lockhart can handle herself. We have to get these people out."

Acaelus shoved him down the hallway. "*We* need to get out. I printed Lockhart to help Kearns handle the crew, but you and I are going to cast our maps back and exit this situation, because I don't know what's happened here, and I'm not risking your map."

Tarquin dug his heels in, drawing his father to a halt. "We can't just leave. I'm not going to allow the Conservators to run us off before I have proof the mining process is safe."

"If this was the Conservators, then we'd already be dead. All the nonfamily printing bays just went active, and I *do not know* who is coming out of those bays. We have to leave. Kearns and Lockhart will handle the rest."

Tarquin rubbed his eyes in frustration. "We can't abandon the mission."

"We can, and we are. Come. This is hardly the place for an argument."

Acaelus jerked on his arm. Tarquin stumbled after him, mind reeling. Sixth Cradle was supposed to be his mission. Supposed to be the moment Tarquin stood up for his family and finally squashed all those squalid rumors Ex. Sharp had started when she'd claimed the relkatite mining process was killing worlds.

While a great deal of what his family had to do to ensure their survival was distasteful, Tarquin was absolutely certain the mining process was safe. He'd refined it himself. Mining Sixth Cradle and leaving it green and thriving was meant to be the final nail in the coffin of those accusations. The one thing he could do for his family that was *useful*.

He wouldn't run. Not this time. Not like he had when his mother had died and he'd fled to university to bury himself in his studies, instead of facing the suffering that weighed on his father's and sister's hearts.

"I'm sorry, Dad, I won't—"

"Kearns, carry him," Acaelus said.

Tarquin was thirty-five years old, second in line to the most powerful position in the universe, and Ex. Kearns scooped him up like he was little more than luggage and tossed him over his shoulder without a flash of hesitation, because Acaelus Mercator had demanded it. Kearns's shoulder dug into Tarquin's ribs, pressing a startled grunt out of him. His cheeks burned with indignity.

"I'm not a child," Tarquin snapped, surprised at the edge in his tone. He never raised his voice to his father.

"You are *my* child, and you will do as I say."

Acaelus didn't bother to look at him. Tarquin closed his eyes, letting out a slow sigh of defeat. There was no arguing with his father when he'd made up his mind. He opened his eyes, and temporarily forgot how to breathe. The door to one of the staff printing bays yawned open, and it wasn't people who emerged from that space. Not exactly.

Their faces were close to human, but something had gone off in the printing. A mouth set too far right. An ear sprouting from the side of a neck. An arm that bent the wrong way around. Half a chest cavity missing.

Misprints. Empties. An error in the printer slapping together a hodgepodge of human parts. The *Amaranth* wouldn't have tried putting a neural map into any of those bodies, but whatever had caused the malfunction had also made the ship release the prints instead of disintegrating them into their constituent parts, as was protocol for a misprint.

What was left of those faces twisted, drew into vicious snarls.

"Kearns," Tarquin hissed in a sharp whisper. His voice was alarmed enough that the exemplar turned.

Kearns pulled his sidearm and fired. The earsplitting roar of the shot in such a small space slammed into Tarquin's ears, but his pathways adjusted, keeping him from going temporarily deaf. The misprints shrieked with what throats and lungs they had, and rushed them. Kearns rolled Tarquin off his shoulder and shoved him back.

Tarquin stumbled, but his father caught him and then spun, pushing him ahead. "Run!"

Fear stripped away all his reservations and Tarquin ran, pounding down the hallways for the family's private printing bay, praying that he wouldn't find the same thing there.

Kearns's weapon roared again and again, a staccato rhythm drowning out the screams of the misprints. He looked over his shoulder to find Acaelus right behind him, Kearns farther back, his injured leg slowing him down. Tarquin faced forward and sprinted—the door to the printing bay was *just* ahead.

Kearns's gun fell silent. His father screamed.

Tarquin whirled around. Acaelus was chest-down on the ground, misprints swarming over him, their teeth and nails digging into his skin, ripping free bloody chunks. He took a step toward them, not knowing what he could possibly do, and Acaelus looked up, face set with determination as he flung out a hand.

"Go home!" he ordered.

He met his father's eyes. Acaelus pushed his tongue against the inside of his cheek, making it bulge out in warning. New terror struck Tarquin. High-ranking members of the corporate families often wore small, personal explosive devices on the interior side of a molar to use in case someone intending to crack their neural maps attacked them. Acaelus had one.

Tarquin fled. He burst through the printing bay door and slammed it shut behind him, leaning his back against it, breathing harder than he ever had in his life. The explosion was designed to be small. It whumped against the door, tickling his senses.

A gruesome way to die, but it was swift. Gentler suicide pathways had been tried, but they had a nasty habit of malfunctioning. Pathways remained frustratingly unpredictable at times.

He swallowed. The staff back on Mercator Station would reprint Acaelus the second they received notice that his tracker pathway had been destroyed and his visual feed had cut. His father would be fine. Tarquin forced himself away from the door, shaking.

One of the printing cubicles was lit red to indicate it was in use. He crossed to the map backup station and picked up the crown of electronics, running it between his hands.

Tarquin knew he wasn't what his father had wanted. He lacked the clear-eyed ruthlessness of his elder sister, Leka. He couldn't stand to watch people cower beneath the threat of his ire as Acaelus so often had to do to keep their employees in line. His singular concession to being a Mercator was that his love of geology and subsequent studies had aided the family in their hunt for relkatite.

His father never complained about Tarquin's lack of participation in family politics. Acaelus had given Tarquin everything he'd ever asked for and had only ever asked for one thing in return.

When Naira Sharp had been captured and put to trial, Tarquin had taken the stand to prove her accusations false. As a Mercator, as the foremost expert in his field of study, he had disproved all her allegations that Mercator's mining processes destroyed worlds.

It hadn't stopped the rumors. Hadn't stopped the other families of MERIT from looking askance at Mercator and asking themselves if, maybe, they wouldn't be better off without them.

They needed to mine a cradle world and leave it thriving in their wake to put the rumors to bed once and for all.

Tarquin could still give his father that proof, but he couldn't do it alone. Not with misprints infesting the halls and the potential of a saboteur on the loose. He needed an exemplar.

He set the backup crown down and crossed to the printing bay control console, checking the progress on Lockhart's print. Ninety seconds left. Enough time to compose himself. Enough time, he hoped, to get to the planet after she'd finished printing.

Tarquin had never disobeyed a direct order from his father before, and he hoped he wasn't making a colossal mistake.